THE STONE GALLOWS

The Stone Gallows

C. David Ingram

MYRMIDON

Myrmidon Books Ltd
Rotterdam House
116 Quayside
Newcastle upon Tyne
NE1 3DY

www.myrmidonbooks.com

Published by Myrmidon 2009

A catalogue record for this book is available from the British Library.

ISBN 978-1-905802-20-3

Set in 10/12.25pt Minion by Falcon Oast Graphic Arts Limited,
East Hoathly, East Sussex

Printed and bound in the UK by CPI Mackays, Chatham ME5 8TD

1 3 5 7 9 10 8 6 4 2

LOTTERY FUNDED

For Peter and Robin Ingram

Prologue 1
January 2008

1.

I was going to kill him.

An hour ago, John Coombes – my partner and *supposed* mentor – had been nothing more than a deeply unlikeable human being. Sixty minutes trapped in an unmarked police car with him had caused me to revise my opinion. He was the anti-Christ, my duty to the human race clear: God *wanted* me to kill him. I was sure of it.

It's amazing how quickly people can go from a state of mild irritation to one of homicidal rage. This was the first time the two of us had pulled a surveillance duty together; although I didn't know it at the time, it was also to be the last.

I even knew how I was going to do it. There was a disposable pen sitting on the dashboard and I was going use it to sign my name on the inside of his skull, jamming it through his eye or up his nose in a gratuitous but undeniably spectacular display of violence.

I was going to kill him because he was making a noise.

Not *just* a noise. An irritating, repetitive, childish sound. Like nails scratching a blackboard, or an amphetamine-fed Jack Russell given free rein with a squeaky rubber bone. The kind of noise that makes your soul wince in horror and discomfort until the most hideous act of violence seems like the conduct of an utterly reasonable man.

I'm a reasonable man. I swear.

But. . . even reasonable men have limits, and I was long past mine.

He'd been doing it for at least ten minutes, using a plastic straw to try and suck the melting ice out of his paper cup, making a disgusting *schlurp schurlp* sound, and showed absolutely no sign of stopping.

Any detective who has ever worked surveillance would testify that those ten minutes had been an eternity. Hell, it wasn't as if Coombes had a whiter than white service record. I might even be able to claim that I was performing a public service.

'John?'

I made sure that my voice was calm and reasonable. If he sensed just how irritated I was, he'd keep on doing it. Coombes was that type of guy.

'Yes, Cameron?'

I indicated the straw. 'Do you mind?'

He sighed like I was asking him to donate his entire liver to my alcoholic second cousin, before tossing the cup in the back seat. We settled back into miserable silence.

There is only one rule to surveillance duty and it's mind-bogglingly simple: don't take your eyes off the subject for a second. It doesn't matter if you have been sitting there for an hour, a week, or even a month, you're expected to maintain a constant level of focus. In the past, whole investigations have been abandoned because the people involved haven't taken the job seriously enough. In one memorable incident, a key suspect was lost forever because the two detectives assigned to the case had been in the bookies across the road watching the three fifteen from Newmarket. They lost more than their fifty pounds each way that day, I can tell you.

Of course, none of that mattered to Coombes. He shifted his weight in the passenger seat of our unmarked Mondeo. 'I need to pee.'

I grunted as I turned and fished the paper cup out of the back seat I showed it to him.

He looked at it, then me. 'What do you think I am? An animal?'

'Yeah, I saw that on David Attenborough. The famous cup-peeing gazelle of the Serengeti.'

We were three hours into a six hour shift. I'd been sensible, not over-eating or drinking. Coombes had munched his way through a quarter pounder with cheese, plus fries, plus a bloody chocolate doughnut. And, of course, nearly a litre of caffeine-laced soft drink. Of course he needed to pee. Coombes was always pissing about. You would think a time-served detective would know better.

But then, Detective John Coombes could hardly be described as the shining light of Strathclyde Police. I'd been his partner for about one month, and it had taken me less than two weeks to work out that he was perhaps not as dedicated as one would expect of a public servant. In his mid-forties, he was soft in the gut and work-ethic, with flabby hands and straw blonde hair that was thinning badly. I was supposed to be learning from him but so far all I'd discovered was the best places in Glasgow to get free food. The city had plenty of restaurants and bars where the subtle wave of a warrant card would net you a courtesy Chicken Fried Rice or pint of Heavy, and Coombes seemed to know them all.

Speaking of which... 'There's a pub round the corner,' he said. 'The Docker's. We could take a little break.'

I checked my watch. 'It's after midnight. They won't let us in.'

'The landlord's a friend of mine. Besides, it's only five past. They won't even have had time to hose the vomit out of the toilets yet.'

'Sounds classy.' I pretended to think about it before shaking my head. 'Maybe another time.'

'Come on. You new fish are all the same. We've been watching this bloody guy for two weeks now. He might be dirty, but he's smart. He's not going to do anything that we can pin on him. It's a waste of time. Nobody's going to know if we sneak off for a quick one.'

I wondered if we would be expected to pay for it, or if it was one of the many places where the landlord owed Coombes a 'favour'.

'I'm not comfortable with the idea.'

His face had a disgusted look on it. 'Look, Stone, I'm not peeing in

— 9 —

a paper cup. All I'm saying is, we'll sneak away for one pint. . .' He wagged a finger at me. 'Just one, mind you, and then we'll come back. We can sit here in the cold and the damp and smell each other's body odour and you can hand over to whoever they send to replace us with a clear conscience.'

There was a park less than thirty yards away from where we sat. No lights, no walls, plenty of trees to slip behind. I nodded in its direction. 'You could jump in there. Take you less than sixty seconds.'

He sulked for about two minutes, crossing and uncrossing his legs. Then he opened the car door. 'Fuck it. I'm going for a pint. You can sit here on your lonesome.'

'Don't do it, Coombes.'

He laughed. 'Why? What are you going to do? Report me?'

I took a deep breath. Being a cop is like being part of a big family. Coombes may have been a shifty bastard, but he was *our* shifty bastard. And I was still very much the new boy. If I made a complaint about him, it would be my word against his, and the repercussions for me could be grave. At the very least, it would isolate me from every-body else. Don't work with Stone, they would say, he's a clyping bastard. The worst case scenario was that I would be viewed as a trouble-maker, and probably not be considered for promotion any time in the next thousand years.

I decided to compromise. 'You got your mobile with you?'

Coombes patted his pocket.

'I'll call if anything happens.'

'Good boy.'

The car door slammed and I listened to him whistle as he walked off into the night. 'Arsehole,' I whispered, to myself.

2.

'Little bastard. Fuckin' get it to stop.'
'She's teething, Gaz. She can't help it.'

'It's been greetin' a' day.'

Maria tried to placate him. 'Her gums are sore.'

'My fuckin' ears are sore. Get it to shut the fuck up or I'll gie it something to fuckin' cry about.'

'She can't help it.'

'Fuckin' hell, man.'

Gaz liked to say fuck. It was his favourite word, serving most of his needs in one juicy little syllable. Adjective, noun, verb, intensifier, modifier and convenient thought-gathering pause. Not that he had a great deal of thought to gather. Gary Tiernan was never going to be on Mastermind, even if they allowed him to choose Scottish Ned Culture as his specialist subject.

He hated quiz shows anyway. All those smartarses who wanted to show off how much they knew about something nobody gave a shite about. Great shell-suits of the eighties. The Golden Age of Buckfast Tonic Wine. Seriously, who cared? To Gaz, the only things worth knowing were the three F's. Football, fighting, and of course, fucking.

Even so, it would be cool to be on the telly. Give the lads a laugh. He could imagine himself on that big black bastard seat in his best Burberry baseball cap, the crusty tones of that old fart Magnus Fagness, or whoever the fuck it was.

-And the clock starts. . . now. What does the abbreviation NED stand for?

-Non Educated Delinquent.

-Correct.

-I fuckin' know it's correct, ya bam. Wanty get a fuckin' move on, pal?

It was just after eleven pm. He'd sprang out of bed at the crack of noon, waited until almost one before cracking open his first can of Supersonic. Now the twelve pack that had been in the fridge was gone, as was the pleasant buzz that had lasted throughout the late afternoon and early evening, replaced by a deadly roaring numbness, a slow motion plane crash of a building hangover that would cost him the best part of the next day. Not that it mattered. It wasn't as if he had a job to go to. He stretched on the settee, a thin, *ferrety boy with a narrow face and angry, disappointed eyes.*

The crying. It was doing his fuckin' head in.

Nobody said it would be like this. They waffled on about the joy of having kids, of being a dad. Being part of a tiny little life, watching it grow and learn. The wonder that is fatherhood.

It was all shite. Shite at one end and puke at the other, and constant fucking noise in the middle. A dog would have been better. Nice wee Rottweiler puppy that would wag its tail and learn to fetch a stick. And you could housetrain them. Unlike the wean. Eight months old, didn't talk, didn't walk, didn't smile. All it did was sleep, shit and scream.

And it was still doing it. Deep, gut-busting lungfuls, bellowing its misery like a foghorn. How could something so small make so much noise?

'*I'm fuckin' serious, Maria. If you can't make it shut up, take it into the fuckin' bedroom.*'

Aye, Maria. The girlfriend. Seventeen going on eighteen, one year younger than him. Twelve months ago she'd been just another dirty wee slapper who liked it all ways. The tart had told him she was on the pill. That turned out to be another lie, but he'd gone along for the ride. After she got knocked up, the council had set her up in a two bedroom flat, and it was handy to have another place to crash.

God knows, he'd tried to make it work. Painted the tiny second bedroom yellow. Moved his Playstation in. Bought a big screen TV from Mad Malky Toseland. Played house. And it had been just fine until Maria had dropped the wean. Then she had changed. Aged thirty years overnight. Started talking about saving enough cash for a deposit on a house, of going to college and getting an education. One day, she used the phrase "We Need To Put Something Away For The Baby" seven times. He'd counted. And to top it all, she was still fat from the pregnancy. Not chubby. Not a bit porky. Fucking Jabba fat. It was like shagging an inflatable couch. And there was no squeeze in her fanny either. He'd tried using the back door, but her arse was too padded to allow any worthwhile penetration. (The fact that his penis might have been too small never even crossed Gaz's mind.)

Maria took the baby into the bedroom. He could hear her trying to comfort it from his station on the couch, talking in that sing-song voice that made him want to smack her through a window. *I need to chill*, he thought. *Just calm down. It's no' her fault that the wean's crying all the time.*

He took the remote and flipped through the television channels, hoping to find something calming. Football, or a Bruce Willis movie, or even one of those documentaries about the porn industry that were more about titillation than information. The closest he could find was a film on Channel Four. Some bird standing naked in a window with her back to the camera. *Nice arse.* But then the scene changed to a bunch of old men smoking in a pub, talking in a language he didn't understand. There were subtitles, but they were gone before he could read them. *Bloody foreign movies. What was the point? He bet they didn't show bloody Scottish movies in France.* He stepped over and flipped his Playstation on. *Maybe killing some cops would improve his mood.*

It didn't. Eight minutes later he was bored. Ten minutes later he remembered about the ecstasy.

He'd been saving it for the weekend, when he and some of his mates had planned to go up the town, but the situation was desperate. He went through to the bathroom and opened the medicine cabinet. There they were, four brownish white pills in a grubby cellophane bag. He held each tablet up to the light, examining it between forefinger and thumb. *No pharmacy markings, which meant at least that they weren't aspirin or dog-worming tablets.* They'd been given to him by a loser called Tommy Graham, who owed him twenty pounds for a wee favour. They were a stop-gap, something to discourage Gaz from kicking the shit out of him for not actually paying the money.

Just take the two, Gaz thought. *Two now and two at the weekend.*

Ah, fuck it.

He tossed all four pills into his mouth and washed them down with tap water, before heading back to his settee and his game.

The baby's cries had faded to a dull whimper. Maria came and sat next to him. 'I've rubbed Calpol into her gums. Maybe that'll help her to settle.'

Gaz barely looked up. '*Fuckin' better.*'

Maria watched her boyfriend's face in the glow of the television. He always bit his lip when he was concentrating on something. She said, 'There's an open day at Langside College tomorrow. I was thinking I might go along and see what there was.'

'Oh aye? How are you going to get there?'

'I was going to walk.'

'Aye, right.' He jerked his head in the direction of the bedroom. 'Two miles with Screaming Annie there? That'll be fun.'

'I was hoping you could keep an eye on her. I could go to the shops and get some food.'

He shook his head. 'I can't.'

'How not?'

'Cos I fuckin' can't, alright? I'm busy.'

'Doing what?'

'Stuff.'

'What, like smoking dope and playing video games with your pals?'

'It's none of your business.'

'Gaz, I'm just asking you for a wee bit of help. All you're doing all day is sitting around the flat anyhow. Plus you should spend a bit more time with Sonata Blue.'

He smiled at that. She'd wanted to call it Meg, but he'd been the one that went to the registry office. If it had been a boy, it would have been named after the Rangers first eleven. All of them. 'But what if she needs her nappy changed?'

'I showed you how to do it.'

'Aye, but I can't be changing nappies in front of the guys. They'll think I'm a tosser.'

Maria sighed as she got to her feet. 'Alright, I'll take her with me. I'm going to go and have a shower. Are you coming to bed?'

He shook his head. With her out of the way he could put on a Ben Dover DVD and have a five knuckle shuffle. 'Nah. Maybe in a couple of hours.'

3.

Coombes and I had been on surveillance for two weeks and one day. The subject was a guy called Alan Grierson, and the location was a truck depot in Dalmarnock. Grierson was owner of a haulage firm that had plenty of business in Europe, and he and several of his drivers were suspected of bringing in some less than legal loads. Our snouts painted a fairly depressing picture; as well as the usual few kilos of heroin or hash, Grierson had apparently branched out over the past year into human trafficking. We hadn't figured out every link in the chain, but there had been a sudden influx of Polish girls working the street, and we were pretty sure who was at the bottom of it.

Except that in fifteen days we had learned nothing. Zip. Round the clock surveillance had revealed little of value. Trucks came, trucks went. Every morning, Grierson rolled up in a shiny black Merc, and every night, he went home. Alone. Aside from the occasional trip to the casino, the guy seemed to be a dedicated businessman. If we didn't turn something up by the end of the week, the operation was going to be cancelled.

We weren't just operating on a tip-off. Grierson had been a good boy for the last thirty years, but he did have some form. Way back in the early seventies, he did a two year stretch in Barlinnie for assault and living off immoral earnings. He'd been a pimp, and one night he beat one of his girls halfway to death. Usually, in seventies Glasgow, beating up a hooker warranted no more than a slap on the wrist, but Grierson was unlucky enough to have his case judged by the legendary Harry Thomas. Now, Harry is long since retired and living in a nursing home, but in the seventies he'd put it about a bit. Rumour had it that he liked them to sing nursery rhymes. It's a standing joke in the trade; ask any working girl in Glasgow for a Harry Thomas, and they'll immediately give you a chorus of *Baa Baa Black Sheep*. Just about everybody knew that the girl Grierson had beaten was one of Harry's favourites, and it was no surprise when Harry handed down a hefty sentence.

Of course, that was thirty years ago. Since then Grierson had kept his nose clean, but that didn't exactly make him a model citizen. He socialised with key players in the Glasgow crime scene. His haulage operation was smooth, but he had a reputation as a hard man. Drivers who were late with their loads were rumoured to be punished with broken fingers and broken noses. And, of course, there was the obligatory Tachometer fixing. We had plenty of ex-employees who confirmed Grierson's management strategies, but none who were prepared to go on the record.

All in all, not a very nice guy. Whoever brought him down a peg or two would get a very welcome little feather in their cap – and being the new boy, I needed all the feathers that were going.

I checked my watch. Twelve fifteen AM. I'd dressed in layers: two T-shirts, one fleece and, of course, the standard CID leather jacket. I was still freezing. We couldn't run the heater for fear of draining the battery, and we couldn't run the engine because an idling car attracts attention. At that moment, I would have sold my soul for a cup of soup.

Bloody Coombes. I could imagine him, pint in one hand, pool cue in the other. The bastard was probably laughing at me.

Fuck him. The idea of a nice warm pub was tempting, but I would rather sit here in the cold than be his pal. I just had to keep reminding myself that he was the one in the wrong.

Grierson's business premises were in an industrial estate that had seen better days. Two thirds of the occupants had gone to the wall in the past five years and the rest. . . well, let's just say that it was easy to imagine their owners checking their insurance premiums before leaving lots of unsupervised candles burning. Most of the units were abandoned, the rest just neglected. The only place that was thriving was the haulage depot itself, and that was something else that was suspicious. In a field where most of the players were struggling to break even, Grierson Haulage had declared a pre-tax profit of one point four million pounds in the last financial year.

The depot was forty yards from where I was parked, and consisted of a large yard surrounded by an eight foot high brick wall. Entry was through a set of wrought-iron gates. Since the start of our shift, three trucks had left and one had arrived. This wasn't unusual; import and export is a twenty-four hour business.

I'll say this for him, Grierson worked long hours. Every once in a while he would stay the night, sleeping on a camp bed in his office. He owned a home in Bearsden, but he seemed to only use it at weekends. Mind you, we had all seen his wife. She was the size of an articulated lorry, and nowhere near as attractive.

Twelve twenty. Coombes had been gone for twenty-three minutes. Enough time to empty his bladder, neck a pint of heavy, and rejoin me. There was no sign of him. I guessed he would show up around about half past one, half an hour before our relief was due to arrive, sucking on Extra Strong Mints. If I was lucky, he would bring me back a packet of pork scratchings.

Twelve thirty. Nothing happened.

Twelve forty. Nothing continued to happen.

Twelve fifty. My back was sore, and now I needed to pee. I used the empty McDonalds cup and tossed it out of the window. Coombes was probably on his third drink by now. I had to be satisfied with a Polo mint.

At twelve fifty-five the gates opened, and a familiar black Mercedes moved slowly onto the street. Instead of turning in the direction of Grierson's home, it swung toward me. There was an instant's worth of eye contact as he motored slowly past me; I got a quick image of stubbled jaw and heavy jowls. Hopefully he would assume I was a nobody, just a taxi-driver taking a break.

There was someone else. A passenger. Not enough time for me to get a close look. Just a quick glimpse – straight brown hair, pale face, worried eyes. Definitely female, definitely young, and definitely not somebody we had previously logged.

Showtime.

4.

An hour later, Gaz was more wired than ever. He'd watched his DVD, had his fun and wiped his semen onto the cushions. Now his heart rate had doubled, his vision had trebled and there was a buzzing in his ears that had nothing to do with Sonata's moonlit serenade. Fucking Tommy. Where did he get his stuff? Whatever it was, it wasn't ecstasy. It wasn't even remotely fun.

At least the kid was quiet. Gaz stood over it for a few minutes as it slept in its cot, a tiny thing with a shock of black hair and a thumb corked in its mouth. Every few seconds it whimpered as it slept, scrunching its face up like a bulldog eating a wasp. He wondered how Maria and her stupid friends could spend hours cooing over it.

Christ, his skin itched. Like spiders were crawling all over him, thousands of little burning feet running up and down his torso. It felt like he was on fire. He went through to the bathroom and stuck a thermometer in his mouth. After a few minutes, he took it out and peered at the mercury.

One hundred and six.

Was that good or bad?

He didn't feel so good, that was for sure. Along with the itchy skin and blurred vision, his mouth was dry, his tongue coated with sandpaper. He clenched and unclenched his fists, the muscles in his arms vibrating like guitar strings. He went through to the bedroom, the thermometer still clutched in his sweaty hand.

There she was, his tubby little princess, one hand flung to the side and a trickle of sleep-drool running down her chin. He flicked the tip of her nose. 'Maria, wake up.'

She stirred. He flicked her again, harder this time. Her face wrinkled at the sudden pain and her eyes opened.

'Maria, I don't feel so good.'

'What?'

'I feel sick. I took a couple of eccies and now I think I'm sick.'

'You did what?'

'It was just a couple of E's. But I think they maybe weren't E's. I'm not feeling right.'

'What the hell are you doing taking E at this time of night?'

'I was bored.'

'Where did you get them?'

'Wee Tommy.'

'Wee Tommy? He's a bloody tube. And you're a bloody tube for taking anything off of him. It's probably an antibiotic or something.'

'It doesn't feel like an antibiotic.' He grabbed her hand, pressed it against his forehead. 'I'm burning up.'

She noticed the thermometer in his hand. 'What are you doing with that?'

'I took my temperature.'

Her voice rose. 'With the baby thermometer?'

'What's wrong with that?'

'Nothing. Except that it's a rectal thermometer.'

He looked at it for a second. 'You mean it's been. . .'

She nodded.

'Shite.'

'You Muppet. Did you put that in your mouth?'

'Aye. . . no. What do you think I am? Dolly?'

Dolly Dimple. Glasgow rhyming slang. Gaz clenched his teeth; the stupid bint thought he was simple.

Maria was too busy laughing to notice the look on his face. 'You did. You put it in your mouth.' It was nice for the joke to be on somebody else for a change.

'Fuckin' shut it. Anyhow, you're meant to sterilise these things.'

'Aye, right. You rinse them under the hot tap and put them back in the cupboard for next time.'

He felt sick. Really sick. His gorge rose, acidy breath filling his mouth. He dipped his head and sprayed chunks everywhere, covering the bedside table, the pillowcase, and Maria, in a pea green mess of bile and doner kebab.

'Gaz!' She lunged at him, flailing away with her tiny fists. 'You bastard! You did that deliberately! You fucking BASTARD.' He raised his hands to defend himself, but one of her blows found its way past, a pointly, puke smeared knuckle jabbing straight into his eye. It stung like a mad thing, and he felt vomit schrapneling from her face and arms as she tried to pummel him. Rage filled him. Stupid cunt. Just because he'd been sick on her didn't give her the right to behave like that. He threw her back down on the bed, grabbing her hands and forcing them together over her head, circling both her wrists with one hand, the other free to punch her in the face, once, twice, and three times the charm, her cheek splintering, her nose breaking, her lips smashing underneath his knuckles.

She stopped fighting, her hands going to her injured face. Blood from her nose mixed with the bile on her cheek. He screamed in her face, an inarticulate caveman howl that re-established his place atop the food chain.

There was an answering cry from the baby.

It rose in the air, a piercing, driving noise, wavering like an air-raid siren. Gaz released her wrists, a mad glint in his eye.

'Gaz. . . don't. . .'

He ignored her, storming through to the child's room. The baby lay in its cot, wrapped in a jolly red sleeper suit covered with smiling octopuses. It was hollering its guts out, goggle eyed with misery. He grabbed it by the shoulders, shook it like a terrier shaking a rat. 'FUCKING SHUT IT! FUCKING SHUT IT RIGHT NOW! WAH! WAH! WAH! FUCKING WEE SHITE!'

The baby's head bounced back and forth on its shoulders, and a long slaver of drool hung from its lip, smearing his hands. Disgusted, he flipped it upside down and held it by its ankles, shaking it up and down like he was trying to empty a pillow case. There was a loud CLACK as he smashed the child's head off the bars of the cot.

That got it to shut up.

5.

Before Grierson had gone more than ten yards past where I was parked, I was fumbling in the glove compartment for my mobile. Coombes was three on the speed dial; I mashed buttons with my thumb and thankfully hit the right ones. The Merc was disappearing in the rear view mirror as I waited for him to answer. There was a brief flash of brake lights and then it turned left onto London Road. I keyed the ignition, slammed into first, let the clutch out like it was electrified, glad it wasn't my own car. Tyres squealed as they struggled for purchase on the wet surface.

Coombes answered after four agonising rings. I didn't give him a chance to speak. 'He's on the move. Unknown female passenger.'

'Fuck.'

I heard laughter in the background, The Eagles on the jukebox. In seconds I was past the haulage yard, nearly clipping the kerb on the corner, engine revving too high because I only had two hands and I couldn't steer and talk and change gear all at the same time. 'He's gone up London Road, so we might still have a chance. Pick you up outside.'

I hit the disconnect button and tossed the phone into the backseat. The Docker's was only fifty yards in front of me. By the time I screeched to a halt outside the front door, Coombes was waiting for me.

'Get in, get in, get in!'

The first rule of High Speed Pursuits: screaming everything three times will make it happen faster.

Before his door was halfway shut I abused the clutch for the second time that minute. Grierson had maybe a forty second start on us, but there was still hope. London Road was one of the city's main arteries, stretching for at least six miles. We were on Millikin Street, which ran directly parallel. If he was travelling any distance, there was every chance we could catch him.

I caught a glimpse of something in Coombes' sweaty hand. 'What the fuck is that?'

Rule number two: rhetorical questions are always welcome. I could see perfectly what it was. It was pint of lager. The bloody thing still had a head on it.

'I'd only just got it,' Coombes said. 'I forgot I was holding it.'

'You're an arsehole, you know that?'

For once, the useless fucker didn't argue. I still had to get over onto London Road. The speedometer read fifty. I hit the brakes and swung the car right onto a cross-street, Coombes covering his pint with his left hand, the back end of the car swinging round faster than the front. I wrenched the wheel left and gassed it, overcompensating, the car lurching left again. Coombes, still fumbling with his seatbelt, was thrown to his right and ended up in the well between the seats. He let out a yell as the hand brake jabbed something fleshy. I felt something cold splash into my stomach. 'Coombes, you cunt! Get the fuck away from me!'

'It was an accident!'

'What kind of dozy twat brings a pint on a pursuit?' I yelled.

He scrambled back over to his side of the car, the now-empty pint glass still in his hand. He rolled the window down and tossed it into the night. 'Satisfied?'

'Yeah, I'm fucking thrilled.' I was so wet, I might as well have not bothered peeing into the McDonalds cup. 'Hold on.'

Rule three: zippy dialogue will enhance tension.

I wrenched the wheel left, finally making it back onto London Road, way behind but moving fast.

6.

After thirty years driving of a Hackney round the streets of Glasgow, Frank Madden had developed a sixth sense. He had three grades of customer, and could usually guess which grade each fare was before his cab had pulled to a halt beside them. Best of all were what he called the High-Fliers. The High-Fliers were divided into several sub-groups – the Harassed Businessman, who never had time to wait for change, the

Foreigner, who's lack of knowledge could be conveniently exploited, and the Stupidly Generous, who were… well, stupidly generous. The HF's made up around ten percent of his customer base.

Grade Two had fewer categories. There was Housewife, who would tip exactly fifty pence irrespective of whether he had driven her fifty yards or fifty miles, and there was Practical Man, who always knew the quickest route and would tip between zero and twenty percent, dependant on his mood, amount of traffic and quality of in-cab conversation. Grade twos usually accounted for about sixty percent of his income.

And then there were the Grade Threes, who had no sub-groups. They were the people who clutched their money in their hands and watched the meter with worried eyes. They generally made up thirty percent of his overall business, although over the past few years, he felt that the number had risen.

He'd picked her up on a street corner in Barrowfield, not far away from Celtic Park. Even before he pulled to a halt, he knew that she was almost certainly going to be a Three. It was the area. Barrowfield was like Iraq, the only differences being that George Bush had yet to decide that the place would be better off underneath American control, and people didn't actually live in the burned-out cars that littered the streets. Frank wouldn't have stopped for her, but it had been a slow night, despite the fact that it was pissing down with rain. That was Glasgow on a Tuesday night for you. Every bugger staying home or riding Shanks's Pony. Twenty minutes between each fare, and nobody wanted to go more than a couple of miles. So when the girl with the bag and the baby waved a hand, he'd pulled alongside.

She tossed the bag in and clambered after it, the wee one held against her chest loosely in one arm.

'Where to?'

'The hospital. I think. I don't know.'

He glanced at her in the rear-view mirror. There was something off about her reflection. Her eyes, especially the right one, were swollen, and her lips were puffy. Her nose had an odd, squished look that he'd seen before. The slapper slapped.

'Make up your mind.'

'The hospital.'

'Which hospital?'

'The Royal.'

'You sick?'

She shook her head, indicated the bundle underneath her arm. 'My baby.'

He put the cab in gear and pulled away from the kerb. 'What's wrong with it?'

'My boyfriend hit her head off the side of the cot.'

Frank slammed the brakes on. 'Is she breathing?'

'Aye. But it was pretty hard. I just want to know that she's alright.'

He released the clutch and the vehicle shuddered as it pulled away.

'Why would he do that?'

'He was. . . drunk. And high.'

'Bastard.'

'He hit me as well.'

He risked another glance in his rear-view mirror. 'Thought so.'

They drove in silence for a moment, the only sound the grinding of the gears and the swipe of the windshield wipers. He kept an eye on her in the mirror. Seventeen, maybe eighteen at a push. Sportswear and trainers. In a parallel universe, he might have given her a lift home from the dancing, her in a spangly top and strappy shoes, giggling with her pals after a night on the Bacardi Breezers. He would have preferred that girl to the one that sat in the back of his cab with tears in her eyes.

Kids, he thought. They grow up so fast.

'Has he done something like that before?'

She shook her head.

'He'll do it again. If you go back to him.'

'I won't go back to him.'

'What are you going to do?'

There was no response from the back seat, not that he really expected one. Abuse victims rarely plan ahead. Instead, they snap like brittle little twigs. Sometimes, like this one, they packed their bags and fled, and *sometimes they buried a carving knife in their abuser's back. Either one was good enough for Frank.*

'What about your parents?'

'My mum's dead. My dad threw me out when I got pregnant.'

Frank shook his head. It wouldn't make any difference if he found out his kid had shagged the entire Premiership. He'd never do that. You took care of your own.

'Won't he take you back?'

'I've taken his granddaughter to meet him. He just shuts the door in my face. Says I'm dead to him.'

'There's shelters, you know. I could take you to one.'

The girl shook her head, indicated the sleeping baby. 'I want to go to the hospital. Just to make sure that she's alright.'

Frank nodded. In his thirty years, he reckoned he'd seen it all. A lot had happened in the rear-view mirror. Three births, two deaths (one heart attack, one stroke). Arguing wives and drunk husbands. Randy kids who couldn't keep it in their pants until they got home. In eighty-nine he'd been stabbed by a football fan after an Old Firm game and nearly died. This girl wouldn't be the first teenager he'd dropped off at A & E, and she wouldn't be the last. 'The hospital will keep you right. They'll take care of you. Both of you.'

The girl nodded.

'What's your name, darling?'

'Maria.'

'I won't charge you for this. Not this time.'

Her voice was a whisper. 'Thank you.'

'As long as you promise me that you won't go back to him.'

'I won't.'

'I've got a daughter only a couple of years older than you.' *He pulled down the sun-visor and passed a battered Polaroid through the change window.* 'Kerry. I'd kill anybody who did that to her.'

She studied the picture. 'She's lucky to have a dad like you.'

The bag was lying at her feet, a battered, lumpy hold-all. She'd stuffed as many of Sonata Blue's clothes in as she could, as well as the tiny stuffed tiger that had been a gift from her one and only trip to McDonalds.

'So you're definitely leaving him for good?' Frank asked.

Maria nodded.

'Good for you.'

He brought the cab to a halt. The girl leaned forward, a worried expression on her face. 'Why are we stopping?'

He nodded across the road at the blue outline of a cash machine. 'The missus always says I'm a soft touch. I reckon she's right. You're going to need some cash if you're leaving him.'

She couldn't stop the tears, not now, not in the face of such generosity. Six months of Gaz had caused her to forget that the world didn't revolve around casual cruelty. 'I can't do that. I can't take your money.'

'I'm not talking much. Fifty quid. Enough for a train ticket.'

Ignoring Maria's protests, Frank stepped out and crossed the road, fumbling in the back pocket of his denims, an overweight man in his early fifties whose simple act of kindness would contribute to her death.

7.

Gallowgate, Glasgow. So named because it was where public executions used to take place. Crowds would line the dirt streets and enjoy the wonderful spectator sport that was capital punishment. Corpses would be left to swing until their necks rotted through as a deterrent to others.

Of course, that was a long time ago in a galaxy far, far away. Things were better now. The only thing left from those bad old days was the name: Gallowgate. Abbreviated from Gallow's Gate. Now, it was just another street, lined with banks and cashline points and handy but illegal places to park a taxi while one dives out and dips into one's savings in an act of misplaced charity. Even though the stone hanging tower was still there, nobody had been executed in Gallowgate for over two hundred years.

But everybody knows the old saying: the more things change, the more they stay the same.

8.

London Road. Sixty miles an hour on the speedometer, running the red lights because it was the middle of the night and there was almost nobody there and I'd been on the advanced driving course up at Tulliallen. Coombes had finally managed to belt in and belt up.

No Merc.

There was traffic. Taxis, both hackneys and private hire cars. The occasional civilian enjoying a late night drive. A fire engine. I passed them on the inside, on the outside. Hell, I would have mounted the pavement if I had needed to.

No Merc.

Where was it?

9.

The slam of the taxi door woke Sonata Blue up, and she started to cry. Maria shrieked, covering the top of her baby's head with frantic kisses. 'Thank God. Thank God. You're alright. Thank God.' She hugged the bundle to her, feeling the hot tears on her cheek. 'I'll never let him hurt you again, I promise.'

A car rattled past as the baby hollered and whimpered, Maria soothing it as best she could. Her mother, dead for over ten years, said that a crying baby was a healthy baby, but the sound still tore at her heart. Then, with a desperate, gulping sound – URK! – Sonata threw up all over the back of the cab. Her eyes rolled back in her head and her tiny body convulsed. Maria screamed and clutched the child to her. She looked frantically for the taxi driver. There he was, still across the road, still at that bloody cash machine. She opened the door of the taxi and lurched toward him. 'Help her! She's fitting! She's dying! HELP US!'

Frank turned in the direction of her voice, his knees tensing as he prepared to go to her aid. But by then, it was too late.

10.

Coombes pointed a stubby finger. 'There! Turning onto Farmloan Street!'

I saw it. Black car, Mercedes-shaped. Possibly... *hopefully...* Grierson. I was two hundred yards back, still doing sixty. It took me less than five seconds to reach the junction, even accounting for the time it took me to slow down enough to make the corner, although I won't lie and say that I was fully in control. Later on, traffic cops measured the set of skidmarks I left as being thirty-five metres, a little fact that was gleefully reported in the tabloid press. I almost lost it entering the corner, turning in too soon and clipping the kerb, hard, bouncing off and side-swiping a parked car, the sound of metal on metal and shattering glass filling the car, Coombes screaming some-thing unintelligible at me and me screaming back.

Then I had control again. So did Coombes. 'He's seen us!'

It was Grierson, I was sure of it. He was moving fast now. We'd gained nearly a hundred yards but now the gap was stretching as the Merc flew away. My Bond-style approach to cornering must have tipped him off. Coombes smacked his fist off the dashboard. 'Floor it! Floor it! Floor it!'

I tried to jam the accelerator through the carpet. The overworked Ford protested but did as it was told, picking up speed but definitely not gaining any ground on the more powerful Mercedes. We both watched as it turned left onto Gallowgate. My palms were sticky on the wheel, and I could feel my temples pounding. Coombes was just the same, both hands clenched on the dashboard, teeth bared, a vein sticking out in his neck, all reasonable thought drowned in a flash-flood of adrenaline.

Onto Gallowgate, the speedometer needle not dropping below forty, the tyres pleading for mercy, Grierson a hundred and fifty yards ahead of us and leaving us for dead. The smell of burning clutch filled the car, and it didn't take a detective to figure this was one race we couldn't win. It was another basic rule of surveillance – when the subject's lost, back off. All we'd done was tip Grierson off. But because Coombes had been fucking around before Grierson made his move, I'd tried too hard, caught up in the pursuit, my desire not to lose the subject completely obliterating any sense of responsibility. And it was only then, at fifty-five miles an hour on a city street, that it came back, and I thought *slow down, you're being stupid, at this speed you could hit. . .*

Too late.

11.

Frank turned just in time to see the girl step into the middle of the road. She screamed and turned, raising the hand that didn't hold the baby to her chest as if to ward off the oncoming car. The collision was savage, breaking both legs, flipping her face-down onto the bonnet before slamming her head into the windscreen, the baby trapped between her body and the car and taking the brunt of the impact, also striking the windscreen and then being torn loose from her arms, the cotton bedding she had wrapped it in unravelling as the child flew through the air. Maria was thrown over the car like a rag doll, a mess of arms and legs and blood, landing back on the road, her head a fractured ruin, alive but not for long, her single remaining eye rolling in its shattered orbit and filling with blood, looking for her baby, not finding it, which was just about the only blessing, the lid trembling even as it glazed over in death.

Sonata Blue landed thirty yards away. In pieces.

12.

Coombes screamed. We both did. I slammed on the brakes and twisted the wheel, and it was at that moment that the front right wheel, already weakened from clipping the corner five hundred yards ago, decided to part company from the rest of the car. The axle dug in, flipped us up and over, the car rotating as it slid on its roof. We hit something – a parked car, a traffic island, it didn't really matter what because we were still doing fifty and it wasn't.

Unlike Coombes, I had forgotten to buckle my seatbelt.

There was a hideous, grinding noise and I felt pain in my leg and my arm and my head, three separate explosions of agony, each one a black hole supernova in its own right. Coombes was yammering about how he was bleeding and didn't want to die and all I could think about was how I had seen the blood fly from the girl's legs as the car struck, and how there was now a head-sized hole in the wind-screen and I was covered in her brains and how I prayed that the bundle she had been holding hadn't been a baby.

And then I passed out.

13.

It took them an hour to cut me free from the wreckage, and another hour in A & E to diagnose exactly how many broken bones I had. It turned out to be ten. One hip, one kneecap, one shin. One wrist and four fingers. One jaw. Plus a lump on my head the size of a Volkswagen Beetle. X-rays confirmed a fractured skull.

Coombes had a cut on his cheek.

The pen that had been sitting on the dashboard – the same pen that I had idly thought about stabbing him with – had somehow turned itself into a missile and opened a two-inch gash from his cheekbone to his jaw – less than an inch from his eye, he reminded me several times.

Once we had come to a halt, he had crawled out of the passenger side window leaving my poor smashed body in the footwell. I'm told that he then lit a cigarette. The poor soul obviously needed something to soothe his nerves.

14.

I was unconscious for two whole days, and spent the next two weeks drifting in and out of a morphine-induced stupor. For the next two months I experienced massive confusion and memory loss which the doctors assured me was normal. My initial haziness on the events, and the broken jaw, meant that Coombes had free rein to say anything he wanted to anybody. Well used to being the subject of an internal investigation, he came up with a story that Hans Christian Anderson would have been proud of, had old Hans ever written about fatal car crashes. I actually managed to read a copy of his statement, and it went something like this:

Detective Stone and myself were on surveillance duty in an unmarked vehicle parked outside Grierson Haulage Ltd on Boothe Street. At twelve fifty-five AM, we saw a black Mercedes registration SD05 XKM leave the premises. The vehicle turned left and drove past us, and both Detective Stone and myself saw three passengers. Grierson was driving, there was an unidentified female in the front passenger seat, and an unidentified male in the rear passenger seat. The male passenger was holding a gun to the female passenger's head; as they drove past, we saw him strike her on the back of the head with it. Concerned for her safety, we immediately went to follow, but our unmarked car wouldn't start. I tried to phone for back-up, but my mobile phone would not work properly and refused to connect. Meanwhile, Detective Stone had managed to get our vehicle started and we set out to follow the suspect, however, we were already significantly behind them.

I won't bore you with the rest. Suffice to say that he did a masterful job of covering his arse, and by association, mine.

15.

The media had a field day. The accident made the front page of every newspaper in the land. I kept the story from the *Daily Times*, and every once in a while I read it.

A teenage mother and child were killed early this morning when they were struck by an unmarked police car. Maria McAusland (17) died instantly at the scene of the accident in Glasgow's Gallogate. Her baby, six month old Sonata Blue, was thrown from her arms and also died at the scene. Two police officers were injured: Detective Cameron Stone (30), who is believed to have been driving the unmarked police car at the time, and Detective John Coombes (46). Detective Stone is said to be suffering from serious head injuries and remains in hospital, and Detective Coombes has been discharged after being treated for shock and a severe facial wound.

So far, so fair, although it was a bit of a stretch to refer to the cut on Coombes cheek as 'severe'. But from that point onwards, the tone of the story shifted dramatically.

It is believed that the two detectives were involved in some kind of surveillance operation. Questions are now being asked as to why the unmarked police car was travelling at high speed through a busy area. Reports suggest that there had been a car-chase stretching over a mile through the streets of Glasgow. Of the accident itself, one eyewitness said, 'It was carnage. The poor lassie never even had a chance. They didn't really appear to be fully in control of the car.' Another source who attended the scene claimed that the two detectives smelled strongly of alcohol.

See what I mean?

The kicker was a side-bar article. There was a picture, a young man sitting next to an empty cot, holding a photograph of his girlfriend and baby.

Tragic dad Gary Tiernan (18) is heartbroken over the loss of his daughter and girlfriend. 'Sonata Blue meant the world to both of us. I can't imagine my life without them.'

That's the part I found myself reading most of all.

16.

The memory of that night didn't return until nearly three months later, and even now there are blank spots. It's like seeing things through a dirty window. I get confused about the specifics of that nightmare drive, and my mind is full of vague questions that become even more vague the more I worry at them. Did we overtake the fire engine before or after London Road? Did I clip the kerb on the last corner, or the second last? Sometimes I think she might have had time to scream, but I can't remember hearing anything. Either way, by then everything had run its course. I wanted to step forward and tell the truth, but the Coombes version had become the official version. Nobody would have believed me. Nobody would have *wanted* to.

The inquiry lasted for three months. Grierson was questioned. As a fine, upstanding member of the community, he was shocked to learn that he had been under surveillance. He stated that there had only been two people in the car that night – himself and an employee he was giving a lift home. There had been no gun, no henchman in the back seat. His story was confirmed by his secretary. It was dark, argued his lawyer. The detectives concerned had made a terrible mistake.

And because we all knew that Grierson was a lying sack of shit, nobody believed him.

The taxi-driver was questioned, and footage from traffic surveillance cameras was studied. Both concurred: Maria McAusland had wandered into the middle of the road without looking.

Blood tests showed that I was completely sober at the time of the accident, and nobody thought to test Coombes. The reports of a smell of alcohol raised a few eyebrows, but the fire brigade had managed to destroy most of my clothing cutting me free from the wreckage, and nothing was ever proved. The police did what they did best when the news was bad but the inquiry was inconclusive: closed ranks.

It was decided that due to the lack of evidence, it would be wrong to hold any individual party accountable. The accident was the culmination of a series of events that could not have been prevented. The press screamed blue murder, but the book was closed. After extensive rehabilitation, I was free to return to work.

I tried. I really did.

Prologue 2

August 2008

1.

The woman walked quickly along the corridor, her heels clicking quietly on the tiled floor. In one hand was a clipboard, and she studied the papers on it with a frown that suggested to anybody who was interested that she was terribly busy and could not be disturbed.

Not that there were many people who were interested. It was the middle of the night and the hospital was quiet. Most of the patients were asleep, and those that weren't, drowsy. Staff drifted from one place to the next like somnambulists, usually alone, sometimes in pairs. Some looked at the woman, but the confidence of her stride, and the laminated identification badge that hung from the pocket of her white coat, implied that she had every right to be there. It was a big hospital, too big to question the presence of one unfamiliar face among hundreds.

She had deliberated for a long time over her appearance. Her hair, dyed chestnut brown especially for the occasion, was scraped into a severe bun. A pair of glasses balanced on the tip of her nose, the frames absurdly large for her face. On her feet was a pair of stiletto heels, their height concealed underneath a pair of trousers that were so long that the hems brushed the floor. The time spent in preparation had been worth it; if anybody saw her – really saw her – the description provided to the police would be of a tall, short-sighted woman with brown hair of indeterminate length.

She stopped briefly when she came to a junction in the corridor, tilting her head down so that she could read the sign over the rims of her too-large glasses. The hospital was a maze. Satisfied she was heading in the right direction, she moved off again. It was two minutes past three in the morning.

2.

Ellen Drysdale looked at her watch; four minutes past three. Two hundred and sixty-six minutes before she could go home. Twenty-one thousand, nine hundred and sixty seconds before she could slide between a set of cool, clean sheets and close her eyes.

She was a pretty girl with dark blonde hair that had been yanked behind her head in a clump. Her eyes were red from lack of sleep, and her fingertips were swollen and raw from where she had bitten the nails down to the quick. Night-shift did not agree with her.

Yawning, she tried to focus on the folder in front of her. It was hard to believe that a ten-bedded unit could develop so much paperwork. Care-plans, risk assessments and reviews. Memos to be filed, but only after all staff had signed to confirm they had read them; the trust directors did not believe in taking chances. In the past twelve months there had been ninety-four separate court actions raised against employees, all for abuse, misconduct or negligence. Of those, seventy-three had been dismissed. Twenty had been settled out of court. One had resulted in a spectacular loss in which the trust was forced to pay over two million pounds to the parents of a child who had suffered irreversible brain damage after an asthma attack. The child collapsed in the street after being discharged from Accident and Emergency with borderline symptoms. The junior doctor who had signed the discharge slip was now training to be an estate agent.

Correction, ninety-five complaints. One of them was still waiting to be heard.

She hadn't even been on duty when it happened. She had managed to buy tickets for Boyzone's reunion tour only to find that she was meant to be working on the day of the concert, so she had stopped briefly at work to ask a friend to swap shifts. As she walked across the hospital car-park, a man had collapsed in front of her. Of a heart attack, later tests confirmed.

Ellen had saved his life.

And cracked his rib while resuscitating him.

It's not as easy as it looks on television, where a nurse who still manages to have all her make-up in place despite having been on her feet for a ten-hour shift manages to magically restart the victims' heart after putting about five pounds of pressure on the sternum. Actors do it by moving their wrists, the power coming from the elbow. That's all very well for TV, but try that in the real world and the patient will be dead in about sixty seconds. For success, the motion must come from the shoulders, the rescuer driving down on a vertical plane, elbows and fore-arms locked. Anything else just isn't strong enough. To force blood out of an arrested heart means squeezing it like a sponge, and as the heart is protected by the rib cage, the only way to do this is by compressing the ribs.

Hard.

Too hard, in Ellen's case.

In a growing circle of onlookers, she worked on him for twelve cycles, five compressions for each breath, shouting for help all the time. The bone had given way with a damp crack, and she had felt the snap vibrate sickeningly through the heel of her hand. At that point, two staff from Accident and Emergency made it to the scene and took over. She watched as the man was wheeled into casualty on a trolley, where they zapped him back to life with three hundred and sixty volts of electricity.

Then it was time for the paperwork.

Incident Reports. Accident Reports. Practice Statements.

All in triplicate.

And, of course, after the paperwork came the interviews.

Why had she been wandering around in the car park on her day off?

How did she know the man? Why did she feel it was her responsibility to intervene? When did she last attend a heart-start lecture? Did she feel it was appropriate to begin treatment when there were more qualified people less than one hundred and fifty yards away?

Was it possible that by attempting resuscitation in the car-park, she had shown poor judgement?

Ellen was honest and told them everything. Her argument was clear and persuasive: there hadn't been time. Her actions had probably brought the man just enough time to receive treatment in a more appropriate environment. She also pointed out that had she not attempted to resuscitate the man, she could have left herself and the trust open to charges of professional negligence.

But what about the rib she broke?

Ellen shrugged. Small price to pay.

Unfortunately, the man didn't agree with her and wasted no time in engaging the services of a lawyer.

She was angry. Furious. How dare he? How dare they? Disgusted with the ingratitude of human nature, she would have quit, except she had bills to pay, and nobody hires a nurse who is currently being sued for incompetence.

Which was the reason she transferred to nightshift in one of the quieter departments of the hospital.

3.

Five minutes past three. The woman stopped at the double doors that lead into the maternity unit. She had been there during visiting hours less than two weeks ago, pretending to read the flyers on the notice board, actually watching the numeric keypad that would open the doors. Half a dozen members of staff had entered the unit during the ten minutes she had hovered; only one of them had bothered angling their hand to hide the code.

One Zero Six Six.

She tapped it in quickly. There was a tiny click as the electromagnet that controlled the lock disengaged.

4.

Ellen yawned, coughed quietly into her hand. Of the ten beds, only eight were currently occupied. Sketched onto the whiteboard behind her was the diagrammatic layout of the unit; the names of each individual patient directly adjacent to the corresponding room number. Four names were written in red felt tip; they were ones that the consultant hoped to discharge in the morning.

She wasn't supposed to be alone. The powers that be had set the current staffing levels at one auxiliary and one staff nurse, but the auxiliary had phoned in sick at ten minutes past six. Something about having stomach 'flu. No replacement could be found at such short notice. Ellen didn't mind. There was no heavy lifting, and none of the patients were that sick. They were all strong enough to attend to their own basic care, and once she had finished the night time medicine round, she could spend half the night doing paperwork and the other half secretly reading her Dan Brown novel.

Officially, the unit was part of the Maternity Wing, even though all the action – the birthing suites, the crèche, the pre-admission assessment clinics – took place upstairs. The unit was called the South Wing, and it was used primarily as a short stay ward for new mothers who needed just a couple of extra days to recover, usually because they had lost enough blood while giving birth to necessitate a blood transfusion. The four planned discharges had all received transfusions in the past twenty four hours, and once their blood results confirmed they were fit, they would all be sent home with their little bundles of joy in tow.

Six minutes past three. Ellen yawned again, a real chin-strainer that left the muscles of her jaw feeling like a rubber band that had been stretched far enough to lose its elasticity. It was her fourth night in a row, and she could feel exhaustion digging its blunt claws into her soul. It was unnatural to be awake at this time; scientific research had proved that nightshift workers were more prone to kidney problems, strokes, heart attacks and cancer, not to mention the old favourites: nervous break-downs and suicide. She found it vaguely ironic that some of the people most likely to suffer ill-health as a result of continuous night-shifts were those in the medical profession.

Coffee time.

In the tiny kitchen was a tiny kettle, and in the cupboard over the sink was a selection of tins. Teabags, sugar, coffee whitener. Some out-of-date skimmed milk in the fridge. The tin that usually held the coffee was empty. . . well, almost empty. Some sticky black residue was caked at the bottom, the remains of a thousand different jars of instant. Ellen tried scraping at it with a teaspoon without success. Probably just as well.

Bloody dayshift, she thought. They could have at least left me some-thing to drink. She checked the fridge again, hoping to spot a previously unnoticed carton of Ben and Jerry's. No such luck. All there was was the skimmed milk. She lifted the carton to her nose and inhaled: nasty. Down the sink it went.

There were vending machines downstairs. Crisps, chocolate. Coffee. Cans of Coke. Even – praise Jesus – a Pot Noodle.

She shouldn't leave the unit.

Yeah, but she shouldn't be on duty alone, either.

She would only be gone five minutes. She could nip to the toilet as well; her bladder had been pressing for the last hour. Kill two birds with one stone. It wouldn't matter. If any of the patients needed anything they could hang on for a few seconds.

Back out to the nurses' station, one quick dial of the phone. When she spoke, her voice was low. No point waking people up. 'Joyce? Yeah, it's Ellen… it's like Siberia down here. I'm just nipping downstairs to get a drink. The sods never left me any coffee. . . five minutes, alright?'

Alright.

5.

There was a linen cupboard just inside the door to the unit. The woman crouched in the darkness and listened.

Five minutes, the nurse had said.

A lot could happen in five minutes.

There was the clunk of the telephone receiver being placed into the cradle. Seconds later it was followed by the soft shuffling squeal of rubber soles. Four quick taps, one for each digit of the door code, then a minute squeak of hinges.

Silence.

The woman held her breath and counted to thirty, just in case the nurse had forgotten something. When nothing happened, she eased the door to the cupboard open and walked slowly up the corridor.

She had been there before, seven years and a lifetime ago, and remembered the layout. There was one four-bedded room, one double room, and four single rooms. She was only interested in the single rooms, all of which were occupied. A small glass window was set in each door, and she used it to scrutinise the occupant of each room, studying each woman as she slept. She passed on the first two; in each instance, the occupant in the bed had stirred slightly. That was no good. She needed somebody who was fast asleep. Not just asleep, but dead to the world.

The patient in the third room lay on her back, her head tilted over the pillow, her mouth gaping. Even through the closed door, the woman could hear the snore. But it still wasn't right. Even in the gloom, she could see the mound of the sleeping woman's belly, and knew that the woman was still waiting to give birth. She shook her head and moved on.

She had been counting silently, under her breath. One hundred and eighty seconds had passed since the nurse had left. Three minutes. She knew from experience that nurses work to a different tempo than other people, and that five minutes of their time meant at least fifteen to the rest of the world. Still, it wouldn't do to mess about.

The four-bedded unit was directly across the corridor, the curtains pulled to cover the windows. There was a light cough and the sound of somebody shifting their weight. She froze, but the noise was not repeated. She peered into the window of the last single room.

The occupant of the bed was asleep – not the dreamless, exhausted sleep of the third woman, but not the fitful, light drowse of the first two. And more importantly, unlike the third woman, she wasn't alone.

At the bottom of the bed was a cot, and in the cot was a baby.

Slowly, she eased the handle down and pushed the door open. In a second, she was inside. There was a pair of slippers on the floor. Quickly she tucked one underneath the bottom of the door to prevent it from closing behind her.

She waited, certain that her intrusion would cause the sleeping woman to wake up, or at least stir. Weren't new mothers supposed to sleep lightly so that they could protect their new-borns?

Apparently not. The sleeping woman – a girl, really, not more than eighteen – snored lightly. A bare arm lay on the bedclothes, and in the pale darkness, the woman saw bruises on the inner forearm. Junkie, she thought. She doesn't deserve to be a mum.

Three hundred seconds now. Five minutes were up. Quickly, silently, the woman moved forward and scooped the sleeping infant out of the cot. Tiny black eyes opened, but she hushed it, stroking the child's brow until the eyes closed. One last glance at the sleeping girl, thinking, babies are such a huge responsibility, especially for somebody like you. I'm really doing you a favour.

Then she was gone, stopping only to kick the slipper free and close the door noiselessly behind her.

6.

Ellen returned to the unit three minutes later, loaded down with provisions for the night. The Pot Noodle machine had been out of order, so she had stocked up with two cans of Coke, two packets of crisps, two bars of chocolate. Hardly the kind of nutritious snack that the posters on *the wall advocated, but who the hell wanted salad at half past three in the morning?*

Nobody seemed to have stirred since she had left, which was lucky. Even the babies were sleeping quietly. There were seven of them, four in the single rooms and three in the quad. It was unusual for them to be so quiet, but she wasn't about to look a gift horse in the mouth. She did a round of the unit, checking on everybody one by one, using the glass in each door to view them. The only person that seemed to have moved was the girl in room four; her slippers had been side by side when she had checked earlier, and now one was skew-whiff, on its edge two feet away. The girl must have been up to the toilet briefly before returning to bed. Ellen tried to check on the baby, but all she could make out was the blanket, one end of it trailing over the side of the cot, the rest of it puddled at the bottom. She debated going and adjusting it, before deciding to let sleeping babes lie.

Actually, she was a little surprised that the girl had been up. The poor thing had been exhausted. Hers had been an exceptionally long labour, thirty-six hours, and she had needed not one but three units of blood. The first unit had gone in alright, but the venflon in the crook of her elbow had slipped out of the vein, causing extensive bruising. It had taken a junior doctor four attempts to reset the thing. The poor kid must have felt like a pincushion.

7.

Another toilet, bigger this time. Four wash-hand basins, four cubicles. A poster on the wall reminded people to wash their hands. Empty soap dispensers made the advice impossible to follow.

The woman checked all the cubicles were empty before laying the baby down on the tiled floor of the last one. She knew it wasn't sanitary (especially not in a hospital), but she needed both hands free. There was a paper-towel dispenser fixed to the wall next to the wash-hand basins. Underneath it was a bin, lined with a black plastic bag, half full of. . .

well. . . stuff. Gritting her teeth, she rolled up her sleeve before plunging her arm in, feeling the dampness of used paper, glad she couldn't see exactly what it was her fingers were probing. It was unpleasant enough just to imagine it. . . second hand tissues. . . tampons. . . at any second she expected to feel the sting of a used needle.

After a few seconds of interminable groping, she found what she was looking for. She withdrew her arm, clutching a plastic bag, placing it to one side and rinsing her hand and arm underneath the hot-tap, rubbing vigorously with fresh paper towels until she was dry, if not clean.

She'd hidden the bag earlier in the evening, right at the end of visiting hours, when the corridors and toilets were full of members of the general public making their way home. Using just her fingertips, she emptied its contents. Bottle of baby milk (room temperature, but there was nothing she could do about that. Hopefully, she wouldn't need it) sleep suit. . . baby blanket. . . scissors. . .

Scissors?

Where were the damn scissors?

She remembered packing them, wrapping them carefully in the blanket so that they wouldn't cut her hand. She shook the blanket, listening carefully for the chink of falling metal.

Damn it, where were they? Without them she wouldn't be able to remove the wristband that encircled the baby's wrist – the wristband that emphatically proved that she was not the mother.

No matter. How time flies when you're on the run. She grabbed the sleep suit and the blanket and entered the cubicle, closing the door behind her and picking the baby off the floor so that she could balance it on her knee as she sat on the toilet. The baby was awake now, goggling at her with its blue eyes. 'It's alright, mummy's here. . . mummy's here, shush, shush, my little love.'

Unconvinced, the baby screwed up its face, drew breath to cry. The woman grabbed the bottle of milk and thrust the rubber nipple into its mouth. 'I bet you're hungry. I bet you're starving. Isn't that nice?'

The baby followed its instincts, sucking hungrily at the bottle. Without scissors to cut the child's clothes off, the woman forced the sleep suit directly over the one the infant was already wearing. Then she wrapped it in the blanket and stood up, cradling it in the hollow of her left arm, her right hand holding the rapidly emptying bottle in place.

Took a deep breath.

Thirty seconds to walk to the main entrance to the hospital, and another thirty to get to where she had parked her car. All she had to do was be cool. Hospitals were twenty-four hour places. If people were sick in the middle of the night, the nurses didn't wait until daylight before allowing loved ones to see them. There were all kinds of people wandering about. As long as she was confident, if she walked like she had every right to be there, then she would make it. She remembered some old war movie her husband loved, a scene where the prisoners had to cross open ground before they could disappear into the woods. Now she knew what it felt like. Absurdly, she was tempted to whistle the theme music for the Great Escape.

She left the toilet, started making her way down the corridor, trying to see everything without looking nervous.

Walk. Not too fast, not too slow. Head down, but not too far. Don't look like you're afraid to make eye contact, but don't do it accidentally. Talk to the baby. It's your baby, why wouldn't you talk to it? If anybody asks you why you don't have a pram, tell them you were in such a rush you forgot to put it in the boot of the car.

Out of the corridor and into the main reception area. More people. Nobody was looking. Vending machines, bright lights, lots of chairs. A woman sat with her head in her hands. Behind her, a family cried. Don't look at them. It's bad luck.

'Excuse me!'

The woman felt a bolt of fear. Her arms became rigid.

'Excuse me!'

She stopped, turned. Forced a hideous smile onto her face.

It was a man in a football top, his eye blackened and his right arm in a sling. He was leaning on a vending machine, waving a five pound note at her. 'You don't have any change, do you?'

'I'm sorry, I don't.'

He shook his head, slapped his good hand against the side of the machine. 'You'd think they would provide coffee for those of us that have got to wait.' He nodded at the baby. 'Yours?'

'Mine.'

'I've got five.'

Good for you, she was tempted to say. Instead, she lied. 'My third. He's only four days old. My granny had a stroke yesterday. She's not expected to last the night. I've driven all the way from London so that she can see her great-grandchild.'

The man nodded. 'I'm sorry.'

She thanked him, told him she needed to go.

Nobody stopped her.

8.

As far as Ellen was concerned, the Coca-Cola people were right: you really couldn't beat the feeling. The drink was ice cold, and tasted like heaven. She guzzled the first can in three huge gulps before eating a Mars Bar in what seemed like a single bite.

Jesus, it was time to come off nightshift. Any more of this and she would have a backside the size of Falkirk.

She was confident that the complaint against her would eventually be dismissed. The man had been huge – compressing his chest had been like sinking her hands into soft dough – and her lawyer would exploit the fact, making it plain that it would be nigh on impossible to calculate the correct pressure needed when the subject was so grossly overweight. Too little pressure and the man would have died, right there in the car park, leaving trust officials with the tricky decision over whether to load him onto a trolley and have him taken to the hospital morgue, or to phone Greenpeace and ask them to push the corpse back into the sea.

The Dan Brown novel was tucked into a drawer at the nurses' station. She took it out, sat down and put her feet up. Opened a packet of crisps and a second can of Coke. Maybe she shouldn't be in such a rush to leave night shift. It wasn't as if you got the time to skive like this during the day.

'I'm sorry, I couldn't do it.'

'Jesus!' Ellen sat up, spilling the crisps down her top. She twisted her neck behind her so that she could see where the voice had come from. 'Jesus!'

It was a woman, about the same age as Ellen. Tears stained her cheeks, and she held a bundle out. 'I was going to take it, but I couldn't.' She stepped forward, thrust the child into Ellen's arms. 'Here.'

Dumbfounded, Ellen watched as the woman turned on her heel and ran for the door. The child pulled in her arms, and she looked down to it. It was awfully bulky, and as she looked closer, she saw that it was wearing two layers of clothes. Then she saw the identity tag on the wrist, realised that it was one of her charges, and had to sit down, breathing harshly.

It took her less than two minutes to figure out what happened, and even less time than that to decide never to mention it. If the powers that be could make her feel at fault for saving a man's life, imagine what they could do in a case like this.

She wasted no time stripping off the outer layer of clothing and slipping the baby back into the cot. The exhausted mother barely stirred. Ellen spent the rest of the night sitting in the corridor, where she could see the door, not reading Dan Brown. The first thing she did when matron arrived at ten past seven in the morning was request to return to dayshift.

Chapter 1

Thursday November 13th, 2008

1.1.

She was pretty, with a sulky mouth and short blonde hair cut in a bob. Like all the girls I had seen since entering, she wore white leggings and a plain, short sleeved blue polo shirt that lent the place an air of class that one didn't usually associate with a brothel.

Sorry. Did I say brothel? I do apologise. According to their advert in Yellow Pages, the Champagne Angel Club was "an exclusive Health Spa, deep in the heart of Glasgow, an ideal place to relieve the stress and worry of your busy lifestyle."

To be fair, it did have a swimming pool. And a gym. Even some sunbeds. The fact that it also had a great many private rooms, and seemed to employ an inordinately high number of girls between the ages of 18 and 35 as "massage therapists" was purely co-incidental.

I'd arrived about fifteen minutes ago, paying the girl on the front desk fifty pounds, which I was told covered my admission fee and a short massage. When asked if there was any "therapist" in particular I wanted to be introduced to, I'd given a description: tall, about twenty, with short, blonde hair. No mention of the sulky mouth. I saw her on the street outside, I said. Thought she looked nice.

The receptionist lead me down a short corridor into a room, telling me to change into one of the robes that hung on a peg behind the door. The room itself was square, dominated by a massage table on one side and a small futon on the other. Soothing music drifted from a cheap stereo on top of a small bedside cabinet. I peeked inside the drawer, finding a small dildo, a tube of KY jelly and some condoms. I had no plans to use any of them.

I stripped down to my underwear and put the robe on. Five minutes after that, the girl – she of the sulky mouth and blonde hair – came in. She said hello and made inconsequential small talk while gathering up the small pile of my belongings and placing them in the lower compartment of the cabinet, closing the door firmly on them. Clever. If I had been an undercover cop with a tape recorder in my pocket, there was no way I would have been able to obtain any usable evidence.

She wasted little time getting down to business. 'Mr Stone, why don't you take that robe off and lie face down on the table?'

I did as I was asked. 'Call me Cameron.'

'Alright then, Cameron.' She climbed on top of me, her pelvis against the small of my back, her thighs pressed against my sides. I turned my head and caught a glimpse of the inside of her left arm. No track marks, which was encouraging, although there was always a chance she was left handed, in which case she would shoot up in her right arm instead. From the way she kneaded the muscles in my shoulders like a lump of dough, I suspected that she had no formal training in massage.

Her fingers stopped, hovering over my right thigh. 'Does it hurt?'

I knew what 'it' was. 'I was in a car accident. They had to rebuild my right hip. I've been told that the marks will fade in a few months.'

'Oh.'

The scars were ugly and red-raw, laddering down both the inner and outer aspects of the thigh, the flesh twisted and hairless. I didn't blame her for not wanting to touch them, but I felt a bitter taste rise in my mouth. After all, I was the one that had to live with them.

She leaned in, her breasts pressing against my back, her breath tickling my cheek. 'How does that feel?'

'Nice.'

She worked on, gently rubbing and stimulating my shoulders and upper half. Even though she was more than ten years younger than I was, I found myself responding to her on a physical level. I hadn't been with a woman since the accident, and most of the time I didn't miss it, but there was something about this girl, with her nice figure and her bold, consequence-free availability that I found arousing. I didn't need to wine and dine her, I didn't need to make her laugh, I didn't even need to pretend to be attracted to her. She didn't care who I was, or what I had done. All she was interested in was the money in my wallet.

Simple, easy sex. Anonymous, guiltless and on demand.

Five minutes later, I was glad when she climbed off me. It gave me the chance to count to ten and re-establish a sense of professional objectivity. I sat up on the edge of the table, crossing my legs to disguise my erection. She saw it anyway and smiled.

'You look as if you enjoyed that.'

'I did.'

She cocked her head to one side, and this time the smile didn't stretch to her eyes. 'Would you like anything else?'

I needed to be careful how I answered. Although tempted on a purely physical level, I had little desire and no intention of fucking her. To answer "No" however, meant that our business was concluded and I would be expected to leave. Saying nothing, I crossed over to the cabinet, took my wallet from the inside pocket of my jacket and removed some notes. Then I made sure to place everything except the cash back inside the cabinet and close the door firmly. She watched the whole procedure carefully, evidently making up her mind that I wasn't a cop.

'Alright. It's fifty pounds for full sex. Blow jobs are sixty with a condom, eighty without. One hundred for up the arse. Anything else, we can negotiate.'

I held out five ten pound notes, fanning them like a poker hand so that she could count them. 'How about we just talk?'

'Talking takes up too much time. Wouldn't you rather just fuck?'

'Fifteen minutes. No more. I promise.'

I could see her mind working, trying to figure out if I was a weirdo who wanted something extra kinky, or if I maybe planned to do her some harm. Eventually she took the notes out of my hand. 'Fifteen minutes.'

I put the robe on and checked my watch; it was just after eleven at night. It had taken nearly a month to find her, and now that I had, I didn't want to scare her off by rushing into anything. 'What's your name?'

She shrugged. 'What does it matter?'

'I just wanted to know what to call you.'

'You can call me anything you like.'

'Fine. I'll call you Susan.'

Because I already knew that was her real name.

Her eyes narrowed as she tried to figure out whether I made a lucky guess, or if there something else going on. 'Do I know you from somewhere?'

'No.'

'Are you a cop?'

'I'm a private investigator.' That wasn't quite the truth, but for all intents and purposes, it didn't matter. 'I was hired to pass a message on to you.'

She walked to the door and opened it. 'Get out.'

'Please. I don't mean you any harm. I'm not going to tell anybody that I found you.'

There was a small red button on the wall next to the light switch; she pressed it. 'You're damn right about that.'

I spoke quickly. 'Your real name is Susan McPherson. You're eighteen years old and grew up in Inverness. Your mum and dad asked me to find you because they love you.' I took my jacket out of the cabinet for the second time, rummaging in the pocket, acutely aware of the sound of pounding feet coming from the direction of the corridor. A man the size of a small house materialised in the door just as my fingers closed on the envelope. I tossed it at her. 'This is for you.'

The bouncer lunged across the room. 'Right, pal, time to leave.'

Moving quickly – or at least, as quickly as I could with a gammy leg – I dodged, putting the massage table between the two of us. Susan bent and picked up the envelope. The bouncer – bald, breathing heavily, a spider web tattooed on his neck – faced me across the table. 'I'll come over there, son. I fucking mean it.'

'I'm not here to cause trouble.'

With a grunt, he leaned forward and put both hands on the table, the muscles across his shoulders bunching as he exerted pressure. With a screech, the whole thing moved, bouncing off my upper thighs, forcing me to take a step backwards. And another. And another, until my back was against the wall. A hand the size of a football clutched at my neck. I put both arms up to defend myself, and felt my left wrist grabbed in a vice-like grip. The bouncer's face turned red as he squeezed; there was a nasty clicking noise as bones that had previously occupied their own clearly defined territory were suddenly forced to share space. I screamed, tried to wrench myself free, couldn't. The bouncer leaned forward and grabbed the front of the robe with his free hand, dragging me forward until I lay face down across the surface of the table. Then he transferred his left hand from my wrist to the back of my neck, holding me down, his bodyweight pushing the table against my legs and my legs against the wall, I couldn't move, couldn't breath, couldn't do anything except wait for the blow to fall. . .

'Kenny! Stop!'

Kenny stopped.

The hand on the back of my head let go. The pressure on my back released a little, enough for me to look up and see what was going on.

Susan was staring at me, a sheet of paper in one hand and a Polaroid picture in the other. The envelope – torn open, now – was discarded on the floor. Kenny glowered at me like a Doberman Pinscher ordered to release a particularly juicy trespasser.

'I have a baby brother,' she said, her voice stunned and

disbelieving. 'Mum had a baby.' She turned the picture round and showed it to us: a chubby infant in a blue babygrow. 'See?'

Absurdly, I congratulated her. Kenny didn't.

She waved an impatient hand at the bouncer. 'Oh, for God's sake let him go. He didn't do anything.'

Kenny muttered something underneath his breath, but stepped back. I stood up and started rubbing my wrist. The damn thing was already swelling.

1.2.

Ten minutes later, I was fully dressed, sipping a glass of orange juice. Susan sat opposite me, unable to take her eyes off the Polaroid. 'I can't believe it.'

I said nothing. The club's bar was small and dimly lit, the only other customer a fat man in a business suit. He sat at a nearby table and sipped his glass, a girl on each side to keep him company. He saw me looking and winked, his face growing cold when I didn't reciprocate.

Eventually, Susan put the picture down. 'How did you find me?'

I shrugged. 'Shoe leather.'

'What?'

'It's what we do. Find people.'

William McPherson, Susan's father, had contacted us a month ago, with a photograph and very little else. Just under two years ago, Susan had gone missing from the family home in Bonnydoon, a tiny village thirty miles outside of Inverness, leaving nothing but a hand-written note saying that she was leaving and not to try and find her. Of course, they searched, but once all the obvious places had proved fruitless, there was nowhere left to look. She's over sixteen, the police said. She can do what she wants.

Two months ago a holidaymaking friend claimed to have seen the

McPhersons' missing daughter walking down Argyle Street one Saturday morning. Acutely aware that Glasgow's a hell of a lot bigger than Bonnydoon, Daddy had sold his car and called in the professionals.

Neither my boss nor I had been particularly hopeful of finding Susan; there were too many ifs in the equation. What if the friend had made a mistake, or was playing a cruel joke, or even just making up the story in a misguided attempt to give the McPhersons a little hope? What if Susan had just been passing through, on her way to somewhere else? What if she was in Glasgow, but just didn't want to be found?

Cruelly but necessarily we pointed out the Worst Case Scenario: maybe she was lying at the bottom of a loch somewhere, a tragic victim of an unknown accident or vile, secret crime? One of the few missing people who were truly missing, somehow completely, unequivocally lost? Sometimes, we said, it's better not to know.

Wily McPherson shook his head and pleaded with us to take the case. A gentle, softly spoken man with a lilting highland accent and a sad, bloodhound face. It was easy to see the cost of his daughter's disappearance in the slump of his shoulders and the way he tugged nervously at his greying moustache. I think we agreed to help him not only because he was willing to pay fifty percent of our fee up front, but because we felt sorry for him. People who don't know what it's like say that there's always hope, but the truth is that perpetual, unfulfilled, unjustifiable hope is a terrible thing to live in.

Of course, Joe had delegated most of the hard work to me, the trusty sidekick. I was a new employee, and I suspected that he had used the case as a test, examining my attitude and dedication. Because Joe had given me a job when the rest of the world hadn't wanted to know, I was determined to repay him. I spent my days and nights walking the streets, showing the out-of-date photograph in bars, in homeless shelters, in cafe's. Train stations, bus stations, hospitals. There wasn't a Big Issue vendor in the city I hadn't bought a magazine from. I tried the street girls. Blytheswood Square, Byres Road. The Anderston Centre. It was in Bothwell Street that I finally got a bite. A fifty-year old hooker name Rosie Hawes (aka Rosie the Whore) remembered a girl that looked a lot like Susan working the West End of the town. They'd shared a cigarette one cold night a few months back. 'She talked about going into one of those massage parlours,' Rosie had told me, tucking the fiver I had given her into the cup of her massive bra. 'Said there was less chance of getting the plague in a place like that.'

It was only a hint, but I doggedly pursued it, using my knowledge of the city to check out every club, every massage parlour, every knocking shop and strip club. And then I had my one stroke of luck, spotting Susan walking along Woodlands Road, an area of the city that was notorious for the amount of brothels tucked between lawyers' offices. The hair was shorter, the face two years older (and, I hate to say, twenty years wiser), but there was no doubt in my mind that it was her. After showing her picture to just about everybody in the city, I felt like I could recognise her face blindfold. From there, it was a simple matter to follow her to work, and even simpler to arrange a meeting.

Like I said, shoe leather.

'So how did you end up working in a place like this?' I asked her.

'I just kind of drifted into it. I was homeless when I first came here, sleeping in squats and stuff like that, always cold. I ended up having a one nighter with some rich guy just so as I could have a place to sleep. When I woke up in the morning he'd gone out, to get a loaf of bread to make toast or something. Didn't matter. I cleaned out his flat and hit the road.' She lit a cigarette. 'I realised then and there that there was no reason for me to be cold and hungry all the time, not when I was young and good looking and not too picky.'

'You're still young and good looking.'

She blew a plume of smoke at me. 'Tough luck, pal, your fifteen minutes are up.'

'So why run away in the first place?'

She shrugged. 'Did you read the letter my dad gave you?'

I shook my head. 'I was only hired to find you.'

She took the page out, read through it quickly before tucking it away again. 'I just got sick of them, you know? Mum had an affair with the next door neighbour. Dad knew about it, but just let it go. You could see how miserable he was, but he just didn't have the balls to act, and all the time mum was just making a complete fool of herself. She was talking about leaving dad, of upping sticks and going to run a bar in Ibiza, and everybody in the fucking village was laughing at her. I just got tired of the whole thing and moved on. My boyfriend was a few years older, said that we could make a go of it. I was dumb enough to believe him.'

'Boyfriend?' I'd asked about boyfriends, but her father had been unable to tell me anything. Now I could understand why. At the time, he'd been too concerned about his wife's affair to notice what was going on in his daughter's life.

'Yeah. The bastard ditched me a week after we got here.'

'Sounds like a nice guy.'

'A prince.'

'So why didn't you go back to your parents?'

She shrugged, and in that gesture I realised that for all her adult mannerisms, she was barely more than a kid pretending to be a grown-up. 'I figured I was old enough to look after myself.'

'You were sixteen.'

'Yeah, and about twice as bloody mature as my parents.'

'They want you to go home.'

'Why should I?'

'Because. . . ' I wasn't sure what to say. Even though she was still young, this girl had done things most people couldn't imagine. It had changed her, making her seem not older, but more cynical. She was confusing life experience with maturity, but if I was to tell her that, she wouldn't believe me. 'Because they're sorry.'

'Everybody is, nowadays.'

I looked over at the fat businessman. He whispered in the ear of one of the girls at his side; a second later her hand slid underneath the table and into his lap. Her expression suggested that she would rather fondle a bucket of toads. 'You'd prefer to stay here?'

Anther shrug. 'The money's good.'

I nodded in the direction of the opposite table. 'It can't be that good.'

She watched for a few seconds, her face expressionless. 'You'd be surprised. It beats working in some call centre for six pounds an hour.'

'Your parents love you.' I told her, feeling hopelessly old. It used to be that selling sex was the lowest one could fall, and now this girl, this child, was telling me that it was nothing more than a life-style choice. 'They love you,' I repeated, my voice lame.

'Stop telling me that they love me!'

The other two girls looked up briefly; the fat businessman was too busy enjoying himself. Susan lowered her voice. 'I don't care if they love me! I don't care! I tried to talk to them, I mean really *tried*, but they didn't listen.'

'Which is why they're sorry now.'

'Jesus Christ, you don't get it, do you? How can I go back? How can I face my parents after this? How can I tell them that I once let a guy pee on me for two hundred pounds?'

'You don't. Tell them what you want. They won't care. All they want is to know is that you're safe. When your dad came to hire us, we told him that you could be doing anything. We told him that you could be dead, that you could be working in a place like this. You want to know what he said?'

She nodded.

'"It doesn't matter. She's a good kid, and a smart one. She'll do what it takes to get by." Bonnydoon is two hundred miles away. It's not as if you're going to be running into people that you've met in Glasgow every day of the week. And the guy that paid to. . . you know. . . you think he's going to tell people what he's into? You think he's proud of the fact that he's such a weirdo that he has to pay someone to be a part of his sick little fantasy?'

Whatever I said, I felt that I wasn't going to get through to her. Still, I kept trying. 'Look, you can sit there and pretend that you've been there, done that and bought the fucking T-shirt, but the truth is that you don't know shit. You might at the time have thought you had a good reason to leave, but you know now that's a load of crap. You know that your parents love you but, rather than admit that, you have the nerve to sit here and pretend that you're the one that's the victim in all this. Can you imagine all the worry and hurt you caused them? Can you understand how their lives stopped the minute you went missing?'

I reached into my wallet and took out a business card and a pen, scrawling my home number onto the back before placing the card on the table in front of her. 'Look, if you're scared about facing your parents, call me first and I'll talk to them for you.'

She just sat there, shaking her head as if by doing so she could discount everything I had said. I stood up, angry. 'Fuck it. I said I wasn't going to tell your parents where you were, but I think I will. Because maybe then you'll see. They'll keep looking for you. They'll come down here and ask questions, so unless you decide that you can handle it, then you're going to have to move on. But wherever you go, they're going to keep looking because, for whatever reason, they love you and will forgive anything. . . *anything*. . . you've done. You can't run forever.'

Chapter 2

Friday November 14th, 2008

2.1

Take Control: Glasgow operated from a small grey building on Paisley Road that had originally been a doctors' surgery. Four years ago, a new health centre had been built a couple of hundred yards away, and the doctors had lost no time in decamping to the upgraded facility. *Take Control* lived up to their name and took control, turning the examination rooms into small offices that were ideal for one-to-one counselling. Everything – the reception area, the private rooms, the coffee bar – was painted in soothing earth tones: harvest browns and spring yellows and forest greens. Pamphlets covered every available surface in the reception area – Coping With Loss, Dealing with Depression, So You Think You Might Be Gay? As I sat in the waiting area, I flicked through something called Positively Positive, only to find it was aimed at people who had been diagnosed with HIV.

As soon as I was fit, the police had made me attend mandatory counselling sessions. They didn't help much. Most of the coppers I know would rather chew their own leg off than admit that they were having difficulty dealing with the nasty things they see in the course of the job, and the force itself is still dominated by stereotyped attitudes to mental health. Rather than talk something through, we'd rather keep it to ourselves and hope it goes away on its own. Most of us, including myself at the time, believed that the best way to deal with mental trauma was to buy it a drink. To actually admit we needed help not only defined us as headcases but could actively harm our careers.

The counselling ended when I quit the police force. It was scary. In a few short months I had lost nearly everything. I had been reviled in the media, and when I walked down the street I could feel people staring and talking about me from behind cupped hands. I was completely alone, a social pariah. The worst incident was when an elderly woman spat on me while I was queuing to pay for a loaf of bread in my local supermarket. She grabbed my arm, told me that she had something to say to me, and unloaded right in my face. I just stood there, her saliva on my cheek, saying nothing as she told everybody what I had done. There was nothing I could say; everything she said was technically true. I had been driving too fast. I had mown down a mother and child. In the end I dropped my basket of groceries and walked home.

That night, I tried to commit suicide.

At best, it was a fairly Mickey Mouse attempt. I drank half a bottle of Bushmills and munched my way through a box of paracetamol, also taking a pathetically small chunk out of my left wrist with a blunt kitchen knife. Then I got scared and staggered to the nearest A & E unit, where I was given an activated charcoal drink to neutralise the effects of the paracetamol. I spent three days taking up space in an acute medical ward before being discharged with a referral to my G.P., who in turn suggested a weekly session at *Take Control*.

That was nearly four months ago.

Nobody – not even Joe, my boss – knew about the suicide attempt. When he gave me the job as his assistant, he made it clear from the start that he expected me to be sober, shaved and in a clean suit, on time and keen. Had he known just how unstable I was, he might not have been so forthcoming with the offer. As it turned out, the work helped me get back on a reasonably even keel in a way that the booze, anti-depressants and therapy hadn't.

Yeah, I owed Joe. A lot. As I sat there in the reception area, I made a mental list. A job. A loan. Even more than that, his friendship. Just last week I had dinner with him and his wife, just like I was a regular human being and not the devil incarnate.

'Cameron?'

I looked up, startled. Katy was standing in front of me. She smiled when we made eye contact. 'You looked like you were about to fall asleep.'

'I was out late last night,' I told her. 'Working.'

'Me too.'

I followed her down a short corridor, trying hard not to watch her backside, which twitched prettily from side to side as she walked. In two months I'd noticed that Katy did everything she could to conceal her looks, without success. She was one of these women who couldn't be unattractive if they tried: slim, with a great figure and legs that reached all the way to the floor and back. Her long black hair had been pulled back into a severe ponytail that only accentuated the delicate contour of her neck and jawline. Tucked behind one shapely ear was a ball point pen. Her eyes. . .

Oh, for Christ's sake, stop it, I told myself. Stop thinking of her as a woman and start thinking of her as somebody who can help you. There's a reason she dresses the way she does, and it's to stop guys like you from thinking she's anything more than a counsellor.

At the end of the corridor she showed me into a room that looked more like somebody's lounge than an office. The carpet was thick, and instead of a desk, there were two armchairs in opposite corners of the room, a low coffee table placed between them. The only concession to practicality was a small filing cabinet just beside the door. On the wall directly facing the door was a poster that hadn't been there last week: a kitten clinging desperately to a branch by its claws, its eyes dark pools of desperate fear. The caption advised the kitten to 'Hang On'. Katy followed my gaze. 'I see you've noticed Kitty.'

'Yeah. I'm more of a dog person myself.'

'Me too.' She saw the question in my eyes. 'This isn't my office. It's a guy called Simon Joseph's. I just borrow it two days a week.'

'So Simon's the cat lover.'

'Among other things.'

She sat down on one of the armchairs, taking the pen out from behind her ear and picking up a clipboard that had been sitting on top of the coffee table. It felt like I was being interviewed by a tradesperson – a particularly sexy, attractive plumber, maybe. Perhaps she was going to give me a quote for a new psyche.

'So, Cameron, what's going on with you?'

I shrugged. 'Nothing much.'

'How's the job?'

'Good.'

'How long's it been now?'

'Two months. Nearly three.'

'Do you think you'll stick it?'

I shrugged my shoulders. 'I've no reason not to. Joe's a good boss. I owe him. Plus I enjoy the work.'

She nodded, made a note on her clipboard. 'What about Mark?'

'He's fine. I think.'

'You think? You haven't seen him?'

'I spoke to his mother on the phone. She's asked me to pick him up from school.'

She waited for me to elaborate, letting the silence grow louder between us, obviously hoping that I would feel the need to fill it. I'd often used the same technique myself while interviewing suspects.

She cracked before I did. 'You don't get to see very much of him, do you?'

I took my time answering, not because I resented the question, but because I missed him so much I found it difficult to talk about. Of all the things that had happened, losing Mark has been the worst. 'Not as much as I would like, no.'

'That must be hard. Why can't you seem him more often?'

She knew why, but obviously wanted me to say it. 'His mother won't let me.'

'Why?'

I shrugged. The easy answer was because of the accident, and because Audrey was a complete bitch. That was oversimplifying things just a tad.

The truth was that we had been having problems even before the accident. My memory of the preceding months consisted mainly of slammed doors, raised voices and sullen silences. Audrey had used what had happened as an excuse to move out and take Mark with her. Of course, I didn't know that at the time. Instead, I woke up from my coma to find out that she had written a brief note on the back of a get well soon card.

Katy uncrossed her legs and took a deep breath. 'Cameron, I can't help you unless you start to trust me. You come here week after week but you won't talk to me. You won't communicate about anything – your thoughts, your feelings. . . anything. I've tried to nudge you into telling me about the accident, but you clam up. I can understand why – nobody likes talking about stuff like that, but unless you can open up just a teeny bit, then we're going to spend every Friday morning dancing around each other like nervous teenagers. Now, I know that you're a big macho man who thinks that counselling's for wimps, but humour me. Help me to feel like I'm earning my twelve-fifty an hour.'

'Twelve-fifty? I would have thought. . . '

'We're funded by the NHS, pal. I'm lucky I don't get paid in salt. Now stop messing me about and start talking. Are you still drinking?'

I stared at her, unused to confrontation. 'Not really,' I said. 'I never had a problem with drink. I just used it as something to help.'

'And did it?'

'For a while, yeah. But I realised that I was better off without it.'

'Did you realise or did somebody point it out to you?'

I took my time answering that one, casting my mind back about ten weeks to a rather tense, unpleasant meeting in the Chief Super's office. I'd been back on light duty for less than three weeks, and it was obvious to everybody that it wasn't working out. 'Somebody pointed it out. My superiors asked me to take a leave of absence.'

'Why would they do that? If you had been certified as being fit for duty, why would they suddenly change their minds?'

I realised that I had been neatly backed into a corner. 'Look, I'm not saying I didn't have a problem with drink. I'm saying that for the first few months after the accident I used alcohol as a. . . a coping strategy. Being drunk helped keep my mind off things. And then I realised that I was spending too much time drunk and I dealt with it.'

'You dealt with it.'

The scepticism in her voice pissed me off. 'Yeah. I dealt with it. I stopped drinking. Completely. Now, I might have a glass of wine or a beer at the weekend, but other than that, I don't drink. I don't go out of my way to avoid it because it wasn't the alcohol was the problem. It was everything else. When everybody else was pointing the finger, when the papers were baying for my blood, when people I thought were friends seemed to crawl into the woodwork, hell, when my girl-friend of seven years fucked off and took my little boy with her, it was the booze that was there for me. Is it any wonder I had a. . . a flirtation with booze? It's not as if I've spent the last ten years drinking Buckfast from a brown paper bag while sitting on the steps of some hostel for the homeless. All I did was spend six weeks pissed as a fart, and when I realised that was no way to live I stopped. It was simple as that.'

Her pen scratched furiously on the paper. 'So why quit your job?'

'Because. . . because it wasn't the same. They couldn't treat me the way they always had. I was given a stupid paperwork assignment. They didn't want me out there, dealing with the general public. Not Cameron Stone, the psycho babykiller. Instead, they gave me a desk in the corner and told me to sign forms in triplicate. They said it was only for a few months, until the fuss had died down, but I couldn't hack it. I could tell that they were all embarrassed for me. When they "suggested" that it might be best if I took a few more weeks off, I told them to shove it.'

'Sounds like you really thought things through.'

'I'd been thinking about leaving anyway. I was sick of the whole business, wanted to make a fresh start. Joe had been in touch, letting me know there was a job with him if I wanted it. I just decided that it was time to go.'

She made a note on her clipboard. I tried to read it, but the angle was all wrong, plus her handwriting looked to be about as legible as chickenscratch. She caught me looking. 'So what's it like being a private detective?'

I shrugged. 'I'm not really a private detective. You need to have a licence for that. I'm more a. . . general dogsbody. Donkeywork. Light surveillance. Typing. I make coffee for clients and I do research for Joe. It's not very glamorous at all.'

'Must be a bit of a let-down, after being a copper. Don't you miss the police force?'

'Sometimes. Most of the time I don't. I don't miss the politics, that's for sure. That's the thing about being a cop. Too many chiefs and not enough Indians. Everybody's trying so hard to impress their boss that no actual work gets done. The best we can hope to achieve is mediocrity.'

'That's a very cynical viewpoint.'

'I'm a very cynical person.'

She looked disappointed. 'What makes you believe that?'

'Because I've seen how shitty people can be to each other. I dedicated ten years of my life to helping clean up the kind of mess that most people would rather pretend never happened.'

'And you believe it's made you a cynic.'

'Don't *you*?'

She shook her head earnestly. 'Cameron, I see dozens of guys like you, talking tough, pretending that they're a character from a novel by James Elroy or something like that, so don't be offended when I tell you that I can see past the bullshit. Let me ask you a question. If you really think the world's a sewer, why do you come here every week?'

I shrugged. She obviously thought she knew the answer.

She did. 'It's because, despite the fact that you think everything is bad, you genuinely believe that I can help make you a better person. And if you believe that you can be a better person, then you have to believe that the rest of the world can be a better place. And if you believe that the world can be a better place, then you can't be a cynic.' She grinned like she had found the answer to life, the universe and everything. 'You, my friend, are an optimist.'

She was so happy, I decided not to spoil it for her.

2.2.

Friday afternoon. School. . . was. . . out!

'Daddy!'

My little boy ran toward me with his arms outstretched. His shirt was untucked, the knees of his grey trousers were brown with mud, his hair was a mess, and I had never loved him more. He hit the lower half of my body like a tiny express train and wrapped his arms around my waist. 'Daddy!'

I ruffled his hair, knowing that whatever I did it couldn't get any more tangled. 'Hey, son.'

Whenever I get to see Mark, I end up calling him son every second sentence. I'm overcompensating for my absence, but I can't help it. I'm scared that if I don't keep reminding him, he might forget I'm his father.

He took a step back and looked at me. 'Where have you been?'

I've been begging your mother to let me see you, I wanted to say. I've waited outside the house for you for hours. I've phoned and phoned, only to be told that you're asleep, or at beaver scouts, or out with your mother's new boyfriend.

But that's not the kind of thing you tell a five-year old. 'I've been working a lot.'

'Catching bad guys?'

'Sometimes,' I said. 'Sometimes I just find out where they are.'

'Why don't you catch them?'

'Sometimes they don't need to be caught. Sometimes, the person that's paying me to find them just needs to know where they are.'

'Why?'

'Because. . .' I'd left the car parked in a side street three hundred yards away, and we started walking. All around us were parents and children doing the same thing. The kids that were old enough to make their way home unsupervised laughed and called to each other as they swarmed past on their way to the video arcade or the shopping mall or to smoke dope in the abandoned tyre factory or whatever the hell it is that kids do for fun these days. Mark held on to my hand and for the first time in weeks I felt good. '. . .Because sometimes all people need is to find to each other,' I told him.

We walked. Mark talked and I listened. We covered important subjects like addition and subtraction and who was going to play King Herod in the nativity play (some kid called Keanu Tucker and it just wasn't fair). It had been a dry November, and dry leaves skittered along the gutter in the light breeze.

There was a tug on my hand as Mark slowed down. 'Dad?'

'What, son?'

'I don't like Arnold.'

Arnold was Audrey's new partner. My replacement. I didn't like him either. In fact, I wouldn't have been at all upset to discover that he had been killed by a falling piano. Yet another thing you don't tell a five year old. 'Why not?'

'He makes me do things I don't want to.'

I stopped. Tensed up. Had to stop myself from squeezing his hand too tightly. Don't frighten him, I thought. Just stay nice and calm.

'What kind of things?'

I was surprised by how casual my voice sounded.

'Just things.'

We started walking again, our pace a bit slower than before. From the corner of my eye I noticed that Mark was biting the thumbnail of his free hand. I was scared and angry. I wanted to grab him by the shoulders and shake him, not to hurt or to frighten but to drag answers out of him there and then. What does he do? What does he make *you* do?

It wouldn't work.

In the weeks directly after the accident, I was made to attend counselling sessions with a therapist called Catherine Goodall. I can't remember Catherine's official title, but she had a degree in psychology and was employed full time by Strathclyde police. We both enjoyed the sessions, and after I left the force we kept in touch. As I was no longer her patient, we went on a few dates. The whole thing petered out after a few weeks, but not because we didn't like each other. It was just that the timing was wrong. Cath was halfway through an extremely messy divorce, while I was only just back on the market after being jettisoned by my partner of seven years. Both of us were simply carrying far too much baggage to help the other out.

In addition to counselling traumatised police officers, Catherine also worked for the Family Protection unit, and although it wasn't a field of police work I had been particularly interested in, I listened politely when she talked about it. Something she had said stuck with me.

'In any form of abuse – domestic, physical, sexual – it's not often that a victim will come forward and just admit to being abused. They won't say 'My boyfriend beats me,' or 'My father rapes me.' Sometimes what happens is something I call escalating disclosure. For example, a woman might tell you that she fell down the stairs, then a few minutes later she might tell you that she had an argument with her partner just before she fell. Then a few minutes later, she'll drop in the little fact that her partner might have accidentally pushed her down the stairs. And it goes on like this for a while, until you know exactly what happened.'

Cath had told me this while eating dinner in a second-rate Indian restaurant. We were on our third date and she had been wearing a red silk blouse. On our previous dates, the blouses had been buttoned all the way up to the neck, but on that night, she'd skipped the top three and kept leaning forward as she spoke. Even if I hadn't been interested in a word she was saying, she would have had my complete and undivided attention.

'Of course, the thing about enhanced disclosure is that you can't rush victims of abuse into talking to you. They have to be in control all the time because they often feel like unless they retain complete control, then they've got none at all. If you push them too hard, if you tell them that the bruise on their face that they claimed was caused by their head hitting the banister, actually looks like it was caused by a fist, then they'll clam up. They'll shut down and leave you with nothing.'

I took a bite of my meal. It was meant to be Chicken Tikka Masala, but tasted more like furniture polish and crow.

'So how do you deal with that then?'

'Give them time. You can lead them a little. Tell them that you fell down the stairs when you were a teenager and broke your ankle. Stuff like that. The important thing is not to scare them off.'

The important thing is not to scare them off.

The problem was, I didn't have time. Cath could spend days, weeks, working with abuse victims, steadily chipping away at the lies like a sculptor. I had an hour, maybe ninety minutes before Audrey expected Mark home. And it was bonus time at that; she had only asked me to collect him from school because she had a dentist appointment and her sister was working. How was I supposed to find out what Mark was talking about without scaring him? There had to be a way. I kept my voice as casual as I could. 'You know, I don't really like Arnold either.'

'He's a dickhead.'

'Don't say that word,' I corrected automatically. The car was only a few yards away. It was a Golf GTI, old, dusty, a hundred and twenty thousand miles on the clock. I should have replaced it ages ago, but I'd bought it the same week I had met Audrey and didn't want to trade it in the way she had me. I fully intended to keep it until it died of natural causes.

'He is, though.'

'I suppose you're right.'

'Dickhead, dickhead, dickhead,' chanted Mark. He pulled free from my hand and ran to the car. 'Can we go to McDonalds?'

'Your mum says I'm not to take you to McDonalds. She says you won't eat your dinner.'

Although for a few seconds, I was tempted. I could take him to McDonalds. In Acapulco. I could splurge and buy a couple of airline tickets and leave the country. Then I wouldn't have to worry about Arnold.

'We could go to the park and look at the squirrels instead.' I offered.

The park would be quiet. Peaceful. I could talk to Mark. More importantly, I could listen.

Mark made a face. 'Squirrels are boring.'

'Compromise, then. Park first, then McDonalds. You can have a Happy Meal. As long as you eat all your dinner and don't tell anyone.'

He nodded his head slowly, eyes big at the unexpected chance to pull a fast one over his mother. There are too many secrets in the world, but not all of them are bad.

2.3.

Like every other part-time father I know, I love the concept of the park. A big wide open space where you can let your kids run wild and still keep an eye on them? Yummy mummies in short skirts? Swings and roundabouts and a van where on hot days you can purchase love in the form of vanilla ice cream? Where the biggest inconvenience is forgetting to bring a few crusts of bread for the ducks? What's not to love?

Except when it rains. Then it's hell. Droopy, miserable kids that would rather be playing Grand Theft Auto than spending time with their fathers. Hostile women who think that every glance is the veiled assessment of a time-served member of the plastic-mac brigade.

Today, the park in question was Bannockburn County Park, on the south side of the city and conveniently equidistant from Mark's home, school, and nearest McDonalds (although I have noticed that in Glasgow, everything is equidistant from a McDonalds – even another McDonalds).

More importantly, the weather was good. The sky was clear, the sun casting long shadows as it slipped nearer to the horizon.

For somebody who claimed to be bored by squirrels, Mark made a show of looking for them, craning his neck to look into the treetops as we walked along one of the quieter paths. 'There's one, Daddy!'

'Where?'

'There!' He pointed.

I didn't see it, but pretended that I had. 'He's a big one.'

'Miss Harper says they'll be getting ready to hibersleep for the winter.'

'Hibernate,' I told him. 'Hibernate. Like bears.'

He skipped ahead before stopping to let me catch up. 'Lions and tigers and bears, oh my.'

'Lions and tigers don't hibernate.'

'They would if they lived in Scotland.'

'You're probably right, son.' I said. 'Where did you hear the lions and tigers and bears thing?'

'Dorothy said it. In the Ozzard of Wiz.'

'*Wizard of Oz*,' I said. 'When did you see that?'

'Arnold let me see it. He said that I would like it.'

'And did you?'

His nose wrinkled. 'It was alright. I prefer Star Wars.'

'Did you tell Arnold?'

Mark nodded. He had slipped his hand back into mine. 'He said that Star Wars was okay, but one day I would appreciate the real classics.'

'So he likes the Wizard of Oz?' I asked.

'He's got all these old movies. Millions of them. Some of them are in black and white.' Mark confided in a worried tone. 'I didn't know they made TV's in those colours.'

'They used to. Does he makes you watch them all?'

'He doesn't *make* me. He puts them on and tells me that I'll like it.'

'But you don't?'

'Sometimes I do. I watched E.T. the other day. It was good except for the end. I asked Arnold what would happen to E.T. if he got caught and he said that the scientists would chop him up.' There was disappointment in his voice. 'I wanted to see that, but instead he flew away in his big spaceship.'

I'd kind of hoped for that ending myself. Maybe there was a

director's cut. 'So what are you having for your dinner tonight? Do you know?'

'Chicken salad. I hate chicken salad.'

'Salad's good for you. Full of vegetables.'

'That's what Arnold says. He says I should eat all my vegetables. He won't let me leave the table until all my broccoli is gone. It's not fair. I hate broccoli,' Mark said, stressing the word to make it sound like an elaborate form of torture. 'He likes broccoli, so we have to eat it nearly every night.'

'Every night?'

'Well. . . last night, anyway. And he wouldn't let me get down from the table until it was all finished and I ended up missing the Simpsons.'

The penny dropped. Arnold wasn't a paedophile. He was a disciplinarian. I might hate his guts, but at least he was trying to do right by my son. 'You should eat your broccoli. It's good for you. Full of vitamins.'

'Mum gives me vitamin tablets and lets me eat what I want.'

That sounded like Audrey. Always taking the easy way out.

2.4

Forty minutes later, I pulled up outside my ex's house – or to be more precise, outside my ex's new partner's house.

Audrey had definitely traded up. I hadn't met the new fellow, but I'd seen him from a distance. Arnold was a surgeon. It was easy to imagine Audrey introducing him like that at parties as if he was an expensive new furnishing from Ikea. 'This is Arnold and he is a. . . surgeon.'

Pause for applause.

It was a surgeon's home, that was for sure. One of those new red brick houses with five bedrooms, an integral garage, conservatory, multiple fitted kitchens/tanning salons and a separate floor devoted entirely to the gift-wrapping annex and the bowling alley. The whole manor was situated in a new housing estate designed to appeal exclusively to people with six-figure salaries and two digit morality IQ's. In London, it would set you back nearly a million, and even on the south side of Glasgow, it wouldn't give you much change from five hundred thousand. The lawns and garden were perfect, probably because Audrey the Cow made Arnold the Surgeon pay somebody to do the work for them. No doubt there would be Silas the Gardener, Maria the Maid and Benny the fucking Butler. Maybe I was exaggerating, but I knew from experience that Audrey was a firm believer in outsourcing basic jobs because she was too bloody thick and lazy to do them herself. The only place that she excelled was in the bedroom, and even then it was due to dedicated practice rather than natural talent.

Oh, aye, Audrey had definitely traded up.

Like just about every young couple who are "Doing Well", Audrey and Arnold drove matching four-by-fours that had almost certainly never tasted anything but tarmac. Audrey's was silver, parked alone in the driveway. Arnold's was no doubt in his personal space at his private hospital, the boot stuffed with golf clubs, waiting for its owner to finish his daily quota of breast implants or whatever the hell type of surgery he practised. Mark and I got out of my Golf (cheap, functional, and definitely not in keeping with the area) and walked up the driveway.

The doorbell played the first few bars of Ave Maria. Naturally.

The door was answered by Audrey. She looked good, but then she always did. She'd had her hair cut since I had last saw her, and it fell over her face in a blonde cascade. She always made me think of one of these girls you see on reality TV: pretty but permanently pissed off about nothing.

Just now, the nothing was me. She glared. 'You're late. We agreed five. It's nearly half past.'

'I thought that your dentist appointment might run over.'

'It didn't. I've been sitting here going out of my mind with worry. Don't you ever switch your mobile phone on?' She looked quickly at Mark. 'Go and play, sweetie. Mummy needs to shout at Daddy.'

He looked at me. 'Penguins tomorrow?' he said hopefully.

I bent down and kissed him on the cheek. 'Penguins tomorrow, son.' Saturday was my official day for him. I'd already promised to take him to see the new Disney movie. Which was, apparently, about penguins.

He kissed me back and went to move past, but Audrey reached out a hand and stopped him.

'What's that?' she said, pointing at something in his hand.

It was a plastic dinosaur.

The type you get with a Happy Meal.

His fingers closed over it. 'Daddy got me it.'

'Did Daddy take you to McDonalds?' asked Audrey, in a tone that suggested she would have preferred it if I had taken him for a quick lap-dance.

Mark's eyes flickered from face to face before falling down to the floor. The poor kid was confused. I'd asked him not to tell mummy about the trip to McDonalds, which was really just a question of him managing to keep his mouth shut, but this was a direct question that he had to answer, and we had both told him not to lie.

'I did take him to McDonalds,' I said.

Audrey's eyes didn't leave mine. 'Go and play, Mark.'

'Go on, son.' I patted him on the shoulder. 'I'll see you tomorrow.'

Mark scampered off, the precious dinosaur still clutched in his little hand. Audrey put her hands on her hips. 'Why? Why do you always undermine me?'

'I don't understand. How is taking him to McDonalds undermining you? For Christ's sake, he only had a Happy Meal. I ate most of it.'

'You undermine me because I always have to be the bad parent. Every time he sees you it's with presents and trips to McDonalds all the way. I'm the one that cooks his meals and tucks him in at night and has to tell him that he's not allowed to have a puppy. Don't you get it? It's me. All the time. I'm the one that does the work.'

Now I was getting angry. 'That's not my fault. You buggered off. You left me and took him with you. And it's not like you're the one living in a crappy little one-bedroom flat. You've got Dr bloody Kildare to pick up your bills and pay for your new haircuts. Don't pretend that you're the put-upon single mother, because let me tell you, that just ain't so.'

She threw a glance over my shoulder before stepping out and closing the front door behind her. 'For God's sake, keep your voice down. I don't want Mark to hear us fighting.'

I counted to five, taking slow, deep breaths. 'I'm sorry. I just. . . I'm sorry. I didn't mean to shout.'

'Look, forget it. Just go. Before Arnold comes home.'

The car was still idling at the side of the kerb. I got in and rolled the window down. 'I'm taking him to the cinema tomorrow.'

'Whatever.' She was already walking back toward the house. I was dismissed. The cow. I might not have been perfect, but I didn't deserve that kind of treatment.

'So. . . Audrey?'

She turned back, her face impatient. No doubt I was keeping her from Richard and Judy or Paul O'Grady or Salman Rushdie or who-ever the hell was doing the early evening chat-show on Channel Four. 'What?'

'Mark tells me that Arnold's a friend of Dorothy's?'

As I pulled away, I watched her give me the finger in the rear-view mirror. I felt it was worth it.

2.5.

Except it wasn't. When I showed up on Saturday, nobody was there, and Audrey wouldn't answer her mobile phone. The bitch had gone out, taking Mark with her.

Chapter 3

Monday 17th November

3.1.

Monday morning. The most hated day of the working week. I was hoping for peace and quiet, but it wasn't going to happen. The first thing I heard upon arriving at the office was a tirade of invective. 'Goddam shit-bastard piece of bloody plastic crap!'

Joe, my boss. What he lacked in vocabulary he made up in enthusiasm. I winced as an ominous clattering sound came from the direction of his office. 'Fucking useless waste of money!'

I cautiously approached the open door. 'Joe?'

'I can't get this piece of crap to give me Stuart Lilley's phone number.'

I stepped into the room. The "piece of crap" was actually a new Blackberry that his wife Becky had given to him for his fifty-fifth birthday. Given that Joe had the technical ability of a panda wearing boxing gloves, I hadn't figured out if she meant it to be a joke. I'd given him a bottle of fifteen year old scotch, and he'd definitely had little trouble figuring out how to use that.

He smacked the BlackBerry off the edge of his desk. 'Fuck sake!'

'Stop hitting it!'

'The bloody thing doesn't work!'

'Neither would you if I smacked you off the side of your desk like that.' I took the seat opposite and held out my hand. 'You've probably broken it by now.'

He passed over the offending item. 'I only tapped it,' he said sullenly. 'Besides, I never wanted the bloody thing in the first place. You can't break an old-fashioned diary.'

'How true.' I probed the screen. It wasn't broken, or at least, didn't appear to be. 'What's your code?'

'Code?'

'Entry code. So that only you can access it.' His face was blank. 'To prevent your private information falling into the hands of the dark forces of the night.'

'The dark. . . Cameron, I don't know anything about a bloody access code!'

'Did Becky give you anything with it?'

Grumbling, he fished around in his pocket, eventually coming up with a small booklet and passing it over. The operating instructions.

'Joe. . . '

'What?'

'Did you even look at these?'

'Becky said it was easy to use.'

'Not that easy.' I tried to come up with an appropriate metaphor, failed completely. Joe was instant death to anything with a microchip, with an uncanny ability to make computers crash just by looking at them. Christ knew what Becky had been thinking. I showed the booklet to him. 'See?'

Written across the front cover in heavy black pen was 'Access code: 6960.' I recognised the hand-writing as that of Joe's wife.

He had the grace to look slightly sheepish. 'That's Becky's birthday.'

I used it to enter the system and retrieve the required phone number, scribbling it down on a scrap of paper. 'Joe, just one question. If you don't know how to use it, how come all your phone numbers managed to get in it in the first place?'

'Becky did it,' Joe said, not so much an admission as an accusation. 'She copied them out of my diary.'

'Do you still have the diary?'

He nodded.

'Then maybe you should just use that instead.' I stood up. 'I'm going to make a coffee. Want one?'

'Oh, God, yes, please.'

3.2.

The kitchen was the size of a shoebox, but it was all that we needed. As I waited for the kettle to boil, I spooned instant into two mugs – the Partick Thistle one for Joe and the British Superbikes one for me.

The office was the smallest suite on the seventh floor of a city centre block. It comprised four rooms – a main reception area, Joe's office, the kitchen, and a tiny bathroom. When I wasn't out in the field, I hung out in the reception area, doing whatever it was Joe needed of me – answering phones, computer searches, typing general correspondence. I guess you could call me a secretary.

The phone started ringing. I walked the three inches from the kitchen to my desk and picked it up. 'Banks Investigations.'

The woman had one of those breathy, little-girl voices that were fine on nineteen-fifties movie starlets but don't really cut it in the real world. She sounded muffled, like she was cradling the receiver between her shoulder and her chin, watching her nail polish dry while a Pekinese yapped around her ankles. 'Is that Mr Banks?'

'My name's Cameron Stone. I work for Mr Banks. Can I help you?'

There was a long pause. 'I'd really prefer to talk to Mr Banks.'

'May I ask what it's regarding?'

'I might have some work for him.'

'What's your name, please?'

'Sophie Sloan.'

'Hold on, please.' I put her on hold and dialled zero. 'Joe, there's a potential client on the other line. Name's Sophie Sloan.'

I put her through and headed back to the kitchen. Once it sensed it was being watched, the kettle took another thousand years to finally boil. When it finished, I poured, mixed milk and sugar and took both mugs into the office, catching Joe just as he placed his phone back on the cradle. He took the coffee with both hands and a grateful look on his face. 'You might need to make another one.'

'Uh huh?'

'Miss Sloan was calling from her mobile. She's on her way up.'

'What did she want?'

'Wouldn't say.'

I took the seat opposite him and sipped my coffee. Joe was still poking away at the Blackberry. At any minute, I expected it to spontaneously combust in his hand. He chewed on his lower lip, stabbing away at the screen like he was trying to kebab it. I gave it until the end of the week. If it was lucky.

Eventually he looked up. 'Good weekend?'

'Alright.'

'Wendy had a football game on.' He shook his head. 'Girls playing football. It's fundamentally wrong.'

Wendy was nine, and the apple of her dad's eye. He didn't say it aloud, but he was less than thrilled that she preferred contact sports to My Little Pony.

'What about you?' He asked. 'You do anything with Mark?'

'I was meant to take him out. Showed up at Audrey's on Saturday, but she'd taken him out already.' I tried not to let the frustration seep into my voice, but it was there. I'd waited outside the empty house for nearly an hour, hoping that she had just forgotten about it, knowing in my heart that she was once again using our son as an excuse to hurt me.

'She's a bit of a cow, your ex, isn't she?'

I was spared from having to agree with him by the sound of the door buzzer. Our potential client had arrived. I stood up. 'You want me to let her in and then leave you to it?'

'No. I don't think so. We'll see what she wants.'

3.3.

Sophie Sloan turned out to be stunning. The silly little Marilyn Monroe voice I had heard on the phone had suggested a fluffy blonde in a frilly pink blouse and pleated skirt. Instead, we were treated to a fashion model in a Metallica T-shirt and skin-tight jeans. She carried a small blue handbag whose simplicity was probably inversely related to its retail value, and her hair was very shiny and black, falling down her back in an elaborate French pleat. Her face was strong, with pale skin and a mouth edged in red lipstick. As I showed her into Joe's office, he stood up. I could tell that he liked the look of her.

Hell, so did I.

There was a ring on her third finger. Small, discreet, but with something that caught the light. Married and rich; right up Joe's alley. He held out his hand. 'Mrs Sloan.'

They shook, and Joe waved in my general direction. 'This is my associate, Cameron Stone. You don't mind if he joins us?'

She hesitated, then shrugged as if she didn't care. I held out my hand. Her fingers were slender, but there was surprising strength in them. 'It's a pleasure to meet you, Mrs Sloan. Can I offer you some tea or coffee?'

'No, thank you.' She looked around. 'This isn't what I imagined it would be.'

Joe made the vague but universal gesture that meant "have a seat". 'What did you expect?'

'Oh, I don't know. A bottle of whisky on the window sill. Filing cabinets. You with a week's worth of stubble and a gun tucked in your belt.'

Joe's tastes were less stereotypical. A Partick Thistle calendar on the desk, a picture of him shaking hands with former labour leader John Smith on the wall. Also, framed pictures of the wife and kids. 'It's not like it is in the movies.'

'I guess not.' She sat down opposite the desk. Taking that as our cue, I took the seat next to her.

Joe sat down on the padded leather monstrosity behind the desk and crossed his legs. 'Now, how can we help you, Mrs Sloan?'

'Call me Sophie, please.' She looked at the handbag on her lap, her long fingernails toying absently with the strap. 'I'm. . . I'm not sure you can. I think I made a mistake coming here.'

'Take your time.'

'I'm just being silly. At least, I think I'm just being silly.' Her eyes met his. They begged for his agreement.

Joe's voice was gentle. He was about twenty years older than her, old enough to play the kindly uncle. 'Being silly about what, Sophie?'

She sighed and shook her head, dropping her eyes back to her lap.

'Sophie, a lot of the people that come to us don't really want to be here. Whatever it is, we won't laugh, or think you're stupid, or accuse you of wasting our time.'

'I think my husband is having an affair with my sister.'

Joe leaned forward, put his elbows on the desk. 'But you're not certain.'

'No. No, I'm not.'

'But you're thinking that you would like to be?'

She fumbled in the handbag for a pack of tissues. 'It's been going on for months now. I mean, they work together. . . ' She blew her nose. 'They're always late, or he needs to go over to her place to do some work at home. And sometimes, in bed, I can smell her perfume on him, as if they've been. . . close.'

Infidelity cases are the P.I.'s bread and butter. It's nasty, gutter-ridden work, but as the song goes, we all got bills to pay. Joe said. 'We can certainly look into that for you.'

'It's just that I want to be sure.'

She seemed unable to meet our eyes. Instead, her gaze roamed around the office, taking in all the detail – not that there was much detail to take in. Joe had a few knick-knacks that he liked – his Irn Bru clock, his Newton's Cradle – but apart from that, his office was pretty bare. One of the pictures on the desk attracted her attention. I knew which one she was looking at. It was a family shot – Joe, Becky, the twins, Wendy the footballer. A Jack Russell sat on Joe's lap, grinning at the camera in the witless fashion that only dogs and politicians can achieve. She picked it up. 'I used to know your wife. That's why I chose you.'

'You know Becky?'

She nodded, gave a small smile. 'She was always Mrs Banks to me. That was back when I used to be a nurse. It was before she was famous.'

'She'd be chuffed to hear you describe her as famous.'

'She was always very nice to me.'

Joe grinned. 'Are you sure that we're talking about the same woman? She scares the hell out of me.'

She responded with another smile. That was one of Joe's many talents: helping the nervous to relax. 'She did have a reputation of being. . . forceful.'

'Christ, you're telling me. Let's just say that if she had been aboard, the *Titanic* would have thought twice about sinking.'

This time, the smile was only a polite one. I suspected that she could only be distracted so far. She moved to put the photograph back down, but misjudged. It tumbled off the side of the desk with a clatter. 'I'm sorry.'

'It's alright.'

She bent down to pick it up, and I noticed that her hand was shaking. 'Oh, God, it's broken. I'm so sorry.' As she turned it over, I could see a jagged crack zigzagging across the face of the picture, a triangular piece of glass by her foot. 'I'll replace it.'

'Don't worry about it,' Joe told her.

I could see how embarrassed she was, so I held out a hand and took it from her, quickly removing the back and placing the photograph on the desk, dumping the frame and the broken glass into the waste bucket underneath.

She seemed calmer. 'I just. . . it took me so long to work up the courage to even come here.'

Joe said, 'About your husband. Cameron and myself can certainly

— 83 —

find out whether or not he is cheating on you, if that's what you want. But have you considered asking him directly? I'm not trying to talk myself out of business, but the kind of surveillance we're talking about is expensive, and in most cases, unnecessary. In my experience, most cheating partners will admit to it if they are confronted.'

'I've asked him. I've asked them both. They just laugh at me and tell me I'm being silly. And money isn't an issue. I have some savings. Ian gives me an extremely generous allowance. I suspect it's a more expensive version of the guilty husband who brings home flowers for his wife in an attempt to ease his own conscience.'

'What kind of business are they in?'

'Ian owns a nursing home. *She's* the Clinical Nurse Manager.'

'The what?'

'It's a fancy title for Matron.'

'I see. So obviously they spend a lot of time together.'

'Yes.' The hand had gone back to the strap of the bag, twisting, worrying at it. 'Too much, I think.' She seemed suddenly to be aware of what she was doing and made a point of placing the bag at her feet. 'It's like they have all these secret jokes between them. They talk about work so much I feel completely excluded.'

'I think my wife could tell you how that feels. She won't allow me and Cameron to talk shop, if he comes over for dinner.'

Joe and I looked at each other. I knew what he was looking for, and gave an indifferent shrug. He said, 'Alright, Mrs Sloan. We're happy to look into things, if you are certain that's what you want.'

She seemed to reach a decision. I could almost see her gritting her teeth and squaring her shoulders. 'It is, Mr Banks. It most certainly is.'

He held out a hand and they shook on the deal. He took a pad of paper out of the drawer. 'I'll need to take a few details.'

'Of course. But. . . I wonder if I could have that coffee now?' She said. 'My mouth's awfully dry. I was so nervous.'

'Of course.' Joe looked at me. 'Cam, will you do the honours?'

I smiled as I stood up. The thirty-two-year-old tea boy. I didn't mind. I owed Joe a hell of a lot more than the occasional cuppa.

Chapter 4

4.1.

My father died while questioning a suspect. One minute he was screaming in somebody's face, the next he was lying on the floor turning the same colour as his uniform. CPR kept him alive long enough for the paramedics to arrive, but he arrested again in the ambulance and was dead on arrival. I was four at the time, and I reckon I was about six before I got it through my thick skull that Daddy wasn't coming home. I miss him more now I'm an adult than I ever did as a child.

I think he was a good man. I could be wrong – we tend to idolise the dead until they become caricatures of the person they actually were, and my memories of him are without foundation, mostly based on the stories my mother passed on before she died – but I'm pretty sure about that. He taught me a few things. How to tie my shoelaces. How to bash in the bottoms of my boiled eggs after eating them so that the witches wouldn't be able to make boats. What I remember most is his love of the police force. He wore the uniform with pride. I know that's a cliché, but there's no other way I can describe it. With pride.

So I guess it was inevitable that I would join up. I didn't do it the second I was old enough because Mum was dying, but after she was gone I applied and was accepted. And from then until the day I left in disgrace, I wore the uniform as my father had before me. Even after that night on Gallowgate, and all the shit that came after, I loved the force.

So did Joe. Of course, to those on the outside, it didn't look that way. They thought he was just another cock in an overcrowded hen house, loving the job not for what it was but for the sense of power it gave him.

We first met over ten years ago. I was twenty, just graduated from the police training college up at Tulliallan, still soaking wet behind the ears, still having the time of my life. My first station was in Glasgow's Pollokshaws, and I was what they called a 'Woollysuit' – a probationary constable. My job was pretty simple. I was expected to do what I was told, when I was told, and how I was told.

Joe, on the other hand, was forty-five, a C.I.D. detective with something of a reputation. The word was that he was the copper that Ian Rankin based John Rebus on.

Of course, I guessed straight away that was bullshit. The first Rebus story was published in the mid-eighties, and that meant that Joe would have been about twenty at the time. Twenty is too young to be a legend, unless you're a footballer or a singer in a rock and roll band.

The whole thing didn't seem to bother him. As a detective, he was something of a cliché. His hobbies included horses, boozing and womanising, and of course, solving crime. He even looked the part, stamping about the station in a snazzy leather jacket, cracking jokes with people he liked and shouting at people he didn't.

I'm six-foot five, so I already stood out, but it was Joe that gave me the nickname that would follow me the rest of my career. I was eating lunch in the canteen with the other probies when he stopped at the table. We went quiet, anticipating a bawling out. We were normally so far below his radar that he only acknowledged us to point out how we screwed up. But this time it was something else. He looked at all of us and singled me out. 'You. Gigantor. You got some civvies in your locker?'

I nodded. 'Sir.'

'Go and change. I want your help. I've cleared it with your supervisor.'

'Sir.'

I did as I was told. Before I even left the changing room, the name had stuck to me like a fly on shite. In the space of a month, it had been abbreviated to 'Gantor'. It didn't bother me. Could have been much, much worse.

Joe was waiting for me outside the locker room. 'Come on. We're going for a drive.'

I fell in step as we made our way to the car park. 'Where to, sir?'

'Social call.'

We commandeered a pool car, and Joe told me to drive, 'So as I can tell you what's going on.

'We're going to see a couple of lads. Jerry and Derek McConnell. They're twins, and they're about the same size as you. They're seventeen years old, and they've both got juvenile arrest records as long as my arm. . . in fact, as long as your arm. Vandalism, fighting, anti-social behaviour, car theft. Both of them have been caught carrying blades. Do you remember the case of Vijay Sarwar?'

I did. Two years ago, the poor kid had been stabbed on his way home from school and damn near died. It happened on a street full of witnesses, but all of them were Indian and under the age of fourteen and wouldn't say a word. The incident aggravated racial tensions in the area, and the media didn't help by implying that the police didn't take what had happened as seriously as they would have if it had been a white boy that had been attacked.

Joe nodded. 'That was Jerry and Derek. But nobody will go on the record for fear of reprisals. And even if they did, both boys were under sixteen at the time. All they'd get is a slap on the wrists and learn not to get caught.

'I only found out about the Vijay Sarwar thing because I've been digging into their backgrounds anyway. There's been a spate of muggings on Pollokshaws Road over the past five weeks. Always on a Friday or Saturday, always early in the morning, sometime between the hours of three fifteen and three forty-five, always in the five hundred yards between the Esso garage and the bingo hall, which, coincidentally or not, is also where Jerry and Derek live. You know what I'm thinking?'

I did. 'The three o'clock bus.'

'Clever lad.'

Glasgow's a town that lives for the weekend, and throughout the nineties, late night buses ran all over the city. For the princely sum of one pound seventy-five, you could always get home after a night out. The Pollokshaws bus route terminated right in the middle of that particular area. The time frame was perfect as well.

Joe continued. 'All the victims were passengers on that bus, so I showed the McDonnell brothers' mugshots to some of the drivers, and they all confirm that the boys are also frequent fliers, always getting off at that stop. I reckon they have a night out on the town and then use the bus journey home to pick a victim. Of course, a good defence lawyer will point out that there is absolutely no law against two of our great city's youths using public transport to travel home after a pleasant evening of drinking mint juleps at the youth club disco.'

I almost laughed at that, but managed to keep it in check, my eyes fixed firmly on the road. From the speed of his speech and the way he didn't pause to check whether or not I was listening, I suspected that Detective Banks was the kind of guy that preferred all questions to be left until the end of the presentation.

'Every single victim has been female and alone. There's been nine incidents that we know about, and the assailants are described as being unusually tall, wearing hooded tops and scarves. That sound like anybody I've described to you?'

I guessed I wasn't supposed to answer, so I nodded, keeping my eyes on the road. You weren't allowed to smoke while on duty, but that didn't stop Joe from lighting a cigarette. He pointed it at me while he talked. 'So far, the attacks show a classic pattern of escalating violence. The first two victims were just relieved of personal property, the next two were struck from behind before being forced to the ground. Since then, they've started frog-marching girls to cashline machines, forcing them to withdraw more cash, and then knocking seven shades of shit out of them.' He puffed on his cigarette. 'Their last attack showed another escalation.'

'In what way sir?'

'Sexual. On Saturday night they grabbed a twenty year old girl and went through the usual routine. Cash and then a kicking. But then they dragged her to a piece of wasteground and ripped her top off. Told her they were going to rape her, that she was asking for it going about dressed like a tart. Of course, she fought back, managed to pull the scarf off one of them. She recognised Jerry McConnell. She said she scratched hell out of his cheek.'

He blew out a plume of smoke. 'I personally wouldn't be sorry if she'd scratched the little bastard's eye out.'

'What happened then?'

He shrugged. 'She ran. . . all the way to the A & E department of the Western Infirmary. She told them what had happened, and I was the one that interviewed her. The poor lass was a mess. They really did a job on her. Broken nose, broken cheekbone, fractured wrist. She agreed that she would testify against them, but she phoned me this morning in tears. After a bit of prompting, she told me that she got a message saying that if she did testify against them, they would do to her wee sister what they failed to do to her. Her wee sister's only thirteen, by the way.'

'So. . . nice guys, then.'

'Salt of the earth. And of course, you know how defence lawyers treat a young woman who goes out and has a couple of drinks in anything more revealing than a suit of armour. They'll say she was begging for it, then changed her mind halfway through.'

'But there would have been DNA under her fingernails.'

Joe shook his head. 'You know what A&E's like at half past four on a Sunday morning. Half the bloody city's there with an alcohol related injury. It was a student nurse who admitted her, and nobody thought a thing about preserving any evidence. It was scrubbed away, down the plug hole like Partick Thistle's chances of avoiding relegation.'

I drove in silence. My mouth was dry, and my heart tripped along in my chest. In my four weeks on the job, this was by far the most exciting thing that had happened. Perhaps too exciting. Everything that Joe had said seemed to contradict what I had learned in training, but I wanted to be a part of it, just so I could see what was going to happen.

'What if. . . what if the girl is lying?' I said. Joe looked at me. 'I mean, I believe you and everything, but it sounds like we don't really have probable cause to arrest them.'

'That's why I told you it was a social call.'

'But what if she's. . . I don't know. . . like an ex girlfriend. Suppose she just made everything up to screw them over?'

'I saw this lassie. She didn't make up the two black eyes, or the broken wrist.' He shifted in his seat. 'Look, son, I understand if you don't want to be a part of this. You're new to the force, and they teach you to do things a certain way. If that's the case, just drop me off and head back to the station. but there's a few things you have to understand. Imagine you're rolling a dice. What are your chances of rolling a six?'

'One in six?'

'Clever lad. Now, what are your chances of rolling another six right after?'

'One in. . . thirty six. Something like that.'

'Right. And another six after that?'

'One in. . .' Mental arithmetic wasn't my strong point. 'One hundred and eighty-two?'

'In the ballpark. Now, my point is this. For our first six, we have two violent young men with antisocial tendencies. Our next six, they live directly in the area that these crimes occurred. All the victims report that their attackers were abnormally tall – that's another six. We have three separate bus drivers, all who swear blind that our boys were on the bus every single time. They remember them, you know, the drivers. Say that they're the kind of lads that always sit up at the back of the top deck so that they can have a smoke and cause trouble. So that's another three sixes right there. And for our final roll of the dice, we have our victim actually recognising one of her attackers. Now, lets do the math. That's six by the power of seven... works out to something like one hundred and fifty thousand to one that it's not them. And those, Cameron, are betting odds.'

I said nothing. I was surprised that he knew my name.

'Now, the thing is that there will always be some scumbag lawyer that will be able to claim that all I have is circumstantial evidence, and they would be right. And because they're both still young, even if we got a conviction, we'd be lucky to get more than a couple of months in a young offenders unit. But I think that everybody could agree that both Jerry and Derek are headed down a slippery slope, and perhaps by intervening now, we might be able to prevent not just further attacks on members of the general public, but possibly even prevent these two young mean wasting what might turn out to be relatively productive lives.

'I'm not going to lie to you; things could get a little rough. But it's up to you to decide what kind of cop you want to be. Whether you want to be the rule follower, or the one that does what's right.'

Put like that, it didn't take me long to decide. 'I'm in.'

4.2.

After Joe's description of the McConnells, I expected a tenement flat with wet rot and used needles on the stairwell, a couch mouldering on the street outside. Instead, they lived in a smart detached house in a new estate. But it wasn't a complete contradiction. Compared to those of neighbouring properties, the garden was unkempt, the grass long, the weeds rampant. Joe nodded as we pulled to a halt outside. 'Mummy inherited a nice wee sum and decided to invest in some property. Guess she's used to having the council do all the maintenance.'

'Where is mummy, do you think?'

'She's got a job in a bar. Long hours. Uses it as an excuse every time the boys get into trouble. Daddy's been gone for years. He saw which direction the boys were heading and moved onwards and upwards.' Joe stubbed the cigarette out in the ashtray, and then, remembering he was in a pool car, emptied the ashtray out of the window. 'Come on. Let's go pay our respects.'

Walking up the path, he spoke softly. 'All I want from you is to stand in the corner and look pretty. I spoke to some of the officers that have interviewed them. Gerry's bad enough, but Derek's supposed to be a fucking headcase. Keep your eyes open and your mouth shut. I don't think they'll try anything, but with idiots like these, you never can tell.'

It took forty seconds of persistent knocking before the door was answered. A stick insect with a towel wrapped around his waist and a can of lager in his hand said, 'I wis takin' a bath.'

There was a livid scratch running down his left cheek.

'Gerry, is it?' Joe waved his badge as he pushed past and into the house. 'Where's Derek?'

There was a frown as Gerry registered the badge. 'What do you want? We haven't done nothing.'

'Just a wee chat. Where's your brother?'

'Listening to music with headphones on. That's how I had to get out the fucking bath.'

'Where? Living room? Kitchen? Shed at the bottom of the garden?'

Gerry pointed sullenly. 'Living room.'

'After you.'

'It's through there. I'll just go and put some clothes on.'

The kid made to go back up the stairs, but Joe put a hand on his arm. 'That won't be necessary. We're not going to be long.'

Gerry grumbled as he led us into the living room. The place was a tip, with old newspapers and half eaten plates of food littering the floor. Derek was sitting on a settee eating crisps, an oversized pair of headphones balanced on his head. He whipped them off as we entered the room and I caught a quick burble of techno before he hit the off switch. 'Who the fuck are you?'

Joe waved his badge for the second time, directing Jerry to the opposite end of the settee. The kid sat down, the towel riding up and falling open. Not a pretty sight, but at least there wasn't much to look at.

They weren't identical, but the facial resemblance was there. Both had high foreheads and monobrows. Joe had said they were my height, but after seeing Jerry standing upright, I put them at a couple of inches taller. They were certainly big enough and ugly enough to scare the shit out of the average person. It didn't worry me. I'd been strong before, but four months of torture up at the police training college at Tulliallan had left me in better physical shape than I had ever been in my life. They were willow trees compared to my oak. If it came to a one on one fight, I'd break them in half.

Joe swiped an empty pizza box off an armchair onto the floor, checking there was nothing unpleasant that could stain the seat of his trousers before sitting down. 'You know, it wouldn't kill you guys to do a bit of a clean up around here.'

'Mum's at work.'

'And wouldn't it be a surprise for her to come home to a nice tidy house?'

The two boys looked at each other and laughed. 'Fuck that.'

'I bet she's proud of you.' Joe reached into his pocket. 'Anyhoo, I didn't come here to chat. I was wondering if you knew this lassie.'

He passed a Polaroid to Gerry, who studied it. I was only three months in the job, but I saw his eyes flick to his brother and back, and understood the significance.

'No, pal. Never seen her.'

'What about your brother?'

This time, Derek's face didn't give him away. He gave the picture a cursory glance before shaking his head and passing it back.

'That's strange. Her name's Louise Brennan. She lives less than two hundred yards away. Walks her dog past your house every single day.'

Derek gestured to the closed blinds. 'Do I look like I give a fuck what goes on outside?'

'Fair enough.' Joe passed another picture over her. 'What about this one?'

This time, both their faces remained clear. They looked at the picture a long time before shaking their heads. Derek said, 'Looks like somebody hit her with a bus.'

'Close enough. It's actually the same lassie. The first picture was the "before", and what you've got there in your hands is the "after". Doctors say that she might need reconstructive surgery on her nose.'

'That's fuck all to do with us, pal.'

'So why's she saying that it was you two fine gentleman?'

'Dunno.'

'Go out much at the weekend?'

A smirk passed between the two brothers. Any doubts I had as to their guilt disappeared. Derek ate a crisp. 'We mostly stay at home and read our bibles.'

'I'm sure you do. What happened to your face, Gerry?'

'Walked into a door.'

'A door with false nails?' Joe slapped his knees with both hands. 'Let's cut the bullshit. I know that it was you two.'

Derek crossed his legs and studied his fingernails. 'Aye, well. Knowing something and being able to prove it are two different things. That's how you've not arrested us. You know she's not going to testify, and even if you make her, she'll just say that she made a mistake. So why don't you just fuck off back to your sty and leave us alone?'

Joe looked at me. 'Don't you love it? We're pigs, so we must live in a sty?'

Derek said, 'You're a pair of fucking wankers is what you are. You think you can come into my house and play it fucking cool? Try and scare us? Even if you could prove anything, the worst we're going to get is a year or so in borstal. Warm beds, good food. We'd fucking own the place. We're fucking laughing at you.'

This from a seventeen year old boy.

He stood up. 'You can both just fuck off. Tell Louise she's a good lassie for doing what as she's told. Maybe one night I'll go round and pay her a visit. I'll wait until she's not quite such a swamp donkey though. . . mind you, they do say ugly birds try harder. She might not be so choosy this time.'

The expression on Joe's face never changed, but there was something. . . a deadening of the eyes, the muscle in his jaw. He sighed and got to his feet. 'It's a slippery slope you're on, lads.'

'Thank you, Mr Policeman, for showing us the error of our ways.'

I moved for the door, disappointed that our social call hadn't had a more conclusive ending. Then something made me hesitate. I turned, just in time to see Joe knee Derek in the balls, the impact like a concrete ball wrapped in wet blankets bouncing off a wall. Derek went down, his mouth opening and closing like a fish. Gerry was up in a shot, the towel falling to his feet. I intercepted him as he moved toward Joe, seizing him, putting his arm up his back like I had been taught.

Joe loomed over the fallen boy. 'Did you think we were finished? Did you think that we were just going to go home?' He planted a vicious kick into Derek's side. 'We're just getting started, son.'

Gerry struggled in my hold, so I increased my grip, jamming his arm further up his back. I had my left hand on his neck, ready to stick my thumb into his brachial artery, a nasty little trick they don't teach you in Tulliallan but I had discovered on my own. I kept him facing his brother on the floor while Joe proceeded to do to Derek what Derek had done to nine people before him. I made him watch, having to watch myself, not wanting to but perversely enjoying it all the same. This was what it was all about. No paperwork, no warrants, no fucking hours wasted outside the High Court waiting to testify only to see some arsehole that we knew beyond a shadow of a doubt was guilty walk away because some dumb twat had forgotten to sign a report in triplicate or whatever.

I've seen, given and received a few kickings since then, but in over ten years, nothing has ever come close. Joe fucked Derek up bigstyle. Ugly, indelicate, but that's the only way I can describe it. While the boy struggled for breath, Joe flipped him onto his front and kneeled on his back, forcing the arm until the shoulder cracked loudly. Then Joe went to work on the hand, snapping the thumb and fingers one by one like a fistful of twiglets. At some point between the index finger and the pinkie, Derek passed out from the pain.

Joe got to his feet and turned his attention to Gerry. 'That's your brother in a cast for the next month. So I guess the question remains. . . what are we going to do with you?'

Gerry was white with fear. 'Oh Jesus. . . Oh Jesus *Christ*. . . you can't. . . you can't *do* that. We're just kids. . .'

'YOU ARE NOT FUCKING KIDS!' Joe screamed in his face. 'YOU FORFEITED YOUR RIGHT TO CHILDHOOD!' Spittle landed on Jerry's face. And mine. 'You forfeited your right to be children the second you started to commit adult crimes!'

'I'm sorry. . .'

'I don't fucking care that you're sorry. Louise Brennan doesn't know that you're sorry. She doesn't care. Sorry isn't going to make up for what you did to her. Sorry is just a word that cunts like you use to weasel out of accepting responsibility for things that you should never have done in the first place.'

Joe looked at me. 'Let him go.'

I released my prisoner. Gerry spared me one terrified glance before turning his attention back to Joe. 'Please. . . please don't. . .'

'Oh, shut up.' Joe's voice was toneless. He went and sat back down on the armchair. 'I know that Derek's the brains behind the two of you.'

Gerry bent and picked up the towel, tucking it back around his waist. He nodded frantically, agreeing with Joe.

'Now, my colleague and I are going to go in a couple of moments, and you can then dial emergency services and get some help for your brother. I think he's going to need it. They'll want to know what happened, and I don't care what you tell them.' He nodded at the scratch on Gerry's cheek. 'Tell them he walked into a fucking door. Anyhoo, the point is that I have a dozen witnesses that will swear blind that both of us were elsewhere, and besides, everybody knows that the pair of you are pond life. Derek was right. Knowing that something is the truth and being able to prove it are two very different things.' He looked at the mess at his feet without the slightest trace of pity. 'You really did bring this on yourselves, you know.'

Gerry nodded. He was at the stage where he would agree to anything that was said. If Joe suggested that it would be fun to get out the baby oil and grease him up, he'd have run to the bathroom in his eagerness to help.

Joe stood up and studied Derek. His chest was moving; the kid was breathing alright. Joe turned his attention to Gerry. 'Now, I won't waste anybody's time by saying that it's up to you to turn your life around. What I will point out is that I can always come back, and the next time, I'll hand out some real punishment. To both of you. So if you and your dumb little buddy find yourselves contemplating getting up to something naughty, just remember. . . I'll find you.'

4.3.

We made it half a mile before I had to stop the car. I pulled in at a bus stop, opened the door and threw up all over the tarmac. I could feel Joe's eyes boring into the back of my head. 'Sorry, sir.'

'That's OK. And it's Joe. While it's just the two of us. You can go back to sir when we get back to the station.'

I wiped my mouth with the back of my hand. 'I don't know what came over me.'

'It's shock.' He held out his right hand in front of him. I noticed a barely perceptible tremor. 'I feel a little bit like that myself.' He checked his watch. 'It's nearly knocking off time. Let's make a little detour. Take the next right.'

Joe directed me to a pub called Yesterday's Promise. Never had a drinking establishment been so aptly named. It was on the edge of a mostly abandoned industrial estate and had obviously collapsed onto hard times. Once it might have been a place for tired workers to go at the end of a long day, but as the businesses had moved out, so had the clientele. Exterior paint had long since peeled away to the bare wood, and the once white walls were now a dirty shade of grey. Joe caught me looking and said, 'I know, it's a shithole. . . which means there's not much chance of running into management types.'

Once my eyes had adjusted to the gloom, the place was better on the inside than I expected. Yesterday's Promise was never going to make the Good Pub Guide – the promise of yesterday apparently failing to become the reality of today – but it was reasonably clean, with polished wood tables and an impressive selection of whisky. The place was deserted except for a barman who was about five feet tall, with a pointy nose and prominent teeth that made me think of a rat.

I was going to order a Coke, but before I could speak, Joe put a ten down on the bar. 'Two half and halves, Des, and get one for yourself.' He looked at me. 'Why don't you go and grab us that table in the corner?'

I did as I was asked, taking a seat where I could watch the bar. Ratman – Des, as Joe had called him – prepared our drinks, the ten pound note disappearing into the till with not even an offer of any change. They chatted for a few seconds before Joe brought the drinks over. He sat down opposite me and polished off the whisky in one go. 'Christ, I needed that.'

I didn't especially want to have an alcoholic drink – I was still a probationary constable, remember – but my mouth was a desert. I took the tiniest sip of the lager, but my thirst outweighed my sense and I ended up downing half of it in one go. Now that the adrenaline was leaving my system, I was angry. Things had gone too far. Way too far.

But what could I say? Joe was the senior officer, and I had watched without even trying to intervene. And hadn't there been a little voice in the back of my mind all along, whispering that the little shit was only getting what he deserved? Wasn't that what I was really angry about?

Joe seemed to know what I was thinking. 'I'm sorry. I didn't plan for that. I didn't go in there with the intention putting the kid in a cast.'

'But you meant all along to hurt him. I mean, why else were we there?'

Joe nodded soberly. 'You're right. I'm sorry.'

'I could lose my job for this!'

'That's not going to happen. Guys like Gerry and Derek don't call the police. That's not their style. Besides, I wasn't kidding. I really can get a dozen people that will confirm we were elsewhere.'

'But we could have waited! Got enough evidence to put them away!'

For the first time, I saw a shadow of anger on his face. 'For how long, Cameron? How long would you wait? Until they beat somebody else up? All it takes is one lucky punch to kill someone. Maybe you'd rather wait until they succeeded in raping some poor lass like they tried with Louise Brennan?'

'No, but. . . ' I had no answers.

'Cameron, I'm not proud of what I just did, and I don't want you to be thinking that's the way I conduct myself. Most of the time, I behave myself. But every once in a while there comes along something that can't be resolved by procedure. I didn't walk into that room with the intention of hurting Derek as badly as that. I thought a wee slap on the face would be enough. But I. . . '

'You lost it.'

'I didn't lose it.'

'You fucking well did.' That was the only way I could account for the sickening level of violence. I remembered the sound Derek's arm had made. 'You lost it.'

'That's not true, Cameron. It's just. . . after what Derek said, I realised that this guy wasn't going to respond to a slap. He was just going to keep doing exactly what he wanted. What he did to that lassie meant nothing to him. Gerry's nobody. He's a follower, not a leader. But Derek. . . he's got all the makings of a serious psychopath. I'm not talking about your garden variety nutjob. I'm taking about a predatory sexual killer, the kind of guy that rapes and tortures and abuses and kills for the fun of it. Like Fred bloody West. And of course, in Gerry he's got a perfect audience. I could be wrong, but I think there's every chance that in a few years we'll be watching Derek's neighbours being interviewed on the evening news. They'll be the ones saying he was such a quiet man, always said hello.'

I said nothing. All I wanted to do was finish my drink, go back home and put this day behind me. Once again, Joe seemed to read my face. 'Look, Cam, I'm sorry. The only regret I have about this afternoon is putting you in the position I have. You're young, you haven't been in the job long. . . it was too soon.'

'Let's just forget about it.'

'That might be for the best.'

4.4.

Of course, we didn't just forget about it. I never told anybody what happened that afternoon. For the next few days, I expected to feel a hand on my shoulder, hauling me off to a disciplinary hearing. I kept my head down and my profile low, knowing that if what we had done ever came to light, it wouldn't just be a question of losing my job. We'd been told what happened to crooked cops in jail, and I had no desire to find out first hand.

It never happened. Two mornings later, my supervisor pulled me to one side and asked how things had gone. I almost blurted out the truth, but managed not to. 'Fine. It was just a routine thing.'

'Oh, aye?'

'Aye.'

'Joe tell you not to talk about it?'

'Sir.'

I love that word. It's neither a confirmation or a denial. It just makes people think that you're listening.

'Well, whatever it was, you did well. Joe said that you've got the makings of a good copper. And I know for a fact that he's not easy to impress.'

'Sir.'

High praise indeed, but it was a while before I forgave Joe for that particular afternoon. I was young, remember, and not as cynical as I am now. At the time, I believed that there had to be a better solution. Now that I'm older, I'm not so sure. I've seen a thousand kids like the McConnells, and most of them continue to re-offend, the escalating violence of their crimes proof of Joe's theory.

I won't lie to you; it didn't quite work out the way we hoped. Derek McConnell died in a McDonalds toilet with a needle in his vein and a Quarterpounder in his cold dead fingers. Gerry is currently doing a four year stretch for breaking and entering. But while they didn't exactly straighten up and fly right, neither of them went on to commit the sort of crimes that we thought they might.

One thing does bother me. I read somewhere that America didn't have a serious heroin problem until after Vietnam, but the common use of the drug as a painkiller, coupled with ignorance about it's addictive nature, contributed to thousands of soldiers being discharged with a monkey on their backs. The supply was created to meet the sudden demand, and a world-wide heroin culture was born. My point is this: if we hadn't hurt Derek as badly as we did, he might not have become addicted. But then, maybe he would have carried on doing what he did to Louise Brennan. So I guess the end justifies the means.

At least, that's what I believe. Most of the time.

Chapter 5

5.1.

Sophie gave me a quick, nervous smile as I placed a mug of coffee on the desk in front of her. Before I could settle back into my chair, the phone rang again. Not wanting to disturb them, I went back through to the reception area and took it at my own desk. It turned out to be a current client who wanted to know why Joe's expenses included twenty pounds for admission to a notorious Glasgow strip club called Cleopatra's Zoo. I explained that it was because that was where Joe had followed her husband – as she would know if she had bothered to read the weekly report we sent her.

Next question: why did Joe have to go inside?

Answer: because the Clatty Panda (as it was known by the locals, possibly due to the prescence of some amazingly tacky neon that showed a panda doing a hula dance with a girl in a bikini) was a wee bit more than a strip club. It was a knocking shop.

Again: why did Joe have to go inside?

Answer: you hired us to find out whether or not your husband was being unfaithful. Just because it's bought and paid for doesn't mean it's not infidelity.

After huffing and puffing and threatening to blow our office down, the woman told us to carry on with what we were doing.

I didn't want to disturb Joe again, so I noodled away at a bit of routine paperwork. After ten minutes, the door to his office opened, and the two of them headed to the front door. Joe was smiling.

'Cameron, we're taking Mrs Sloan as a client as of now.'

'Of course.' I nodded at her. 'If there's anything we can do, don't hesitate to give us a wee call.'

She looked at me again, and again I was struck by just how attractive she was.

'I can't help but feel I've seen you somewhere before.'

She probably had. Ten months ago, my face had been on the front page of almost every newspaper in the land. Of course, for most of that time, I was in a morphine-induced coma, so I pretty much slept through my fifteen minutes of fame.

'I really don't think so,' I lied.

Joe said his goodbyes and showed her out the front door. Then he turned to me. 'Who was that on the phone?'

'Betsy Hegarty. She wanted to query your expenses.'

He made a face. 'Again?'

'She's disappointed that three weeks of evening surveillance hasn't discovered anything more exciting than the occasional trip to a strip club.'

'That's because it's hardly grounds for divorce.'

Stephen Hegarty was the chief exec for one of Scotland's top law firms, and two years ago he divorced his wife in favour of his twenty-six year old secretary. So far, so boring. Things got interesting six months ago, when the secretary (who had recently been promoted to wife status) hired us to find out whether or not he was playing away from home. Joe and I suspected that she'd got bored and wanted out, but needed it to be his fault instead of hers, so that she could benefit from a no-doubt favourable pre-nuptial agreement.

Joe asked, 'What did she want us to do?'

'Proceed as normal.'

'I'm fed up with her. I don't often do this, but I think I'll tell Mrs Hegarty that we'll not 'proceed as normal' until we receive payment for the work we've already done. As soon as her cheque clears, I'll tell her to take a hike. We don't need the work and I definitely don't need the hassle.'

Joe took the seat opposite my desk, dragging the Blackberry out of his pocket. I watched him, trying to stop myself from grinning. He noticed. 'Stop it. I'll have to learn to use it sometime.' He poked at the screen with a finger like a surgeon's scalpel – a blind, drunk surgeon, that was. 'How the bloody hell do I do this again?'

It took me three minutes of patient explaining before we managed to find the right telephone number for Mrs Hegarty. As Joe was connected to our soon-to-be-ex client, the door to the office opened. It was Sophie Sloan. She pointed at the door to Joe's office. 'I forgot my bag.'

I moved to stand up. 'Let me help you.'

Joe's voice was sharp. 'Mrs Hegarty, I don't appreciate having my methods questioned.' He covered the mouthpiece of the phone and waved at me, then the computer. 'Cam, pull up a copy of the last report we sent her. We'll see if we can make this stupid bitch see sense.'

Sophie's mouth fell open. I harrumphed as loudly as I could, but Joe was too wrapped up in defending his investigative techniques to notice. I gave Sophie an embarrassed smile and waved a hand in the general direction of Joe's office. She got the message and went to collect her bag. I tapped away at the computer keyboard and swung the monitor around to face Joe. He prodded at it with a stubby finger. 'No, Mrs Hegarty, that's not correct. We round our hours *up*, not *down*. We're like plumbers in that respect.'

I stood up and walked round my desk. Sophie opened the door to Joe's office as I got to it, the expensive-looking bag in her hand. 'Does he speak like that to all his clients?'

'No, not at all. He's really quite patient.' I ushered her to the door.

Joe slammed the phone down. 'Goddam silly cunt.'

He turned to see both Sophie and myself looking at him. The man didn't even have the grace to blush. 'Well, she is.'

5.2.

Sophie Sloan had written a cheque for nearly two thousand pounds, and Joe wasted no time in sending me to the bank with it, telling me to take the rest of the afternoon off and to meet him back at the office at six. With some unexpected free time, I found myself at a loose end. I bought an overpriced sandwich and ate it while I wandered around a shopping mall. There was a sale on in HMV, so I ended up buying a couple of CD's I would probably never listen to, and an autobiography of Bob Dylan I would probably never read. Four PM found me parking the Golf outside Audrey's house. She answered the door with a smile which disappeared the second she realised who it was.

'What do you want?'

'I was hoping to see Mark.'

'He's not here. My sister's got him.'

I loved the way she said that, as if Mark was a possession instead of a child. 'I thought I was taking him out on Saturday.'

She shrugged. 'I forgot.'

There was no offer of apology, but then, apologies weren't Audrey's style. I knew it was bullshit, but let it go, mainly because if I confronted her on it, if I called her to task over all the shitty things she had done, I might not be able to put a lid on it. Custody's an ugly thing, requiring both sets of parents to walk on eggshells. If I let Audrey provoke me into a public screaming match, she would have more justification than ever to prevent me from seeing my son.

I said, 'When's he coming back? Maybe I could take him out tonight.' Even as Audrey shook her head, I remembered that I had promised Joe to meet him. 'I forgot. I can't.'

'You can take him out on Saturday.'

'You'll forget again.'

'I won't.' She went to close the door. 'Pick him up at eleven.'

'Audrey. . . '

The door hesitated. 'What?'

'It's not. . . ' I was going to say fair, but managed to stop myself. There's nothing worse than an adult whining like a child. 'It's not right to use Mark to get at me.'

'I'm not.'

'You are. You forget when we make arrangements. . . ' I only just stopped myself from surrounding the word forget with air quotes. '. . .or you say that he's not feeling well, or that you promised to take him to the Zoo. Apart from the other day, it's been over a month since I saw him.'

She peered over my shoulder, as if gauging how many of her neighbours were watching. The door opened a little. 'Look, why don't you come in and talk? I'll make you a cup of coffee.'

'Thank you.'

She lead me through the house and abandoned me in a conservatory that looked like the "after" in an episode of Changing Rooms. Lace curtains, whicker furniture, a plasma TV the size of a football field. A couple of minutes later she bought two mugs of coffee through. I took a sip; too sweet. I don't take sugar, and I was pretty sure that Audrey hadn't forgotten.

She sat down on one of the whicker chairs and crossed one denim-clad leg over the other. I didn't have to see the label to know that her jeans hadn't been bought at a supermarket. 'So? How're things going?'

'Fine.'

'Still taking the anti-depressants?'

'I've stopped. They made me feel thirsty all the time.'

Fake concern crossed her face. 'Are you sure that's wise?'

'I don't want to be on them for the rest of my life.'

'That's great. That's wonderful. I'm so proud of the way you've managed to put your life back together.'

With absolutely no fucking help from you, I nearly said. 'I'm doing alright. One day at a time and all that.'

'Wonderful.'

'How's Archie?'

She wasn't the only one that could pretend to forget something.

'Arnold, you mean?' She waved a hand. 'He's away. A medical conference in London. Some new way of replacing heart valves or something. Bo-oooring.'

'I would imagine it would be quite a thrill if you were one of the people who needed a new heart valve.'

'I'd forgotten what a sarky bugger you are.'

'How's Mark?'

'He's alright. He misses his. . . misses Arnold.'

That hurt. Right down to the core. 'I miss him too. Mark, I mean.' I smiled to make her think I was joking. 'I'm not so keen on Arnold.'

'I know. And I promise you'll get to see him.'

'When?'

'Saturday. Oh. . . wait. . . can we make it Saturday afternoon? It's just that Arnold's flight lands at eleven. I need to go to the airport and pick him up.'

'And what if his flight's late?' As I rather suspected that it would be. I would roll up and spend my afternoon sitting in front of an empty house. Again. Once bitten, twice shy.

'It won't be.' She said. 'You think I don't want you to see Mark, don't you?'

'It's crossed my mind.'

'That's not true. It's. . . '

'It's what?'

'It's Arnold. He's asked me to marry him, and he thinks it might be better if he adopted Mark.'

I had to stop myself from jumping to my feet. 'That's not going to happen. I won't allow it.'

'Cameron, we have to think of what's best for our son.'

'That's the thing. Mark's our son. He's nothing to do with Arnold. If you hadn't decided to walk out on me we wouldn't even be having this conversation.' I didn't want to go over old ground. 'Audrey, I will never allow Arnold to adopt Mark. Never. I'm his dad, and I have rights.'

Christ, I sounded like a character in a soap opera. I half-expected the theme music to Eastenders to start playing.

'Look, Cameron, I agree with you. You're his dad. I'm just telling you what Arnold feels.'

'Well, you just tell Arnold to get that idea out of his head.'

'I will, I promise.'

I counted to five. No way would I allow anything like that to happen. No way. When I could speak normally, I said, 'Maybe I could go and pick Mark up from Lynne's.'

Lynne was the sister, and an even bigger slapper than Audrey. She liked me about as much as she liked a full blown case of gonorrhoea, although, to be fair, she probably didn't see me as frequently.

'She still with that guy Andy?' I asked.

'No. And they're out. They've gone to see *Get Fish*.' Audrey put her coffee cup to one side and crossed her legs. 'I've got the place to myself for the rest of the afternoon.'

'Lucky you.' I stood up. 'Look, I'll come back Saturday morning.'

'Leaving so soon?'

'I can't think of a reason to stick around.'

'I can.' She stood up and walked over, pressing herself against me. 'I can think of a damn good reason to stay.'

I could smell perfume in her hair, sweet but with something spicy in it. 'You really are a twisted bitch.'

She put her hands on my sides. 'Come on. For old times sake. Arnold's good at the whole providing thing, but he's definitely lacking in certain. . . key. . . areas.'

Even as my brain recoiled in shock, I could feel my body responding. She put a finger on my lips before standing up on her tip-toes and kissing me. 'Come on. Can't you remember how good it was between us?'

It had been something, that was for sure. Occasionally great. But it wasn't what you would call good. Even when we were a couple, the physical side of our relationship had never been mutual. We never gave the other anything, just took. I couldn't describe it as making love, or even fucking. It was just one intensely pleasurable fight with winners on both sides.

And she made me remember that, her lips on mine, gentle, then hard, biting my lower lip, her hand sliding down my chest and into my trousers, twisting hard enough to make me gasp. . .

. . .then my phone was ringing. I broke away, turning my body to the side so that Audrey couldn't see her effect on me. 'Hello?'

'Is that Mr Stone?'

'It is.'

'This is Cheryl Reynolds of Virgin Mobile. You've been with us for nearly a year and as a valued customer we'd like to offer you an exclusive deal on a new mobile phone. . .'

'Cheryl, I'm so glad you called. . .' By then I was almost sprinting for the door. Saved by the bell. I wasn't sure if I actually needed a new phone, but in this life you have to take your rescues as they are offered.

Chapter 6.

6.1.

'We'll take your car,' Joe said. 'The heater's still broken in mine.'

As instructed, I'd drifted back to the office at about half past five. Joe was waiting for me, smelling of single malt. It was easy to guess how he spent his afternoon. Directly across the road from the office was a fairly decent pub and a bookies. With such wonderful facilities less than a hundred yards away, it was a wonder that he ever bothered to go home.

Because it was my car, and because Joe was probably not fit, I drove, which was exactly what Joe had intended. He told me to head for Giffnock. Progress was slow. Everybody in Glasgow wanted home.

'Good afternoon?' I asked.

Joe patted his inside pocket. 'Troubled Youth. Came second in the Three-fifteen from Kempton at nine to one. Excellent afternoon.'

'Your dedication knows no bounds.'

'What's the point of owning your own business if you can't play hooky every once in a while?' Joe didn't wait for an answer. 'What about you?'

'I drove over to Audrey's place to see Mark.'

'How did it go?'

'He wasn't there.' I decided not to tell him what had happened. 'That reminds me. I think I'm getting a new phone.'

'Why?'

'It's on a free trial or something,' I lied. 'She phoned while I was driving, so I couldn't really talk. Anyway, what's the plan?'

'The usual. We're going to sit outside in the cold and try to catch people with their trousers down.'

'You'd think millions of years of evolution would have come up with a better system of catching people out.'

'I hope not. We'd be out of a job.'

That was Joe's biggest fear, that the rampant advance of technology would make guys like us redundant. I suppose it made sense, what with his almost phobic dislike of anything with buttons. I said, 'So what did I miss in your little meeting with Mrs Sloan this morning?'

'Nothing much. The husband's name is Ian, and the sister is called Maureen. We're off to Maureen's house. Apparently the two of them sometimes spend the evening together doing "paperwork".' He waved a buff-coloured file at me. 'Everything we need to know is in here.'

'So what do you think? You think there's something in it, or you think she's your average paranoid wife?'

Joe took his time. 'I think there's probably something in it. You know what it's like in this job. They only come to us as a last resort, and by then it's just a question of us confirming what they already know.'

'Have you ever found a case where the person you're following is completely clean?'

'Oh, yeah. It's rare, but it happens. I remember one job, the husband was completely convinced that his wife was screwing around on him. Turned out, she was working as a Samaritan but hadn't wanted to tell him. He went mental. He was a total arsehole, thought that any kind of charity work was a waste of time. I think in the end she eventually left him.' He looked at me sideways. 'What about you?'

'What about me what?'

'You think that a man and a woman should commit themselves to the same person for the rest of their lives?'

'If you'd asked me that two years ago I would have said yes. Nowadays, I'm not so sure.'

'Were you ever unfaithful to Audrey?'

'No. What about you and Becky?'

'No. I've always talked a good game, but that's as far as it goes.' Joe replied. 'We've been together for nearly thirty years. I'm not saying I don't window-shop, but I wouldn't screw up what I have for the sake of some bimbo.'

'Fair enough.'

He grinned at me. 'But I could be tempted by the lovely Mrs Sloan.'

'I think she's more in my age group, Granddad.'

'She's about ten years older than you, son. Mind you, they do say that there's nothing better than an older woman.'

'I'm sure you're right,' I said. 'Although when you get to your age, they must be bloody hard to find.'

6.2.

Maureen Black lived on a quiet little cul de sac in Giffnock. I knew the area quite well. Until the mid-eighties most of the houses had been owned by the local council. Right-to-buy clauses caused the property values to appreciate wildly, and now it was the kind of place that estate agents described as being "Ideal For the Growing Family".

Except that Maureen's family wasn't growing but shrinking. Joe filled me in on what Sophie Sloan had told him. Eighteen months ago Maureen's husband of ten years had left her. There were no kids, and divorce ensued. She bought half of the house from under him and he invested the money in a convertible. It was so tragic it was almost Greek.

Joe summed up Sophie Sloan's fears about her sister rather neatly. 'You know what they say about recently divorced women. They're so eager to prove it was a fluke they'll seduce anything in trousers.'

All day long it had been overcast and gloomy, and with no blue sky to help eke out the daylight, darkness fell quickly. We reached our destination just after half past six. 'Just cruise by,' Joe instructed me. 'See if anybody's home yet.'

The house itself was a neat little semi, with a living/dining room and a kitchen on the ground floor; two, possibly three bedrooms plus a bathroom upstairs. A driveway extended down one sandstone wall, ending in a fence that presumably lead to a back garden. The front garden was neat, with little in the way of flowers. Estate Agent parlance would describe it as "Low Maintenance". It would bloody well have to be, now Maureen was on her own and working full time.

No car in the driveway.

'The living room light's on,' I said.

'She might have left it like that. Make people think she's already home when it gets dark.'

I turned at the bottom of the road, found a space about fifty yards away that wasn't directly underneath a street lamp, turned the engine off. We settled in to wait.

'I have a question.' I said.

'What?'

'If Sophie Sloan's a qualified nurse, why isn't she the. . . whatchma-callit. . . clinical matron type thingy at her husband's home?'

'She gave up her nursing registration when she had a kid. Wanted to be a full time mum.'

'She didn't strike me as being the mumsy type.'

'The kid died. About six months ago. Leukaemia, I think. I didn't want to pry.'

'Poor woman.'

Yet another person with a shrinking family.

Joe turned to face me. 'I remember reading that something like fifty percent of couples who lose a child under the age of five go on to split up. You have to admit, all the triggers are there. Losing the kid will have left this incredibly raw wound, so Sophie and Ian are possibly not getting along as well as they should. Throw into the equation a recently single sister-in-law... it's like all the planets lining up in a row. It's inevitable that something's going to give.'

'It's shitty.'

'I agree. But the world's a shitty place.' Joe reached out and switched the radio on, started pressing buttons randomly. 'How the hell do I get this thing tuned to Radio Scotland?'

'You don't. It only gets Radio Two.'

'You mean I need to sit and listen to Terry Bloody Wogan?'

'Hopefully not.' I said. 'He does the breakfast show.'

'Can't you change it?'

I assumed he meant the station the car stereo was tuned to and not the BBC's daytime line-up. 'There's an instruction manual in the glove compartment.'

Joe started rummaging around. He withdrew a book the size of a paperback novel. 'Is this it?'

'That's the owner's manual. The manual for the stereo's bigger than that.'

'Bigger? How can it be bigger?'

'I guess the stereo's more complicated than the car.'

Grumbling, he gave up. I covered a grin. We settled in to wait. The minutes ticked by. Lights went on in the surrounding houses as families came home from work. It was damp, but that didn't stop a few kids starting a game of football at the end of the street, using a street light for one goal post and some poor sod's car for the other. Joe and I chatted quietly, our eyes on the house. Joe thought that Glasgow Rangers were spending too much money on outside talent and failing to foster home-grown players. I feigned an interest as best I could. I'm not much of a football fan, but to Joe it was a religion. I wasn't expected to agree, but not to have an opinion was sacrilege.

Tired of his moaning, I fiddled with the radio, eventually pressing enough buttons to find Radio Scotland just in time for the seven o'clock news bulletin. An investigation was to be launched into the cost of the investigation into the cost of building the Scottish Parliament. A body had been found dumped in a bin behind a notorious Paisley strip club called Diamonds and Pearls; police were investigating. We both pricked our ears up at that one; Paisley was less than six miles away from where we were parked. Five years ago it was the kind of case that we might have been assigned to.

'You ever miss it? Being a copper, I mean.'

'Sometimes,' Joe grunted. 'Mostly not. It's all politics now. Politics and budgets. What about you?'

'Yeah.' Every day. 'I mean, no offence and all, but sometimes I wish I hadn't left.'

'None taken. You could always go back.'

'I doubt it. I've made my bed. Now I'll probably die in it.'

'Maybe you should move. Head for the east coast. A change of scenery would do you good.'

'I'm a Glasgow boy, Joe.'

'Alright then, don't leave Glasgow. You could live in the city and work somewhere else. Become a community copper for one of these villages that tie four sheep to a lamp post and call it a leisure centre.'

'Nah, you're alright.' I reached forward and turned up the volume, hoping to distract him. 'I've not heard this song in years.'

'Who's it by?'

I didn't know. It was one of those one hit wonders that dominates a season before disappearing forever. 'Can't remember.'

'It's shite.'

It was.

A car pulled into the driveway of Maureen Black's house. It was impossible to tell the colour; darkness makes everything the same shade of grey. I could see it was a hatchback, maybe a Ford Fiesta. Joe leaned forward as I turned the radio down again.

'Aye, aye.' There was the sound of pages riffling as he flipped through his file. 'Margaret's supposed to drive a blue Three-Oh-Six.'

'I could tell it was a Peugeot.' I lied.

We lost sight of the car as it parked at the far end of the driveway, hidden from view by the house. A few seconds later a woman appeared and let herself in through the front door. I got a glimpse of

C. DAVID INGRAM

dark hair, pale skin. The hair wasn't as long as Sophie's, but there was a resemblance. 'Hello, Maureen,' I said, softly.

'No sign of the husband.'

'He might be following. She's left enough space in the driveway for another vehicle. What did Sophie say Ian drove?'

Joe flipped through his notes. 'BMW. She said they had one each.'

Of course he drove a BMW. He was, after all, the boss.

We watched in silence. The front bedroom light came on for about five minutes, then went off again, then back on for another five. Then off. It was easy to imagine what was going on. Shower, then change. Now she would be downstairs, maybe preparing something to eat, maybe reaching for a takeaway menu as she slumped in front of the television, or maybe. . . just maybe. . . opening a bottle of wine and making sure that she had two clean glasses.

Joe nudged me. 'Look.'

A saloon car was approaching the house. 'That's a BMW.' I said.

The left indicator came on and the car slowed as it approached the house. 'Oh, Matron,' I said in my best Kenneth Williams voice. 'What a naughty girl you are.'

Except that she wasn't. The Beamer pulled into the driveway of the house next door. Doors slammed. Mum, Dad, two kids. Plus a whole load of shopping. We both sat back in disappointment.

'I suppose we should be glad,' I said.

'I suppose. The longer we sit here, the more we earn.'

'You're such a cynic.'

6.3.

At ten to eight, Joe's mobile phone rang. I kept my eyes on the house, eavesdropping, pretending not to, trying to figure out what was being said from Joe's side of the conversation alone. Eventually he hung up.

'That was Sophie Sloan. She was calling to say that her husband had just arrived home. They're sending out for a curry. There's no point in us sitting here all evening.'

'And here was me just getting comfortable.'

'Take me home, Jeeves.'

I started the engine. 'You want me to take you back to the office so that you can drive home yourself?' Inwardly, I hoped that he would say no. I had my doubts over whether or not he would pass a breath test

'Nah. I'll get a taxi in the morning. You can drop me at the house.'

'No problem.' It was only five miles out of my way. Five miles there, five miles back. But then, he did give me the afternoon off. I had nothing to complain about.

Curry sounded like a damn good idea. I decided to make a detour.

6.4.

Home was a tenement flat in Craghill Road. Parking was on-street, in the first available space. Tonight, the first available space was nearly four hundred yards away, between a Vauxhall Astra with a cracked rear-windscreen and a transit van that looked like it had just been dragged out of a canal.

I got out of the car and made sure that the door was locked. It had been months since I had washed it and a heavy layer of dust was caked along the sides. That was good; if the local kids got the impression that somebody cared then the windows probably wouldn't survive the night. I started walking, the plastic bag that contained my dinner in my left hand, my right hand buried in the pocket of my jacket, clutching a heavy, chain-link dog lead that I had tied a knot in, creating a borderline-legal, but potentially devastating weapon. Don't believe what the politicians tell you; Glasgow may be a beautiful city, but like every beautiful city, it has a nasty side.

I just happened to live slap-bang in the middle of it.

No rain. I kept my pace up, ignoring the few pedestrians, making sure that I didn't make any accidental eye-contact and provoke a fight – not just because my face was one of the most hated in the country, but because some of the locals would pick a fight for the hell of it. Back in my days as a police officer, the area around Craghill Road was known as Little Bosnia.

Except that the conflict in Bosnia was long over, and this place still looked like a war-zone.

The streets were pot-holed and narrow, lined with tenement flats that seemed to absorb the small amount of light the night sky had to offer, enveloping everything in a depressing curtain of perpetual greyness. Every second lamp post was dim, destroyed by a well-placed half brick no doubt thrown by a local hero. Broken plastic and glass crunched underfoot as I negotiated the cracked and pitted pavements. I had a theory that the street lights were vandalised because most of the locals actively craved the darkness, the better to hide their nefarious lifestyles and dirty deeds done dead cheap. Furtive-looking kids loitered on almost every street corner, hair unkempt, faces pale, eyes scanning the middle distance for their drugs connection, or the patrolling police car that would blow the deal.

I had less than fifty yards to go when I spotted them: two rail thin youths who looked as if they had last eaten some time about the turn of the millennium, loitering like stray dogs outside the off-licence that was directly across the road from my flat. Sportswear, baseball caps, and expensive-looking trainers. I paid no attention to them; they were always there, part of the local scenery, peddling small time drugs and buying alcohol for anybody that might look younger than eighteen. Just a couple of aimless kids who would drift through life until it finally caught up with them. I was so used to the sight of them that I barely noticed them, if that makes any sense.

Big mistake.

I covered the last few yards to the communal door to my tenement, taking my hand out of my pocket, feeling for where I had attached my keys to the belt hook of my trousers. It didn't register that both of them had started to cross the road just as I slid the front door key into the lock and pushed open the door. I made my way up the stairway that led to the individual flats, taking my time, blissfully unaware of the front door swinging slowly closed behind me.

Slowly enough for my two little pals to reach it before it could latch shut.

I was halfway up the first flight of stairs before I heard – too late – the gentle scuffing of rubber on concrete. As I began to turn, somebody grabbed the neck of my jacket and wrenched me back. I stumbled, my foot searching for solid ground and finding only air, my body twisting to the right, glancing off somebody else, a fist jabbing me hard in the kidney. My foot landed half on, half off one of the stairs, then slid off, the ankle turning underneath me as it hit the stair below, my knee buckling as my lower body tried to bend in three directions at once. All sense of balance was gone and I tumbled heavily back down the staircase, not far enough to break anything but plenty far enough to knock the wind out of me. I landed in a heap at the bottom.

They stood over me. 'Give us your wallet.'

Struggling for breath, I made it to my hands and knees.

'I said, give us your wallet.' One of them swung a foot, kicking me right in the stomach. I folded, rolling on my side and going foetal, the cold stonework against my face, unable to inhale for the leaden pain in my abdomen. In a bizarre moment of clarity, I found myself thanking God that Reebok didn't fit their trainers with steel toecaps. My back hurt. My shoulder hurt. My right leg felt as if it had been dipped in fire. Even my eyelids hurt.

Click.

I quickly forgot about my pain as I recognised the sound.

Flick-knife.

Opening.

A cool blade was laid against my cheek. A voice spoke softly in my ear. 'Wallet. Now.'

'OK,' I gasped. 'Just. . . just let me get up.'

They stepped back and I lurched to my feet, using the stone wall to prop myself upright. The world was fading in and out, the strip light that illuminated the close pulsating – bright, dark, bright, dark. I gulped air and worked hard on not passing out. When I was sure that I could remain upright, I risked a closer look at my assailants.

Wished I hadn't bothered.

They were both skinny and ugly. Shaved heads, bad skin. The one that held the flick-knife had a Glasgow Rangers tattoo on the back of his knuckles; the other one was wearing a Celtic top. It was heartening to see the young people of Glasgow putting their differences to one side.

'I'm gonny count to ten,' said Flick-Knife. 'After that, I'll cut your bollocks off.'

Although unconvinced of his ability to reach such lofty numerical heights, I decided not to try and find out, slipping my hand inside my jacket and removing my wallet. 'There you go.'

Celtic Bhouy took the wallet from my outstretched fingers and flipped through it. He held up a solitary five-pound note and looked at me in disgust. 'This all you've got?'

I was beginning to get my breath back. It still hurt like hell, but I could feel the adrenaline flooding my system, possibilities opening as my brain finally stepped into gear. I had a choice: fight or flight. You would think that fifty billion years of evolution might have provided a third option.

I chose. 'There's two fifties in the wee compartment.'

'Whit wee compartment?'

'Behind the Donor card,' I said. 'It's got a tiny zipper.'

Celtic Bhouy's brow furrowed in concentration as he fumbled away with his thick fingers, turning the wallet this way and that as he tried to find the non-existent section I was talking about. I almost laughed as he ripped the Donor card from its mounting and tossed it to the ground.

'It's there! You had your hand on it.' I told him, doing my best to stir things up.

It was all too much for Flick-Knife. He stretched out and grabbed the wallet from his hapless crony. 'For fuck's sake. You're bloody useless, you are.'

Engrossed in the search, neither of them noticed as I slipped my right hand into my pocket. I gripped the dog lead, feeling for the nylon loop. I'd never used the thing in anger, but in theory, if I pulled, then the whole thing would come smoothly out of my pocket with no snagging or catching. I sagged against the wall, tilting the right side of my body away from them, breaking into a coughing fit in case the sound of the metal chain links sliding over each other tipped them off.

It didn't.

As I slowly took my hand from my pocket, the chain fell down the side of my leg, loose, heavy, ready to do some damage.

And not a moment too soon. Flick-Knife threw the wallet away and brandished his weapon at me. 'Lying bastard. You're having us on.'

I waited, my left hand at my mouth, the chain still hidden by my body, my eyes on the knife. If he moved, I would have one shot, and one shot only. Whatever else happened, I had to take care of the knife.

He leapt forward, right arm a blur, aimed straight at my side. If I'd been any slower, he would have gutted me. As it was, I twisted just a fraction too late; the tip of the blade glanced off the side of my stomach but didn't penetrate the skin. Instead, it snagged in the material of my jacket, tearing it with a harsh ripping sound. I swung my left elbow forward into his chest, an awkward, lumbering blow that probably hurt about as much a flea bite but caused him to stagger back. I brought my right hand up, swinging the chain as hard as I could, the angle completely wrong but it was all I could do. He must have sensed movement in the corner of his eye, raising his left hand to ward off the blow. The chain wrapped around his wrist and I pulled, hard, sending him reeling off balance, planting my foot in his backside and pushing, sending him pinwheeling into his companion. I yelled as I finally got a clear shot with the chain, swinging it as hard as I could, gravity adding momentum to the knot at the end. There was a thwack as it struck Flick-Knife's right shoulder blade, the thin material of his shell-suit providing no protection whatsoever. He screamed in pain and leapt forward directly into his pal, the two of them landing in a confused tangle of limbs at my feet.

My turn.

I swung for them, again and again, not bothering to aim, not really needing to, just leaning forward and walloping away with all my strength. Shins, thighs, calves, buttocks– the chain made a thwopping noise every time it made contact. Flick-Knife howled in agony and his weapon skittered across the concrete, coming to rest at the bottom of the stairs.

I collapsed back against the wall, my exhaustion real this time, a dull throbbing pain in my shoulder. From somewhere upstairs, I heard a door open. One of my neighbours was taking an interest.

'Help! It's me!' I called. Then I realised how meaningless that was. 'Cameron! I'm in the Second Floor Left! Call the police!'

There was a slamming sound. Shouting my name had been a mistake. I was never going to win any popularity contests, not tonight, not in this city. Had I been on fire, most of my neighbours would probably break out the marshmallows.

I took my mobile phone out of my pocket and dialled. Instead of a soothing voice asking me the nature of my emergency, I got a hiss of meaningless static. Concrete might be great for building tenement flats, but it's hell on telephone reception. Disgusted, I flipped my Nokia closed, only to look up to see Flick-Knife had rolled over and was watching me, a nasty cut bleeding away underneath his left eye. God knew how that had happened; all my efforts had been concentrated on his back. His companion was still foetal, hands clenched between his thighs, a high-pitched wailing sound emanating from behind his clenched teeth.

Flick-Knife and I looked at each other balefully. 'Little bastard,' I told him. 'What did you want to go and do that for?'

He shrugged. 'Easy money.'

'You've got to be kidding,' I said. 'Nobody round here *has* any.'

I wasn't sure what to do. Although I had gained the upper hand, I was still outnumbered. Meanwhile, the adrenaline was leaving my body, making me feel shivery and ill. My head throbbed, and the lights seemed overly bright. If I had to stand there for much longer, I was probably going to throw up on my two captives.

Which would be an ideal way to defuse the situation.

Flick-Knife levered himself upright and grabbed his pal by the ear. 'Come on, Shabsy. Time for us to go.'

I waved the dog chain feebly. 'Don't move.'

His lower lip twitched upward in a sneer; he knew I didn't have it in me. 'Fuck you, Stone.'

Shabsy lumbered to his feet. His pain tolerance must have been much lower than his pal's; although there was barely a mark on him, silent tears ran down his face. His eyes burned into mine. I raised the chain. 'Don't even think about it.'

Flick-Knife bent slowly to where his blade lay on the ground, his eyes on me all the time. 'I'm takin' this back.'

Of course he was. Why leave evidence lying around?

Leaning on each other, the two of them trudged their way to the door. I let them go, too sore and nauseous to do anything else. They were just punks. Craghill's a closed community, assault cases nothing more than an everyday occurrence. Even if their identities could be discovered, friends and relatives would swear blithely that on the evening of the 'alleged' attack, my assailants had been at bible class, or maybe volunteering at the local old-folks home. Without witnesses, it was an unwinnable case, and as an ex-copper, nobody understood that better than me.

After a few minutes, I felt slightly better. Well enough to cover the last few steps to my flat, where I planned to assess the damage in the privacy of my own bathroom. Moving like I had a damn good case of arthritis, I grabbed my wallet. The plastic bag that held my dinner lay where I had dropped it. I picked it up, surprised to find that apart from some minor seepage, the foil containers were still sealed. It was my first – and last – lucky break of the evening.

As I trudged up the stairs, it occurred to me; how had Flick-Knife known my name? Although my face had been plastered over the front

C. DAVID INGRAM

page of every newspaper in the land, the accident had been months ago, and neither of my attackers looked as they had much interest in current events. They seemed more the type to dispense with the pesky front part of the paper and head straight to the sports pages at the back.

I lost interest the minute I reached the front door to my flat, where somebody – possibly my two pals – had left me an unpleasant little surprise.

6. 5.

Somebody had daubed the words BABY KILLER across my front door. The letters were large and looked like they had been made in a hurry. The paint had run in thick, messy drips. I stood and looked at it for thirty seconds, anger passing through my body like a wave, rising, peaking and then subsiding into a trough.

Actually, the paint was a very pleasant shade of red, although probably more suited to interior work. This wasn't the first time it had happened. A couple of months ago, the message had been 'MURDERER.' If I recalled correctly, it had been in exactly the same shade.

Same paint shade equals same artist. I was glad to see that four months away from real police work hadn't damaged my uncanny talent for deductive reasoning.

Including my own, there were eleven flats in the block. Two on the ground floor, three each on the first second and third floors. Bottom Left had been empty since I had moved in, but every other flat was occupied. There were families, singletons, couples, and of course, the obligatory little old lady with the scruffy cat collection.

I wondered who the culprit was. I doubted it was Flick-Knife and Shabsy. Anything more than a kicking was probably too imaginative for them. It was far more likely that the mystery artist was one of my own neighbours. Almost everybody in the block hated me. If Ian

Huntley had moved into the empty flat, the little old lady on the top floor would have welcomed him by baking him a nice cake and warning him to stay away from the nasty fellow on the second floor. Even her cats gave me the evil eye when they passed me on the stairs.

I knocked on the door to the flat opposite me, folded my arms, and waited. After a few seconds, Lee opened the door. In his hand was an empty can of lager, crushed flat in the middle. Something – probably a ball point pen – had been used to punch a group of tiny holes through the side of the can, creating a convenient hash delivery system. I gestured at the paint on my door. 'Know anything about this, Lee?'

The door opened wider as Lee stepped out, craning his neck to admire the artwork. He wore an unbuttoned Hawaiian shirt over a pair of stained Y-fronts, and an odour of skunk followed him about like cheap aftershave. Manky dreadlocks hung halfway down his skinny back. Music drifted from his open door, funky guitars and a saxophone. He told people he was a sociology student, but as far as I could tell, his days consisted of smoking dope and watching porn.

Maybe I was being unfair. A friend once told me that sociology was a Mickey-Mouse subject. It was always possible that drugs and self-abuse were part of the course.

He shook his head and smiled. 'Man, somebody's got a grudge against you.'

Thanks, Einstein. 'Have you been out at all today, Lee?'

'What's it to you?'

'Maybe you could tell me when it was done.'

He shook his head. 'Jane was over.' He winked at me. 'Spent the day in bed, if you know what I mean.'

Jane was his "girlfriend" – supposedly. According to Lee, she was married, stunning, and wanted nothing more than an affair. Nobody had ever seen her, and everybody thought that he was full of it.

'Is she still here? Maybe she saw something when she arrived.'

'She left. About an hour ago. With a satisfied grin on her face.'

'And you didn't hear anything?'

'A bit of shouting a few minutes ago. Nothing special.'

I resisted the impulse to kick the stupid little stoner in the balls. 'That was me. Two kids tried to make off with my wallet. I'm talking about earlier. I want to know who did this.'

The stupid little stoner gave me a stupid little grin. 'Still playing detective? Far as I remember, you're not a cop anymore.'

'I'm not a babykiller, either.'

Although, technically, I was. Just because it was an accident didn't mean it didn't count.

'Whatever.' Lee turned to go. I snatched a quick glance at his hands. If he was the mystery message-leaver, maybe he had been too wasted to scrub the paint off his fingernails. But there was nothing in-criminating – a few months worth of grime, but no tell-tale paint residue. He went into his flat and shut the door behind him. The smell of hash lingered, not quite strong enough to overshadow the smell of cat urine.

I unlocked my own door and stepped in the hallway. I would deal with the graffiti, but not this very second. Right now, I was going to eat the takeaway I had picked up on my way home. Chicken Jaipuri. Hot, spicy, full of onions and mushrooms. The high point of a distinctly average day.

Except when I peeled the lid off the foil container, I found that they had given me Lamb Korma by mistake. Instead of chargrilled chicken in a sunset of red sauce, I had lumpy grey meat poking out of a glutinous yellow sludge that reminded me of bile.

I never had liked Mondays.

6.6.

Only one of my neighbours didn't hate me. Liz. Top Left, the flat above and across from mine. I had almost removed the paint when she showed up an hour later, smelling of white wine and teetering along on a pair of improbably high heels that would have looked great on a six foot tall fashion model but just looked dangerous on her. She stopped on the landing and watched me as I scrubbed away with a rag soaked in white spirit. 'What did it say?'

'That I was a wonderful man and they hoped I would live here for ever and ever.'

'You'd think they could have slipped a note underneath your door.'

'Perhaps they didn't have any paper available,' I said. 'You look nice.'

A black dress decorated with a pleasing pattern of flowers stopped just above the knee. Her complexion was always light, and she wore very little make-up. Her face was round and usually smiling, and her body was about a thousand times more attractive than the stick-insects that grace the covers of the fashion mags, possibly because there was nothing contrived in the way she carried herself. She wasn't trying to be sexy; she just achieved it naturally. I would never mess up a good thing, but every once in a while I caught myself thinking about her in a way that you don't normally think about your friends. It was the Irish accent that did it for me.

She sat down on the steps, pulling off the high heels to massage her feet. 'Jesus, that's better. I was on a date.'

'Who was it this time?'

'A junior doctor.'

I looked at my watch. Ten forty. 'It can't have gone that well.'

'It didn't. Turns out, he's looking for a Barbara Windsor.'

She must have guessed by my face that I didn't get it.

'You know. A naughty nurse. A bit of slap and tickle in the linen cupboard.'

'I thought you might have meant a seventy year old woman.'

'Aye, well. He's welcome to her. Halfway through the meal he leaned forward and started to lick my ear. Asked me what colour knickers I had on.' She looked at me matter-of-factly. 'You're all bloody useless, you know.'

I scrubbed away serenely. 'I know.'

'I mean, for God's sake, have you ever done anything like that?'

'Not recently.'

'I stood up and walked out.'

I clenched my fist in a gesture of female solidarity. 'You go, girl.'

She laughed. 'What have you been up to today? Apart from graffiti removal?'

'This and that. Bit of the other. Went to see Mark.'

'Really? How'd that go?'

'Not well. He wasn't there. I ran into his mother instead.'

'Your ex?'

'That's the one.'

'I thought you looked depressed.'

I shook my head. 'I'm fine. I always look depressed.'

'How true.'

'She made a pass at me.'

God knows why that slipped out.

Liz stopped massaging her feet. 'What did you do?'

'I ran for the hills.' I neglected to mention that it had taken a phone call to prompt my tactical retreat.

'Good man. That's crap you don't need. I mean, what was she thinking? She uses Mark as a. . . a bargaining chip and then thinks you'll drop your trousers the second she feels horny?'

'Seems like it.'

'Dirty bitch.' She stood up. 'I'm starving. I think I'll make some toast. Want some?'

I shook my head. After the takeaway disappointment, I'd eaten an entire tin of spaghetti hoops. 'I thought you went out for dinner.'

'Yeah. To one of those places where they give you a lettuce leaf with a bit of grated parmesan on it and expect you to believe it's a salad.'

'There's Korma if you want it.'

'What's wrong with it?'

'It was meant to be Jaipuri. They gave me the wrong thing.'

She almost knocked me over on her way to my kitchen. 'Not your day, is it?'

Chapter 7

Tuesday 18th November

7.1.

Insomnia's a bitch.

Even before I smacked a one ton car into roughly one hundred and eighty pounds of mother and child, I had difficulty sleeping. Every day I wake up at the crack of dawn, too hot, too cold, too damn bright to do anything but get up.

This morning was no different. My eyes snapped open at three minutes past five, despite the fact that I had only drifted off to sleep some time after half past one. I lay there, nestled in the warmth of my bed, hoping that maybe this time it would be different and I would be able to go back to sleep. As always, habit triumphed over ambition, and ten minutes later I found myself dressing silently in the dark.

I felt like shit. It was cold and my body ached from the previous evening's tumble down the stairs. I did a series of stretching exercises, the pain flaring like a struck match before subsiding into embers. After five minutes, I stopped hoping for death and started planning for life.

And life – at least my life – begins with coffee.

Three heaped spoons of instant, four of sugar, all maxed into one tiny cup without milk. For the rest of the day, I'd take it white with no sugar, but the first time round I needed something to kick-start me and give me the energy boost necessary for my morning exercise. I used to jog, but the surgeons had advised me that the repeated impact would place additional strain on the collection of pins and wires that held what was left of my hip together. Instead, I do twelve miles on an exercise bike, working my upper body with a set of dumbbells. I was fairly sure that it was good for me because it hurt like hell.

By six fifteen I was showered, hungry, and feeling slightly better about the world. As I spooned more coffee into a mug, there came a knock on my door. Five seconds later, Liz shambled into my kitchen wearing a pink dressing gown and fluffy slippers. 'I've ran out of milk.'

I opened the fridge and took out half a pint. She shook her head when I offered it to her. 'And coffee. And bread.'

I rolled my eyes. 'There's a soup kitchen down the street.'

'No good. They've figured out that I'm not actually homeless.'

Instead of a nice, wooden kitchen table, I have some plastic patio furniture that looks like it has been rescued from a tip. She slumped onto a dirty chair, her hair a rats' nest, her eyes full sleep. She looked at me and groaned. Not a morning person, is Liz.

'You on an early shift?'

She nodded. 'I've got three hips and an elbow.'

'Mutant.'

She ignored me. It was a joke she had heard about five million times before, the price of being a theatre nurse specialising in orthopaedic surgery. 'You want to go and see the new Tom Cruise movie tonight? I was going to go with the junior doctor but he told me that Tom was symbolic of everything that was wrong with Hollywood today.'

'The bastard. No wonder you walked out on him.' I grabbed another mug from the draining board. I'd been feeding her breakfast a few times a week for the last couple of months, the two of us slipping into a comfortable routine like an old married couple.

She yawned. 'So. Cinema. Tom Cruise. Car chases. Acrobatics. A dazzling smile with perfect white teeth. You game or what?'

'I'd like to, but I'll need to see what the boss has planned for me.' She looked like she wanted to ask, so I changed the subject. 'Why is it you have to drag me to every single movie Tom Cruise makes, and yet you wouldn't go and see that Martin Scorsese one with me?'

She shrugged. 'I like Tom. I'm taller than him.'

'Chipmunks are taller than him. And they also have perfect white teeth. Smaller ones, but it's still a dazzling smile.'

'Shut up.'

I did as I was told, filling her mug and handing it to her. 'You want some toast?'

'Urggh.'

'So that's a "no" then.'

'I'm just bored with toast. I could eat a Big Mac.'

'I'm sorry, we're fresh out.'

Liz is one of those people that can eat anything for breakfast – pizza, curry, chocolate. One morning the two of us walked to Burger King at seven am. I stuck to the breakfast menu, but Liz wanted the works – Whopper, fries and a milkshake. Turns out, Burger King aren't as keen on you having it your way as their advertising campaign would have you believe.

I made toast for myself. Four slices, the butter taken directly from the fridge and carved onto it in thick yellow wedges before being topped with Marmite. Just because I exercise every day doesn't mean I'm obsessive about my health. I hate salad and don't take vitamins. Mentally, it's important to eat food you like. A plate of whole-wheat soy bread and a glass of lemongrass juice would probably be enough to make me want to kill myself, and with my history it's a risk I just can't afford.

Liz rummaged in the fridge, eventually surfacing with a pork pie that looked like it might have been there since the war. 'Can I eat this?'

I frowned. 'I can't remember buying it.'

'Maybe it belonged to the previous tenant.'

That was actually more plausible than it sounded. Whoever lived in the flat before me must have left in a hurry, because they had left everything behind, including a mouldy bridesmaid's dress and my lovely kitchen furniture. 'She might come looking for it.'

'Well if she asks, tell her it went out of date.' She fumbled with the wrapper. 'It *is* out of date.'

'How out of date?'

'Five days.'

'Throw it away.'

'These things are loaded with preservatives. Did you see that thing about the French fries? Some documentary I saw. They put them in a box and they were fine almost two months later. Just a bit fusty.'

She dumped the pie on a plate and started to eat it. I watched, appalled. The meat was the colour of bubblegum. 'Jesus, Liz, you'll catch food poisoning. You're supposed to be a nurse.'

'I never said I was a good one. For God's sake, listen to yourself. And you're coming to the cinema with me whether you like it or not. It'll do you good to spend time with another human being. There's a seven o'clock showing. Alright?'

I bowed my head. 'Yes, dear.'

7.2

He must have been waiting for me to leave the flat.

I saw the car first, parked in a disabled space, a dusty brown Rover that was even more anonymous than my Golf. As I went to move past, the occupant leaned across and opened the passenger door directly in my path. A voice I recognised said, 'Get in.'

Harper.

My mood nose-dived. 'What do you want?'

'I thought I might buy you breakfast.'

'I've already eaten.'

'Then you can watch me eat.'

I thought about just walking by. God knows, I wanted to. Harper only ever looked me up when there was dirty work that he didn't have the sack to do himself. But we both knew that I wouldn't. I got in the car. He smiled as he started the engine and pulled away from the kerb.

Although he was wearing a newish suit and a nice shirt, it didn't alter the fact that Kenny Harper was one ugly prick. He had a face like a bulldog licking piss off a thistle. His skull was all planes and angles, the features a rudimentary afterthought, slapped on like a child's Mr Potato Head. One ear was slightly higher than the other, one eye squinted to the left and down towards a nose that looked like a lump of putty. Instead of a suit, he should have been draped in animal skins and living in a muddy pit. Every once in a while, the villagers could toss him a nice juicy virgin to appease his rage.

There had to be *some* in the Glasgow area.

We hadn't liked each other when I'd been an active member of the force, and we didn't like each other now. But that didn't alter the fact that I was always broke and he always wasn't. I'd done a few jobs for him over the past few months – mainly small stuff, the kind of work that cops wish they could get away with but can't in these politically correct times. Teenage yobs causing a disturbance outside your local? Nasty drug dealer hanging around outside the amusement arcade that your thirteen year old son thinks is the centre of the universe? Wish you could just give them a good hard kick in the balls and tell them to piss off? Speak to Detective Harper. A quiet word in his ear and your problem could disappear as if by magic.

Except it wasn't magic. It was me.

The first few times, I'd enjoyed it. It was like being a cop again, but free from the shackles imposed by today's criminal-friendly society. I even glamorised it in my mind, thinking of myself as some kind of vigilante dispensing street justice. I knew it was wrong, though, and told Harper I wanted out. Every time I did something for him, I felt myself stepping further over the line. He was OK about it, but continued to offer me the occasional bit of work. And the sad thing is, I was usually tempted by it. Usually because he seemed to know just when I was running low on cash. That's how he was – a stone cold bastard who knew the value of everything and the price of nothing.

He steered with one hand as he lit a cigarette. 'You keeping busy, Stone?'

'I'm getting by.'

'How's Joe?'

'Fine.' I didn't say anything else. Harper and I might not have been the best of mates, but we were bosom buddies compared to how he and Joe felt about each other. They'd been partners and friends, and then one day, they were neither. Nobody knew the reason. It was weird, because they both had similar backgrounds and investigative methods.

Harper said, 'I got one of his wife's books out of the library.'

A few years ago, Becky Banks had discovered a talent for writing. Her speciality was historical sagas; the unconventional but feisty lass who stands up to the corrupt land owner and marries the boss's son, but only after losing her real love in a mill accident/ fall from a horse/ burning orphanage. They sold well, and Becky had become something of a minor celebrity.

'I never had you down as the romantic type,' I said.

'There was a picture of a poppy field on the cover,' he told me. 'I thought it was a war story.'

'I believe you. Thousands wouldn't.'

'It was shite.'

I ignored him, suspecting that any fiction that didn't start with the lines "I always thought that the letters in your magazine were probably made up, but a few weeks ago I was holidaying in Spain when two of the most beautiful girls I have ever seen knocked on the door of my hotel room and asked if they could borrow some suntan lotion" was probably outwith his literary sphere.

We headed north, possibly making for the McDonalds on the edge of the industrial estate. His cigarette smelled good. He kept his eyes on the road, his jaw clamped on the filter like the hero of a seventies cop drama, which in his imagination he probably was. 'I used to work with Joe, you know. It came as no surprise to me when he went into P.I. work. He was the type.'

He was just trying to bait me. I ignored it, watching the scenery go by. The morning traffic was heavy but flowing well.

'You know what I mean. A bit of a maverick. Didn't like to follow the rules. Played it fast and loose.'

'Yeah. It's a shame he quit,' I said. 'He could have had his own TV show. You know – the loner cop who's always getting thrown off the case for pissing off "Somebody In Authority". The kind of guy whose partner gets killed halfway through the season.' I looked sidelong at Harper. 'That would have been a tragedy.'

'Now. Be nice. I'm the one that's paying for breakfast.'

'What a prince.'

I was right: we were heading for the McDonalds. He stopped at the drive-thru window. 'You sure you don't want anything?'

'A double sausage muffin meal. White coffee.'

'Your wish is my command.'

Five minutes later, we pulled over at a quiet little lay-by. The morning traffic droned past while we ate our food. I wiped my greasy fingers on the underside of the car seat. 'What do you want, Harper?'

'You remember Jason Campbell? Instead of a custodial sentence the judge let him off easy and sent him to Leverndyke Hospital to make wicker baskets?'

I nodded.

'He's out now. Managed to convince the trick cyclist that he's not a danger to the public. He's back living at his mum's house.'

'I thought she was dying. I seem to remember his lawyer whining about terminal cancer.'

'Not any more.'

It took me a second to figure it out. 'Poor lad. When did it happen?'

'Last month. Jason got sprung just in time to hold her withered claw as she stepped into the light. I suspect that Mummy's condition perhaps contributed to the decision to release him. You know, compassion and all that crap.' Harper spat the word compassion like it was a particularly virulent strain of genital warts.

I wanted one of his cigarettes. Like most ex-cops, I'm also an ex-smoker. Those little coffin nails can be so comforting. 'I take it you want me to go and pay him a visit?'

He nodded. 'Find out why he's been spending his time parked out-side St John's High School instead of at home sniffing through Mummy's knicker drawer like a good little perv.'

'You have such a nice way of putting things.'

'It's my gift. And while you're at it, you could perhaps make him see the error of his ways. Perhaps you could even suggest that he sells his mother's house and moves to somewhere where his type are made more welcome. Cambodia, for example.'

'Welcome the way that Gary Glitter was welcome?'

He turned to look at me. 'I don't fucking care what he does, as long as he feels an urgent desire to get the fuck out of my patch.'

'Why can't you do it yourself?'

'Jason's done some work for me in the past. He used to be one of my snouts. And I, unlike you, still have a career to worry about.'

It was a cheap shot. 'One day I'll get caught. You can't be coming to me with this kind of work all the time.'

'What makes you think I do?'

Part of me wanted to say no, but it would have been pointless. Harper no doubt had half a dozen other people lined up to do the same work. There's plenty of guys willing to do a dirty job for the right price, and it wasn't as if Jason was going to discover a cure for cancer.

I scrunched up the wrapper that had been wrapped around my muffin. 'How much?'

'How much do you want?'

There was no point in aiming low. 'A grand.'

'What do you think this is? Charity?'

'Eight hundred.'

'Two hundred. I could get a couple of crack addicts to do it for one.'

'But I won't fuck it up. They'll either kill him or get caught. And if they get caught, you know they won't hesitate to name their sponsor.'

'Three.'

I wondered where the money was coming from. There's a lot of slush out there, and it's easy to find if you know where to look. Once I arrested a nineteen year old boy for dealing heroin outside a secondary school. He had a bundle of notes more than half an inch thick hidden inside his training shoe. I asked him how much was there and he couldn't tell me because he didn't know. The final total turned out to be over five grand. Five grand in non-sequential used notes. It would have been so easy to say that it was three, and keep the rest.

I know what you're thinking, and I didn't. I never did. There's a line between getting paid in dirty cash for a job well done, and actually stealing. It's fine, but it's there.

I pretended to think about the amount. 'Five.'

'Three fifty. And that's my final answer. If you don't like it, I'll phone a friend.'

'It'll do.'

We shook on the deal. Harper grinned slyly. 'I'd have gone to four.'

'I'd have done it for free.'

That wiped the smile off his face. He started the ignition. 'Don't wipe your fucking greasy hands on my seats again.'

7.3.

I usually beat Joe to work, but my breakfast meeting with Harper had caused me to run a little late. By the time I arrived, he was already on his first cup of coffee. I walked in to the reception area that doubled as my office to find him sitting at my desk checking his reflection in a tiny hand held mirror that he snapped shut and stuffed into a pocket the second he saw me.

I pretended not to notice. 'Morning, boss. What's with the suit?'

Joe was very much of the trousers, shirt and leather jacket school of dress, and he wore a suit like a monkey wears a tie – that is to say, infrequently and badly. The suit in question was Italian, expensive, and cut to fit a man twenty years younger and twenty pounds lighter, which, in all fairness, he probably had been when he purchased it. For him to wear one by choice meant only one thing: money.

Corporate money.

'I'm meeting some people for lunch. Harald and Ginsell International Holdings.' he replied.

'Who are they and what do they do?'

'They're something to do with the Internet. I think. They're about to build a new call centre in Westerhouse and they want to discuss internal security.'

Westerhouse was one of the city's rougher areas. A call centre would mean some jobs, but it would also be one more target for the local criminals. 'Are you going to advise them that the best way to secure the place would be to build somewhere else?'

'Ha ha. This is why I'm the boss and you're the trusty sidekick.'

'I've always thought of myself more as being the comedy relief.'

'Really?' Joe raised an eyebrow. 'When does that start, then?'

'Now who's laughing.'

He stood up and allowed me to sit down. 'There was a message from Sophie Sloan on the answering machine when I got in. Want to hear it?'

I nodded. Joe pressed a button on the machine, naturally managing to select the wrong one. A digitised voice informed us that it was Friday, two fifteen am. One day I would have to get round to programming the right date and time into it.

'Maybe you should try the one marked "play",' I said quietly.

He shot me a sour look. 'Shut up.'

I mimed zipping my lips closed. This time, he managed to hit the right button. Sophie Sloan's voice was so whispery quiet, I had to strain to hear it.

'Hi. It's me. Mrs Sloan. I forgot to tell you, my husband's going away on business. Today. It's some big conference down in London. He'll be there until Thursday. I'm sorry, I made a mistake, I thought it was next month. I don't want you thinking I'm wasting your time.'

She concluded with a few inconsequential remarks, telling us that she had phoned the office because she didn't want to wake Joe up, but she had woken up at four in the morning and she just knew that she wouldn't be able to get back to sleep unless she told us.

We looked at each other. 'What do you think?' Joe said.

'I think Mrs Sloan is perhaps rather highly strung.'

'I suspect you're right. I phoned her a couple of minutes ago, and she couldn't apologise enough for calling in the middle of the night. She says that the conference is an annual thing, but she got confused about the dates.' Joe shook his head. 'The poor woman is so wrapped up in her problems she doesn't know if it's New York or New Year.'

'She's just concerned. Anybody can make a mistake like that.'

He stood up and started to walk from one end of the room to the other, his hands clasped behind his back. 'The expense account won't stand for us following him to London, so it does limit our options, at least for the next couple of days. But there's plenty of other things we can do.'

I mentally raised an eyebrow. By 'we', I rather suspected he meant me. 'So, what are we going to do?'

'The husband is supposedly away for the next few days on business? Any thoughts about that?'

'Yeah. Where's the sister in all this?'

'Exactly. The business trip is, after all, a classic. How many men have used it as an excuse to set up an away game with their secretary?'

His constant pacing was beginning to irritate. I resisted the urge to tell him to sit back down. 'Let's look at it like this. There's three potential scenarios. Ian Sloan might be telling the truth, in which case he really is in London. Or, he could be telling the truth, but the sister could be there as well, and it could be a mixture of business and pleasure. Finally, he's not at a conference, he's not in London, and as usual, the wife really is the last to know.'

'You forgot the secret mystery option. He could be at the conference, without the sister, but is secretly prowling the streets of Soho in search of hookers, rent boys or other creatures of the night.'

'There is that, yeah. I mean, if he can be unfaithful to his wife, then he could definitely be unfaithful to his mistress.'

I remembered an opinion poll I had once heard on the radio. Seventy percent of men who were questioned confirmed that they would sleep with Claudia Schiffer if it was guaranteed their wife or girlfriend would never find out about it. Fifty percent of women would sleep with Brad Pitt. Perhaps the concept of monogamy is similar to the idea of International Waters: the second you get more than twenty miles from your significant other then all bets are off.

The conference story was easy enough to prove. I said, 'Did Sophie have any information? Where the conference was, what hotel he was staying at?'

'She told me that the conference is at the Millennium Dome,' Joe said. 'I phoned the event organisers, and they confirmed that a place – for one – had been booked in the name of Ian Sloan. I threw the name of Maureen Black at them, but they had never heard of her.' He checked a piece of notepaper that lay on his desk. 'He's staying at a Traveller's Lodge in Knightsbridge. One single room. And again, there's no reciprocal booking for a Maureen Black.'

'Traveller's Lodge. How nice for him.' My knowledge of London's geography was poor, but I seemed to remember that Knightsbridge was only a brief kerb crawl from Soho. 'What's the conference about?'

'"Committing to the Future: Anticipating the Needs of an Ageing Population."'

I repeated it aloud. 'That's a hell of a mouthful. Why don't they just call it "The Annual Granny Farming Conference"?'

'It's probably against EU regulations. You know, because if they refer to themselves as farmers, then we would have to institute a cull at the age of sixty-five or something because Great Britain produces too many elderly people and it destabilises the economy of Lithuania or something.'

'And that would be just a tragedy.' I said. 'Joe, I'm not sure Lithuania's in the EU. Hell, I'm not sure it's even in Europe. Or that it's even a country. It's probably a state of Russia or something. Some mad little dictator's holiday warzone.'

He laughed, then his face turned serious. 'What did you think of her?'

'Sophie Sloan?' I took a little time to formulate an answer. 'She's very. . . intense? Is that the word I want?'

'It's *a* word, that's for sure. Something about her bothers me. You know how you brought the pair of us coffee yesterday morning, then you had to go and take that phone call?'

I nodded.

'She popped a pill with her coffee. Told me it was an anti-depressant.'

'You think maybe it was something else?'

'Damned if I know. I read an article the other day that said that Prozac was the most commonly prescribed drug in Britain.' He looked at me. 'You were on that for a while, weren't you? After the accident? What was it like? Does it work?'

I shrugged. 'Hard to tell.'

'Did it mess about with your motor skills? Make you clumsy? I'm thinking of the way she dropped that picture.'

'Yes. No. Don't forget, at the same time I was taking Prozac, I was also on about a bottle of Bushmills a day. My fine motor skills were fucked to the sky, as was my grasp of reality.'

He nodded slowly. 'Right after she took it, it was like she was stoned or something. Remember how slowly she spoke? Like she was having to remember every single word that came out of her mouth. And she's a beautiful woman, but you can tell she's not paying attention to herself. Her hair needed washing, and she looked like she hadn't been sleeping.'

'Yeah, but all that's in keeping with somebody who's worried about the state of their marriage,' I said. 'You're bound to lose a little sleep if you think that your partner's playing away from home.'

'Yeah, I suppose. . .'

'Anyway, she's not paying us to look into her, is she? All we want to know is if the husband is knocking off the sister. What Sophie Sloan does with her private life is up to her.'

He nodded and stood up. 'You're right. I just think she's weird. Anyhoo, what are we going to do today?'

I hazarded a guess. 'You're going to wine and dine potential clients and I'm going to stay in the office and work?'

'Spoken like a true trusty sidekick.' He turned around. 'How would you like to go out to Ian Sloan's nursing home and have a poke around?'

'Seriously?'

'Yeah, why not? See what the local gossip is.'

'Jesus, Joe, I don't know what I'm looking for. Are you sure you don't want to do it yourself?'

He indicated the suit. 'I'm busy, remember?'

'Bollocks. You're scared they'll keep you in.'

7.4.

Inch Meadows Care Centre turned out to be a bugger to find. Sophie Sloan had given us an address in Eaglesham, but after stopping twice to ask directions, once at a petrol station where the assistant was barely able to drag his gaze from his copy of *Kerrang*, and again at a post office where the attendant looked like she might have failed the audition to be an extra in *Deliverance* for being too inbred, I eventually discovered it by chance on a back road nearly two miles away from the village. It turned out to be a large brick building in about two acres of land. I didn't spot any BMW's in the half-full car park, but I recognised a maroon Peugeot that almost certainly belonged to Maureen Black. I slid into the space next to it and took a minute to catch my bearings. Before leaving the office, Joe and I had spent an hour or so discussing our plan, looking for pitfalls, trying to anticipate any problems. I felt fairly confident; the risks were fairly low. At the very worst, I would be told to sling my hook and leave. I got out of the car, walked to the front door and rang the bell.

It was answered by a girl in her early twenties. She wore a brown tunic top and a pair of dark blue trousers, her hair tied back in a neat ponytail. 'Hi. Can I help you?'

In my experience, you're more likely to give yourself away if you sound like you know exactly what you're talking about. 'Um. . . Hi. My name is Jack. Jack Hill. I'm. . . I was wondering. . . I'm thinking that maybe my father needs long term care and I was driving past and I just wondered if I could ask a few questions.'

A smile that was professional rather than welcoming appeared on her face as she opened the door wider. 'Of course. Why don't you come in and have a seat? I'll let the boss know that you're here.'

I was escorted down a short corridor and shown into a small lounge. The girl offered coffee before disappearing, and I made myself comfy on a lumpy armchair that looked old enough to be a paying resident.

Like most people under the age of fifty, I didn't know what to expect. Nursing homes have this stigma attached to them. For most of us, they represent the end of the line, the final, unwinnable battle between age and youth. A diet of boil-in-the-bag fish and steamed cabbage. Days spent complaining about the youth of today, in between domino tournaments and exciting rounds of bingo. I wondered what I would be like as an old man, whether I would be the kind of jolly old soul that handed out toffees to children on a seemingly random basis, or if I would be a crotchety old git who spent his days writing letters to the local council. I was just remembering that I hated toffee when a head was poked round the door. 'Mr. . . Hall?'

I stood up again. 'Mr Hill. Jack Hill.'

I recognised the woman I had seen from a distance last night. Close up, she was almost as attractive as her sister, but with an added warmth. She wore a dark business suit over a peach blouse, and when she spoke, her voice was pleasant, with none of Sophie's hesitancy. 'My name's Maureen Black. I'm the clinical nurse manager for Inch Meadows. Stacy told me that you were looking for a care home for your father?'

I shrugged. 'I think so. I don't know.'

She smiled. 'Perhaps we better talk in my office. Won't you come this way?'

C. DAVID INGRAM

'Sure.'

She kept a running commentary as walked back down the corridor. 'Inch Meadows has been open for nearly nine years. The home itself consists of two wings of thirty beds each. The West Wing is for residents that we class as Elderly Frail, and the East Wing is for residents who have some form of dementia. Of course, it's a guideline rather than a rule. Sometimes a frail resident goes on to develop cognitive problems, but that doesn't mean that we kick them out of one room and move them into another. That wouldn't be very fair at all. Ah, here we are.'

She showed me into an office and we sat down. Behind her was a window that looked into a large dining room. Staff were escorting residents through for lunch. The majority of them were in wheel-chairs, except for a few poor souls who seemed to be in overstuffed armchairs, limbs contracted, eyes vacant. A few walked, either hunched over zimmer frames or leaning on walking sticks, a staff member by their side to guide them, or to catch them if they fell.

Maureen turned to see what I was looking at. 'Most of our residents have difficulty mobilising, so we need to help them.' She reached into a drawer and took out a form. 'Anyway, I was wondering if I could ask you a few questions about your father?'

'Of course.'

'What's his name?'

'Andrew Hill.'

I did my best to help her complete her form, answering questions that Joe and I had spent an hour trying to anticipate. My father was supposedly seventy five years old, and had suffered from mild Alzheimer's for the last three. He'd been living in sheltered housing, and I had taken him with me to attend my sister's wedding in Devon. Unfortunately, Dad had suffered a severe stroke that had left him completely paralysed down his left side, and we had been told that he would now need nursing care for the rest of his life. They hoped to transfer him to a local hospital, but it might take some time before they could make that happen. While my sister stayed with him in England, I was hoping to arrange a nursing home place for him.

She nodded as I spoke, appearing to swallow the story hook, line and sinker. 'Quite a few of the residents have similar medical backgrounds. Does the stroke seem to have affected his behaviour at all?'

'It's hard to tell. He's more confused than normal, but they say that might just be after-effects. It's difficult to understand what he says. The doctors say that might improve, although they can't be sure.'

'That's the thing about brain injuries. Those of us in the medical profession like to pretend that we know everything but the truth of the matter is that when it comes to something like a stroke, we're still operating very much on a "best guess" format.'

The girl that had opened the front door pushed her way through the office doors with a mug of coffee. 'Maureen, the pharmacy's on line one. And I'm sorry, but I really can't cover that shift tomorrow.'

'Thank you, Stacy. That's alright. Tell the pharmacy I'll call them back.'

We watched her go. I took a sip of my coffee; it was awful. No doubt the place saved money by buying cheap instant by the truckload. Maureen said, 'Shelly's one of the staff nurses.'

'How many staff do you have?'

'Plenty. We try to have one carer or nurse for every five residents during the day shift– that's eight am to eight pm.'

'Long hours.' I decided to flirt a little. 'I bet you don't have much time for a social life.'

She shrugged. 'People hear on the news that there's a shortage of trained nurses, but they don't realise that it's a real, genuine problem. About ten minutes before you arrived I was told that one of my regulars has broken their ankle, so I'm trying to find a replacement at short notice.'

'What happens if you can't?'

'We hire an agency nurse.'

'Isn't that expensive?'

She shrugged. 'Money is no object when it comes to our residents.'

C. DAVID INGRAM

Bollocks, I thought. 'Who owns the place? Is it one of these big companies. . . BUPA, or Eastern Star?'

She smiled at that. 'I think you must mean Southern Cross. No, Inch Meadows is privately owned by a man called Ian Sloan. My brother-in-law, actually. I'd introduce you, but he's away on business. BUPA offered to buy the home last year, but Ian turned them down. Anyway, would you like to have a wee look around?'

I put my coffee down, glad to be offered an excuse to abandon it. 'That would be great, thank you.'

She showed me out of the office and into a corridor that was painted a dark, uriney yellow. 'Inch Meadows is actually shaped a little bit like a capital "H". The bit we're in just now is the horizontal bar, and it includes such things as the dining room, the hairdresser's, the laundry, the admin office. . . stuff like that. The residents' rooms make up the legs of the "H", and like I said, there's thirty on each side. At the top and bottom of each leg is a large and small sitting room. Once they're up and dressed, most of our residents like to spend time in the sitting rooms.'

'Do they all have their own rooms, or are there shared rooms?'

'We used to have a few double rooms and a couple of triple rooms, but the law changed recently, so now every room is a single with its own en suite bathroom.' She stopped outside a door and took a large bunch of keys out of her pocket. 'There's nobody staying in here just now, so nobody's going to mind if we have a wee peek.'

The room itself was about as big as a moderately sized bedroom. A single bed ran down one wall, and a large armchair faced a portable television that stood on top of a chest of drawers. A few faded pictures of nothing in particular graced the wall. I wondered if the reason there was nobody staying in the room was because the most recent tenant had died of depression, and they had yet to move somebody else in.

'Of course, if your father had a favourite item of furniture, we'd encourage him to bring it with him, as long as it fitted.' Margaret said. 'We try to do whatever we can to make it seem like home. You

— 146 —

wouldn't be able to tell me whether or not he would be privately funded or if the DSS would be helping to meet his fees?'

I gave her the answer that Joe and I had agreed. 'He'd be privately funded. He has a fair amount of savings, and I could help out. How much would it cost if he was to become a resident?'

'Six hundred and fifty pounds a week,' Maureen said, without the slightest hint of embarrassment. 'I know that it seems like a lot, but the amount is actually agreed with the local council. Of course, a lot of our residents are funded by public money.'

It did seem a lot. But I wasn't there to judge. I made a show of looking around. 'It's a nice enough room, anyway.' I gestured at a door at the far end of the room. 'And is this the bathroom?'

'It is.' Maureen opened the door, revealing a small water closet. A large yellow object that looked like a Nan bread made out of cotton wool lay on the floor. There was a yellow stain in the middle of it. She stepped forward quickly, peeled a disposable plastic bag from a small roll that was on top of the toilet cistern, and stuffed the Nan bread inside it. 'I'm so sorry about that. I'll need to speak to the girls and tell them to be more careful.'

To be honest, I wasn't exactly sure what I had seen, but I nodded and shrugged non-commitedly. Then the smell hit me and I realised that the Nan bread was actually a used incontinence pad. 'Don't worry about it. I'm sure things like that can't be helped.'

'Yes, well.' Her mouth was turned down, her eyes sour. 'It's always annoying when something like that happens.' She breathed heavily through her nose and led me out of the room. We made our way towards the end of the corridor, me trailing behind like a dutiful student. Maureen kept up the sales pitch, such as it was. 'Of course, there's plenty of bathrooms and things like that. I'm taking you to the large lounge for this wing so that you can see what it's like. We've just had it painted, so it looks lovely.'

Trying not to pass out from excitement, I followed her into a room that was large enough for at least thirty people. "Lovely" turned out to be a slight exaggeration. Whoever had been in charge of the decorating was either completely colour-blind or a big fan of the worst aspects of daytime television makeover shows. The walls were almost the same shade of yellow as the corridors, but in an attempt to inject some life into the mess, somebody had painted large pink and orange spots every few inches. The effect was enough to have any normal person reaching for the paracetamol, so Christ knew what it would do to somebody whose grasp of reality was already tenuous.

'It's very. . . bright.'

'Isn't it,' Maureen said. 'I chose the colours myself. You wouldn't think they would work, but they do, don't they?'

I was unsure if I would be able to keep my tone neutral, so I nodded as I looked around. Warm rugs for cold knees were thrown casually over the back of armchairs that had been arranged in groups of about four or five. I brushed one of the chairs with my hand and realised that although they looked like they were fabric, they were actually made of some non-absorbent plastic. One wall was dominated by a large screen television, and beside it I saw a cheap stereo unit. Beside that was a stack of CD's. Daniel O'Donnell, Sydney Devine, Foster and Allen. God save me from getting old, if it meant having to live in a place like this. Listening to Daniel singing *Danny Boy* while trying to avoid looking at the seizure-inducing walls would destroy whatever was left of my sanity.

'Albert, are you not going through for your lunch?'

The tone was friendly, but the pitch was at least ten decibels above normal. I turned to see Maureen addressing a man who sat in one of the armchairs. He was in his eighties at least, wearing a tweed jacket with leather patches on his elbows. He looked briefly at me before facing the woman in front of him and shaking his head. 'No. Not today.'

'Why not?'

'Don't want to.'

'Stewart won't be there. He's out with his daughter.'

'I don't like Stewart.'

'Well, he's not going to be there,' Maureen said patiently. 'He's out.'

'He chews with his mouth open. It's a vile habit. Vile.'

'He's *out*, Albert.'

The old man shook his head resolutely.

'How about I get the girls to bring you something on a tray then?'

The old man nodded. 'That would be acceptable.' His eyes crossed briefly over to me again before returning to her. 'Who's that then?'

'This is Mr Hill. His father might be coming to live with us. Wouldn't that be nice? Another man for you to talk to?' She lowered her voice and turned to me. 'We've got forty-six female residents and only twelve men. He's a wee bit outnumbered here.'

'It depends,' Albert said. 'If he behaves the way some of them behave. . .' He muttered something unintelligible to himself. I doubted it was friendly.

I held out a hand to the old man. His grip was surprisingly firm, and I made sure to raise my voice. 'It's nice to meet you. How are you today?'

'I'm fine. Fine. But I want to go to bed. It's getting late.'

'It's lunchtime, Albert,' Maureen said. 'You'd spend all day in bed if you could. Anyway, Mr Hill, we best be getting on.'

We headed back to her office. The dining room was completely full by now. Staff milled from table to table as they fetched and carried for the residents. I watched as one girl tried to feed three people at the same time. One old lady sat at a table by herself, a male member of staff spooning something from a bowl into her mouth. As I watched, she spat the whole mess back out onto the floor. The boy patiently wiped her mouth with a napkin and tried again. The window was open a fraction, and the noise was a cacophony of dozens of unrelated conversations. People howled and gibbered for no apparent reason.

It was awful. A hellhole. I couldn't imagine condemning somebody I cared about to a place like this.

Both my parents had died nice and quickly, Dad from his heart attack, Mum from one of those evil but incredibly polite cancers that waited until it had sank bony fingers into every single internal organ before announcing its presence and then spreading through the body like wildfire. She survived for two weeks from diagnosis to death, eventually shuffling off her mortal coil while she slept in a private room in a seven bedded hospice that seemed to have twice as many staff members as Inch Meadows.

Maybe I was being unreasonable. This was a world I had never seen. I never had to sit and watch somebody I loved deteriorate slowly, their personality being stripped away layer by layer, until there was nothing left but the shell. I never had to clean up piss and shit, I never had to see the way that Death sometimes teases his victims, not taking them cleanly but toying with them, stealing pieces of them a little at a time, their minds, their bodies, their dignity, their souls.

Yeah, maybe I was being naive.

I turned my eyes away to find Maureen watching me. She said quietly, 'I know that it's not very nice.'

I tried a weak smile. 'You know, you're a terrible sales person.'

'I don't believe in lying to people. We're committed to trying to give our residents the very best we have available, but it can be very hard sometimes.'

Suddenly there was a shriek. I looked over Maureen's shoulder to see the elderly lady that was being fed by herself reach over and claw at the boy's face. 'You bastard bastard BASTARD!'

'It's alright, Bessie, it's just lunchtime.' The boy soothed her as best he could, stroking her hand and speaking gently to her. Eventually she calmed.

I said, 'Are all care homes like this?'

'Some of them aren't as good, I hate to say. I know that you will probably think I'm biased, but I genuinely believe that Inch Meadows is the best care home in the area. Every other day you see something on the news about how life expectancy has gone up? Twenty years ago a woman would live until she was seventy-three, and now the average age of death is eighty-one?'

I nodded.

'Thing is that although people are living longer, they're not enjoying good health. There's more dementia, more strokes, more cardiac problems. Of our fifty-nine residents, only five of them can walk without using a stick. Forty two of them need two people or more to lift them. And that, I'm afraid, is about average. It's a lot of work. Nursing homes are becoming more and more like long-term stay hospital wards, except that we have much fewer trained staff available.' She seemed to realise she was dragging on. 'I'm sorry. I'm drifting off at a tangent. I promise you that if your father were to become a resident, he would get the very best of care we could offer.'

Another shriek came from the dining room. It was accompanied by the sound of crockery smashing and a yelp of pain from the male care assistant. Maureen looked over her shoulder. 'I better get out there.' She was already getting to her feet. 'Before Bessie kills somebody.'

7.5.

Five minutes later I was back in my car, glad to see Inch Meadows disappearing in my rear-view mirror. The time was nearly half past one, and despite having two breakfasts, my own stomach was growling. I stopped at the same petrol station that I had asked directions at earlier in the day. It was one of these large rural places that sell everything from disposable barbecues to emergency plumbing supplies. The *Kerrang*-reading assistant had been replaced by a bored looking girl with bright pink nails and enough chewing gum to choke a donkey. Wary of petrol station food, I bought a packet of crisps and a chocolate muffin, working on the principal that as neither of them required to be refrigerated, they were unlikely to be a suitable breeding ground for salmonella.

Pink Nails held out her hand. 'Two forty-four.'

'You're kidding me.'

'The muffin's one ninety-nine.'

I forked over the money. 'What, does it unwrap itself?'

A smile crossed her face. 'You'd think so, at that price.'

She seemed to be a little bit more on the ball than the fellow she had replaced, so I decided to cast a line and see if anything came back.

'I was looking for a nursing home that's meant to be near here? Inch Meadows?'

She nodded and pointed in the direction I had already come from. 'It's about a mile.'

'Do you know it?'

'My cousin works there.'

'Any good?'

'What, my cousin?' Again, she smiled. She was in her twenties, quite pretty if you could get past the cud in her mouth. 'Very, if you believe what the graffiti on the bus shelter says.'

'I meant the home,' I said. 'I'm looking for a place for my father.'

'Gemma says it's alright.' Her nose wrinkled. 'Don't know if I would fancy it, though.'

'Why not?'

She shrugged non-committally. 'You know. Old people moaning about how cold it is in the middle of summer. And the money's crap.'

I wondered how much Pink Nails made an hour. 'Suppose you could be right.'

'She says that the matron's a bit of a bitch.'

'What, to the residents?'

'To the staff. Mind you, Gemma's a lazy cow, so maybe she needs a good kick up the bum.'

I pretended to think. 'My dad's social worker said the owner was a woman called. . . Margaret Brown? Black? Something like that?'

'Maureen. And I think she's just the matron. The owner's a man. Sometimes he stops on his way there. Drives a big Range Rover.'

'I was at a nursing home in Clarkston where the matron was married to the owner. The whole place was a big family business.'

The girl was shaking her head. 'Don't think so.'

I waited. If there was any local gossip about the relationship between Maureen Black and Ian Sloan – or even Sophie, for that matter– I had given Pink Nails a perfect opportunity to fill me in.

She said nothing. Either she didn't know or she wasn't telling.

7.6.

Lunch was a solitary affair.

I ate in the car. The hubbub of the dining room had left me craving some calmness and serenity, and I had eventually found some on a farm-track a couple of miles outside the village of Eaglesham. The main road was a quarter-mile behind me, the silence broken only by the occasional drone of a distant car. I was surrounded by nothing but fields and sky, the breeze ruffling the grass and rolling the clouds slowly toward the horizon.

My exorbitantly-priced chocolate muffin tasted like it had been left to mature down the back of an abandoned settee. I gave up halfway through, heaving it out of the car window and into the muddy ditch that ran alongside the track, where it sank like a stone. I sighed in frustration, beating a tattoo on the steering wheel with my fingertips.

The whole bloody trip had been pointless.

I wasn't quite sure what I had expected, but I felt like I had learned nothing. Eaglesham was a small village, and a place like Inch Meadows would occupy a fairly prominent role in the local community. As well as calling at the petrol station, I'd also bought stamps at the local post office and asked for directions at the local grocery, surreptitiously bringing the conversation round to include Maureen Black and Ian Sloan. If the two of them were the subject of local gossip, then by all rights I should have turned up something of value, but each time I had been met with polite indifference. That left two options: either Ian and Maureen were very discreet, or there was simply nothing going on.

I hoped for the latter. Maureen had struck me as being hard-working and likeable, and even though I barely knew her, I didn't want to think of her being the 'other' woman. Joe's comments of the previous evening – about how infidelity investigations almost always had an unhappy ending – had depressed me. It would be nice to prove him wrong.

There was one final trick up my sleeve. On a small table just inside the front door of the nursing home had been a pile of business cards, and force of habit had led me to slip one into my pocket. I took it out and used my mobile to dial the number, asking to be put through to the person in charge. Within seconds, a familiar voice came on the line. 'Hello?'

'Maureen, I'm sorry to trouble you. This is Jack Hill. You showed me round about an hour ago?'

'Hello, Mr Hill. How can I help you?'

I gave a laugh that sounded every bit as false as I wanted it to. 'Well, the thing is, I was hoping to. . . I was wondering if maybe I could. . .'

Her voice was cool. 'Could what, Mr Hill?'

'It's just that you seemed like a nice person and I wondered if you would perhaps let me buy you dinner some time?'

There was silence on the other end of the line. I counted under my breath, making it all the way up to seven before she said, 'Oh.'

'I'm sorry. I shouldn't have asked.'

'No, no. I'm very flattered. It's just. . . unexpected.'

I gave another false laugh. 'I know. Believe me, I didn't come out with the intention of asking anyone out, but you seemed like a nice person and I just thought. . . my divorce has just been finalised and Pam – that's my sister – keeps telling me I should get out more. I hope you're not offended or anything.' I was speaking quickly now, hoping to create the impression of a shy man who had started babbling to fill an ever-increasing void of silence. To be honest, it wasn't a stone's throw away from the truth. 'Of course, I quite understand that you might not want to go out with a potential client, so I assure you that we'll find another care home for my father if that's the case. . .'

'Mr Hill. . .'

'Jack.'

'Mr Hill, I'm afraid that you've put me in quite an awkward situation. Even if I wasn't already seeing somebody, it would be inappropriate for me to go out with you. I hope you understand.'

I sighed. 'Of course. I can only apologise.'

'I think it's probably best if we forget all about it.'

I assured her that I would, allowing her to disengage from the conversation with the minimum of embarrassment. When I eventually flipped my phone closed, it was with mixed feelings. Yet another inconclusive conversation. She had claimed to be seeing somebody, but she might just have been trying to let me down gently. Even if she had been interested, it still didn't exclude the possibility that she was bumping uglies with the boss. I tucked my phone into my pocket and started the engine, secure in the knowledge that time hadn't dulled my ability to make stupid decisions.

7.7

Glasgow's a big place, but if you avoid the town centre and the motorways, it's easy enough to get around. It's got the schizophrenic nature of all large cities, with multi-million pound housing estates being built across the road from council slums. Tapas Bars were side by side with bookies and sectarian pubs. Men in tracksuits and baseball caps rubbed shoulders with fur-coated women in the most expensive stores the city had to offer.

By three twenty, I was in Jordanhill. It was one of the more expensive districts: trendy restaurants and wine bars, huge flats with bay windows. Designer boutiques instead of cut-price off-licences. Every second car vehicle seemed to be a massive Land Rover driven by a tiny blonde.

I spotted Jason Campbell fairly quickly. He was parked directly outside the school gates in a tasty little Mercedes soft-top that had probably belonged to his rich mother. The top was down, despite the September coolness, and he had one arm slung casually over the door, drumming his fingers on the paintwork. From behind a pair of sunglasses, his eyes were fixed on the school.

Waiting for the show.

There are plenty of characters in this world with reprehensible traits, but Jason was one of the few people that managed to combine multiple nasty habits – drug-dealing and paedophilia – into something altogether more unpleasant. Back in ninety-nine, he was caught having sex with a twelve year old girl that he had lured back to his flat not with the promise of sweeties or puppies, but with hash and ecstasy. Investigation showed that she wasn't the first of his victims. The fact that he was here, now, suggested that she wouldn't be his last.

The prosecution hadn't gone as well as we had hoped. The girl was one of these kids that dress and act six years older than they actually are, and on the witness stand Jason managed to portray himself as a cross between a choir boy and the school swot. His lawyer managed to get a tame psychiatrist to say that Jason's behaviour was the result of childhood trauma and painkiller addiction, and instead of getting sent to Barlinnie prison, where guys like him were punished by not the system, but their peers, he went to a secure psychiatric unit.

I parked directly behind him, wondering how exactly he had managed to convince a psychiatrist that he was no longer a danger to the public. From what I remembered, he was smart, and didn't show the crawling servility that a lot of paedophiles do. It didn't do any harm that he looked a little like a young Keanu Reeves. The people responsible for his care – psyches and social workers – were predominantly female, and were possibly more easily charmed.

I checked my watch. Three-twenty-five. I wondered if he was waiting for a specific pupil, if he had somebody already dangling from his hook, or if he was just window shopping. Good looking guy in his own car? He wouldn't need to say a thing. They would come to him.

It was easy to visualise. I could almost picture it. One of the more precocious kids, wearing a miniskirt that was more like a belt, would approach. Call her Little Miss Sweet Thing, or LMST for short.

–Nice car, mister.

–You like it?

–Yeah, it's cool.

–Thanks.

At this point, Jason would take a drag on the dooby he was keeping on the low-down, out of sight below the sill of the car window. Little Miss Sweet Thing's eyes would grow wide.

–Is that a joint?

–Why, yes, I believe it is.

LMST would look around, to make sure that nobody was looking. Jason would take another hit before offering it to her.

–You want some?

–I'll get caught.

–Not if you get in the car. They'll think I'm just your big brother giving you a lift.

LMST hesitates. She's had all the warnings about getting in cars with strangers, but she's a big girl. She can take care of herself. And besides, nobody that cute could be dangerous.

–Okay then.

. . . And so on.

I got out of my car and walked the few yards to his, opening the passenger door and sliding in beside him before he had the chance to say yea or nae. 'Hello, Jason.'

His face twisted, emotions coming and going like images on a television screen. First anger, then fear. Finally, dull recognition. At least he remembered my face, if not my name. 'What do you want?'

'Just a chat.'

'I haven't done anything!'

I took a second to organise my thoughts. Close up, Jason had changed a little since the last time I saw him. There was still the puppy-dog eyes, the floppy hair, but now there was a hardness to the face, an edge to his glittering smile. Mind you, I'd wager that Keanu would look the same, had he had ever spent a few months playing Dodge-the-Soap-Dropper in the showers of a secure psyche ward.

He was starting to get cocky. 'My life is no longer any of your business. I'd like you to get out of my car.'

'No.'

'I'll report you.'

I looked over at the school. 'Be sure to tell them exactly where the incident occurred. I suspect they might have a few questions as to why you would be parked here.'

'I'm waiting for my girlfriend, who just happens to be a teacher here.'

'I don't believe you.'

'Then you can wait and meet her.'

I checked my watch. Three twenty-seven. On the radio, Steve Wright was just reading out a bunch of factoids. Black and Decker handheld electric saws were the serial killer's choice for dismemberment. There was a pack of Silk Cut on the dashboard. I picked it up and slipped a cigarette between my lips, pushing the button for the car's built-in cigarette lighter. 'When did you get out?'

'Six weeks ago.'

'And you already have a girlfriend? I'm impressed. Does she know about your past?'

He didn't reply. The little fucker was lying. I was sure of it. He was back to his old tricks, using grass and coke to troll for underage pussy. The cigarette lighter clicked to let me know it was ready. At the same time as I used my left elbow to push the button that locked the door, I grabbed his left wrist with my right hand. Then I reached across and took the metal filament out of its socket with my left hand. Jason saw what I had in mind and scrabbled at the door handle, forgetting that his car had central locking. When I had pushed the snib with my elbow, all the other locks in the Merc had followed suit. Holding him as tightly as I could, I pressed the metal filament against the back of his hand. There was a sizzle and the smell of burning. A tiny wisp of black smoke. Jason squealed like a piglet in a microwave.

I took it away. Lit my cigarette. The tobacco hit me like an express train and I felt the sudden light-headedness that comes after a period of abstinence. It was good. Better than good. Great. That's what I love and hate about smoking; all the cancer studies in the world can't alter the fact that it tastes. . . fucking. . . marvellous.

I slipped the filament back into its socket. Jason had his hand pressed to his chest, like a lion guarding an injured paw. No doubt he would like to find a tiny innocent lamb to help draw out that troublesome thorn.

'Let me see.' I moved to take his hand, and he cringed away from me. 'I'm not going to hurt you, you prick.'

He let me take his hand. On the back of it was a small, circular burn, the flesh seared a dark, blackish red. 'You'll live. More's the pity.'

'You bastard.'

I felt totally comfortable with the label. That was the upshot of Harper's little jobs: they were always spiritually rewarding. Just because Campbell had conned some doe-eyed little junior doctor into believing he was a changed man didn't mean that he'd crawled any higher up the food chain.

The school bell rang. Within seconds, the kids were swarming out of the main gates. Blazers flapping, ties askew, shouting, challenging each other. And of course, the girls. Short skirts, kinky boots, shirts tied at the middle to expose tiny flat tummies. I watched Jason watching them. He was like a deer in headlights.

'Time to move on, Jason. Go home and don't come back.'

He turned to face me. 'I really am waiting for somebody.'

'Who?'

Before he could answer, she arrived. Mid-thirties, wearing the standard sensible combo of white blouse and dark skirt. She had a jacket slung over one shoulder and carried a cheap leather briefcase. As she made her way over to the car, I saw that she had one of these bland rabbit faces that only really express negative emotions – fear, worry, unhappiness.

She saw me first, then Jason. 'Hello, dear.' Her eyes turned back to me, filled with curiosity. Worried curiosity.

Jason said, 'Gwen, this is. . . a friend of mine. . .'

The asshole couldn't remember my name. Maybe that was just as well. I got out of the car, walked round the back to her side, extending my hand as I went. 'Andy.'

Curiosity had been replaced by doubt. Then she stepped forward, good manners overcoming her initial hesitation. 'Nice to meet you.' Her palm was slightly moist, the nails clipped extremely short.

'I was just driving past when I saw Jason. I thought I would stop and say hello.'

'How do you two know each other?'

I decided to let Jason field that one. He did it with his usual style. 'We were in prison together.'

'Oh. I see. Well, it's nice to see that you're out.'

I could tell she was dying to ask. 'It's nice to be out.'

'Were you. . . in for a long time?'

'Twelve years.'

Her eyes crossed in worry, and she unconsciously rubbed her hand against her skirt.

'It was meant to be seventeen, but I've been a good little boy.'

'My goodness. What did. . .'

'Shoplifting.'

'I see.' She looked over at Jason, and a touch of schoolmarm crept into her voice. 'Jason, we'll be late if we don't get going.'

I held up my hands. 'I won't keep you, I promise. Just let me speak to your man here and I'll be on your way.'

'Certainly.'

But she held her ground, foot tapping slightly in a sensible black shoe, obviously not wanting to move out of earshot just in case I was planning to ask her boyfriend to help me knock over a bank. I glared at Jason until he took the hint and got out of the car. We walked about ten yards away, keeping our voices low. Miss Gwen watched us flintily, possibly concerned that I might suddenly stab her boyfriend in the heart with a shiv made out of an HB pencil.

'Jason, what the fuck are you playing at?'

'I told you. She's my girlfriend.'

'Where the hell did you meet her?'

'In an Internet chat room. I told her I was an airline pilot, she told me she was an airline hostess. When we agreed to meet up for real, we both had a bit of explaining to do.'

'Jesus wept.'

'Look, I know what it looks like, alright? But I swear, there's nothing like that. It's just a normal relationship.'

I wanted to punch him, to put him down on the ground and stamp on his face. The psychologists are full of shit. Leopards can't change their spots and paedophiles can't control their behaviour. 'Dump her. Dump her or I'll do it for you.'

'What?'

'I don't know what kind of sick, twisted game you're playing, but she's not like you. She's not some little schemie. She's got values. Don't lead her on like this. Messing her about could screw up her career.'

'I'm not leading her on.'

'Does she know what you were in for?'

He said nothing.

'What did you tell her? Some pathetic little white collar crime? Stealing the company pension fund?'

'I swear to you, I'm a changed man.'

'The only thing that guys like you change is their stories.'

Behind us, a couple of kids lounged by the school gate, probably waiting for teacher to disappear so that they could light up. Gwen had got into the passenger seat of the Merc. Jason heard the slam of the car door and started to back away. 'You leave me alone. I don't want anything to do with you.'

He turned, bolted for the car, lunging behind the wheel and grinding the ignition. I called out, hoping she could hear me over the rev of the engine. 'He's a paedophile, Gwen. He's a beast.'

There was a squeal of tyres. Twin dark tracks of burnt rubber were burned onto the surface of the road as the Merc fishtailed away from the kerb.

The two kids stared at me, a boy and girl of about twelve.

'What's that teacher's name?' I asked.

'Miss Morris.'

'Miss Morris's boyfriend is a paedophile.'

'Fuckin' everybody's a paedo these days, pal,' said the boy. 'You're probably a fuckin' paedo an' all.' He looked at his pal. 'He probably wants to give us a sweetie and show us some puppies.'

'Fuck that. If he gives me a cigarette I'll show him my fanny.'

The two of them screamed laughter and ran for it. I watched them go, hoping that they weren't as jaded as they sounded.

7.8.

When I finally made it back to the office at just after half past four, Joe wasn't there. Instead, I found a message on the answer machine. In the background, I could hear chatter and music. Pub life.

'Cam. We're in the Scotia, but I don't know for how long. We're going to hit the town to celebrate. You're welcome to join us, but I don't know where we're going yet. The lads want to see the city, so I was thinking about packing us all in a cab and heading to the West End. Give us a call on my mobile and we'll arrange to meet.'

Great. Except that when I dialled him, I got a bland female voice explaining that the person I was trying to call wasn't available. The useless pillock had switched his mobile off. He probably thought it was still switched on, and when we finally met up tomorrow morning he would have an insulted air, as if I deliberately hurt his feelings by not coming out to play.

It didn't matter anyway. I had made plans for the evening – or rather, Liz had made plans for me. Since there was little of value I could do at the office, I headed home. By five thirty I had showered and dressed in a nice shirt and a pair of almost clean jeans. When I looked about as presentable as I could hope for, I knocked on her door. She opened it in her underwear. 'Jesus!'

Clothed, she looked good, but in red lacy bra and cami-knickers she looked amazing. Sexy. Damn sexy. All the curves in the right places. I pointedly looked away. 'Sorry,' I lied.

She ducked behind the door, peeping out from behind it. 'I thought you were Katrina. She's been over twice already.'

Katrina lived in the bottom floor flat. Hated me but liked Liz. 'I got home early. Thought I could take you out for a meal before we went to the cinema.'

'Ten minutes?'

'No problem.'

And it wasn't. But then, she had given me something to think about while I waited.

7.9.

Exactly twelve minutes later, she knocked on my door. 'Ready?'

'Ready.'

We headed out of the flat. She'd dressed in a pair of blue jeans and a red T-shirt that told everybody she was an angel by daylight. It was getting dark. As we walked along Paisley Road, she grabbed my arm. 'Himalayan Heaven?'

The Himalaya was a restaurant that was almost halfway between the flat and the cinema. We'd eaten there a few times before, and while it wasn't the best curryhouse in Glasgow, it was by no means the worst. Liz was on first name terms with the owners, the Singhs. Two years ago, their youngest son had been knocked off his scooter while delivering a takeaway. Liz had been part of the team that glued him back together, earning their eternal gratitude and a lifetime's supply of cut-price meals.

We were shown to a table in a quiet corner, near to a stereo that was playing a sitar version of 'Hey Jude'. Within minutes a small mountain of snacks had materialised.

'How were your three hips and an elbow?' I asked.

'Fine. They also tossed us an ankle at the last minute. We fused it, but that's pretty much all we could do.' She said. 'Chronic arthritis.'

'And what about your junior doctor friend? Did you happen to come across him on your travels?'

'I spotted him on the far side of the canteen. He didn't even have the good grace to look embarrassed.'

'Some people don't embarrass easily.'

She dipped a piece of chicken chaat into pakora sauce, before tearing into it like she was a cavewoman and it was a particularly tasty piece of the very last woolly mammoth. 'What about you? You have a good day?'

'Yeah, I suppose.'

'What did you do?'

I thought about Jason. 'Paid a visit to an old friend.'

'Who?'

'Somebody I used to work with.'

She pointed a chicken bone at me. 'Now you're being all mysterious. What are you up to?'

I shrugged. 'Just trying to clean up the streets of the big bad city.'

She clasped her hands together and fluttered her eyelashes. 'My hero.'

'Just doing my job, Ma'am.'

'You ever thought about rejoining the police force?'

I took my time answering. The truth was, I missed it every day. 'I'm not sure I'd be welcome.'

'Why not?'

I didn't particularly want to answer her, so I "accidentally" dropped a piece of pakora into the dip, before making a big fuss about fishing it out. Unfortunately, my cunning plan to distract her failed. She pointed the chicken bone at me. 'Stop farting around. Why not?'

'I just don't want to.'

'For God's sake, Cameron.' She picked the last of the meat from the bone and tossed it on her plate, shiny chicken juice on her chin. 'I bet they would be glad to welcome an experienced copper like you back.'

'Somehow I very much doubt it.'

Thankfully, the waiter brought our drinks over – a pint for Liz and mineral water for me. As usual, he plonked the pint down in front of me, following the basic rules regarding beverage consumption in Scotland: Man equals Lager; Woman equals Water. I waited until he left before reversing them, resisting the urge to lick the condensation from the side of the glass off my fingers.

7.10.

One Chicken Jaipuri, one Lamb Tikka Garam Masala and *way* too many pakoras later, we made our way to the cinema, walking with the ponderously slow steps of the chronically overfed. The drizzle had let up for a while, and the streets were quiet. Pretty much nothing happens in Glasgow on a Wednesday evening. Even the drunks have to take a night off once in a while.

The cinema was one of those soulless multiplexes that specialise in cramming as many screens as possible into a small space. We bought a couple of Cokes before making our way into the auditorium. The place was almost deserted, so we chose seats nearer to the back, directly in the middle. I'm always careful where I sit; with my height it's easy to piss people off.

After three minutes, Liz wriggled in her seat. 'I want some Maltesers.'

'You're kidding.'

'I like to finish a meal with something sweet.'

'You practically ate an entire sheep.'

She giggled. 'I'm going to the snack bar. Want anything?'

'I think I'm good, thanks.' Actually that was an overstatement. I was so full that it wouldn't matter if Tom Cruise was battling terrorists or a giant, robotic bunny rabbit; I was probably going to sleep all the way through it.

I waited for her to return, listening to the piped-in music, while adverts flashed up on screen. Half-price sale on at Tile-It-All; I'd apparently be crazy to miss it. Behind me, the swing doors banged, and I turned my head, thinking it was Liz returning.

Instead, it was another couple. The lights were dim, but I could see that they were both young and good looking. They made their way to seats a few rows in front of us, his arm on her waist, either guiding her or copping a feel.

Liz came back just as the lights dimmed, slouching back into the seat next to me. Not only had she bought Maltesers, but she had got a quadruple scoop sundae. And two spoons. I shook my head in mock protest. 'You can't be serious.'

'I had to go to the ice cream counter. Had to.'

'Was there some kind of medical emergency?'

'The counter assistant had a heart attack.'

'So you helped to resuscitate him?'

She shook her head. 'I helped myself to the Chocolate Cookie Dough.'

'Good thinking.'

She opened the bag of Maltesers and scattered some over the ice cream before pressing a spoon into my hand. 'Guess who I saw?'

'Who?'

'My Junior Doc. The one that thinks Tom Cruise is symptomatic of Hollywood's decline. He's with a student nurse. I mean, that's just *slumming*.'

'The bastard.'

She passed the ice cream over to me and took out her mobile phone, thumb blurring as she tapped a message.

'What are you doing?'

'I'm asking my friend Jenny to ruin his evening. He's on call tonight. I'm sure she can think of a reason to drag him back to work.'

'Hell really doth hath no fury,' I said, glad that I hadn't been forced to stand Liz up. God only knows how she would have punished me.

A few minutes later, just as the movie started, there came the unmistakable sound of a pager going off. Liz and I laughed silently in the darkness as her unwitting victim rushed past.

7.11.

Three hours and several thousand explosions later, the movie was over and we were home, standing outside the door to my flat. No fresh graffiti on my door today, but the pink splodge remained. Apart from the sound of squeaking bedsprings from somewhere behind Lee's front door, the place was silent.

Liz said, 'You want a coffee? I actually bought some today.'

'Sure.'

I followed her upstairs. At the front door, she turned to face me. 'I should warn you, the place is a tip.'

She wasn't kidding. I'd never been in her flat before, and it came as a surprise to find out that it was at least half as big again as my own. The settee itself was a lumpy green thing that looked like it had seen better millenniums. Clothes – tops, bras, knickers – spilled out of drawers and peeped from underneath the coffee table. Liz instructed me to sit while she went to the kitchen. I did as I was told, trying not to look too closely at her underwear. The settee was surprisingly comfortable.

I don't know what I expected, but there were stacks of books. John Irving, Stephen King, Dickens, Ian Rankin. Very eclectic taste. I picked a Joanne Harris – Chocolat – off the top of one pile, only to find the pages stuck together. No doubt *with* chocolate. I found it easy to imagine Liz sitting there, reading her books, munching away.

She came back with the coffee, pressing a mug into my hands before sitting down next to me. A gap of about two feet separated us. She kicked off her shoes and tucked her feet underneath her, completely comfortable on her home turf.

I, of course, wasn't.

Late at night, invited in for coffee. . . was I missing something? I thought we were just friends, but perhaps I had misread the situation. Perhaps she wanted more from me?

Or perhaps I was letting my own attraction to her lead me on. I'd seen *When Harry met Sally*, knew that Liz probably believed that we could be friends without the awkward question of sex getting in the way.

Except that – for me, at least- the awkward question of sex was getting in the way.

There hadn't been anybody for a long time. Since Audrey. There had been opportunities, of course. The girl at therapy, the client that took a shine to me – I'd been polite but distant. I was too wrapped up in being a miserable bastard.

Except that, with Liz, I wasn't such a miserable bastard. I liked her as a person, knew that she liked me – as a friend.

Maybe there was more to it than that.

Liz picked a remote control off the arm of the settee. 'You want to watch some television?'

'Sure.'

She flicked it on, cycling through the channels. Football on BBC One, Jeremy Paxman shouting at a hapless politician on Two. STV had one of these crappy interactive game shows. Find the hidden word and phone in.

'Boring,' Liz said, pointing and flicking with the remote.

Channel Four had a subtitled movie. Intense French people staring at a plate of cheese.

Five had what they called an "Adult Thriller", which was really just a polite term for a soft core porno movie. The only thing less realistic than the breasts was the acting.

Liz left it there. And was it my imagination, or had she scooted a few inches closer to me?

We talked. I can't remember what we talked about, but we laughed and drank our coffee. I relaxed; she relaxed even further. Then she said, 'Can I ask you something?'

'Sure.'

'What happened?'

I put down my coffee mug. 'You didn't see it?'

'See what?'

The accident had been caught by two separate traffic cameras. The

TV stations were obliged to edit the footage, but an uncut video clip surfaced on YouTube and got downloaded into several million homes before being yanked. Why anybody would want to watch something like that was beyond me.

Liz shook her head as I explained. 'I didn't mean that. I mean after. How did you end up here?'

'I was suspended while they did an internal investigation. It took them a while, and for a long time I didn't know what was happening.'

I told her about the head injury, the broken bones, the weeks of confusion. I even told her about the way Coombes tailored the truth to suit himself.

'Did they help you at all?' she asked.

'In what way?'

'You know. Support you. Like a counsellor.'

'I went a few times. It was hard. Her office was at the station, so I had to walk past all my colleagues to get there. I could see them thinking, 'There goes Stone.' They wouldn't look at me. Some of them were friendly, some of them weren't, but you could tell that they were all relieved that it was me and not them.

'It was like, I spent my time sitting at home. And I couldn't talk to anybody because I knew that whether or not it was my fault, it was me that did it. I kept replaying the whole incident over and over in my head, trying to see if there was any way I could have made things come out a different way. I mean, now I know the difference, that it was just one of those split second things that nobody could have helped, but at the time, I just blamed myself.

'The rest is just a cliché. I started drinking. There wasn't much else to do. I couldn't go outside, not with half the country wanting to string me up by the balls, so I used to sit on my settee and watch Fern and Phil with a bottle of Bushmills in my hand. Before long, the drink had taken over.

'So they completed the investigation and concluded that I wasn't to blame, but with the case being so notorious, I was taken off investigative duty and given a job riding a desk. They didn't want me out there, dealing with the public. And for a while I was glad of it, a simple, nine to five job where nobody hassled me. The police are very forgiving. I used to go in without shaving, stinking of drink, and they would just turn a blind eye. I think that the general opinion was that I'd had a hell of a time and I just needed a few months to pull myself together. And I thought they were right.

'But I couldn't stop drinking. I was up to about two bottles of Bushmills a day. Barely able to function.' I looked at Liz's face briefly, wondering if I would see a trace of embarrassment. There wasn't one. 'I. . . wasn't looking after myself. You know. . . eating crap, not changing my clothes. . . not washing. It must have been like sharing offices with a tramp.

'One morning I got called into the Chief's office. I must have been a state. Trembling, two weeks worth of stubble. The red-eyed wonderboy. He told me that he was suspending me again, that I needed to get myself together. I threw up all over his desk.

Liz reached forward and took my hand. It surprised me, and I held on tightly. I'd never talked of this to anybody. There were so many things I wanted to forget. The smell of vomit, the shame that I felt then and still feel now. Most of all, it was the disgust in the Chief's eyes.

I wanted to forget, but I couldn't. It wasn't just that I was unable to. Forgetting would have been an insult. It was only the knowledge of how far I could fall that kept me from stepping over that ledge again.

'I. . . uh.' My mouth was dry. 'That's not all.'

'You don't have to tell me.'

I knew that. But it wouldn't do any harm. 'I had a breakdown.'

She nodded.

'There's a blank period where I can't really remember what happened. I've been told things, but I don't know. . . it's like you ever watch a film, and all the way through it you think it's new to you, and then five minutes from the end you realise that you've seen it before?'

'I have.'

'It's like that. Remember Coombes? My partner? Lazy bastard, on the take. I fucking hated him. And he knew that I knew he was on the take, but I didn't have any evidence so we had spent weeks dancing around each other. . . he viewed what had happened as an excuse to get rid of me. He said some pretty ugly things about me throughout the whole disciplinary hearing. . . like I was a loose cannon and unable to follow orders and shit like that.' I closed my eyes. 'So, that afternoon, I apparently stormed out of the Chief's office in a rage, just as Coombs was walking down the corridor. He said something, some snarky comment and it was just an issue of him being in the wrong place at the wrong time.'

'What did you do to him?'

'I broke his nose.'

'Oh dear.'

I'd hurt Coombs pretty badly that day, catching him unaware, punching him to the ground, stamping on him before pulling his arm up his back until he screamed like a woman. The whole thing took me less than five seconds.

If I could remember it, it might have been worth it. Just.

Liz said, 'So they fired you.'

'No,' I told her. 'They didn't fire me. I left. There was a lot of people who were sympathetic. They all suspected that Coombes was dirty, and they'd all seen his campaign against me, so they discouraged him from pressing charges against me and they let me walk away. And that's exactly what I did. I went home and climbed inside a bottle and I didn't sober up for a month.'

'But you don't drink now?'

I shook my head. 'Not much. I think I was just using the booze as an anaesthetic. There came a day when I wasn't as thirsty. I sobered up, had a bath and went and asked Joe for a job.' I shrugged, as if to say, and here I am.

In reality, it hadn't been quite that simple. For the first couple of weeks of working for Joe I wanted nothing more than to crawl back inside the bottle. Every face I saw, every person I spoke to, I felt like they were judging me. It took a couple of months before I stopped automatically checking behind me when I walked down the street. I was lucky; Joe understood what I was worried about and was patient. Anybody else would have fired my pathetic ass.

We sat together in silence for a few minutes. Then she pulled me toward her and kissed me gently on the lips. I didn't know what it meant – if it was supposed to offer comfort – but I kissed her back. Her tongue touched mine, and I felt her hand on my neck. She let out a little moan before pulling away. 'Do you want to stay the night?'

I nodded and kissed her again. She stood up, took me by the hand, and led me to the bedroom.

Chapter 8

Wednesday 19th November

8.1

For once, I didn't wake up at the crack of dawn. I slept all the way through until quarter to seven. When I finally did open my eyes, I spent a pleasantly confused few seconds wondering where I was. The bed may have been comfortable, but it wasn't mine.

I looked to my left; Liz was beside me, hair spread across the pillow in a blonde wave. I shut my eyes and pretended to roll over in my sleep so that my elbow nudged her gently. When I opened them, her eyes were open. Emerald green. Nice way to start the day.

'Morning.'

She kissed me briefly on the lips. 'Morning.'

'How are you?'

'OK.'

She sighed and snuggled closer; I lifted my left elbow so that she could lie with her head in the crook of my arm. Her body pressed against mine, soft and warm and sexy.

Hell of a nice way to start the day.

After a few minutes of lying like that, she lifted her head. 'You OK?'

'I'm good.'

'Any regrets?'

'None.'

'You know how it is. You spend the night with somebody and then all of a sudden everything's different.'

'Everything *is* different,' I told her. 'Everything is better.'

'You know yesterday, when I opened the door and I wasn't. . . you know. Dressed?'

'Yeah?'

'I knew that it was you.'

'I forgot to thank you for that.'

'Don't mention it.'

We drifted off for another ten minutes. The sex had been good – excellent, in fact – but for me, there had been something else as well. There had been nobody but Audrey for a long time, and things had been very different between us. Animalistic and unfulfilling. I'd forgotten that there it could be tenderness as well.

'Cameron?'

'Uh huh?'

'I don't want to freak you out, but what happens now?'

'What do you want to happen?'

'I like you.'

'Thank God for that. I wasn't quite sure.'

She poked me gently in the side. 'You know what I mean.'

'I do, yeah. And I like you. A lot. Have done ever since I moved in.'

'How much is a lot?'

'Enough to break it off with Jessica Alba.'

'Who?'

'She's an actress.'

'Will you stop taking the piss? I don't do stuff like this. I don't sleep with somebody on the first date. Ever. But I've broken my own rules and now I want some answers.'

'Alright. The truth is that you are the best thing I've got in my life just now, and I'm looking forward to getting to know you better. The sex was great, but even if we had talked all night and I had slept on your sofa, I'd still feel the same. If you tell me now that you want to pursue a relationship, but you have no intention of sleeping with me again for the next five years, then I'd probably still be sleeping on your couch in five years time. I like you, Liz. Not what we can do with each other. Sex is good, but if you begin a relationship by defining it as a sexual one then it probably won't work. And whatever happens, I like you for everything you are. You might be sexy – damn sexy, by the way – but you're also funny and smart and kind. I'd be daft if I thought that sex was all you had to offer.'

She was silent for a few minutes. Then, 'If you begin a relationship by defining it as a sexual one then it probably won't work. . . Wow. That's deep.'

'Read it in *Cosmo*.'

We drifted away again. Warm. Safe. Happy.

This time, it was me to break the silence. 'It wasn't really our first date, you know. We've been friends for a while. All we did was move on.'

'You're just saying that so I'll sleep with you again.'

'Not *just* so you'll sleep with me. So that you don't go feeling guilty for what we did.'

'What did we do?'

'You know. . .'

'I can't remember.' She giggled and rolled on top of me. 'You'll need to remind me.'

Like I said, a hell of a nice way to start the day.

8.2.

Late for work again. If I wasn't careful it could become a habit.

The office block that Banks Investigations was situated in included underground parking, and as lease holders, we were allocated two spaces side by side. Joe's space was empty. Even though I was an hour and a half later than usual, I'd still managed to beat him into work.

I got up to the office, made the coffee and sorted the mail. It included a cheque from a satisfied client to the value of ten thousand pounds. I remembered typing up the invoice; the actual amount was nine thousand, six hundred and fifty pounds. He had included a note, telling us to think of the extra as a bonus. The day just kept getting better and better.

When Joe hadn't arrived by ten, I called him at home. The phone rang for a full two minutes before he picked up. The second I heard his voice, I knew why he was late. He sounded like he had been ridden hard and put away drunk. 'Morning, boss.'

'Morning. I think.'

'Good night, was it?'

'Probably.'

'I see.' It was easy to imagine him leaning against the wall of his hallway with red cheeks and dark circles underneath his eyes. 'Where did you go?'

'I took Gary and Barry out on the town.'

'Gary and Barry?'

'I swear. Gary and Barry. The Harald and Ginsel guys. You should have seen them. They wore matching suits and had identical mobile phones. And a fine line in bullshit. Kept telling me how much they enjoyed interfacing in an informal environment.'

'Where did you take them?'

'Everywhere. We started out in the Bermuda Triangle.'

The Bermuda Triangle consisted of three pubs: The Scotia Bar, The Clutha Vaults, and the Victoria, all within a hundred yards of each other on Stockwell Street. So called because of the number of good men that had been lost there. 'Where else?'

'Can't really remember. We finished the night in the Panda.'

'Classy,' I said. He meant Cleopatra's Zoo, the notorious 'Gentleman's Club' that doubled as a knocking shop. 'You can't interface in a more informal environment than that.'

'I seem to remember buying a lot of tequila shooters.'

'You really know how to entertain your clients.'

'You'd think they had never been to a strip club before.'

'Did they behave themselves?'

'Both of them disappeared for a suspiciously long time, and when they came back, they had smiles on their faces. Gave me a handshake guarantee on the contract.'

'Who did they go with? Any idea?'

'Starla.'

I knew the girl he meant. She was dirty brunette that would do it all for a choc ice. I had no doubt that Barry and Gary had enjoyed interfacing with her on an informal basis. 'When do you get something in writing?'

'They said they would get the contracts ready for signing today. I'm meeting them for dinner at their hotel tonight. I'm not sure my liver's up to it.'

Joe was selling himself short. His liver was probably the fittest part of his body. Had to be, the amount of exercise it got.

'So are you coming in to the office at all today?'

'Maybe later this afternoon. When I feel better.'

'I've got something that will make you feel better. A cheque from Victor Leslie for ten grand.'

'Ten grand? I thought it was less than that.'

'Victor was extremely impressed with our diligence.'

'You're right. I do feel better.'

'Want me to put it in the bank?'

'Yeah. And the extra's yours. Like a bonus. Fair enough?'

'Fair enough. What do you want me to do for the rest of the day?'

'You got anything you can do?'

'You mean, do I have routine busywork I can be pressing on with while you spend the rest of the day recovering from your hangover?'

'Don't forget that this is a work-related hangover. I got it because I gave up my precious evening to entertain two potential clients. I would much rather have spent the evening with my lovely wife. It wouldn't hurt you to make a few sacrifices like I do.'

'Since when is taking two clients out on the piss a sacrifice? And I thought Becky was at the London Book Fair?'

'Fuck you, Stone.' He was laughing when as he spoke. 'She's due back tonight. Did you go to the granny farm?'

'Yeah.' I told him everything that happened, including my clumsy attempt to ask Maureen Black out.'

He chortled. 'So she shot you down in flames. I knew I should have done it.'

'You wouldn't have fared any better.'

'I've been told I have a certain charm.' He paused, gave a series of hacking coughs. Joe smoked about thirty a day, and the Panda was notorious for overdoing it on the dry ice. His lungs would need a rest. 'Anyhoo. There's probably not a lot you can do right now, not with Ian Sloan being away in London. Is all the paperwork up to date?'

'Just about.'

'Then take the day off. Alright?'

'Cheers, boss. Give me a phone if anything crops up.'

I hung up, aware how lucky I was to have a boss like Joe. The day (well, most of it, anyway) stretched out before me, full of promise.

Life was good.

I should have known something bad was going to happen.

8.3.

The first thing I did after depositing Leslie's cheque in the company account was phone Liz and ask her if she wanted to go out for lunch. She sounded pleased to hear from me. 'I can't. I'm doing a back shift. They phoned half an hour ago.'

I tried and failed to think of something to say that didn't sound disappointed and needy. 'That's a shame.'

'I'll be home at ten. You could make me a late supper.'

'What would you like?'

'You. Covered in chocolate sauce.'

Fair enough. 'You can have that for after. How about I make

you. . .' I hesitated. '. . . smoked salmon and branglemashed eggs?'

'That sounds very posh.'

'It's not.'

'What the hell are branglemashed eggs?'

'Uh. . . they're like scrambled eggs.'

'Like?'

'Alright then. They are scrambled eggs.'

'I see. And you think that giving them a different name makes them more impressive?'

'That was the general idea.'

'Alright then. Branglemash away. And can I suggest one alteration?'

'What's that?'

'Bacon. I'm not a big fan of fish. They're underwater aliens.'

'Bacon and Eggs.' I pretended to be disappointed. 'You're easily satisfied.'

'Not that easily, Buster,' she said. 'Don't forget the chocolate sauce.'

I hung up and tucked my phone into my pocket, aware that I had a clownish grin on my face. I snickered to myself as I drove down Renfield Street.

What next, that was the question. It was too nice to go home and spend the day on the couch reading Stephen King novels. For the past five days there had been a run of clear days where the low autumn sun divided the landscape into patches of light and shadow. In the sunlight, it could almost have been late August, but in shadow you could sense the approaching winter. For some reason, I found myself thinking of the park, and wishing that I had a dog. That would be fine, to watch a golden Lab bouncing around the golden leaves.

Finer still if Mark could watch with me.

I was still pissed off about Saturday, about sitting in the cold outside Audrey's house feeling like a fool, hoping that she had just taken Mark with her while she nipped down to the shops to buy a pint of milk. Worse than feeling foolish was the sensation of impotent, frustrated anger. Audrey had the entire week to turn Mark against me;

I relied on a few precious weekend hours to undo the damage. My mistake of the other day – thinking that Arnold might be up to something nasty – had been unpleasant, and afterward I had found myself wondering about my reaction. I had jumped to a conclusion based on nothing more than a throwaway remark from a seven year old. Was it possible that I was so desperate to prove Audrey an unfit mother that I had wanted there to be a problem? If so, then I should be ashamed of myself.

That was a matter for another day. Thinking about Mark had called another, younger child to mind. There was something itching at the back of my subconscious. I'd ignored the itch for a while now, procrastinating, always finding something better to do. Now that I had most of the day to myself, it was time.

I had to go back to where it all began.

8.4.

Gallowgate, Glasgow.

It had been a while.

I hadn't been back since the night of the accident, which in itself was quite a feat. Glasgow's a small city, small enough that it's hard to avoid a particular place just because it makes your balls want to crawl back up inside your body.

I did the math in my head. Ten months, six days. And about eight hours, give or take a few minutes. Happy Cammieverysorry.

It was busier in daylight. Cars were parked nose to tail on both sides of the street. Buses lurched back and forth in a squeal of hydraulic brakes and exhaust fumes. Pedestrians moved from shop to shop, looking for anything and everything. Because it was a weekday, the Barras market was closed, but there were plenty of other places to buy discount leather goods and bootleg compact discs.

I watched.

There was a transit van double parked on the spot where it had happened, an Asian man unloading boxes and carrying them into a shop. It was slow work, because he could only carry two boxes at a time and he had to lock the back of the van between trips to prevent some opportunist lightening his load.

Glasgow is a city of opportunists. And optimists. And people like me.

I looked at the road and wondered if there had been blood. Of course there had been. There had been blood on the windscreen of the car. Lots of it. And brains. It had been raining that night. How long had it taken to wash away? If I asked one of the Scene of Crime Officers to gown up in a white plastic suit to swab the area and look at things underneath an ultraviolet light, would there still be any trace? Would there be anything left of Maria, of baby Sonata Blue?

Probably not.

It would be so easy to get out, to go over to the spot, to walk on the ground where it had happened. To remember them. They deserved it.

And yet, I couldn't make myself do it. I just couldn't.

Pathetic.

I thought about my own life, and how much I would give to change the past.

Anything.

Almost anything.

The guilt was crushing. My good mood was gone, and rightly so. I shouldn't be happy. I didn't deserve it. Maria McAuseland wasn't happy. Neither was her daughter.

They were just dead.

Because of me.

The Asian man finished unloading his van and drove away. I stayed in the car. All I was doing was raking over old coals. Maria and Sonata were dead and gone, and it was my fault; that was how it was and how it would stay. To expect some kind of epiphany to release me from my guilt was self-serving and tasteless. I gave myself a mental kick up the backside. It didn't help much, but I felt a little weight lift from my shoulders.

Three kids made their way along the street in matching hooded tops and track suit bottoms. On their feet were brightly coloured training shoes that were probably endorsed by their favourite football stars. As they walked past the spot where the accident had happened, one of them casually spat into the middle of the road. I felt the sudden heat of white hot rage. It would be so easy to start the engine and chase the little bastard down. How fast could he run in his expensive footballer's trainers?

Chill. Just because somebody is ignorant and dirty is not an excuse to mow them down like a vengeful maniac. They were just three kids playing hooky from school. In five years time, Mark could be one of them, especially if his mother continued with her current strategy of giving him everything he wanted except attention.

Mark would be at school right now. I'd asked Audrey if he got good or bad reports, and her response had been vague to say the least. To me, he seemed bright enough, always questioning the why or the how of things, and I knew for a fact that he could read because he knew the menu at McDonalds like the back of his hand, able to understand meal-deals and promotional offers with a speed that was scary and slightly depressing. He could probably program the DVD recorder as well.

The three boys had moved on, to be replaced by two teenage girls in tight jeans and boots. Both of them were smoking, cigarettes held prominently between two forefingers so that everybody could see how cool they were. As they flicked ash onto the tarmac, I wondered if any-body from the east end of Glasgow ever bothered going to school. The question was more than rhetorical; a closer look told me that there were hundreds of kids wandering the streets, some with parents, some mooching around with friends. None were in school uniform.

I remembered something that Mark had said to me the other day. At the time, I hadn't really paid much attention – we had been in the queue at McDonalds and I was trying to figure out whether or not salad came with a Happy Meal or was extra – but it had obviously sunk home. Today was some kind of in-service training day, and the schools were closed. It took me less than three seconds to dial

Audrey's number. As usual, she sounded overjoyed to hear from me. 'What do you want?'

I decided to make small talk to butter her up. 'How are you?'

'Oh, I'm just fine.'

Except that something in her tone told me that she was being sarcastic. I waited.

'Your bloody son managed to drop an entire bottle of tomato juice all over my new settee. Instead of picking the damn thing up, he ran to fetch me, which would have been fine except I was in the fucking shower. By the time I got there the thing was soaked.'

I smiled. 'That's terrible.'

'It's going to stain.'

'What colour is the settee?'

'Originally? Cream.'

Good lad. 'I thought that club soda was supposed to help.'

'Well thank you, Mr Good Housekeeping. Was there a reason you called or did you just want to pass on some handy housekeeping tips?'

'I got an unexpected day off and I remembered that Mark had the day off school as well. I wondered if perhaps you wanted him out from under your feet for a while.'

'Mark's never "under my feet",' Audrey said. Although her tone suggested that he was more in her firing line.

'Where is he now?'

'In his bedroom. Playing with drain-cleaner, hopefully. Did you know that Domestos kills ninety-nine point nine percent of all known children dead?'

Appalled, I said nothing. After a short silence, she said, 'I'm sorry. That was an awful thing to say.'

She was right, but now wasn't the time to point out Audrey's flaws as a parent. 'Maybe I could take him out for a while? I could come by and collect him.' I pretended that an idea had just struck me. 'I could take him to see that *Get Fish!* movie.'

'He's seen it. My sister took him.'

'It was just an idea. Come on, Audrey. You could go to the Tanning

Salon. You were looking kind of pale the last time I saw you.'

'You know, you can't just come and pick him up when you feel like it.'

I decided that it wouldn't be wise to point out that she was the one who behaved like that. 'Please, Audrey.'

'Alright. But have him back by five, and no McDonalds, alright?'

'Alright.'

It would be Burger King instead.

8.5.

I didn't even need ring the doorbell. The car had barely come to a halt before Mark flew out of the house and jumped in. He kissed me on the cheek before fastening his seatbelt.

Audrey watched from the living room window. I nodded at her. She didn't nod back, so I pulled away. 'It's nice to see you.'

'Mummy's cross with me 'cos I spilled.'

Yeah, well, kids spill stuff, I thought. Mummy was daft for buying cream-coloured furniture. 'I'm sure you didn't mean it.'

'It fell out of my hand.'

I examined him from the corner of my eye. He was a gorgeous kid, with blonde hair and the best of his mother's features. It was possible that in a few years he might have picked up her habit of looking pissed off at anything and everything, but for now he was just a gap-toothed little boy in a Teenage Mutant Ninja Turtle T-shirt and a pair of blue jeans that looked like they had been purchased from BabyGap. 'What do you want to do today?'

'*Get Fish!*'

'Your mum told me that you had seen it.'

'I did see it. I went with Auntie Lynne and Uncle Keith.'

'Who's Uncle Keith?'

'Auntie Lynne's new friend.'

No doubt he was a new boyfriend. In the past six months, there had also been Uncle Graham, Uncle Andrew and Auntie Jill. At least it was his aunt and not his mum. 'What's Uncle Keith like?'

'I didn't like him. He kept pinching Auntie Lynne and making her squeal.' He fidgeted in the seat next to me. 'They took me to see *Get Fish!*'

'Was it good?'

'Brilliant. It's really, really funny. It's the best film ever made.'

'What do you want to go and see today?'

He looked at me like I was crazy. '*Get Fish!*'

'Again?'

'Yes!'

'What's it about?'

'A penguin.'

'A penguin?'

'His name's Fish.'

'Why's his name Fish?'

''Cos he lives with fish.'

'I see.'

I didn't. Maybe you had to be five to get it.

'I want to go and see it again.'

What the hell. It sounded like a pleasant, inoffensive way to spend a couple of hours, and I felt like I could use something inoffensive.

'You know, I read somewhere that Eskimos eat penguins.'

'What's an Eskimo?'

'They're men who live at the North Pole. In igloos.'

I suspected that was perhaps a stereotyped oversimplification, but decided to keep it simple.

'What's an igloo?'

'It's a house made of snow and ice,' I said. It was time to move on, or else we would quickly head into "Why is the sky blue?" territory. 'You hungry?'

'Starving. Can we go to McDonalds?'

'I promised your mother that we wouldn't.'

He pooched his lower lip out. Not quite ready to go into a sulk, but definitely less than pleased with the situation.

'How about Burger King instead?' I asked. 'Would that meet His Lordship's dietary requirements?'

Strangely enough, it would.

8.6.

'Dad?'

I fished what seemed to be an entire raw onion out of my burger with thumb and forefinger. 'Yes?'

'Do people really eat penguins?'

'I was joking. I'm not sure if they do or don't. They probably do.' Possibly because there weren't anywhere near as many fast-food restaurants in the Arctic Circle.

'Do you think they taste like chicken?'

'I very much doubt it.'

Mark took a bite of his Whopper, holding it with both hands. A dab of mayonnaise was on his chin. 'Mum won't let me have a puppy.'

'She told me.'

'She's mean.'

'No, she's not,' I lied. 'Puppies take a lot of looking after, and you're at school all day.'

'Yeah, but *she's* home.'

'Yeah, but *she's* busy.'

Yeah. Watching Jerry and Trisha and Jeremy Kyle.

Mark took another bite. We'd had a minor tantrum because Burger King didn't have any free balloons to give away, but we seemed to have bounced back nicely.

'Da-ad?'

I swear, you could hear the hyphen. 'Uh huh?'

'You like puppies, don't you?'

I could see where this was going. 'I do. But I'm usually at work all day. A puppy would be very sad and lonely in my little flat, because it would have nobody to talk to or play with. You wouldn't want a puppy to be sad, would you?'

'You could get two puppies. Then they wouldn't get lonely.'

'Yes they would. And my flat's too small. Puppies need to run about a lot. They need exercise.'

'There's a park near your flat.'

I knew the one he meant. It was a tiny, rancid square of mud, littered with used needles and empty bottles of Buckfast, surrounded on all four sides by major roads. Any puppy going there would either get squashed by traffic or catch hepatitis, if it wasn't doused in lighter fuel and burned for the entertainment of the lurking teenagers. I explained about the roads, but left out the rest.

'Da-ad?'

'Yes, son?'

'Can you get pet penguins?'

'I don't think so. You only ever see them in zoos.'

'I bet they don't need as much. . . exercise,' I heard him shaping the word with his mouth, trying it out for size. Clever lad. 'They don't walk very fast.'

'I'm sure your mother would be thrilled if I got you a penguin.'

Hell, why not go the whole hog and get him a polar bear? If I was lucky, it would eat Arnold for dinner.

And Audrey for dessert.

'Da-ad?'

That hyphen again. Enough. I had to get him off the subject of pets. 'Ma-ark?'

'What?'

I'd sent him to get napkins while I waited for our meals, and he'd come back with about fifteen straws. As he watched, I picked one up, tore open the top and blew it at him. He giggled. 'Cool! Can I try?'

'Sure.'

He blew the straw at a skinny bloke clearing the table next to us. The kid gave me a dirty, why-can't-you-control-your-child-in-public kind of look before moving away. I picked the rest of the straws off the table.

'Don't blow them at other people.'

'Why not?'

I decided to ignore the question. Three seconds later, Mark was studying the tray the meal had come on. There was a large sheet of paper lining the tray; on it was printed a picture of two kids in a convertible. The background was deserted country highway and blue skies. Both the kids had shiny, American grins and smooth, zit-free complexions, and you could tell they were just as happy as happy could be. The girl (blonde, naturally) was drinking a can of Coke and the boy had a burger the size of Texas in his hand. An advertising slogan advised us that life was just peachy.

Mark pointed at the girl. 'She looks like Mum.'

'Uh huh? You think so?' I couldn't see it myself. But then, the girl in the picture was smiling. Maybe Audrey smiled more when I wasn't around. 'Listen, Mark, you know how your mum and I don't live together anymore?'

'Yeah.'

'How does that make you feel?'

He shrugged. 'Dunno.'

'You know that I love you, don't you?'

'Yeah.'

Say it back, I willed him. He was too busy looking at the girl. Idly he touched her hair with a finger stained by tomato sauce.

'Mark, do you like it when we see each other?'

'Yeah.'

I waited, but there was nothing else forthcoming. 'You know how Arnold is Mummy's friend?'

'Yeah.'

'How would you feel if Arnold was your daddy?' I swallowed, feeling dryness in my throat. 'Instead of me?'

'Dunno.'

Christ, this hurt more than I ever thought it could. Maybe I was expecting too much from him. They say that children of separated parents mature faster, but it was doubtful he understood that if Audrey had her way then I would be playing second fiddle to Arnold.

Mark looked up at me. 'Does that mean I wouldn't see you anymore?' For the first time since he had got into the car, I felt like I had his complete and undivided attention.

'Of course not. We'll always see each other. I'll make sure of it.'

'Cool.'

It was hardly a tearful declaration of love, but it would have to do.

8.7

Get Fish! turned out to be pretty good; one of those rare films that's as entertaining for the parents as it is for the kids. The cinema was busier than I expected it to be. A lot of people had used the in-service training day as an excuse to take the kids out, perhaps, like me, thinking that the place was going to be quieter.

The movie finished just after four PM, and I decided to take him home, rather than risk his mother's wrath by pushing my luck. I strapped him into the car and started to drive slowly. After giving me a top-ten of his favourite bits of the film, he went oddly quiet.

'What's up, Champ?

'How come you and mum don't live together?'

In twelve months, he'd never asked that. I wondered if it was because he was getting older, or if he was the only kid in his class with separated parents. Somehow, I doubted it. 'Why do you want to know?'

He shrugged. 'Dunno. How come?'

'We. . . we weren't very happy together. And then I was in that car accident and was sick for a while. I had to stay in hospital for a long time so that I could get better. Mummy got used to looking after you by herself and when they let me out of the hospital we both thought that it would be better if I didn't come back to live with you.' I realised what I had said. 'You and mummy,' I amended.

I didn't want him to think that it was his fault.

'Why not?'

I tried to think of an answer and couldn't. How do you explain the complexities of adult relationships to a child? Mark didn't have the insight to understand, and I lacked the ability to simplify it so that he could.

Subject change. 'So what do you want to do on Saturday?' I gave him a warning look. 'Don't say "*Get Fish!*"'

'Dunno.'

'You want to go to Laser Quest? Pizza Hut for lunch?'

'Yeah!'

Laser Quest was one of those places where you wore an electronic backpack and ran about like a nutcase shooting bolts of light at people you had never met. Great fun. It felt like somebody took a syringe of testosterone and injected it directly into your brain.

'I might bring a friend,' I said casually.

'Who?'

'Her name's Liz. She lives next door to me.'

'Is she your girlfriend?'

'She's a friend friend.'

'Is she nice?'

'No. She's horrible. I'm scared of her. You better be nice to her or she'll put you in a cooking pot and eat you.'

He smiled. With the gap between his front teeth, he just looked sweet. 'Does she have any children?'

'No.' At least, none that I had heard about. 'She might not want to come anyway.'

'She can come,' Mark said. 'If she's nice.'

'Of course she's nice. I wouldn't be friends with somebody nasty.'

'Auntie Lynne's nasty.'

'What, to you? Is she nasty to you?'

He shook his head violently. 'Uncle Keith said it. I heard him telling her she was a nasty B-word.'

I studied him carefully. 'Uncle Keith said she was a nasty bitch?'

'Yeah, but he was laughing at the time. They were both laughing.'

I decided not to pursue the conversation any further, instead making a mental note to ask Audrey whether she really thought her tart of a sister was a suitable babysitter.

8.8.

I arrived home to find the message light on my answer machine blinking. I hit play and listened to about fifteen seconds of static before there was the clunk of a dropped receiver. Second time around, I turned the volume up as far as it would go. I was rewarded with the sound of somebody breathing heavily and a set of high heels clipping along a corridor. There was also a soft ping, as if a lift had just arrived. At a guess, I thought maybe the call had originated from a hospital.

Liz.

That didn't make sense; she only had my mobile number. There was no reason to give her my home number when she lived less than twenty yards away. I checked my mobile phone for messages just the same. Nothing new. I sent her a quick text anyway – *luking4wrd 2c-ing u 2 nite*. Three minutes later, my phone beeped as it received a reply. I read it and blushed. I was quickly learning that my neighbour was a girl of many appetites.

So. . . not Liz then.

I picked up the phone and dialled 1471; a computerised voice told me that I had been called at three-fifteen pm and that the caller had withheld their number. With so little information available, I gave up. Whoever it had been would have to call back.

I spent the next hour cleaning my flat, spending most of my time in the living room and bedroom. Usually I'm fairly relaxed about tidiness, but I felt like I was on a promise and didn't want to jeopardise it by having dirty laundry lying on the floor. I gave up after spending ten whole minutes scrubbing at a stain on the coffee table. Any girl who could eat an out-of-date pork pie for breakfast was unlikely to be discouraged by such trivialities.

The phone rang again and I picked it up. I heard breathing, slightly snuffled, as if somebody had a nasty cold. Probably the same mystery caller that had failed to leave a message earlier. 'Hello?'

Nothing.

'Listen, whoever that is, I'm going to hang up and pull the cord out of the wall, OK?'

Silently, I started to count to five. Made it all the way to three.

'Mr Stone?'

The voice was familiar– not the kind of familiarity of an old friend, but the type where you know that you spoke to its owner recently, but just can't quite remember. 'Who's calling?'

Whoever it was, they sounded on the verge of tears. 'Excuse me, is that Mr Stone?'

'It is.'

'I'm Susan Mc Pherson? From the other night?'

I remembered. Teenage runaway. I'd told her off and then left her my card. 'How can I help you, Susan?'

'Can you come and meet me?'

'I'm not sure. . .'

'Please. I really need your help.'

'This isn't exactly a good time.'

'You were right. I'm just a kid.' There was desperation in her voice. 'Please. I really need some help.'

Mentally I sighed. 'Alright. Tomorrow.'

'Tonight. Now.'

'Susan, I can't just drop everything.'

'Please.'

Her voice sounded desperate. 'Alright. Where are you?'

'The Western.'

'The Western what?'

'The Western Infirmary. The hospital.'

'Susan, what's going on?'

She was crying now. 'Just come.'

I tried to get some more information out of her, but the last sound I heard before the line disconnected was sobbing.

8.9.

Glasgow's Western Infirmary occupied a ten acre site in the heart of the city, surrounded on every side by major roads, the University, and the internationally famous Kelvinhall art gallery. To keep pace as the city had grown, the hospital had been forced to expand by slotting new wings and units into the available space between the established buildings. The result was a confusion of architectural styles; post-modern concrete and glass clashing with classic Victorian sandstone.

And, just for a bonus, a complete lack of available parking.

There was a visitors' car park, which I spent a joyful ten minutes circling in the vain hope that somebody would be leaving just as I happened to be passing. It proved to be a futile exercise. On my fifth orbit I worked out that there would be at least another thirty available spaces if the people who drove SUVs could learn how to park. The clincher was a brand new Land Rover Discovery that was abandoned across four disabled spaces; with no disabled sticker, I could only assume that the owner was either mentally challenged or a colossal dickhead, or possibly even a consultant. Maybe even a combination of all three.

I eventually gave up and headed into the surrounding streets, where in their infinite wisdom, Glasgow City Council had seen fit to levy some truly extortionate parking fees: fifty pence for ten minutes, no waiting, no loading, no happiness. It didn't seem to be a deterrent; cars were lined up nose to tail, street after street after street. After another ten minutes of cruising, which was taking me further and further away from the hospital, I thought *screw it* and headed back, eventually finding a space in an alleyway between office blocks, less than a hundred yards away from the main hospital entrance. I left the car directly in front of the emergency exit for a well-known firm of

Sheriff Officers. I had visions of them rattling the door handle in vain, trapped inside while their office blazed around them. Perhaps it wasn't impossible to redeem myself in the eyes of the press after all.

Susan hadn't given me any details of her admission, so I followed the signs that led to the main entrance. The receptionist was a harassed woman in her mid-fifties, hiding behind a glass screen and a permanent scowl. I took my place in the queue, behind an elderly man who told me that he was visiting an friend who didn't have long to go. He seemed quite chipper about it, perhaps relieved it wasn't him.

After five minutes of slowly shuffling forward, it was my turn. The receptionist glared at me. 'Yes?'

I gave her Susan's full name and she tapped at the computer key-board in front of her. 'Ward Twelve.' She looked at her watch pointedly. 'And you've got less than three minutes.'

'That's an awfully specific diagnosis.'

She looked down her nose at me, and her tone could have sliced a hole in her little glass screen. 'I mean until the end of visiting hours.'

Ward Twelve turned out to be at the opposite end of the hospital. I walked quickly, against the flow of people on their way home. Even though I followed the signs, I got lost in the labyrinth of corridors and dead ends. By the time I found what I was looking for, visiting time was over. On the plus side, I had managed to locate the mortuary. You never know when things like that are going to come in handy.

The sign on the door said that Ward Twelve was something called Acute Medicine. I wondered what they meant by acute. Wasn't it just a tiny step down from Intensive Care? I was assuming that if Susan was able to make telephone calls, then she was at least mobile, but then I remembered that some hospitals had trolleys that could be wheeled to a patient's bedside and then plugged into the wall. Or maybe she had been breaking the rules and using her mobile. For all I knew she could be completely helpless, getting bed-bathed and tube-fed. I took a deep breath and pushed my way through the double doors.

Even though it was a different unit in a different hospital, the memories came flooding back. The smell – antiseptic cabbage – triggered nostalgic recollections of inedible meals and lukewarm cups of tea. It also kicked off other, less pleasant memories. I don't remember being unconscious, but I could vividly recall the terrified, disconnected feeling I had when I woke up. It lasted for days. My leg was in a plaster cast, and every time I dozed off into natural sleep (which was regular and frequent: I was on enough drugs to tranquillise an entire stable of horses) I would forget everything I had been told. I spent the first two weeks of my recovery thinking that I was paralysed from the waist down. A nurse took pity on me and wrote a list of things that she thought I might like to remember, sticking it to the wall with Blu-Tack so that it would be the first thing I saw when I woke up:

1. My name was Cameron Stone.

2. I was in a car accident.

3. I was not paralysed. I had a broken hip. The rehab would be painful, but I would walk again.

4. I had a beautiful little boy called Mark who loved his Daddy very much.

Eventually, my memory returned (mostly), but I was grateful for this simple act of kindness, especially as it was becoming increasingly obvious to the rest of the nation that I was an extremely bad person. The month in bed didn't do me much harm; as I was very fit beforehand, my muscles didn't atrophy or degrade to any significant extent. As soon as it was possible, I was out of bed and exercising. Desperate to be discharged, I worked hard at the physiotherapy, ignoring the pain, skipping ahead with the exercises. I got myself fit in record time.

Physically fit, that is. Mentally, I wasn't doing so well. I was still trying to come to terms with the accident, with the media attention, and most of all with the fact that Audrey had used it as an excuse to pack her bags and leave.

I snapped back to the present. Ward Twelve seemed to consist of two corridors running parallel to each other, connected by two horizontal bars, almost like a square version of a capital letter 'A'.

Separate rooms – singles, doubles, four-bedded mini-wards – lined the outside of the corridors. I found the nurses' station directly in the middle of the lower bar.

Unfortunately I didn't find a nurse.

'Hello? Anybody there?'

'Mr Stone? Is that you?'

'Susy?' I couldn't tell where the voice was coming from. 'Where are you?'

'Room eighteen.'

She was waiting for me as I rounded the corner, leaning against the doorframe in a hospital nightie and a pink dressing gown that had seen better days. But then, so had she. I came to a sudden stop. 'Jesus Christ, Susan, what happened?'

'I got beaten up.'

That was the understatement of the year. Her face was a mess of bruises, dark blue and black, yellowing underneath the eyes. A large white dressing covered her forehead, and her nose appeared to be strapped in place with surgical tape. I felt a sudden stab of anger – not at her, but at whoever was responsible. She may have chosen a high-risk occupation, but she was just a kid. 'Who did this to you, Susy?'

'Can we maybe talk in my room?'

'Sure.' I followed her in. She sat down on the bed, arranging the pillows behind her and crossing her legs like the teenager she was. I made myself as comfortable as possible in a plastic-covered armchair. 'Susan, I'm so sorry. Whoever did this to you is an animal.'

'It was Kenny.'

She said it as if she expected me to know who that was. I did a quick mental search, sorting through the index cards in my brain, cross referencing them until I made the connection. 'Kenny the bouncer?'

'That's the one.'

'Why?'

She shrugged. 'All that stuff you said about me just being a kid. . . I know you think that I wasn't listening, but I was. After you left the bar, I just sat there. You know, thinking things over. He came looking for me. I told him I was thinking about going home.'

'And he beat you up?'

She shook her head. 'Not then. He seemed O.K. about it at first. Not exactly thrilled – Kenny's a paying customer as well as an employee – but he didn't seem bothered.'

'But later?'

'Yeah. I decided to go home, went through to get my jacket. He pulled me into one of the empty rooms, put some tape on my mouth, and then beat the living crap out of me. You've seen the size of him. I didn't have a chance.'

'Why?'

She shrugged. 'Dunno. He said that if I left, he'd hunt me down and kill me.'

I shook my head in wonder. 'For Chrissake. He can't make you stay. You want to leave, then leave.'

'I can't.'

'Of course you can.'

She shook her head. 'I really can't. It's not just me, you see. It's Rose. I can't leave her. I can't do it.'

I began to get an extremely nasty feeling. 'Who's Rose?'

'Rose is another girl who works at the massage parlour. I look after her. She's. . . she's got problems. Like, big problems.'

'What do you mean, problems?'

'It's like, she's not very smart. She needs a lot of help. She's two years older than me, but she's like a toddler. She's like that movie with Tom Cruise?'

I shook my head, mystified.

'It's like Tom's got this brother that he needs to look after, and the brother can't do much for himself, he's like artistic or something.'

It clicked. *Rainman*. 'Autistic.'

'What?'

'The word you're looking for. It's *autistic*.'

'Yeah, well, Rose works in the parlour as well. They don't put her out front, though. It's only customers that Kenny trusts that get to spend time with her.'

'Why? What does Rose do that you don't?'

Her lip curled. 'Everything. Anything.'

'What do you mean, anything?'

'I mean anything. You wouldn't believe some of the sick things that people want to do. I told you about the guy that I let pee on me? I would never have allowed that, but I was stupid. He told me to lie down on the floor and close my eyes and open my mouth and I did. By the time I figured out what was going on it was too late. How dumb can you get? I don't mind getting fucked for cash, but there's guys out there who want girls to do stuff that's really horrible and nasty. I mean sick. I mean disgusting. It's the kind of stuff that nobody in her right mind would ever agree to.' She looked me dead in the eye. 'I mean, you wouldn't believe it.'

Unfortunately, I would. In my time as a cop, I'd seen some pretty unpleasant things, including a man who celebrated his daughter's seventh birthday by raping and donkey-punching her into a coma, and a fourteen year old boy who died from internal bleeding after allowing his technical teacher to insert a screwdriver into his anus. I have nothing against most forms of sexual activity, but I was sadly familiar with the weird sickness that infects a small minority of us. I like to think I'm a pretty open-minded guy, but for me, the key word is consensual. It has to be mutually gratifying for all parties.

Kids can't give consent.

Neither could Susy's friend, from the sound of it.

Susy continued. 'Thing is, Rose doesn't really know what's going on. She's like a child. She doesn't do it for the money. She does it because she thinks that she has to, that unless she does whatever Kenny wants her to then there won't be any food or anywhere to sleep.'

'Where does she stay?'

'We all stay in a bed-sit flat in Victoria Road. There's six of us. The other four are a bit older than me and Rose. They don't like us much because we're so young. I look after Rose most of the time, take her to work with me, make sure that she eats something and washes and stuff. She's a good kid, but it's hard.'

'I don't mean to sound harsh, but why is this your problem?'

'Because Kenny knows that I look after Rose. He said that if I left then he would kill her as well. I don't want that on my conscience.'

'Doesn't Rose have any family?'

'I don't think so. I heard that she grew up in orphanages and stuff, that her parents abandoned her when she was a baby. That might be one of the reasons she's so fucked up. She didn't have a stable childhood.'

'Even so, there must be somebody. A social worker, something like that?'

Susy shook her head impatiently. 'She's got nobody. Nobody knows her last name, and she won't tell us. For all I know, she might not even know that she has one. And even if she does, nobody wants her.'

I tried to process what Susy was saying. It was hard to believe that in this day and age there could be somebody like the girl she was describing. The news is always full of stories of abuse and neglect, but the truth is that these are the exceptional cases. Nobody is truly alone in this world, unless they want to be, or unless they can't reach out for whatever reason.

Maybe it wasn't so hard. It's true that crime has no class barrier, but it's also true that a lot of people with troubled childhoods go on to live troubled lives. Take my two attackers from the previous night. I wasn't excusing them, or condoning their actions, but it was probable that they had received very little in the way of education or guidance. How can we expect people to respect others and obey the law and each other when we pay footballers and pop stars millions of pounds a year to act like animals?

I was getting too philosophical. Here was I bemoaning society when Susy had a very real, very pressing problem.

'So what do you think is going to happen?' I asked. 'You can't just take her away. She's not some puppy that you can abandon in the wild and fool yourself into believing that you've somehow rescued her.'

'I know that. I don't know what I'm going to do.' She uncrossed her legs, bringing her knees up to her chin and wrapping her arms around them. 'That's why I called you. I was hoping you could do something.'

Shit. The last thing I needed in my life was a crusade, but I had a nasty feeling I had been backed into a corner. Susy watched me, her expression an uneasy mix: fear, despair and resignation, but also pitiable, unspoken hope. It was easy to guess what that hope was. Maybe I could be the one that would make all the bad things go away.

If I agreed to help.

There was a clock on the wall, and every tick of the second hand sounded like the banging of a gavel. Answer the question! Answer the question! Answer the question or I'll hold you in contempt!

'Mr Stone?'

'I think we're beyond that now. My first name's Cameron.'

'I want to go home. I want to meet my baby brother. I've got nobody else.' She paused, then said, 'Neither does Rose.'

In my opinion, the worst kind of blackmail is emotional. The heart coerces the brain into helping, and when it all goes tits-up (as things inevitably do), you can't even hold your blackmailer responsible because it's not as if they put a gun to your head.

That said, I felt hugely sorry for this girl. She'd made a shedload of bad decisions, one after the other, each mistake compounding the previous until she was up to her neck in shit. And it wasn't as if my hands were entirely clean. I'd made a few quid doing Harper's dirty work. Maybe this was what the kaftan-wearers called Karma. Universal payback. I owed somebody somewhere, and the bill was due. Don't they say that what goes around comes around?

I sighed. 'I'll see what I can do, alright? I'm not promising anything.'

Susy flashed a quick smile at me before bursting into tears. The door opened and a nurse put her head in. 'Hi Susy. I just wondered if. . .' She saw me and ground to a halt. 'What's going on?'

Susy wiped her nose on the sleeve of the dressing gown. 'He's a friend of mine.'

'Of course he is. I often cry when my friends visit as well.'

I stood up, walked over and offered my hand. 'Cameron Stone.'

She ignored the hand, giving me a very obvious once-over. 'Visiting time was over almost half an hour ago, Mr Stone. You'll have to leave.'

I looked to Susan for help, but she was still snuffling on the bed. 'Please, just a while longer. I've only been here about ten minutes.'

The nurse gave me a wintry little smile. 'I'm afraid not.'

Susy raised her head. The tears had caused the tape on her nose to start peeling. 'He really is a friend. He's going to try and help me.'

The nurse folded her arms and gave Susy a thoughtful look. 'I thought you fell down the stairs?' Her tone was sceptical but not unkind. 'Why would you need help?'

When Susy didn't answer, the nurse looked at me. 'What about you, Mr Stone? Any idea? Because I've been doing this job for a long time and I find myself worrying more and more about the increasing number of young women who seem unable to negotiate a simple staircase. Especially when the staircase in question appears to be able to punch people in the face.'

From the corner of my eye I caught Susy shaking her head frantically at me.

'Um. . . '

'Sister, please, I promise you. Cameron's a friend. He's going to help me. He's going to make sure that I don't. . . fall down any more staircases.'

I rummaged through my wallet before handing over a business card. The nurse looked at it, then me, for a long time before sighing in exasperation and checking the fob watch that hung from her lapel. 'Right. Two minutes, then I'm coming back.' She pointed a finger at me. 'By that time, Mr Stone, I expect you to be on your way.'

We watched as she closed the door behind her.

'Cow,' Suzy said dismissively.

'Cow, nothing,' I told her. 'She's trying to help. You need all the friends you can get.'

'I just don't like being bossed around.'

'Yeah, well get used to it. If you want me to help you then you're going to have to do exactly what I say. Besides, I'm the one that's getting the bum's rush.'

'The what?'

'The bum's rush. Thrown out.'

'Is that some kind of disease?'

8.10.

I headed home. Liz came round at half past ten, and we shared a late supper. We made love on my sofa and then sprawled about watching trash television until about one AM. Then we showered and made love again before drifting off to sleep. It was a nice night, right up to the point where somebody tried to kill us.

Chapter 9

Thursday 20th November

9.1.

When I woke, Liz was asleep beside me, a huddle under the bed-clothes. Somehow, she had managed to wrap the quilt around her top half, leaving my torso bare. I shivered and smiled to myself as she let out a long, trumpeting snore that sounded more like a wild pig snorkelling for truffles than the gentle waft of rose petals being blown through a fan. I leaned in to kiss her cheek, only to notice that she had drooled all over her pillow.

A dribbling, snoring, warmth-stealer. Nobody's perfect. To tell the truth, it was a relief to sleep with somebody who didn't worry about bodily functions. Audrey had been so neurotic she would go into another room to blow her nose.

I lifted my head and looked at the digital clock on the night-table. Twenty-seven minutes past two. For me, it wasn't an unfamiliar time of night. The only difference was, it hadn't been bad dreams that had awoken me, or the usual guilt that had kept me awake. It had been something else. I listened, trying to figure out what it was.

A noise. A slow, pattering splash, like rain falling onto concrete from an overflowing gutter.

Maybe Liz had left a tap running in the bathroom. The basin could be quite slow to drain; it was easy to imagine the water level slowly rising, spilling over the edge and onto the tiled floor below.

I swung my legs over the side of the bed, pushing myself upright. 'Waszup?'

She must have felt me shift position. I decided not to blame her for anything. 'I think I left a tap running in the bathroom.'

'Oh.'

I was halfway to the door when she said, 'What's that smell?'

I shook my head, then realised that she probably couldn't see. 'I don't know.'

'Maybe you left the gas on?'

'I don't have gas.'

She sat up in bed. 'It smells like gas.'

She was right – sort of. Without any form of context, it was just an unfamiliar odour, heavy and cloying in the nostrils. No doubt it would have been just as confusing to try and identify the scent of bacon frying while standing in the middle of a garage forecourt. To my sleep-addled brain, it was just a funny smell. 'I'll go and check the kitchen.'

She sat up in bed, letting the quilt fall away from her breasts and raking a hand through her hair. In the half-light of the bedroom, she looked amazing. 'Hurry back.'

Damn right I would. Grinning, I stepped through the bedroom door. The flat was a fairly standard layout, comprising an entrance hall that led off to separate rooms. Yawning, I went into the bathroom on my left, checking the taps, only to find them tightly closed. I got down on my knees and felt behind the washbasin, running my hand up and down the pipes in a fruitless search for leaks. The only thing I found was a combination of dust and bathroom crud, smeared all over my fingertips. I rinsed them in the sink, marvelling at how something so easy to get on your hands could be so difficult to remove.

By now, I was starting to wake up. I drifted through to the kitchen, wondering if perhaps somehow the pipes were leaking underneath the sink. I even peered behind the refrigerator to see if the mystery noise was coming from there.

It wasn't. All I found was a crust of bread so mouldy it should have been contributing to the rent. Meanwhile, the pitter-patter sound continued. Wherever it was, it didn't sound like it was coming from the kitchen.

Maybe a pipe had burst in the flat directly above me, and the sound I heard was of water leaking through my ceiling. Perhaps the Old Lady of a Thousand Cats had finally kicked it while filling the kettle for her seventy-ninth cup of tea that day. The police would force the door and find her only true friends gently nibbling her be-cardiganed corpse as it lay in a pool of water on the kitchen floor. I'm not by nature a vindictive person, but the idea was not without its attractions. She really was a sullen old cow.

Moving faster now, I checked the living room, with no success. I stepped back into the hallway and listened – hard.

Somewhere, somehow, liquid was flowing. I wasn't imagining it.

And the smell was getting stronger.

Something caught my attention. I stared, narrowing my eyes as if that would somehow compensate for the poor light. It didn't, but after a few seconds, I managed to discern what it was had so captivated me. Had the inside of my front door not been painted a very light shade of brown, I would never have noticed.

Somebody had inserted a length of tubing through my letterbox.

Now that I had something visual to focus on, my hearing followed suit. The sound was coming from that direction. The smell – the eye-watering, mouth-gagging, almost recognisable odour – seemed to emanate from the carpet at my front door.

Time seemed to slow as my brain finally kicked into gear and made a rapid series of connections.

Middle of the night.

The most hated man in Glasgow.

Small, one bedroom flat on the second floor.

With only one door.

The reason I had made the bacon-frying-on-a-garage-forecourt link was because on a subconscious level I had recognised the smell.

Petrol.

Shit.

'Liz?' I called softly.

No answer. She must have gone back to sleep. I suspected that it would be an extremely short nap.

Options.

Somewhat limited.

I could kick the front door open and barge my way out there, arms flailing, screaming like a banshee, hell bent on kicking ass and taking names.

Only problem was, the front door opened inward. To pass through it, I was going to have to stand in the danger zone, spending vulnerable seconds fumbling with the mortise lock, the chain, and the deadbolt. Knowing my luck, it would be at that moment that my uninvited guest decided to make his presence felt by tossing a match. I would go up in a puff of smoke. And besides, what if there was more than one person out there? What if there were five of them, or ten, or twenty, all standing there with their zippo lighters drawn? You don't pour petrol through somebody's letter box as a prank. Whoever was out there wanted me corpsified in the most terminal sense of the word. Not just merely dead, but really most sincerely dead. Even if I was able to overpower them, the chances of the petrol igniting were pretty high. If I was on the other side of the door when the flames went up, that would still leave Liz trapped.

I very much doubted that my conscience could bear the weight of another death.

But what else could I do? We were on the second floor. If we had been on the first floor, a pair of broken ankles would be an acceptable price to pay for our lives, but the extra storey was too far to jump. If it didn't kill us outright, the fall would almost certainly fuck us up beyond all repair.

Plan B: hide in bed and die like a man. Take Liz in my arms and try to kiss the fear away from her lovely lips.

Yeah, right. Romantic in theory but probably pretty horrible in practice. We would be squealing, roasted pigs in a blanket.

Besides, I very much doubted Liz would be in a kissing mood.

Even as I dithered over my course of action, fate decided for me. The letterbox rattled as my midnight caller dragged the length of tubing out. There was the scuffing of a shoe, and then a rattle, followed by the harsh dry scratch, concluded by the guttering sputter of a freshly-lit match.

I watched, horrified, as a hand pushed my letterbox open.

9.2.

'Fuck!'

It was meant to sound like a shout of combined warning and anger, Neanderthal man to Neanderthal woman, *Come quickly, the cave's under attack by a giant sabre-tooth.*

Except it didn't quite come out like that. Instead, a pathetic, breathy squeak passed my lips. There was no way in hell Liz could have heard it, especially over the *whoof!* of the petrol sodden carpet at the base of my door igniting. Blue-orange flame raced toward me, stopping less than twelve inches away.

'FUCK!'

Better, that time. Sudden heat licked at my knees and broke my paralysis. I dived back into the bedroom and kicked the door shut behind me. 'The flat's on fire!'

'What?'

'The fucking flat's on fucking fire!'

'There's no need to fucking swear at me!'

I ripped the bedclothes off her, wadding them up and pressing them to the base of the door. 'We're on fire! You hear me? The hall-way's on fire and there's no way out!'

She sat upright, pushing her knees against the mattress so that her back was right against the wall. Her voice was full of fear. 'Why's it on fire?'

'I don't know! I didn't ask!'

'What do you mean, there's no way out?'

This time, I ignored her, looking around frantically for my mobile phone. Then I remembered: it was in the pocket of my jeans.

Which were crumpled up at the foot of the couch.

In the fucking living room.

Mum always told me to put my clothes tidily on a chair in my bedroom. Now was hardly the ideal time to wish that I had listened to her.

'Liz, you got your phone nearby?'

She nodded. 'It's in my flat.'

Crisis always brings out my sarcastic side. 'So it's within arm's length, then, is it?'

She shook her head, eyes wide.

I bounced over to the window. Nobody around. All I saw were parked cars, pools of yellow light from the few working streetlights. A glimpse of a fox as it crossed the road. I grabbed the sill, tried to force it upward. The damn thing was painted shut. I punched the glass as hard as I could. My fist bounced off, pain shooting up my arm. I stepped back, did a half-arsed scissor kick, my heel thudding as it impacted the glass. A splintering crack appeared. I repeated the move and the window caved in, a chunk of glass opening a gash in my ankle as it fell. I wrapped my hand in a T-shirt, using it to knock the remaining pieces of glass out of the window frame, the sudden chill of the night air on my chest. 'Help! Help us! We're on fire!'

Somewhere, a dog barked.

'Please! Help! Call the fire brigade!'

Below me, there was the sound of a door opening. A hunched, hooded figure scurried off into the night. I screamed, but it didn't look up. The arsonist. It was unlikely they would be calling emergency services. I watched as the figure ran across the road and dived into a car. Headlights flickered into life. Tyres screamed as it peeled away from the kerb. The car was low and sleek.

Jason Campbell. The cunt. If I lived through this, then he wouldn't.

Liz howled. 'Cam! For God's sake!'

I turned and looked at the door. Despite all the bedding I had piled up at the base, the first tendrils of smoke were beginning to creep through and rise like dark, hungry fingers. I could hear the fire, roaring its way through my home like a beast. It was easy to imagine the flames establishing base camp in the hallway before spreading like a virus into the other rooms, destroying everything before them in a furious conflagration of heat and energy. Something – the television, a light bulb, it didn't matter – exploded with a tinkling smash and Liz screamed, a hand raised to her mouth.

I looked to the window again. 'We're going to have to jump.'

'Are you crazy? I'm scared of heights.'

'Yeah, well, I'm scared of dying.'

A few lights had gone on in the flats on the opposite side of the road. I caught sight of somebody leaning out of their window, speaking urgently into a telephone. Although it was always possible that they were just letting their pals know about all the excitement, I decided to hope for the best and assume that they were calling emergency services.

The nearest fire station was just over a mile away. Say sixty seconds for the call to be patched through, and another one hundred and twenty seconds for the firemen to suit up, figure out where the hell they were going, and get on board their fire engine. Then maybe another ninety seconds to get here – and that was an extremely generous projection. The streets round me were narrow, lined with parked cars. And besides, sometimes they had to wait for a police escort because the local kids would stone them to pieces.

Of course, that was assuming that they weren't already attending another call-out.

All in all, the earliest possible time I could expect to see a fire engine was a hopelessly optimistic four and a half minutes.

My toaster was set for less. If we jumped, we would die. If we stayed, we would die slowly.

I had a limited selection of bedclothes. Three sheets, three quilt covers. One set for use, the rest in storage. I threw open the wardrobe next to the bed and started pawing my way through the contents of the top shelf, tossing items over my shoulder in my search.

'What are you doing?' Liz screamed at me.

'We need to make a rope.'

'Out of what? Bermuda Shorts?'

'There's sheets in here. And quilt covers.'

'They won't be strong enough!'

She was probably right. Unfortunately, it was the only idea I had, and I was in no mood to debate. If she had a better plan, she was free to raise it at any time in the next four and a half minutes.

From the direction of the living room came another explosion that was as loud as a gunshot. Dimly, I wondered if it was the television that I had just finished paying for. I nearly screamed in triumph as I found the spare bedclothes tucked all the way at the back of the wardrobe. I swept them all onto the floor and bent down, my hands flying as I remembered my old cub-scout lessons in how to tie a reef knot, right over left and left over right.

A standard double-sheet is about six foot long by about six foot wide, totalling a diagonal length of about eight feet in total. By tying them corner to opposite corner, I was able to maximise the available length. Even so, I still lost about one foot of each sheet or quilt-cover for each knot, meaning that the total usable length of rope I got was about six feet per item of bedclothing. I needed more length, as much as I possibly could. I grabbed the quilt that had been on the bed from where I had used it to block the crack at the base of the door, stripping it of its cover. I finished by dragging the sheet off the bed.

In total, it took me about ninety seconds to tie all six items together.

Thirty-six feet – maybe. Maybe my math was out and my makeshift rope would come to an abrupt halt a spine-breaking distance from the ground.

We were on the second floor.

I wondered how high that was.

Decided it didn't matter.

I had to make myself shout over the roar of the flames. 'Liz! I'm going to lower you down.'

She shook her head mutely.

The smoke was getting worse. When I had lifted the quilt to strip the cover, I must have missed sealing the crack when I put it back. My eyes were stinging, my throat burning. 'Liz! Look at the door!'

Terrified, she raised her eyes. The smoke was pouring in, billowing from underneath the quilt, somehow managing to squeeze through the keyhole. I watched in horror as the paint on the door itself started to blister.

'Liz, it's not going to hold. We'll die if we stay here.' I bent down, taking hold of her arm, drawing her to her feet, trying to make my hold on her firm enough to reassure but not tight enough to frighten. 'Liz, you have to do this.'

'Just leave me!'

'You know I can't do that.'

'You'll drop me.'

I held a hand up to her cheek and stroked it, marvelling that even now, she looked beautiful. 'Liz, I can't do that, either. I won't. I promise.'

'You promise?'

I kissed her, hard, briefly. 'I promise.'

Her eyes searched my face one last time, questioning me, looking for an answer that would not be found until she was safe – or dead.

'You better not.'

'Thatta girl.' I pushed her to the window, watched as she swung first one leg and then the other over the sill, until she was sitting with both feet dangling into the cold night air. She turned to look at me over her shoulder. 'What do I do?'

'Put your hands over your head.' I demonstrated. 'Like that.'

She did as she was told. I placed the end of the rope in her right hand. She rotated her wrist, wrapping the sheet around it, taking more of the length than I cared for. I said nothing; this would either work or it wouldn't. She grabbed the section of rope above her right wrist with her left hand. 'What now?'

'I'm holding it. Just let your bottom slide over the edge and I'll catch you.'

'You're kidding.'

'I'm strong.'

'I can't do it.'

'Please, Liz. Do it for me. I promise, I won't drop you.'

'Please don't make me do this,' she babbled, at the stage of panic where she would say anything. 'Just don't make me do this. I'll do anything else you want. I love you.'

Time was running short.

I raised my foot, placed it against the small of her back, and pushed her out of the window.

9.3.

Of all the times to say those words. If we survived this, we needed to have a talk.

9.4.

She only fell about two feet before the slack ran out in my makeshift rope, but even then she gained sufficient momentum to almost pull me out of the window after her. I was wrenched forward, my waist bouncing off the window frame, my arms almost dragged out of their sockets by the sudden weight. I could hear her screaming, and when I tilted my neck forward, I saw her dangling below me, arms raised above her head, holding on for dear life. Underneath her was the ground, incredibly hard and a hell of a long way down. Something flashed in my peripheral vision and I turned my head. Orange flames were shooting from the window of my kitchen. I decided there and then to wave goodbye to my security deposit.

'Get me down!' Liz screamed.

She was right. I had to stop daydreaming (or, indeed, nightmaring) and get busy. I started to lower the rope, hand over hand, making sure that I had a good fistful of material each time. Before long, my shoulders started to burn and my back ache. At a guess, Liz weighed between one-twenty and one-forty pounds, significantly heavier than anything I usually lifted. My exercise routine consisted of fast reps with no more than thirty kilos on the bar; I was strong, but not prepared for this. We both hung on for grim death as I inched her down the front of the building. Every time she swung close enough, she kicked out with her feet, doing her best to stop herself from being scraped along the sandstone. Grunting with exertion, I closed my eyes and put my mind to the task, counting off each handful as it passed. Time seemed to slow, the world becoming nothing but sensation; the pain in my hands and arms, the heat on my back, the fear in my heart. My eyes stung and my lungs felt as if they had been filled with acid.

And then I dropped her.

I don't know what happened. Perhaps my grip on the sheets wasn't as tight as I thought. Perhaps my hand spasmed and relaxed its hold. Perhaps I wasn't as strong as I thought I was, or I lost concentration. All I knew was that suddenly the sheets started running loose through my fingers and she was falling. She didn't scream but howl, like a hunted animal who almost makes it to freedom only to have it snatched away at the very last moment. I think I screamed as well, frantically trying to catch hold of the makeshift rope as it whipped through my fingers. I managed to grasp it but couldn't hold on, my palms and fingers burning as the cotton dragged between them. I willed myself to dig deeper, to ignore the pain and reach inside to find the reserve of strength that heroes talk about but real people rarely discover.

And then. . . nothing.

The tension on the rope was gone. So was the screaming.

I opened my eyes. Liz lay on the ground in a crumpled heap.

9.5.

She had been less than halfway down when she fell. Maybe twenty-five feet in all. She had probably landed on her feet, the bones of her lower body accordioning upwards like a badly shuffled deck of cards, multiple fractures to the lower back, pelvis and hips, everything below the knee a splintered mess of fragmented bone.

Wheelchair case. For life. Probably still able to feel pain and move her arms. If she was lucky, she would be able to change her colostomy bag unaided.

Of course, she might have twisted as she fell, landing on her back, or her skull. On her back, she might still survive, but the nerves of the spinal cord wouldn't. And the skull?

It didn't bear thinking about, but I thought about it anyway.

9.6

I had to get down there. I had to know how badly she was hurt.

My fears about the rope being too short had proved groundless; in the end, it had been just long enough. What I had badly under-estimated was my strength. I thought that just because I could do two hundred forearm curls with a twenty kilo dumbbell, I was qualified to pretend I was Fireman Sam.

The paint on the inside of the door was gone, melted by the heat on the opposite side, replaced by a blackened, bubbled surface of carbon. One of the panels finally collapsed in on itself. The fresh oxygen caused a huge gout of flame to shoot twelve feet across the room before retreating; I felt my eyebrows singe and the hairs in my nostrils crisp. The fire itself sounded like a terrible, ravening beast; something that had been locked away in Dante's seventh level of hell, suddenly given free reign to wreak havoc upon earth. As I watched, it poured itself through the inside of the door, spreading up to the ceiling.

I tried to remember everything I knew about pyrotechnics. It wasn't much; my childhood may have been spent setting fire to anything and everything I could get my hands on, but I had been far too busy riding my BMX through the flames to stop and look at the mechanics of it. As a copper, I had attended my fair share of house fires, but I usually arrived after the fact, when all that was left was a pile of smoking rubble and a few black-faced survivors, who usually weren't in the mood to talk about it, and a stumbling, shambling drunk who was disappointed that his chips weren't ready.

One thing I did remember was the fire triangle. To burn, a fire needs three elements; oxygen, fuel, and heat. Take one of these things away, and it will die. Supply all three in abundance, it will thrive.

This one was thriving. This one was as lively as a basket of puppies on crack.

By lingering directly in front of an open window, I might as well have been hiding underneath a tree in the middle of a thunderstorm.

I risked one last look. Liz hadn't moved. She lay on the concrete like a rag doll that had been tossed aside by an angry child. Somewhere in the distance, a siren rose. The makeshift rope dangled down the side of the building, twisting slowly in the breeze. I looked around frantically for something to tie on to, something strong that was too large to be dragged out of the window.

The bed frame. Metal. Thank God for Ikea.

Grunting, I pushed it as close to the window as I could, looping the end of the sheet around the frame before swing my legs over the windowsill and grasping the sheet in my hands. Even though the fire seemed to be moving faster than I was, I couldn't stop myself from pausing on the way out and sparing a final glance at the flat that had been my home for less than four months. All that could be seen through the rapidly disintegrating doorframe was a raging conflagration of flickering orange. I swung myself out of the window, feeling my arms take the strain. By leaning back I managed to make my body almost horizontal, the stone wall of the building cool on the soles of my feet. As quickly and as carefully as I could, I started to walk backwards down the side of the building, fully aware that flames could already be eating their way through the fragile cotton.

It was the longest walk of my life.

At any second, I expected to feel myself falling. By turning my neck, I could see the ground below me. Liz hadn't moved. Somebody was standing over her, holding what might have been a mobile phone in one hand. I had a nasty feeling it wasn't being used to call emergency services. I looked away, trying to focus my mind to the task in hand.

It took forever to reach the first floor window, and when I did, I nearly lost my balance as the bare soles of my feet struggled to find purchase on the smooth glass. After the choking smoke, the night air was cool and sweet in my lungs. The muscles in my arms felt taut, stretched like piano wires, ready to give way at any second. I held the rope with both hands in front of me, the loose end hanging down between my thighs, making sure to move only one limb at a time, having to consider every stage to make sure I didn't fall.

After what felt like at least twenty minutes, I stopped looking down. The ground didn't seem to be getting any closer anyway. For every foot I moved, it seemed to retreat a yard. When I did next risk a look down, I saw that the man on the ground – he was as big as a whale, and dressed in a pure white shell-suit that made him look like a giant marshmallow – had his camera phone trained on me. Whether I lived or died, I was going to be an Internet star. Again.

Focus.

Left hand. Left leg. Right leg. Right hand. Repeat ad infinitum.

Thick black smoke was pouring from the window above me. The fire had taken hold of my bedroom. I wondered how much longer the cotton could last.

Left hand, left leg, right leg, right hand.

And. . . again.

The rope twitched once in my hands, then went slack.

I started to fall.

9.7.

So this was it. I was going to die. My life was going to be over. I tried to think happy thoughts about the good times – taking Mark to the park. . . being with Liz for the first time. . . swapping one-liners with Joe – but all I could feel was a terrible, swooping terror. I remembered Maria McAusland, and how the eyewitnesses said that she lived for a few seconds after I hit her with the car. Had she felt this way? Did she experience the same horror, the same feeling of anti-climax? Maybe her pain had been too great, too overwhelming for any rational thought at all. Maybe I would meet her in the afterlife, and she could tell me.

I doubted it; there was a terrible poetry about being killed in a fall. It seemed to serve as a metaphor for my final destination. Babykillers don't get to go to heaven.

They go down the way instead.

9.8.

The impact was something of an anti-climax.

That's not to say that it wasn't hard. The wind was knocked out of me in a sudden rush, and for a few seconds I was unable to breathe, sucking hopelessly at the air like a fish out of water. Then my lungs kicked back in, the sudden rush of oxygen leaving me light headed and dizzy. My heart pounded in my chest, like an engine forced to rev too hard and too long, until it was only a stroke away from complete shutdown.

I was still alive. It may seem kind of obvious, but it wasn't at the time. I was genuinely shocked. Tom Cruise and Jackie Chan may be able to plummet fifty feet in slow motion and roll to their feet with little more than a sprained ankle and a photogenic gash on the cheek, but in real life things don't work that way. Falls tend to be sudden, brutal and extremely messy, especially when the landing zone happens to be actual concrete instead of a grey-painted crash-mat. Anything over ten feet breaks bones. Anything over twenty and your days of playing pocket-pool in the public parks are over.

Anything over thirty, and the ambulance crew will scrape you up with a spatula.

I'd fallen fifteen, maybe twenty feet, and nothing was broken. Everything hurt like hell – my hands and feet were somehow numb and tingling at the same time, and my back felt like a loan shark had used it for base-ball bat practice – but everything seemed to be working, albeit in a slightly off-kilter, disconnected way. To be honest, I relished the pain as a confirmation I was still alive. Slowly, I raised my right arm and made a fist. It was like making a telephone inquiry to a particularly incompetent call-centre: only after the message from my brain had been bounced to half a dozen wrong extensions did the fingers in my hand eventually do as they were told.

But they got there in the end.

Now that I was satisfied that I hadn't died, the next question was, why not?

The answer was simple. Something had broken my fall. A fat guy.

Not just a fat guy, but the fat guy that had decided to use his camera phone to shoot our escape. In his bid to get a better shot, he must have been standing directly below me and, when I fell, I landed directly on top of him. Lucky for me, not so lucky for him. He was out cold, breathing through his nose, making the wet snuffly noises that obese people make when they've passed out after eating six Whoppers and a litre of Chunky Monkey ice-cream. Other than checking that he was breathing, I ignored him. By using his camera phone, he had taken our moment of desperation and turned it into something amusing he could sell for profit.

To be brutally honest, I wasn't overly concerned with the fat fuck.

Especially when I had more important people to worry about.

I rolled over onto my knees, ignoring the sudden stab of pain in my legs. . . my arms. . . just about everywhere, really. The sudden chill of the concrete made me realise for the first time that I was starkbollock naked. So was Liz, for that matter. She lay about five feet away. I almost fell as I lurched over and grabbed her by the shoulder. 'Liz! Liz, can you hear me?'

Groaning, she opened her eyes and looked into mine. 'Cam. . .' Her mouth twisted and her hand flew to her leg. 'JESUS!'

I looked. Wished I hadn't. Forced myself to look again. 'Um. . . that's maybe not so good.'

She squeezed her eyes tightly shut. 'How bad is it?'

I wasn't quite sure how one quantifies such things. 'It's bad.'

'How much of the bone is sticking out?'

'A lot.' To me, it looked like a hell of a lot. A lot of white bone and a lot of sticky red blood, the two colours contrasting brilliantly in the dim light. The bone was jagged, like a shard of glass. 'Maybe a couple of inches.'

'You need to reduce it.'

'I need to what?'

She gritted her teeth against the pain. 'You need to push it back in.'

Yeah, right. I thought they only did stuff like that on television. 'Are you sure that's a good idea?'

'Cameron, if you don't do this for me I'll never sleep with you again!'

Given that attempted murder places an additional strain on blossoming relationships, I was already having doubts on that score. Nevertheless, this was her field. If she told me the bone had to go in, then she was probably right. 'What should I do?'

'Just take hold on either side.'

The blood was warm on my hands as I did as I was told.

Liz coached me between squeals of pain. 'That's it. . . just there. . .put your thumbs on either side. . . now push.'

I pushed. Liz screamed. I yelped. The bone slid back below the skin, leaving only the wound. My yell of triumph was cut short by the realisation that she had passed out.

9.9.

Things moved fairly quickly after that. The fire brigade arrived, sirens blaring, and handed out coarse woollen blankets to cover our shame. Then a couple of paramedics rolled up and seemed slightly disappointed that nobody was dead. Fat Guy regained consciousness and started yelling that somebody had stolen his mobile phone. (Nobody had stolen it; I'd kicked the thing down a drain.) Between that and bitching about his pain, he made so much noise that the paramedics hit him with a sedative, leaving him notably calmer and glassy-eyed. By this time, a small crowd of onlookers had gathered. They applauded as three husky firemen assisted the two medics to lift him onto a stretcher, and somebody gave the ambulance driver directions to the nearest beach, so that their precious cargo could be returned to its natural element.

As walking wounded, I was allowed to share an ambulance with Liz. She woke up screaming during the ride to the hospital. They gave her something for the pain that sent her right back to sleep. I was then given a stern telling off about resetting the leg– apparently it wasn't the accepted practice (well, duh), and I could have done all sorts of damage – before a grudging acknowledgement that I had done rather a good job.

We were separated at the hospital. I was shown into an examination room and given a thorough going-over by a doctor who looked like he was about seventy-two hours into a sixty hour shift. When I asked him about Liz, he shrugged. Satisfied that I was unlikely to die in the next few hours, he admitted me to a general hospital ward 'for observation'. They gave me a single room, which I knew from experience was a fairly valuable hospital commodity. Although grateful, I knew what it meant. Less than ten minutes after I climbed into bed, the cops showed up. I spent the next two hours giving two detectives a report on what had happened. When we reached the point where I listed all the people that might have a grudge against me, the officer's pen ran out of ink.

9.10.

I woke up to find a nurse fastening a blood-pressure cuff to my arm. She saw my eyes open. 'Morning.'

'Morning.'

She pointed to her name-badge. 'My name's Harriet. I'm your named nurse for today. How are you feeling?'

I shifted my head on the pillows, the movement highlighting a pain in the area behind my left eye. It wasn't quite a migraine, but more like the throb of a hangover. Not just an ordinary, bog-standard hangover, either, but one of these brain-smashing, bowel-quivering bastards that are completely immune to over-the-counter medicine. My eyeballs felt like somebody had inflated them with a bicycle pump and my mouth tasted like a decomposing cigar that had been marinated in the sweat of a Las Vegas poker player.

All in all, a rough start to the day.

'I've felt better.'

'From what I hear, you had quite an exciting night.' She moved quickly, poking a thermometer underneath my arm, making rapid-fire notes on a clipboard. 'You'll be glad to know that your oxygen saturation levels are much better.'

'Oh. Good.' With no idea what she was talking about, I forced myself to relax as she poked and prodded at my body. She was pretty but tiny, only slightly taller than me even though I was lying on a hospital bed. Her ears were beet-red, as if she had spent the morning scrubbing them with carbolic soap and cold water. 'What time is it?' I asked.

She checked the fob watch that dangled from the front of her white tunic. 'Ten past eleven.'

For a moment I was confused, wondering if I had lost an entire day. 'It's still Thursday, right?'

'That's right. You were asleep when I came on duty.'

I tried to do some fast mental arithmetic to figure out how much sleep I had got in the last two nights, but the numbers eluded me. 'I've got a headache.'

'I can give you some Kapake, if you like.'

I had no idea what Kapake was, but I was working on the principal that if I had never heard of it, then it was probably something good. I nodded to let her know that I liked. 'Thank you.'

Two minutes later, she was back with something fizzing in a plastic glass. 'I got you dispersible ones because your throat is still going to feel a little raw.' She pressed the drink into my hands and bent over me, fussing with the oxygen mask that I had forgotten was there. 'And the doctor says that you don't need to use this if you don't want to. If you find yourself becoming short of breath, let me know and we can put it back on.' She hung the mask on a little hook next to the bed and stood back. 'There's somebody waiting to see you. He was quite insistent.'

'Is he a police officer?'

She nodded. 'I think so.'

Great. Another two hours of going round in circles. That would do my headache a world of good. I raised the glass in a toast, draining it in one long swallow, nearly choking on the bitter taste. 'Thanks. Can you tell me about the girl that was admitted with me? I think she had a broken leg.'

Harriet nodded and smiled. 'She's in ward seventeen. She's going to be fine.'

'Can I see her?'

'Maybe later.'

I gave her what I liked to think was a winning look. 'Pretty please with sugar on top?'

For a few seconds, I thought that she was buying it. Unfortunately it was at that moment I spoiled things by breaking into a fit of coughing so loud it sounded like I was trying to choke up a donkey. Harriet tutted at me before moving to put the oxygen mask back on. I waved her back. 'Don't worry, I'm fine.'

'You want me to tell that man you're awake?'

'Not really,' I told her. 'But I suppose you better.'

9.11.

The first thing my visitor said when he saw me was, 'Jesus, don't tell me you've got a room of your own, you lucky bastard.'

The day just kept getting better and better. I hung my head and tried to look sicker than I really was. 'Joe.'

He grabbed hold of my hand and squeezed it like he was checking to see if it was ripe. 'You'll do anything to get a bloody day off.'

I raised a ghost of a smile. His response to stuff like this was predictably macho: lots of jokes to distract the victim from the emotional and physical pain. Although glad to see him, I wasn't sure that I would survive. 'How did you find out?'

'When I couldn't raise you on your mobile phone, I went round to your flat… or rather, what's left of it. Did we leave the grill on again?'

'Something like that.' I told him what had happened, going over the details the way I had done last night with the two coppers. I concluded with our dramatic escape.

Joe said, 'Fuck me, Mr Bond. I suppose you'll want to refer to me as 'M' now.'

'I have another nick-name for you.' I said. 'Several, actually.'

'I'm sure you do.' He patted me on the arm and sat down on the edge of the bed, despite the fact that there was a perfectly good chair less than three feet away. His thigh accidentally brushed mine and he jerked it away as if it had burned him. Although a fundamentally good man, Joe is ill at ease with how tactile society has become, especially between two men. Anything more than a handshake was conclusive proof of rampant homosexuality. I was actually glad of the accidental contact; Joe was much easier to handle when he was uncomfortable than when he was firing on all cylinders.

He slapped his own thighs to confirm his masculinity. 'So. . . the police interviewed you.'

'Yes they did.'

'Any names come up?'

'Dozens. I'm not a popular man, Joe. You know that.'

'Anybody in particular?'

I shrugged. It didn't fool Joe for a second. He dipped his head and looked me dead in the eye. 'Anybody whose name you didn't feel like sharing with the police?'

Yeah. Jason Campbell. I'd given the matter some thought, and come up with a feasible explanation of how he could have done it. After he high-tailed it away from our little after-school discussion group, I'd sat in my car for a short while. No particular reason; I'd tapped out a quick text message to Liz, then phoned my service provider to buy some more air-time credit. I'd checked the log book of the car, wanting to know when the next MOT was due. All in all, maybe five minutes. Not long.

Long enough.

Jason could have driven around the corner and then turfed the girlfriend out on the street. From there, it would have been a simple matter to follow me home and figure out which flat I stayed in. Then it would be a case of waiting for darkness. Hell, he could even kill a little time by making a quick trip to a nearby petrol station and investing in a length of rubber tubing and a petrol can. There were two such places within half a mile of my flat, open twenty four hours a day, three hundred and sixty-three days a year.

As the kids say, *Easy-peasy, lemon-squeezy*.

I had good reasons for not mentioning his name to the police. Firstly, I didn't want to have to explain why he might have a grudge against me. A decent lawyer would make mincemeat of my claims to have seen him fleeing the scene of the crime – it was dark, the distance was significant, I was under extreme stress; was it not possible, ladies and gentleman of the jury, that Mr Stone *wanted* to see the accused? The bottom line was, the police might be able to build a solid case against him, but only while simultaneously doing the same thing with me.

Second was Harper. There may have been little love lost between us, but I had absolutely no intention of dropping him in it. Especially as I had yet to collect my money.

Lastly, there was the nature of the crime itself. Arson is a sneaky, cowardly act; easy to commit because you don't make direct contact with your victims. It's simply a more extreme version of harassment, like slashing somebody's tyres. Jason probably hadn't even considered the potential consequences of his act.

But he would. I planned to make sure of that. For Liz's sake as well as my own peace of mind.

I told Joe everything. I told him about the work I did for Harper. I told him about meeting Jason outside the school, and how I had branded his hand with his own cigarette lighter. Turned out, Joe already knew most of it anyway, and was somewhat less than impressed. 'You want to watch Harper. He's a bastard.'

'He says equally complimentary things about you.'

'I just bet he does.' Joe's right hand crept into the inside pocket of his jacket and then stopped. I knew what he was reaching for: his cigarettes. Yet another habit that alienated him from today's accelerated, health-conscious society. 'So when are you getting out?'

'Can you buy me some clothes? And let me stay in your spare room?'

He nodded.

I pushed myself upright in the bed. 'Today.'

9.12

When I told the staff that I planned to discharge myself, Harriet the Nurse quickly turned into Harriet the Spy, wasting no time in reporting my intentions to a member of the medical staff. I had a terse conversation with a Senior Registrar called Dr Dilawari about how irresponsible I was being. Didn't I know that I needed at least another twenty-four hours observation before they could give me the all-clear? Didn't I know how hard all the staff had worked looking after me? Was I not grateful for that? Did I not want to express my gratitude by staying until I was fit for discharge?

Probably, yes, very, and no. In that order. Dilawari sat in a hurt silence for a few minutes, possibly hoping that he could guilt me into staying. When he finally accepted that hell wasn't going to freeze over, he produced a disclaimer so comprehensive that it would absolve the Hospital Trust of liability under just about any circumstances; if I were to collapse within a week of leaving the hospital, and the attending medical staff, instead of loading me into an ambulance and driving me to hospital, accidentally amputated my head, then it would be my own sweet fault. I signed his disclaimer without protest, hoping that whoever was trying to kill me would take at least seven days to plan the next attempt.

The truth was that I was very much aware that I was discharging myself against medical advice. Although I felt like shit, I didn't have time to lie about in bed waiting to get better. I had to find the person or persons responsible for last night's shenanigans. Also, I had no intention of forgetting about Susan McPherson. Agreeing to help her may not have been my wisest decision, but that didn't alter the fact that she was in a world of trouble and I had given my word.

While this was going on, Joe made a brief shopping trip and returned with new clothes for me. Just the basics: plain black T-shirt, blue jeans, socks and underwear. While he waited outside, I dressed as quickly as I could. The T-shirt was a size too small, making me look like I had more muscle tone than I actually had, and the jeans were about an inch too short. Luckily, the shoes he had bought were hi-tops which came all the way up my ankles, so it wasn't obvious. I dressed as quickly as I could, desperate to lose the feeling of vulnerability caused by wandering about in NHS-issue pyjamas. The new clothes might have been a gift, but they were mine, and I could be reasonably sure that nobody had pissed or died in them.

I thanked the nurses and said my goodbyes, making sure that they knew that my decision to leave had absolutely nothing to do with the care I had received. A few of them didn't recognise me; all of them were too busy to do anything more than wave.

9.13.

Liz had also been given a single room. I found her sitting upright in bed concentrating on something that might have been shepherd's pie. She was in a standard hospital night-gown – yellow roses on a pink background - but somehow she still managed to look good. When she saw me standing in the doorway she put down her fork and smiled. 'Hi.'

'Hi. How are you?'

'I'm fine. I'm just peachy. It's a fairly standard fracture of the tibia. I get to take the next two months off work. Paid, of course. I can catch up on my reading.' She noticed my outfit and gave me a searching look. 'Please tell me you haven't discharged yourself.'

I nodded without enthusiasm. Something told me that she was going to give me the same lecture that Dilawari had. Only difference was, I cared about what Liz thought of me.

She didn't waste any time letting me know. 'You arsehole. I was trying to sort us out with a shared room. We could have had nooners.'

I looked at her leg, which was hanging from a sling six inches above the bedclothes. 'I think we're a while away from that.'

She winked at me. 'You would be surprised at what you can achieve when your heart's set on it.'

I was shocked. Well, not quite shocked. More surprised. I'd wanted to see her, not just because I wanted to reassure myself that she really was alright, but because I wanted to give her the chance to dump me quickly and cleanly. 'Doesn't it bother you? That somebody tried to kill us last night?'

She picked up the fork and shovelled more of the pie into her mouth. 'Actually, I find it rather a turn-on.'

'You can't be serious. Because of me you're going to spend the next. . .' I waved a vague arm in the direction of her leg, '. . . two months in a cast. We both very nearly died last night. Are you seriously telling me that you're still interested?'

She pointed at the chair next to her bed with the fork. 'Sit down and shut up.'

I did as I was told. She shovelled the final piece of pie into her mouth, making me wait for what she had to say.

'First of all, it's four weeks, not two months. Second, yes I do find it a turn on. You should have realised by now that if you were an accountant or an Internet Support Engineer, I wouldn't have the slightest interest in you. I like bad boys. I'm not proud of it, but there you are. It might get me in trouble sometimes, but I can't help it. And thirdly. . . ' she looked at me archly, '. . . interested in what?'

'Interested in. . . me?' I said. 'You and me? Us?'

She clutched her hands to her breasts and fluttered her eyelashes. 'As in, do I want us to live together in a little house and have identical twins and a Labrador called Binky? I could bake cakes and you could mow the lawn at weekends? Is that kind of what you had in mind?'

I wasn't sure how to answer that, so I didn't. She put her hand on my arm. 'Look, I'll admit that the idea is not without its attractions. But let's not get carried away. We hardly know each other. Just because we're sexually compatible doesn't mean we can go planning a future together. So let's just go on as we are – two people who are more than friends and less than partners.'

'Why did you say that you loved me?'

'Because. . . I was scared. I've never said those words to a bloke before. People say stupid things when they're frightened. I thought I was going to die, and I didn't want to die without having said it.' She shook her head. 'Look, don't go reading too much into it. I say it to my friends all the time. Let's not be one of those stupid couples who break up because one of them says the wrong thing at the wrong time. There's more important things in the world.'

People did do stupid things in times of stress. I could testify to that. I decided to let the matter drop. 'So what happens now?'

'We carry on as we were. Boyfriend and girlfriend. We can go out on dates and rent videos. You can bring a bottle of wine over and I'll cook for you. But let's not put so much pressure on ourselves that we screw things up before we've had a chance. How does that sound?'

'It sounds good to me. But aren't you worried you'll get hurt?'

'Don't flatter yourself, pal.'

'I mean physically.'

'I know.' She shrugged, the nightie slipping off one of her shoulders and showing off pale, perfect skin. I was suddenly extremely grateful that she didn't want to break up with me. 'Of course I'm worried. But let's not forget: you saved our lives last night. You kept it together when every other man I've been with in my life would have dived underneath the bedclothes and hid. That makes me a very lucky girl. Besides, I'm quite sure that what happened last night is a fairly infrequent occurrence.'

I decided not to tell her about my near-miss on the stairwell two days earlier. For all we knew, I could just be having a run of bad luck. Instead, I bent over and kissed her cheek. She turned her lips to mine, and we stayed like that for a few seconds. When we finally separated, she whispered in my ear, 'Besides, you just might be worth it.'

Chapter 10

10.1.

Joe was waiting for me in the car park, behind the wheel of the Jag he had owned for the past thousand years. He watched me climb into my seat, noticing the smile on my face. 'You know, for a man who lost his home and all his possessions in a fire less than twelve hours ago, you seem awfully chipper. Who is she?'

'She's just a friend.'

'Who is she?'

'She's just a friend.'

'Who is she?'

'She's. . . just. . . a. . . friend.' I repeated. 'Is this how you used to question suspects? Hammer away at them until they finally cracked?'

'Who is she?'

I tried to distract him. 'What the hell happened between you and Harper?'

'Who is she?'

'Joe, I swear to God, let it drop. Or I'll kill you.'

'Don't do that. You might get blood on your fancy new outfit.' Joe keyed the ignition and the Jag started with an unhealthy grinding noise that he had previously assured me was completely innocent. 'Correction. My fancy new outfit. Now. . . who is she?'

I sighed. 'Her name's Liz. She's a nurse.'

'Christ, that didn't take you long.'

'She lives... lived... up the stairs from me. She spent the night at my place. I helped her to get out, but she hurt her leg.'

When I had first told Joe about my escape, I had carefully edited Liz out of the story, still under the illusion that I might have a private life. This time, I told him the complete version.

Joe looked impressed. 'She must be quite a lass to climb down a rope,' he told me. 'Especially being registered blind and all.'

'Ha ha.'

He put the car in gear and pulled out of the parking space. 'It's just a shame that her guide dog got barbecued.'

I ignored him, staring moodily out of the window, oblivious to the passing scenery. Joe drove as if there was a glass of whisky balanced on the dashboard, which up until a few years ago, there probably had been. We headed east, through the city's industrial heart, making our way to Newton Mearns, where the people who *owned* the city's industrial heart lived. Joe clicked the radio on to Clyde Two FM and seventies music – Bread, Supertramp, Pink Floyd – provided a soundtrack. When he next spoke, Joe sounded almost humble. 'I'm glad you're OK, mate.'

I found myself absurdly touched. 'Thanks, boss.'

'I can't afford to train a new assistant.'

10.2.

Unlike her husband, Becky Banks was warmth personified. She enveloped me in a hug the second I stepped through the front door. 'Cameron. You must be so upset.'

I hugged her back. She was tall and slim, dressed in a cerise silk blouse and flowing skirt. Her blonde hair was elegant but looked natural, and her face was smooth with baby blue eyes. It was no wonder her publishers loved her; if you asked the average romantic fiction reader to describe an average romantic fiction novelist, they would have come up with someone like Becky. Completing the image was a pair of granny glasses that dangled from a string around her neck. It was easy to imagine her sitting at a typewriter and sipping herbal tea as her busy fingers breathed life into her fictional creations.

When I saw the two of them together, I often wondered what they saw in each other. Becky was cultured and graceful, a glass of wine in the garden in a summer breeze. Joe was the opposite: whisky and cigarettes, greyhounds and pubs with sawdust on the floor. Yet they had been together for nearly thirty years, with four lovely, well-adjusted daughters. Their oldest daughter was married – happily, it went without saying – and lived in Kidderminster, propagating the eagerly awaited first grandchild. The twins were about to finish University (both in the top five percent of their classes), and the youngest seemed to be as likeable an example of a ten-year-old girl as one could reasonably wish for without seeming greedy.

Even the house Joe lived in seemed to reflect his luck. It was a four bedroomed bungalow in one of Glasgow's more expensive suburbs, all whitewashed walls and well-trimmed hedges. Inside it was just as nice: dark wood, light rooms and high ceilings. Joe once told me that he'd lived there almost all his life, inheriting it when his parents passed on.

Reading this, you might think I was jealous of Joe. Nothing could be further from the truth. He was the first to admit how lucky he was, and I knew that luck alone hadn't bought him the comfort and security that he enjoyed. All his life, he'd grafted, putting his heart and soul into everything he took on board. The snide rumours about his days as a supposedly corrupt cop were nothing more than groundless gossip spread by people who didn't have his ability or charm. Although he occasionally showed poor judgement (Derek and Gary were just one of many such examples) Joe had been one of the best cops in the division. His conviction rate was one of the highest in the country, and he had refused promotion on numerous occasions, preferring to stay a detective. He had little use for the bullshit politics that seemed to grow ever more abundantly the higher you climbed the tree.

Becky finally let me go. 'You can stay as long as you like. It'll be nice to have a little company now the girls have gone back to university. How about a cup of coffee?'

Coffee sounded good.

'Why don't you go into the lounge, then?'

I followed Joe into a room at the front of the house, collapsing in an settee that seemed to be larger than my car. It was like being enveloped in a large, leathery marshmallow, and as I shifted my position, the thing squeaked and squalled beneath me. Eventually I was comfortable – too comfortable. A lot had happened in the last couple of days and I could feel my eyelids drooping underneath the weight of it all. From the direction of the kitchen, I could hear Becky humming to herself as she clinked mugs and boiled water. There was a picture on the coffee table. I picked it up and studied it, finding myself looking at a group of women. Three rows of ten, to be exact, tallest at the back, the front row seated so that nobody obscured anybody else. They were all young, and their faces were a mixture of expressions: ambition, hope, relief. I turned the picture over, wondering if there was a list of names. Instead, there was a hand-written note: *Me and the gang – Rotten Row, Class of '78.*

I looked at Joe and raised my eyebrows.

'It's Becky's graduating class from nursing school,' he said. 'I think she's in the back row, on the left.'

Becky swept into the room, carrying two mugs of coffee. 'Oh, for goodness sake, you're not looking at that old thing, are you?' She passed out the drinks and took the picture from my hand, turning it so that she could examine it. 'That was taken about a hundred years ago.'

'Joe said that it was your nursing class.'

She shot her husband a vexed look. 'Not my nursing, but my midwifery.' She pointed with a nail that had also been painted a light shade of cerise. 'That's me there. The two women on my left are my friends Myra Dollar and Bessie Longfellow. . .'

Something rang in my mind and I looked at Joe, surprised that he hadn't heard the same set of bells. 'Didn't Sophie Sloan say that she used to know Becky? Back in the day?'

Joe nearly dropped his coffee cup. 'That's right! I completely forgot.'

Becky was looking from one of us to the other. 'Sophie Sloan? What's going on?'

Joe explained. 'Sophie Sloan. She's a client. Used to be a nurse at the R.A.H. She said that she used to know you.'

'I don't remember her.'

'Her husband runs a local nursing home. Inch Meadows.'

'I've heard of the place.' Becky sat where she was, her fingernail still touching the glass of the photoframe. 'Was she in Cardiology?'

'I don't think so. I don't know how she knew you.'

'I'll try and remember her.'

But the expression on her face wasn't hopeful.

10.3.

I spent a little time napping and drifting around the house, the events of the past twelve hours catching up with me. Joe wasn't much better; after another long night of drinking, he'd finally locked the Harald and Ginsel people into a deal. He popped out for an hour in the afternoon and returned with five hundred cash, which he gave to me. I tried not to take it, only to be rebuffed.

'Shut up. I was going to give you a bonus anyway. It should tide you over for a couple of weeks.'

Later in the afternoon, I borrowed Becky's car – a smart little Mini convertible that was a huge amount of fun to drive but made me feel like a male hairdresser – and made my way to my flat, or rather, what was left of it. Apart from the ceiling of the unoccupied flat below, the rest of the tenement was undamaged, although a vile smell of burned plastic filled the landings. I passed Crazy Cat Lady on the stairs; she harrumphed and gave me a look that I suspect was intended to stop my heart in its tracks. By the time I had made my way up both flights, I was breathing heavily and wishing for Nurse Harriet's oxygen. I guessed it would take a couple of days to flush the smoke out of my lungs.

There was a policeman standing outside the blackened ruin that had been my front door. He told me that the fire investigators had left. Because the fire had burned so quickly and fiercely, it had consumed what there was for fuel before dying out almost as rapidly as it began. After some sweet-talking, he let me have a look inside.

It was pretty fucking grim.

Just about everything I owned had been destroyed. I floated through the rooms, hardly hearing the warnings about being careful I didn't fall through the floor. My CD collection had been reduced to a pile of melted plastic, with the occasionally recognisable scrap of casing. I picked one up and gave a hollow little laugh: Dan Reed Network's 'The Heat'. My books were nothing but a pile of ash, the settee a blackened husk. It seemed like a lifetime ago that Liz and I had laughed and made love on that very same sofa. Next to it was a charred lump that was out of place with my memories. It took a few seconds before I realised what it was: my denims. Liz had helped me out of them less than twenty four hours ago. I picked the remnants up. They were sodden from water the fire brigade had sprayed into the place, and it took brief seconds for them disintegrate into a soggy mush. As they fell to pieces, I was left holding what remained of my wallet. On the outside, it was badly damaged, but it had been made of good quality leather. Maybe I had been lucky. I peeked inside, handling it as gently as I had ever handled a piece of physical evidence, ready for the contents to dissolve the way the jeans had, hoping against hope that my photograph of Mark had survived.

It had.

I drew it out with steady fingers, surgeon's fingers. It had been taken on his fourth birthday, him sitting on my knee and stuffing his face with cake. Audrey hovered in the background, the very top of her head missing because she had misjudged how long she had to position herself before the automatic timer made the shot. I have – had – many pictures of him, but this one was my favourite because it was one of the three of us together, and every time I looked at it I was reminded of better days. After the accident, the press had somehow got hold of a copy of the picture, and it had been featured in several of the national newspapers.

I held it up to the light, the detritus of my life forgotten. Sure, the edges were scorched and black, but everything else was fine. In it, we were smiling. It had been a good day. Audrey and I seemed to have managed to put our differences to one side, and were joking and laughing the way we had when we first met. Mark had been a joy, delighting in his presents and the sense of occasion. We'd taken him to Edinburgh zoo to see the penguin parade.

I looked at it for a long time before I realised that I was crying.

10.4.

I found one other thing before calling it quits. My keys had been in the lock of the front door when the whole thing went up in flames. Although the door was destroyed, the fitting for the lock appeared to have survived. The key-ring itself – a leather swatch that Mark had 'given' me for Father's day – was nothing more than a dried out scrag of dust and ash, but the keys themselves looked to be alright. I took the key for my car and the key for the office. The rest I abandoned. I had no use for them. My only regret was that I was unable to use them to close the door on this part of my life.

10.5.

I caught up with Jason Campbell in the pub.

Actually, that wasn't not quite true. Jason lived Jordanhill, a part of the city that was too posh to be classified as the West End and too affluent to count as a suburb. It was less than three miles from what remained of my flat in Craghill, but just as the river divided the two areas in a geographical sense, wealth – or the lack of it – illustrated the differences between the two neighbourhoods. Jordanhill was rich. Craghill wasn't.

I checked his house first. Apart from the time he spent in the secure Psych unit, Jason had grown up in his mother's three story mansion on Jordanhill Road. Except it wasn't so much on the road as back from the road, directly in the middle of two acres of grounds. In a city where a goddamn parking space recently sold for more than sixty-eight thousand pounds, two acres was more than just a garden. It was a fucking republic.

I'd expected there to be some form of controlled entry, but there had been nothing; just an open front gate, which I breezed straight through. A driveway of white gravel – at least, it looked like gravel to my untrained eye, but for all I knew might have been the pulverised bones of paupers – crunched underneath the tyres of my Golf as I cruised slowly up a gentle hill toward the house. Surrounded on both sides by tall hedges the driveway was slightly curved, making me conclude that it eventually looped back on itself and led back to the main entrance.

Soon I was out of sight from any passing traffic. Good. I brought the car to a halt in the shadow of a beech tree and decided to walk the rest of the way.

The Mercedes was parked diagonally outside the front door of the house, buried up to the wheel rims in white stones. Whoever had last driven it had stopped in a hurry. As I passed the windows of the dining room, I kept my eyes peeled for any sense of movement, but saw nothing. I climbed a short flight of stone steps, stepped into a vestibule and rang the doorbell.

Nothing.

I listened carefully, hoping for a sign there was somebody home, hearing only the hum of traffic from the main road and the breeze as it shuffled the leaves on the trees. I bent down and gently pushed the letterbox open, pressing my ear to it, unconcerned that I was committing a grievous invasion of privacy. If somebody were to open the door now, there could be no justification for what I was doing. I would look like a tawdry little snooper.

Never mind. They do say that the best form of defence is offence. If Jason had opened the door, I planned to go in hard and fast, striking first with no intention of asking questions later.

Even as I stood there with my ear pressed against the cold metal, I heard nothing. No music, no running water, not even the settling noises old houses like to make at the end of the day. After thirty seconds I was pretty sure that nobody was home.

But that didn't mean there was nothing to learn. The vestibule was small, really nothing more than an alcove for visitors to shelter from the rain while they waited for the front door to be answered. I was standing on a dusty mat that might have once been a deep vibrant red, but over the seasons had faded to a wan shade of pink. Tucked in the corner was an empty umbrella stand, and because I was bending down, my back cricked and my ear against the cold metal of the letterbox, I could see directly behind it, which is something a less inquisitive person would not have been able to do.

Tucked behind the umbrella stand was an envelope. Quickly, I fished it out and opened it. Jason's handwriting was small and almost impossible to read, the ink frequently blotching then fading. It was as if a dozen spiders had run across the page, and for the first time in my life I wondered if there was something in the theory that penmanship was indicative of character.

Betty

I'm writing this now because I'll probably be too bladdered to remember to write it when I get home – I'm going to watch the game in the Anchor. Please would you spend your time in the kitchen, dining room and living room, and don't use the Hoover or washing machine because I need my rest! Here's your monthly 'bonus', and as always, I appreciate your discretion.

Jason.

Clipped to the note were five twenty pound notes, which I slipped into my wallet, figuring the bastard owed me for what he had done to my flat. 'Betty' was obviously some kind of cleaning woman, and I wondered how much discretion she needed to display to earn such a substantial monthly bonus.

I hesitated on the doorstep, planning my next move. It would be easy enough to break into the house and wait for Jason to come home. I could spend my time sniffing through his underwear drawer. Not tempting, but if he owned a secret stash of kiddie porn, underneath his stained boxers was an obvious hiding place. I also wondered what I would learn if I was to mess about with the computer that I would almost certainly find; no doubt it would be the kind of thing the police would be interested in. Guys like Jason never change their spots, developing instead more and more ways to camouflage their activities. Even if I didn't find anything, I could always hook up to the Internet and spend a while downloading the kind of images that would send Jason straight back to Barlinnie. Go directly to jail, do not pass go, do not stop to admire your collection of dirty pictures.

In the end, though, I decided against it. Jason might not be alone when he returned from the pub. Just because I wanted to have a little chat didn't mean that I wanted to involve any third party in our little quarrel. Plus I knew where he was; the Anchor was less than three hundred yards away. I made my way quickly back to the car, suddenly deciding that I deserved a pint. It had, after all, been a rough day.

10.6.

The Anchor was on the corner of Jordanhill Road and McTeague Street, and was a fairly typical Glasgow pub. Its full name was John's Anchor, and although the bar had been there since the late thirties, it had absolutely no connection with Glasgow's shipbuilding history. Instead, local legend claimed that it had originally been named

Kinniver's, after the first landlord, John Kinniver. All his life John had wanted to emigrate to America, but his wife Florence persuaded him to remain in Scotland and open a pub. She got her way in the end, selfishly dying of influenza just after John had ploughed their entire nest-egg into the bar. He always planned to sell up when the place showed a profit, but the depression and the war put paid to that. He tried to find a buyer, but nobody was interested. In the late fifties, he gave up on his dreams of a new life abroad and changed the name of his bar to John's Anchor, in reference to his late wife – as in, 'The fucking bitch hung an anchor around my neck.'

Of course, now it was owned by one of these chains that strive to make their pubs all things to all people, and in doing so manage to suck dry any charm and individuality a place once had. A chalkboard on the wall inside the door advertised the different theme nights. Ladies Night. Karaoke Night. Seventies Night. And let's not forget the Family Afternoon, where if you bought a main course you could have a child's course absolutely FREE!

Tonight was Football Night, and the place was packed. Two men for every girl, and the girls could be subdivided into actual fans and ones that had tagged along with their boyfriends. Every table and barstool was occupied, and those that couldn't find a seat had to stand. As well as the projector screen, there were numerous plasma televisions scattered throughout the bar, meaning that wherever you looked you could enjoy the antics of twenty-two overpaid little upstarts who would earn more in a week than I probably would in my life. Every touch of the ball and run for position was criticised and commented upon by the audience. Opinions were freely offered and rejected. I had no idea who was playing who, and cared even less. I took my time as I shouldered my way through the crowd, keeping an eye out for my quarry. If he spotted me and panicked, that was fine. If he remained oblivious to my presence, even better.

In the end, I nearly tripped over him. It was nearly three deep at the bar, but suddenly the crowd did an unpredictable little shuffle, leaving me standing less than two feet from his back. I tried to keep my distance, but as people ebbed and flowed around me, I was forced behind him. If he looked round, he would see my face six inches from his own. Although a confrontation at this point was not part of my plans, it would be entertaining to see how he would react.

His head was tilted to the right, fixated on the nearest television screen. His hair was secured in a tight little pony-tail that made him look like a photographer that specialised in porn-masquerading-as-art. In his right hand was a half empty bottle of beer. A friend once told me that the reason beer manufacturers placed labels on the necks of their bottles was so that their brand name wouldn't be obscured by the hands of the consumer as they held the bottle. I wondered how the advertising people at Budweiser would feel if they discovered that Bud Ice was the beer of choice for the discerning paedophile arsonist.

Probably not very happy.

I sidled round to Jason's left, managing to place a buffer between us without losing my place at the bar. Catching the bartender's eye, I ordered a pint of Guinness, trying to pitch my voice low enough to avoid attracting Jason's attention and loud enough not to force the bartender to ask me to repeat myself. Sixty seconds later, a drink was placed in front of me.

Guinness is important. Every man likes to receive a bit of head from time to time, but there is such a thing as too much. This was one of those times. The bartender – a speccy, spotty student who looked like he might be studying social sciences en route to a deeply productive career as a social worker – had poured at least two inches of foam on the top of my pint. Had I not been acutely conscious of causing a scene and attracting unwanted attention, I would have said something. He banged the till and handed me my change, ignoring my dirty look, already concentrating on the next order. Defeated, I made my way over to the quietest corner of the place I could find that still had a view of Jason, and sipped my pint.

The damn thing tasted like it had been watered down.

10.7.

An hour later, the football was over. Somebody won. Somebody else lost. I didn't care; most of my attention had been focused on Jason. It was gratifying to observe that in a bar full of friendly faces, he seemed completely alone. Nobody talked to him, nobody looked at him, and nobody clapped him on the shoulder or commiserated with him when one of the players scored the winning goal. I wondered if people subconsciously *knew* he was an unpleasant person; if he somehow exuded a fundamental sense of wrong that kept him separate him from the rest of the world, the same way that a pack of dogs can sense when one of their own has turned rabid.

Nobody spoke to me either. Perhaps Jason wasn't the only person who seemed out of place.

Five minutes after the final whistle, Jason was on the move. He finished his drink and left the pub. Thirty seconds later, I followed, keeping to the shadows as much as possible. It had started to drizzle, and my jacket – one I had purchased from a nearby supermarket that very afternoon – turned out to be as waterproof as toilet paper. Before long I was soaked to the skin, and the chill of the night quickly set in. If Jason was out for any length of time, I was probably going to catch pneumonia. Liz would get the afternoon playmate she claimed to want.

I had thought that Jason would head straight home, but I was wrong. Instead of turning right when he stepped out of the pub, he turned left and started to head further up Jordanhill Road. The streets were quiet but not deserted – a few late night voyagers wandered the streets, and the occasional taxi splashed through the shallow puddles at the edge of the road. I kept my distance, making no particular effort to be quiet and somehow managing to be quiet anyway.

I was going to hurt him. I *needed* to hurt him.

I needed him to understand just how angry I was, to look into my face and know fear. I wanted him to look into my eyes and know how it was to be seconds from death.

I wanted him to suffer.

It wouldn't be enough, of course. In those desperate minutes before escaping the flat I had been frightened not just for myself but for Liz as well. Jason had nobody, so he had nobody to lose. And even if he did, I had no intention of putting them in harm's way, the way Jason had with Liz. I might be a petty, vindictive bastard, but I'm not completely without a conscience. Whatever happened between Jason and I was strictly between the two of us.

I had no idea what I was going to do.

We made our way through the sleeping streets, past the silent houses and late night travellers. Jason walked at a reasonable pace, but he seemed aimless, zigzagging up one sidestreet and down the other, his attention focused on his mobile phone as he tap-tap-tapped a text message. After twenty minutes, I estimated that we had covered just over half a mile as the crow flew, heading in the general direction of the city centre. I half-expected him to flag down one of the many passing taxis, in which case everything would be over. He didn't. He just kept cruising the streets, a man with no particular place to go and all the time in the world to get there.

After another five minutes, he turned onto Dumbarton Road. Kelvingrove Park was on his left. His pace slowed even further, and I could see his head bobbing as he glanced around. I was about fifty yards back, so I crossed the road and ducked behind a parked car. Not a moment too soon, either. I barely got myself under cover when he did a complete three-sixty, taking his time about it. For a second I thought he saw me anyway. I dipped my head out of sight, convinced that he would panic and run. After a slow count of ten, I popped my head back up. I was just in time to see him climb over the wall that surrounded the park and disappear into the shadows.

In seconds, I was up and across the road. The wall was high, about six feet, but there was a small energy substation that served as an ideal starter platform for the would-be intruder. I climbed on top, managing to hook my arms over the top of the wall, scrabbling with my feet to find purchase. It was easier than I had expected. Some of the stones themselves had eroded, creating small footholds, and it took only a few seconds for me to scramble over.

I stood where I had landed, in complete darkness, feeling the earth beneath my shoes, smelling the soil and the air. It was different, somehow. Cleaner. I like to think that parks are separate from the rest of the city, somehow existing in their own place and time. The traffic and the noise and the kebab shops were behind me, and I was alone with nature.

And Jason, of course. I didn't intend to forget about him.

10.8.

I listened intently. The undergrowth was heavy, and if I didn't get a fix on my target I would lose him. After a few seconds I was able to tune out the ambient noise of the traffic and focus on other things. . . the soft hoot of an owl, the skittering of some small animal running for cover. . . and footsteps, in front and slightly to the right, fading into the distance. I moved quickly, the wet earth quickly soaking through my cheap trainers as I bulldozed my way through the shrubs and the trees and the long grass. Before I had gone twenty yards I burst onto a small path. The going was easier now, and I broke into a jog, my trainers squishing softly as the first few paces forced the worst of the moisture out of the soles. Before long, I was able to make out Jason, a darker silhouette flitting among the shadows. My hip was starting to ache, and I slowed my pace slightly.

There were no lights, but I didn't need them. As my eyes adjusted to the dark I was able to see more and more. The path curved in a shallow loop as it climbed a slight incline. The trees were thinning out, and as we got higher, more and more of the city became visible. In the middle ground, I could see the river Clyde as it picked its way across the landscape winding through the warzone that was Craghill. The redundant shipyards with their idle cranes were a reminder of better days. Further upstream I could make out the Merchant city, expensive flats for rich people who would piss and moan about having the destitution and dereliction of the defunct industrial belt on their doorstep, unaware that the very things that made them rich also gave birth to such poverty. For them, Craghill was just a shortcut to pass through in their Audi's and BMW's; a convenient route to somewhere else where they could dispose of their disposable incomes; cappuccino bars and frapaccino lounges and retail outlet stores where they could buy cut-price designer handbags for fifty times the amount a child in the third-world earned making the damn things in the first place.

Further south was the suburbs: Castlemilk and Clarkeston, Giffnock and Graemestone, rich and poor, chalk and cheese. I couldn't tell where one district ended and another began. The view was beautiful: softly glowing lights shimmering in the darkness. If I hadn't known the city like an ex-lover, I would have been impressed.

From a distance, I guess that anything can look good.

10.9.

Two minutes later, I realised that Jason wasn't out to appreciate the scenery. The path opened out into a small parking area, lined with trees and trash buckets. A car was parked at one end. A crowd of onlookers surrounded it. There were four of them, one at each window, noses pressed to the glass, hands forming a pair of blinkers on each side of their faces to cut down on ambient glare. When I figured out what was going on, I was simultaneously disgusted, amused and intrigued.

Doggers.

Of course, I'd heard of it. I'd read the disapproving articles in the *Daily Mail* with my tongue firmly in my cheek, somewhat sceptical that such a tawdry practice could have managed to insinuate itself in our culture. The idea of providing a free sex show for the entertainment of strangers was fundamentally weird, and even with the dubious thrill of having an audience I really couldn't see the appeal of having sex in a Fiat Punto. Most of my teenage sexual encounters had consisted of an uncomfortable grope in whatever car my mother had owned at the time. It didn't matter if we used the front or the back seat; there just wasn't enough room for my six-foot five inches of spotty hormonal lust. In one memorable incident I managed to persuade my willing partner to bend over the bonnet of the car. I was busy giving her the business when the handbrake cable snapped. The car rolled forward, nearly flattening us both and killing the mood outright.

I watched as Jason walked to the car with a spring in his step. One of the watchers looked up and raised a hand in recognition before shifting a few inches to one side, creating a space. As Jason slipped in next to him, the man – he was fat and short and looked like a Star Trek fan – patted him on the shoulder. They were friends, or at least acquaintances. That explained Jason's compulsive message checking: he'd been waiting for information on his rendezvous.

I drifted into the shadows behind a tree and watched the show. The passenger side window was open just a crack, and from it came a variety of sounds: thumping, creaking, the occasional moan and muttered curse. I wasn't close enough to see much more than the rocking of the suspension and the occasional outline of a flailing limb, like a drowning octopus, and I honestly can't say I regretted it.

After about ten minutes, the moans and thuds ceased. The engine started and the car drove away into the night. I wondered who they were. A married couple desperate to spice things up but too cautious to try swinging? A couple cheating on their respective partners, the whole thing giving them an even bigger thrill? I decided that I was happier not knowing.

Now that it was over, I half expected the watchers to linger, perhaps analysing the performance the way people discuss a movie. It didn't happen. The tail lights had barely disappeared into the night when three of the men started walking – two in the same direction the car had taken, the other simply disappearing, presumably along a path similar to the one on which I had followed Jason. The park was a rabbit warren of tiny little trails and tracks. In less than two minutes, all that was left was Jason and his tubby little friend. They seemed to be talking about something, so I kept my head down and duck-walked a little closer, keeping a tree between us. Unless I did something stupid like stepped on a dry twig or a hedgehog or something, I would remain undetected. I strained my ears to make out what they were saying.

Turned out, I needn't have bothered.

'. . . doesn't light properly. I'll need to get it replaced, but I'm holding off until after the summer.'

'I had a combi-boiler installed last year.'

'Are they any good?'

'They're alright. Make a lot of noise. . .'

What a disappointment. It was depressing to learn that sexual deviants are just as boring as the rest of us.

10.11.

Ten minutes of suicidally dull chit-chat later, they said their good-byes. By then, I had learned that Star Trek fan's name was Liam and he lived with his mother. I could probably have figured out that particular detail on my own.

Liam started off in the same direction as the car. Jason went back the way he came, passing perilously close to my hiding place. Luckily the tree was one of those oaks that grow to about ten thousand years old and looked big enough to house an entire army of Ewoks. As he passed, I sidled around the trunk. The light drizzle that I had cursed was now my ally; the leaves underneath my feet were damp enough not to rustle as I shuffled through them. In seconds, he was thirty yards away. I fell in behind him, closing the gap quickly. Now was the time to make my move. It was the middle of the night, and given that the park was supposed to be closed to the general public, the only people in the immediate vicinity were unlikely to be fine upstanding citizens. Jason would have to shout very loudly and run very quickly before finding anybody that would help him.

I had no intention of allowing him to do so.

He hummed as he walked, some tune that I remembered Daryl Hannah whistling in a Tarantino movie a few years back. In the movie, she'd been dressed as a nurse, on her way to give a lethal injection to Uma Thurman, who was in a coma in some hospital. Daryl had looked damn fine, and Uma had made the sexiest coma victim I'd ever seen.

Talk about irony. It should have been me singing the song, because I was the one playing the Daryl Hannah role. Instead of a lethal injection, all I had was my fists, but it didn't matter. By the time I was done, Jason was going to wish he was in a fucking coma.

Or dead.

Tired, bored, and cold, I decided that it was time to act. There wasn't a soul around for five hundred yards, and it was unlikely I would get such a clear window of opportunity again. Jason was twenty yards in front of me. I broke into a jog, closing the distance rapidly. At ten yards I accelerated to a run, ignoring the yowl of protest from my hip. He heard me and started to turn. Too slow. He got halfway round before I hit him amidships in a savage tackle, burrowing my shoulder into the soft part between his waist and his ribcage. I ploughed straight through him like a bowling ball picking up a spare, hardly losing momentum, my feet getting ahead of me, running faster to compensate. The run turned into a stumble and then it all became too much; my knee buckled and I was sprawling, throwing my hands out to stop the fall, the tiny jagged stones chewing through the flesh of my outstretched palms like cheese in a grater. I ignored the pain, rolling to my feet and turning. Jason was behind me, head down, on hands and knees, coughing. I ran at him, driving the side of my foot into his stomach like I was punting a rugby ball and going for a world record in distance. His arms and legs collapsed and he went face down in the dirt. I straddled him, grabbing him by that stupid little pony-tail and jerking his head up, bending his spine in a backwards arch. He screamed and coughed, spraying saliva. There was dirt on his cheek. I screamed at him. 'Jason, you bastard! Why'd you do it?'

'I haven't got any money! Don't hurt me!'

'You prick! That was my flat! My stuff! My girlfriend!'

'What! What flat? What stuff?'

I turned his head halfway round, jamming his cheek into the soil, leaning forward so that he could see me. His eyes were crazy and wide. But then, so were mine, probably. 'You burned down my flat. You fucking burned up all my stuff.'

He started to shake his head from side to side. 'I swear, I didn't. I didn't touch your fucking flat.'

'You were there, you piece of shit. I fucking saw you!'

'I was never anywhere near your flat! I don't know where you live,' he blubbered. 'I don't even know your fucking name!'

I pressed down on his shoulders, driving him further into the ground. He screamed. My mind was an abyss, filled only with the gladiatorial roar of conquest, the barbarian in me proud of my revenge. As it had been on the night of the accident, all my common sense was gone and only the adrenaline was left. I wanted to hurt him. I wanted kill him. I wanted to make the cunt cry like a baby. I seized his arm and forced it up his back. He screamed again, but this time it wasn't fear but pain.

'Please! PLEASE!'

Something click/crunched in his shoulder and he howled. I eased off, just a fraction, leaning close into his ear. 'I saw you, you turd.'

'Saw me do what, ya fuckin' psycho? I don't know what you're talking about. I swear. Don't hurt me anymore.'

I was about a heartbeat away from an aneurysm. 'DON'T FUCKING LIE TO ME!'

'I'm not lying. Whatever you think I did, I didn't.'

'Liar.' I reapplied pressure on the arm, jamming it further and further toward his shoulders until I felt the bone itself bend, just the tiniest fraction, seeking a compromise I had no intention of giving. By now, Jason had quit screaming. Instead he was making a high pitched mewing sound, like a nest of starving chicks. He sucked air desperately, his eyes bulging with terror.

And then it broke.

And so did he. His eyes rolled like the tumblers on a fruit machine before coming up empty, his body going limp beneath me as he passed out from the pain.

10.12.

I waited and listened, planning to fade into the background if there was any indication that our scuffle had attracted anybody's attention. It hadn't. The moon slid out from behind the clouds, and the silence, broken by the sound of anger and pain, healed itself. I made a slow count to a hundred, the only noise the patter of falling water.

It was just me, Jason and the rain.

He lay at my feet. I pressed my finger to his neck, feeling a faint but steady pulse. Still alive. How wonderful for society.

On the edge of the path was a brightly coloured yellow bin. Grimacing with distaste, I rummaged for a few seconds, finding what I was looking for wrapped in a brown paper bag underneath an empty pizza box. I removed it from the bin and examined it. Mississippi Steamer. Pineapple flavour. High in alcohol content and low in price, the beverage of choice for the city's homeless alcoholics and dis-enfranchised teens. Also known as Jakey Juice. There was still at least half a litre of fluid swishing around in the bottle. Wishing I had some gloves, I unscrewed the cap and sniffed. The stench of spoiled fruit juice caused my eyes to water and my stomach to grumble.

Jason was still unconscious at my feet. I rolled him onto his back and upended the bottle, pouring the contents over him, starting at the top and working my way down, making sure that not a drop was wasted. Then I reversed my grip on the bottle, holding it by the neck as I smashed it on the edge of the trash bin, leaving me with the world's most popular makeshift weapon. Moonlight glittered as it bounced off the jagged edges.

Behind me, Jason moaned.

I turned to face him. His eyelids were fluttering. Both hands moved to wipe the stuff off his cheeks, but only one of them made it. The other flapped uselessly at his side, like a bird with a broken wing. He whinnied in pain. I got down so that his head was almost between my knees, the damp seeping through the material of my budget denims. With my left hand, I pinched his earlobe as hard as I could, causing his eyes to spring open. They were muddy and confused. That would never do.

I wanted – *needed* – Jason's complete and undivided attention.

By leaning over him, I could encircle his throat with my left hand, driving my thumb and forefinger deep into the flesh. His good hand grasped weakly at my wrist. I ignored it. With my right hand I skimmed the remains of the bottle in front of his face and explained how I planned to use it to remove his eyeballs if he didn't stop fucking around.

He got the point, going limp immediately. His eyes tracked the jagged glass. I waved the bottle at him, using it as a visual aid to underline my words. 'I don't particularly want to kill you, but I should warn you that doing so would not be the tragedy that you no doubt think it to be. I suspect that very few people would miss you.' A thought struck me. 'Although I'm quite sure that Betty the Cleaner would miss the regular bonuses. What is it you do that makes her discretion so appreciated?'

He didn't answer quickly enough, so I sliced a tiny line into the skin of his forehead, quickly subduing his lamentable attempt to struggle. The shallower the wound, the more it bleeds, and this one was no exception. Within seconds, his forehead was smeared red. I used the sleeve of my jacket to wipe it away, wishing that I had thought to wear gloves. 'Seriously, what's the deal between you and Betty?'

into his forehead, the skin dimpling and then puncturing, a tiny bead
of blood swelling from the perforation. 'And?'

'And she knows lots of girls.' He saw the look in my eye. 'Not kids.
The ones that are over sixteen. Sometimes I go and pick her up and
she. . . introduces me.'

'You're kidding me.' I found myself seriously considering cutting
his face off. It was only the fear of finding something even less
pleasant underneath that stopped me.

He shrugged. 'You wouldn't believe what these kids are like. Since
the Internet was invented, all people want to do is have sex. I'm not
committing any crime.

'You are if they're under eighteen.'

His eyes flickered left, and then right. 'They're not. All sixth
formers.'

'I guess that makes you a stand-up guy. I wish I had a sister so that
I could give you her phone number,' I said. 'Besides, I know that you're
fucking lying to me. You said sixteen first of all. I bet you think that if
the shit goes down and you end up in court you can argue that they
looked eighteen. You can turn those big puppy dog eyes in the
direction of the jury and explain how you're actually the victim? How
some nasty, morally bankrupt girl lied to a man no doubt grieving
the death of his dear sainted mother, who made the mistake of turning to a comely young lady for comfort and emotional support. Is that
about right?'

He said nothing. He didn't need to.

'Jason, you're a scumbag. I hate to be so plain, but there you go.
When I spoke to you yesterday afternoon, I was just passing on what
everybody thinks of you. There was no need for you to do what you
did.'

'What I did. . . I didn't do anything.'

— 252 —

'Yes, you did,' I said patiently. 'You followed me home and burned down my flat. Last night.' I patted him affectionately on the cheek. 'I don't mind – it was a shithole, really – but I was in it at the time. As was a close friend of mine. Now I can understand why you might hold a grudge, but seriously, all you did was demonstrate the sort of stupidity and ineptitude that got you locked up in the first place, and by putting my friend's life in danger you made yourself much more important to me than you originally were.'

'I swear, I don't know what you're talking about.'

'Jason, I saw you.'

'You didn't. I was at home last night. I had no where else to be.'

'Bullshit. I suppose it was just a co-incidence that your car was parked down the street when my flat went up in flames.'

He tried to shake his head, but I held him down. 'I don't know. I didn't burn your flat down. I swear it. I can't be the only person in Glasgow who drives a Mercedes.'

'You're the only one who's threatened to kill me in the past forty-eight hours. And that's quite a coinkydink, isn't it?'

We carried on like this for another five minutes or so. He kept denying it, and I kept pressing him. Eventually I dropped the matter, deciding that I had made my point. I found his mobile phone in his inside pocket and checked the display. Three bars; good reception. He wouldn't have any difficulty phoning for an ambulance.

I told him that I was going to let him go – on two conditions. He nodded. Anything.

'One. Move the fuck out of Glasgow. You've got money, so it won't be a problem. If I don't see your house in the property pages by this time next week I'm going to find you and break your other arm. Alright?'

Alright.

'Two. You might be entertaining some silly ideas about revenge. It's alright to think these things, but to act on them would be very, very silly. There are so many things I could do to you. I have so many friends that can act on my behalf. I have friends in the police department, I have friends on the street. You got off easy tonight. Your arm will heal. I could have happily taken a hammer to your joints, but I like to think of myself as a kind person. Fuck with me again, I'll do something you won't walk away from. Understand?'

He understood. I tossed his mobile phone onto the ground next to him. 'Phone an ambulance. Tell them that you tripped and fell. They won't believe you, but that's their problem and not yours. You mention my name, I'll kill you. Do you think I'm kidding?'

He didn't.

Chapter 11

Friday 21st November

11.1

I woke up the next morning a changed man. My lungs, which had spent the last twenty-four hours feeling like a deployed airbag, felt clean and refreshed. The air seemed to shimmer with the promise the new day had to offer. It was time to move on from all the shit that had been holding me back. Instead of thinking of the loss of my flat as a tragedy, I would see it as an excuse to move on. I would find somewhere better. Nicer. Christ knew, it wouldn't be hard. I was a lucky man. I had a great job with a good boss. A nice girlfriend. A beautiful son. It was time to stop wallowing in self-pity and start getting on with my life.

I hummed as I shaved

After the excitement of the past couple of days, it was good to get back to what passed for normal in my life. Joe and I spent the morning in the office, going through the nuts-and-bolts work that comprised maybe seventy percent of his business. Sophie Sloan wasn't the only active case we were investigating. We had several other clients, all of whom believed they were more important than anybody else. I spent most of my time on the telephone, chasing down avenues as they wound their way into various blind alleys and dead ends.

I wanted to show Joe how much I appreciated the bed and the loan, so I took him out to lunch. We ended up spending the afternoon in the pub, playing pool and talking bullshit, the line between employer and employee becoming ever more blurred as the drinks flowed. After his third drink, Joe mentioned something that caught my attention.

'You ever think about the future, Cameron?'

I lined up a stripe, aiming for the corner pocket. 'Not really. I find that it happens soon enough.'

'I think about it a lot. I'm going to be a granddad soon. You find yourself wanting to leave something behind. Not just money, but more. A. . . a *legacy*, if you will. An empire.'

'An *empire*?' I straightened, clapping my hand to my cheek and pretending to be concerned. 'Joe. . . are you dying?'

'Fuck off.'

'It's just that you sounded very serious for a second. I thought you were going to tell me that you had a terminal disease.' I eyed the glass in his hand. 'Like liver failure.'

'I *am* serious. I've been thinking about expanding the business to include a diligence department.'

Even though I wasn't really concentrating on the game, I bent to the shot again. 'What, like Sheriff Officers?'

'And Messengers at Arms. I've got the contacts; I think it would be a good little moneyspinner.'

Sheriff Officers and Messengers were the Scottish version of Baillifs, only with significantly more legal power. It wasn't a popular job, but neither was it a bad one. I shot. Missed. The cue-ball bounced awkwardly and hid against the top cushion.

Joe sighed and shook his head. 'You're shite at this.'

'Yeah, well, I never claimed to be Steve bloody Davies, did I?'

Joe leaned down and cued up, aiming for an almost-impossible yellow at the opposite end of the table. 'I'd need to have somebody to run the department.'

It wasn't often I didn't know what to say. '. . . Are you serious?'

He looked up at me. 'You'd have to do the exams. Once you passed them, I'd form a separate company. We'd be partners. Not *equal* partners, 'cos I'd be the money, and would take a bigger chunk of the profits, but there would be enough to go around. We recruit people as we need them, and you can run it.'

'Christ, Joe. . . that's a hell of an offer.' I was so moved, I had to look away for a second. 'Why would you offer something like that to a guy like me?'

He shrugged. 'I like you. I liked your dad.'

I took a few minutes. I'd always known that Joe and my dad had been pals, but he'd never really talked about it. I wondered if Joe had made the offer out of some misplaced sense of obligation, and said so.

'Bullshit.'

'So why me, then?'

'Like I said, I like you. More importantly, I trust you. Never do business with somebody you don't trust.'

'How do you know you can trust me?'

Joe looked me straight in the eye and made his shot without taking his gaze from mine. 'Because I only ever pick winners.'

I knew the effect he was going for, of course; even men over the age of fifty occasionally aspire for a moment of Scorsese-inspired cool. Unfortunately, it didn't work out the way he planned it. The cue ball trickled slowly down the table and rolled sedately past its target. Joe looked stricken.

I couldn't help but laugh. 'I hope you're better at business than you are at pool.'

11.2.

The boy walked quickly, his rucksack over one shoulder, the knees of his trousers stained dark with lunchtime playground mud. His lower lip was set in a pout he had inherited from his mother. He was angry. It was mummy's fault he was walking. She'd been late four times that week, rolling up at the school gates after all the other mummies had been and gone. It wasn't fair; the other children had started calling him the boy that nobody wanted. Just yesterday, his favourite teacher, Miss Kenwood, had offered him a lift and he'd had to say no because he knew that if he just waited just a little while longer, his mother would arrive. And he was right: ten minutes later she showed up in a bad mood and yelled at him for not fastening his seatbelt quickly enough.

He hated her. She wasn't like the other mothers, who smiled and laughed and wore pretty dresses and smelled of flowers. Instead, she smelled of cigarettes and mobile phones and she never stopped telling him that she gave up her career so that she could look after him.

This afternoon, when she'd been late again, he'd started walking. He knew that it was naughty – he'd been told he must wait – and decided that he didn't care. Just for once, she could be the one who waited outside the school gates in the rain. He was a big boy and could find his own way home, and if she got a fright then maybe she would show up at the same time as all the other mothers. Maybe he should stay out all night, and when he finally came home she would give him a big cuddle and tell him that she was sorry that she was late and sorry for making him stand in the rain all by himself and then all the other kids would stop laughing at him.

Behind him, a car beeped its horn. He turned and looked over his shoulder, watching as it pulled level with him, the window sliding down. 'Mark! Hello.'

Mark stopped and said nothing. They'd talked about Stranger Danger at school.

'I was just driving past and I saw you there. Your mummy asked me to give you a lift because she's late.'

'She's always late.'

'I know. She's very sorry. She asked me to buy you a Big Mac to show you just how sorry she is.'

'I don't know you.'

'I'm a friend of your mummy's.'

'I've never seen you before.'

'I know. But I know your mummy, and your daddy. I'm friends with them both.'

'Where's my dad? Where's Auntie Lynne?'

'Your dad's at work. I don't know where Auntie Lynne is.'

Mark shook his head and looked round. 'I don't know you. They said that if I didn't know who it was then I wasn't to get into the car.'

'I know. And you're very clever and a very good boy. But your mummy can't come and collect you today. She told me to show you this.'

There was something in the driver's hand: a picture. Mark recognised it at once; him, mummy and daddy. They'd gone to the zoo that day and watched the penguin parade. It was the last day that the three of them had done anything together. Then daddy had his accident and everything had changed.

He stepped forward and took the picture. 'Are you a friend of mummy's?'

'I'm a friend of both your mummy and your daddy.'

'Why isn't daddy here?'

'He's working.'

'That's a nice car.'

'Thank you.'

'My daddy has a Golf. Mummy has a Land Rover.'

'I know. I've seen them. They're not as nice as mine, are they?'

'How fast can it go?'

'A thousand miles an hour.'

'Really?'

'Really.'

Mark didn't know what to do. He didn't know this person, but they claimed to know him, and they had a photograph. Strangers were bad. They wanted to do bad things to him. He didn't know the exact nature of the bad things, but his friend Josh had told him that some people had a beast living inside of them that made them do nasty stuff to kids. They would bite him and watch him bleed and then throw him off a bridge with his head bashed in and his pockets full of stones. The police might catch them, but it didn't really matter, because they just told the judge about the beast inside that controlled them and made them do things that they didn't really want to and instead of going to prison for ever and *ever, they were sent to a special hospital where they got electric shocks that were supposed to cure them but didn't and then they had their names put on a list and then they were allowed to go home and kill again.*

He looked carefully at the person behind the wheel. 'Are you on the File?'

'The what?'

'It's a list of bad people.'

'No, I'm not.'

'I shouldn't get in a car with a stranger.'

'Of course you shouldn't. But I'm not a stranger. I'm a friend of your mum and dad's. Just the other day your dad was telling me that he'd like me to meet you.'

'Are you his new friend? The one that was coming to play Laser Quest with us?'

'Why, yes. Yes, I am.'

Mark shrugged his shoulders and got into the car.

11.3

We drifted back to the office at about quarter to five, making our way through the streets of Glasgow, checking out the girls and laughing at the students. The weekend was approaching fast and I'd already made plans. I had phoned Audrey just to let her know I was still alive and intended seeing Mark as the two of us had previously agreed. She'd sounded disappointed but I felt it was unlikely she would mess me around the way she had last weekend. Her attitude might have been different if the media had known the truth about the fire, but for once I seemed to have caught a break so far, all the reports made the incident sound like nothing more than an accident. My plan was to take Mark to the hospital to meet Liz, and then on to Laser Quest as promised. I even managed to get Audrey to agree to let me take him out for a proper meal – 'As long as you go to a place where there's menus and cutlery and salad.'

I was thinking Pizza Hut. Both Mark and my wallet would appreciate it.

Back at the office, the two of us got in the lift and pressed the button for the fourth floor, sagging against the walls as the doors closed. Joe checked he had enough change for a taxi home. I did the same, before realising I no longer had a home to go to.

The concept didn't seem as depressing as it had yesterday.

After a few moments, the lift reached its destination, the doors sliding open to reveal the foyer we shared with the accountants next door to us. A man was leaning against the wall beside the artificial Yucca plant. He watched Joe take out his keys.

'Excuse me, are you Mr Banks?'

Surprise guests are rarely welcome in this business. Upon hearing his name, Joe reflexively dipped his hand to his pocket, where I knew he kept a set of knuckle-dusters. I slipped my own hand into my jacket, surreptitiously feeling for the metal links of my trusty dog lead. Joe said, 'Do I know you?'

The man's tone was not aggressive. 'I think you know my wife.'

We both relaxed slightly, although Joe kept his hand where it was. 'How can I help you?'

'I want to know why she hired you.'

'I'm afraid we're not in a position to talk about our work.'

'Please, you have to help me. I'm worried about her.'

Joe looked over his shoulder and caught my eye. I could tell what he was thinking: more than likely the man was worried about getting caught shagging his secretary, or sister, or golf buddy. 'As I said, we can't discuss our cases.'

'I'll pay you for your time.'

Joe shook his head. 'It's a clear conflict of interest. I won't help you.'

The man turned his attention to me. 'Please. I want to know what's going on. She's spent a fortune, and I don't know what it's for.'

Joe moved past him. 'Perhaps you better ask her. They say that honesty's the best policy when it comes to marriage.'

As I moved to follow Joe, the man stopped me by putting his hand on my shoulder. 'Please. I need some help.'

I removed the hand, my grip firm but not designed to hurt. 'Whatever it is you have to say, say it to your wife.'

His face twisted in distress. 'I would, except I can't find her.'

Before I could stop myself, I said, 'What's her name?'

Joe shot me a dirty look, his message clear. It didn't matter what her name was.

Except it did.

The man said 'Sophie Sloan.'

11.4.

In the months I had worked for Joe, I had never known a subject of one of his investigations show up on the doorstep. From the look on his face, neither had Joe. He quickly went on the defensive. 'Mr Sloan, I really can't confirm whether or not your wife is a client of ours. If she's missing, I suggest that you contact the police and file a report.'

Sloan held his hands up, palms outwards. 'I'm not here to pick a fight. I just want to know that she's alright. I know that she paid a large sum of money to your company a few days ago.'

'How would you know that?' Joe asked.

'It's a shared account. Both our names. I was able to see who the cheque had been paid to.'

Sighing, Joe shook his head. He stuck his key in the lock and opened the door. 'How long has she been missing?'

'Since yesterday. I was in London on business. I came home,' the man shrugged and turned his palms up. 'She was gone.'

'I guess you better come in. Cameron, will you make some coffee? I have a feeling that we're going to need some.'

The three of us made our way into the office. I tossed my jacket over my chair and proceeded to the kitchen, where I filled the kettle and spooned coffee into the pot. While I waited for the water to boil, I leaned on the door frame, taking a good look at the man we were being paid to spy on. For somebody that was supposed to be shagging his sister-in-law, Ian Sloan was a fairly normal-looking guy. Slightly older than his wife, he wore a suit jacket over a pair of battered jeans and a corduroy shirt. No tie. For some reason, I found myself thinking he looked like the resident professional of the kind of golf club that didn't pride itself on petty discrimination. His voice was soft and filled with concern for the welfare of his wife. Together, they would have made a good-looking couple, the kind of people who would bicker cheerily over the distribution of the Sunday papers while discussing the ideal wine to have with dinner.

Joe hung his jacket on the coat stand and perched on the corner of my desk. 'So she's been missing for twenty-four hours?'

'I'm not sure how long she's been gone,' Sloan said. He sat down on one of the leather settees that served as our waiting area, leaning forward and propping both elbows on his knees, rubbing his eyes with the heels of his hands. It was a gesture of fundamental exhaustion. 'I last spoke to her on the telephone on Wednesday evening. It was a pretty strange conversation.'

'Strange how, Mr Sloan?'

He shook his head, the gesture more confused than negative. 'I couldn't put my finger on it. At first, I thought she had been drinking, but she didn't sound drunk. She sounded. . . distant. Like she was far, far away.'

'Do you mean far, far away in a geographical sense, like she was out of the country, or do you mean it in a. . . a. . .' Joe looked to me for help.

I finished for him. 'Far away in an emotional sense?'

Sloan nodded enthusiastically. 'It was almost like talking to a different person. You know that we lost our little boy?'

Neither Joe or myself said anything. To admit as much was to admit that Sophie was a client.

Our silence went unnoticed, a meaningless blip on the radar of the man's grief. 'He died of leukaemia. Horrible thing. That was nine months ago. He was seven.' Sloan's eyes were distant, perhaps remembering a happier time when his son wasn't dead and his wife wasn't missing, presumed crazy.

Joe said, 'We're sorry for your loss.'

Sloan waved a hand impatiently. 'She was devastated. We both were, but her more so. She was a full time mum, you see, and then all of a sudden she was made redundant. I still had my work, and she resented the fact that I had something to fill the time with.'

I remembered the first time we had met Sophie, and how she had told the same story from the opposite viewpoint.

Behind me, the kettle reached the boil. I quickly filled the pot. So far, all Ian had done was confirm Sophie's story, albeit from his own side of the fence. I left the coffee to percolate and went back to my position at the doorway. In the ten seconds I was gone, Sloan hadn't moved from his defeated slump. His voice was that of somebody who had just survived a major disaster.

'I asked her what was wrong. She wouldn't tell me, not at first, but I persisted. Then she said that she wanted a divorce. I couldn't believe it. I know that couples who lose a child frequently have problems, but the thing was that I thought they were the kind of things that the two of us would face together. I never thought that I was part of the problem.'

He raised his head. 'She's never really got over Luke's death. I would come home from work to find her sitting in his bedroom. He had this toy, this stuffed tiger. . . it was his favourite. . . and she would sit on his bed with it on her knee for hours at a time, just stroking the fur. One day I was downstairs when I heard her voice. I went up, thinking she was talking to me, but she wasn't. She was reading *The Wind in the Willows*, just like she did when she was telling Luke a bedtime story. I didn't know what to say, so I just closed the door and left her to it.'

Joe said, 'You said that you last spoke to her on the telephone? Where were you at the time?'

'In London. At a business conference. I wasn't meant to return until tomorrow, but I was so worried about her I couldn't sleep. I tried to phone her all yesterday, but couldn't get in touch. I made the decision to rent a car and drive overnight. I got back early this morning and there's no trace of her.'

'Where have you looked?'

'Everywhere I can think of. We don't have many friends and I've spoken to them all. Her sister hasn't seen her since Wednesday afternoon.'

'What about her mobile phone?' Joe said. 'Assuming she has one.'

'You know she does,' Sloan said wearily. 'I keep trying it. Always switched off.'

There was a pad of paper sitting on my desk. Without taking his eyes off the man in front of him, Joe scribbled a brief note, probably reminding himself to try the number Sophie had given us the second her husband left. 'What made you think to try the bank account?'

Sloan shrugged. 'I wondered if she had decided to leave me. I thought maybe she had holed up in a hotel somewhere and I might be able to find out where she was.'

'And there was nothing?'

'The cheque she gave you the other day. Also, she made a cash withdrawal on Wednesday afternoon. Five hundred pounds.'

Joe caught my eye again. I could tell what he was thinking. Sloan was convincing. If his concern for his wife was a performance purely for our benefit, then he was a damn fine actor. Unfortunately, the fact remained that Sophie Sloan was a client, and as such we were limited in what we could do.

I spoke first. 'Mr Sloan, I'm sure that you can understand our concerns. We have a professional reputation to maintain, and we certainly can't hand over confidential information. . .'

Sloan burst in. 'Is she in trouble? Is that it? Is she being black-mailed? I saw a film once where a woman hired professional investigators to find out who it was that was trying to blackmail her. Maybe the five hundred pounds is a. . . a down payment?'

Joe said, 'Five hundred pounds isn't a very large sum of money. And besides, do you think your wife had anything she might prefer to keep secret?'

'What kind of thing?'

He took a deep breath. 'I don't know. That would be why it would be a secret.'

From my place at the doorway, I said, 'Mr Sloan, everybody has things they would rather other people didn't find out about.' I was bitterly aware of my own experience. 'Maybe she has a drunk driving conviction, or she posed for Fiesta, or. . .' I spread my hands, as if by doing so I could demonstrate the breadth of possibility.

Sloan wiped a hand across his brow. 'I don't know. She's not a. . . a well woman. She has a history of psychological problems. Some of it stemmed back to her childhood – she had an abusive father, and she took a great deal of drugs when she was a teenager – but the rest. . .' He shook his head slowly. 'I don't know. Anti-depressants. Uppers. Downers. There were days when she was great, but there were others when she could barely function. And ever since Luke died, she's been on some kind of downward spiral. I've been terrified that she might do something stupid. She told me a few months ago that she had thought of abducting a new-born baby from the Maternity Hospital. Said she had a plan and everything. At the time I thought she was kidding, but now I'm not so sure. . .'

Joe and I looked at each other. Neither of us knew what to say.

11.5.

In the car, it was child versus adult. Adult was losing.

'I want a Big Mac. You promised me a Big Mac.'

'I know. But there isn't a McDonalds for miles around.'

'There is. There's one around the corner. I saw it.'

'It's closed.'

'There was cars outside. I saw them, too.'

'*They've run out of Big Macs.*'
'*They never run out of Big Macs.*'
'*They do sometimes.*'
'*No they don't!*'
'*Yes they. . .*' Deep breath. Dontgetangrydontgetangrydontgetangry.
'*Where are we going?*'
'*Home.*'
'*This isn't the way home.*'
'*It's a short cut.*'
'*No, it isn't.*'
'*It's a game.*'
'*What game?*'
'*Hide and seek.*'
'*But we're not hiding. We're driving.*'
'*It's special rules. We get to use a car.*'
'*Is my daddy playing?*'
Gritted teeth. '*I told you. He's at work.*'
'*He's good at hide and seek. He always knows where I'm hiding.*'
'*Maybe this time we'll beat him.*'
'*I don't think so. He's good at finding people.*'
'*I bet he won't find us.*'
'*I bet he will.*'
'*I bet he won't.*'
'*Where are we going?*'
'*To a special hiding place.*'
'*What's so special about it?*'
'*Nobody will ever find us.*'
'*My daddy will.*'
'*I doubt it.*'
'*He will.*'
'*. . . And so on.*'

11.6.

Sloan broke the silence. 'I'm worried that she might have done something stupid. One time I came home to find a suicide note on the kitchen table. It was little more than a few words along the lines of goodbye, cruel world, but it scared the hell out of me. I ran upstairs expecting to find her floating in the bathtub with her wrists open or something.'

'But you didn't,' Joe said.

'No. I didn't, I found her on the bed with a bottle of paracetamol in her hand. I shook her, asked her how many she had taken. She just laughed in my face. I grabbed the bottle and opened it. There were meant to be a hundred and when I counted them, I got ninety-three. I was livid. I didn't know if she had taken the seven and I had disturbed her, or if she had just used the bloody thing as a prop. That's the thing about stuff like this. You don't know if they're serious or if they're just doing it for the attention.'

Briefly, I recalled my own pathetic little suicide attempt. Since then, I'd asked myself the same question a number of times.

Sloan continued. 'I've always tried to be a good husband. I've been patient with her, tried to understand. . . tried to make allowances, but it's been hard.'

How hard, I wondered. Hard enough to drive him into the arms of the sister?

Joe stood up, picked up the cordless phone from my desk. With infinite gentleness, he said, 'Ian, I think you need to contact the police.'

Sloan nodded and reached out for it. Just as his fingertips made contact, my mobile phone rang. His hand jerked in shock. The two of them watched me check the caller I.D.

Audrey. I sighed as I flipped the phone open. As usual, she sounded pissed off about something. 'Where's Mark?'

'I don't know.'

'Don't fuck me around. Where is he?'

'Audrey, I don't know what you're talking about.'

'He was supposed to be waiting for me to collect him after school. He's not there. I've driven all over the fucking place. I spoke to some old git who says he saw a boy like Mark getting into a blue car. Your shit-heap Golf is blue. Where is he?'

A cold thread of fear twisted inside my belly. 'Audrey, I don't have him. I swear.'

Either she didn't listen, or she didn't hear. 'I can't believe you would stoop so low. I mean, I know I'm not going to win mother of the year, but I would never have done something like this to you.'

'Audrey. . .'

'If you don't put him on the phone this minute, I'm going to call the police. You'll be charged with child abduction or child endangerment or whatever the fuck it is and I'll make sure that you never see him again as long as you live.'

'Audrey, are you saying that somebody saw him getting in a car? With a stranger?'

'Somebody saw him getting in *your* car, you bastard.'

'Audrey, I don't have him. Phone the police. Do it now, and then stay at home. I'm coming over.' I handed the phone back to Joe. 'I have to go. Mark's gone missing.'

I left quickly, but not so quickly that I missed the look that passed between Joe and Ian Sloan.

11.7.

Constable Malcolm Jenkins looked at the man and thought, pretentious old bastard.

The old bastard in question was about seventy, wearing a white silk shirt underneath a tweed jacket with leather patches on the elbows. And a cravat, by God! In twenty-seven years on the force, Jenkins had never actually seen a cravat, had believed them to be a fictional item of apparel created by eighteenth century romantic novelists to make their limpid heroes a tad more dashing. It was a jaunty number, tartan, scarlet and emerald green, tied in a foppish little knot around the old git's scrawny chicken neck.

He checked his notebook. 'So, Mr. . . Carruthers. . .'

'Please, just call me Anderson.' The man's voice was clipped and precise. He had claimed to be a retired English teacher. Jenkins, who in his youth had hated the English, teachers, and English teachers, had absolutely no doubt it was true.

Anderson fucking Carruthers, he thought. Jesus wept. 'So what time was it you saw the lad in question?'

'Let me see. . . I took Monty for a walk when Countdown finished. I guess it would have been about twenty past four.'

'You're sure about that?'

Carruthers bridled. 'Quite sure, Constable.'

It was just after seven pm. The two of them were sitting on red leather armchairs in Carruthers' living room, which was overflowing with ornamental plates and pewter pots and a whole load of other tat specifically designed to appeal to pretentious old bastards between the ages of sixty and eighty. It was like leafing through the back pages of the People's Friend, thought Jenkins. The walls were covered in Official Princess Diana Commemorative tea towels and cross-stitches of West Highland Terriers poking furry snouts out from straw baskets.

He passed over the photograph that he had been given by his Sergeant less than forty minutes ago. 'And you're sure it was this lad?'

'I'm fairly certain. I always take Monty into the park, so I was about a hundred and fifty yards away.'

Monty was a real West Highland Terrier, lying on the rug like a hairy rat. Instead of a collar, it was wearing a tartan neckerchief that bore a suspicious resemblance to its owner's cravat. Every time Jenkins shifted his weight, it bared its teeth at him. He fought the urge to step on it. 'That's quite a distance, Mr Carruthers.'

'What are you implying?'

Jenkins sighed silently. Why did he always have to get the irritable coffin dodgers? 'I'm not implying anything, sir. A hundred and fifty yards is quite a distance. I'm not sure I could recognise somebody from there.'

'I'm certain it was the boy.'

'What was he wearing at the time?'

Carruthers looked at Jenkins as if the younger man was an idiot. 'School uniform, of course. Grey trousers. One of those hooded tops.'

'You mean a hoodie?'

'It was a hooded top, officer. I deplore the habit of deliberately shortening words for no apparent reason. I'm quite sure you wouldn't appreciate your name being abbreviated to Malkie.'

And I'm quite sure you wouldn't appreciate your name being abbreviated to Cunt, thought Jenkins. He wondered if he should point out that Monty was obviously a shortened version of Montgomery before deciding that like almost all teachers – retired or not – Carruthers would remain completely oblivious to his own hypocrisy. 'What colour was the hoo. . . the hooded top?'

'Black.'

According to the missing boy's mother, he had been wearing a black hoodie. That conveniently narrowed it down to about eighty percent of the population under the age of twenty-five.

'Mr Carruthers, I need you to tell me exactly what happened.'

'Like I said, I was out walking Monty. I saw the boy talking to some-body in a car. They talked for maybe five minutes, then the boy got in the car and they drove away.'

'Where was this?'

'On the corner between Hawthorne Avenue and Skella Road.'

'Did you see the person driving the car?'

'I did not.'

'Not at all?'

'Not at all.'

'What kind of car was it?'

'It was blue.'

Jenkins took a deep breath. 'What kind of car was it?'

'I don't know. It looked foreign. Not British.'

Jenkins thought about asking the man to clarify Britishness, decided he was happier not knowing. 'But you couldn't tell me the make?'

'No.'

'Was it big or little?'

'Medium.'

'Was it a hatchback? A coupe? A saloon?'

'What's a coupe?'

'It's. . .' He had no idea. 'Just describe the shape of it, if you can.'

'It looked fast. Expensive. It wasn't the kind of car a poor man could afford, if you know what I mean.'

Jenkins sighed. For somebody who obviously prided himself on his ability to dot i's and cross t's, Carruthers had the observational skills of Stevie Wonder on Valium. 'Sir, is there anything of value you could tell me about the car?'

'It had one of those silly little roofs on it.'

'What do you mean?'

'The kind that slides up and down.'

'I see.' Jenkins scratched a note on his pad. 'What happened then?'

'They drove away.'

'And nothing struck you as being unusual?'

'No. I didn't think anything of it.'

'And it was only when Mark's mother stopped you in the street fifteen minutes later did you think there might be a problem?'

The old man nodded. 'Is that the boy's name?'

'Yes. Mark Stone.'

'I'm surprised he isn't called something like Phoenix, or Diesel, or Agamemnon. People today give their children such stupid names. It shouldn't be allowed.'

'I quite agree, Anderson,' Jenkins replied. 'Where were you when she stopped you?'

'Just outside the house. She hit the brakes so hard she nearly clipped the curb. Started yammering on, had I seen her little boy?'

'And you told her what you had seen?'

'Of course. She got very upset.' Carruthers' tone was vaguely surprised. 'Seemed to be quite angry with me for some reason.'

'I'm sure she was just worried about her child.'

'That's no reason to be rude. She was quite the cheeky little madam. No wedding ring on her finger, either.'

Jenkins let it go. 'The blue car. Had you ever seen it before today? Maybe cruising round the neighbourhood like it was looking for something?'

Or someone?

The old man thought about it. 'Maybe. Maybe not. I'm not the kind of person that catalogues every vehicle that goes past, Constable.'

Of course you're not, Jenkins thought. Probably too busy watching Countdown and complaining to Monty about the number of immigrants. He stood up. 'Well, thanks for your time, Mr Carruthers.'

'Has the boy been abducted, do you think?'

'It's too early to be sure. Give us a call if you remember anything else.'

'I will.' Carruthers showed the police officer to the door. 'I'm sure he'll turn up. Give him a clip round the ear and a telling off and he'll learn not to do it again. We're too protective of our children these days. We wrap them in cotton wool and think that we can protect them from the world. We didn't do that in my day. Promote independence, that's the key to bringing up children.'

'Do you have any kids, Mr Carruthers?'

'I never married.'

'I see.' Jenkins put his cap on, wondering who the hell had done all the cross-stitches that hung in the living room. 'I'll certainly pass on your parenting tips to the boy's mother.'

He was sure they would provide a great deal of comfort if he'd been raped and murdered by a paedophile.

11.8.

I was going to kill him.

Arnold the Surgeon sat next to the woman I once thought I was going to marry, the fingers of his left hand entwined with hers in a manner that conveyed possession rather than support. He wore canvas trousers, sandals, and a blue short-sleeved shirt. Designer glasses dangled from the breast pocket by a wiry, almost-invisible leg. I could feel him examining my cheap denims and even cheaper T-shirt (Motto: Fat Men Do It By The Pound), but every time we made eye contact he would flick his gaze into the corner of the room. The prick.

I was going to kill him because he was making a noise.

For the past ten minutes he had relentlessly clicked the top of a retractable ball-point pen. In, out, in, out. Every few seconds he would walk the pen around his knuckles so that it ended up back at the start, his thumb falling on the popper ready for another round.

Click-click. Click-click. Twirl. Click. Twirl-twirl-click-cli. . .

'Arnold?'

'What?'

Even his voice was annoying; rich in timbre with a lilting Inverness accent, it sounded like he was having his scrotum caressed by a latex-gloved scrub-nurse who did porno on the side.

I nodded at the pen. 'Do you mind?'

'Mind what?'

'The clicking. It's irritating.'

He blinked at me in surprise. 'The clicking?'

No *way* was this guy bright enough to be a surgeon. 'Yes. The clicking.'

He did it once more before putting the pen back on the coffee table. 'I'm sorry. It's just a habit I have.'

I smiled my thanks. Audrey glared at me. I smiled at her as well, and she looked away.

Completing our happy little gang of four was a police officer from the Family Liaison Unit, one of the most miserable, thankless specialities in the force. Janice Galloway was about forty, short for a copper, with dark hair scraped back from her face in a bun. Apart from a nose that looked to have been broken on a number of occasions, she was attractive enough. On the third finger of her left hand was a band of white skin where a wedding ring might have sat, and I found myself wondering if she was another casualty of failed relationships. Probably, I concluded. Why else would fate have set her sail on our particular ship of fools?

It was eight pm. Mark had been missing for more than four hours. His mother hadn't spoken to me for the last ninety minutes. It was about the only silver lining in one extremely large cloud.

The first two hours had been a blur. I'd checked every street, shopping arcade and public library within a two mile radius of Mark's school, even bribing a grumbling janitor thirty quid to look in every single class-room of Mark's primary school.

All to no avail.

Upon running out of ideas, I'd drifted over to Audrey's place, finding Arnold's four-by-four parked in the driveway and a police car in the street outside. The three of them brought me up to date, not that there was a lot to catch up on. Audrey had been twenty minutes late collecting Mark from school, he hadn't been there, she'd looked for him, finding instead an old man who claimed to have seen him getting into a blue car. Police had interviewed the gentleman in question and seemed to think his claims had some credibility.

The driver of the blue car was described as "unknown", a phrase guaranteed to strike fear into the heart of every parent in the world.

Upon being told that the blue car had been a foreign convertible, I pulled Galloway to one side and named Jason Campbell as a suspect, telling them that I had picked a fight with him without mentioning it had been at the request of a senior detective. I cast my mind back to last night's adventures in Kelvingrove Park; I'd genuinely believed I had broken Jason's arm, but maybe I had made a mistake. I racked my brain trying to remember whether or not Jason's Merc had been an automatic– difficult to drive with an arm in plaster, but not outwith the realms of possibility.

Sergeant Galloway had immediately called the details in. Since then, there had been nothing to do but wait – and like Tom Petty once said, the waiting was the hardest part.

Tension flowed through the room like the wind on a weather forecaster's map; a mixture of poison-ivy hate and anger between Audrey and myself, dislike from me to Arnold, disdain from Arnold to me. The separate currents of jealousy, hurt and failure were all underpinned by our worry for Mark.

Humans are one of the few species that mate for life. I couldn't help wondering if perhaps the animals were smarter.

My phone rang. The four of us leaned forward. I checked the number on the display. 'Joe.'

Audrey's scowl intensified. I ignored her, flipping my phone open. 'Hi.'

Joe didn't fuck around with casual conversation. 'Any sign?'

'Nothing yet.'

'Ok.' He clicked off.

No sooner had I tucked the phone back into my pocket when Audrey said, 'Do you think you could ask him not to ring?'

Beside her, Arnold had picked up the pen again. He hadn't clicked it yet, but I could tell the bastard was just itching to. He leaned over to peer at the puzzle magazine. Carol Vorderman was on the cover, leaning on the bonnet of a brand new car, banknotes falling from the sky like rain. I could win Up To Twenty-Five Thousand Pounds Worth Of Exciting Prizes. Carol's smile was so wide and inviting and artificial it made me want to kill her as well.

Arnold yawned. The fucker. My voice dripped acid. 'I do hope we're not keeping you up.'

'Cameron. . . ' Audrey said, a warning tone in her voice.

'No, it's no problem. Maybe he should go to bed. We wouldn't want him nodding off on the seventh green tomorrow.'

'Cameron, you're not helping.'

Maybe not. But it was good to see two red spots rise on the arsehole's cheeks. I couldn't tell if he was embarrassed or angry, and cared nothing either way. I'll admit it: getting a perverse thrill from buzzing the man's buttons was petty and small. That didn't stop it from feeling pretty damn good.

Then I looked at my shoes, ashamed of myself. I had nothing to feel good about. Mark was still missing.

11.9.

'I want my mummy!'

'Don't you want to play hide and seek any more?'

'I want my Mummy.'

'I'm afraid she's not here, sweetheart.'

'Mummy! Muuummm!' Small hands bunched themselves into even smaller fists. 'Muuuuuummmmmmy!'

'Shhhh'

'Where is she? Where is she?'

'She's hiding. Just like us.'

'I don't want to play any more. I don't want to play. WHERE'S MY MUMMY?'

'She's coming. She'll be here soon.'

'Why can't she be here now?'

'Because she's got a long way to travel. She was hiding too.'

'I don't like this game. It's cold.'

'Are you cold? Do you want some more of the blanket?'

'I want my mummy.'

'And she's coming. Here, look. Let me tuck you in.'

Mark squiggled. 'There isn't room.'

'There is if you lie very still.'

'I don't want to lie still. I want to go home. I miss my bed. I miss my posters. I miss Bart-Bart.'

'Who's Bart-Bart?'

'He's on a poster my bedroom wall. He's funny. Mummy always says goodnight to him as well as me.'

'Does your mummy ever sing you songs?'

A single shake of the head. Mummy never sang songs for anybody.

'I could sing you a song. Would you like that?'

Mark nodded. He would like that very much.

'Would you like a drink? I've got some Coca-Cola in little cans if you would like.'

Coca-Cola was another thing that Mark would like very much.

'Mummy says that I'm not allowed it. She says it's got too much sugar in it.'

'Then you better finish it before she gets here, then.'

Pop. Fizzle. Small amount of crushed white powder, tipped into the can from a cone made from an envelope.

Mark pointed with his finger. 'What's that?'

'It's extra sugar.'

'Cool.'

11.10.

In the living room, weather conditions had continued to deteriorate. Arnold the Prick had excused himself and gone to bed, citing an early morning triple bypass– it turned out he was a heart surgeon, not a plastic surgeon as I had once supposed. That didn't stop me thinking that the man was a complete tit. Audrey, subtle as ever, made show of wrapping her arms around his neck and clinging to him like ivy, whispering in a voice loud enough for everyone to hear that she would take strength from the knowledge that the man she loved was just few feet away. Arnold left the room with an air of smugness I associated with losing the battle but winning the war.

Stupid bastard. If he was serious about spending the rest of his life with Audrey, he better be like the Viet Cong and learn how to dig in for the long haul.

Now it was just me, her and Constable Galloway to act as a referee. The poor woman sat there and watched us score points off each other, like a spectator to a game of tennis played with verbal hand grenades.

Audrey crossed her legs with a calculated flash of thigh to remind me of things I could no longer possess. 'So how is Joe, then?'

'Fine.'

'And Becky?'

'Fine.'

'And the kids?'

'They're fine too.'

'I wonder how she puts up with him. I'd have kicked him out long ago.'

'I know. I mean, she had the perfect excuse when he had that heart attack.'

Just over two years ago, Joe had suffered a minor cardiac 'event' that had been just serious enough to allow him to leave the force on a full pension. Within two months of retirement, he was bored out of his mind and persuaded Backy to allow him to open the agency. The work proved the ideal compromise: exciting enough to keep him alive but not so stressful as to kill him.

'You've never forgiven me for that, have you?'

I decided not to answer. Her question implied that she still believed her actions were entirely reasonable.

'One thing I've always wondered, Aud. How did you meet Arnold? Was it before or after you decided that I was unsatisfactory husband material?'

Her face twisted viciously, and even before she answered I knew I wasn't going to like what I heard. 'We were together for six months before I left you.'

'Six months?'

'And before that, I had a brief fling with somebody else.'

'Who?'

'You didn't know them.'

Incredible. I shook my head, wondering how I could have been so blind. 'You two. . . triple-timing bitch.'

'Oh, don't get all self-righteous with me. You were so busy with your job that you didn't have any time with me. You practically encouraged me to have an affair.'

'How?'

'You told me that you didn't mind me having male friends.'

'And you took that as encouragement?'

'What was I supposed to think? You were so obsessed with your caseload I could have been sleeping with the entire city and you wouldn't have noticed.'

'It sounds like you *were* sleeping with the entire city.'

She looked at me coldly. 'Think what you like, but you drove me away. If you had given salvaging our relationship half the effort you put in to your job then we might still be together.'

'I wasn't aware that we needed to be salvaged! I thought we were cruising along in a calm sea!'

'Yeah, well, so was the *Titanic*, and then it hit that iceberg! That's what our relationship is like. It's drowned underneath three thousand feet of water with nothing but barnacles and camera crews from the Discovery channel to remind us of it.'

The nautical theme was becoming tiresome. 'You encouraged me! You pushed me to chase promotion. I told you again and again that I wanted to spend more time with you, and you just kept saying that it would be worth it in the end.'

'I knew that you wanted to make Detective. I was just trying to make you happy.'

'I wanted to be a father! I wanted to be a husband. *Your* husband!' I shook my head in disbelief. 'I can't believe you. You're twisting what happened and making yourself into the victim. You bitch. You stone cold, conniving little bitch.'

She opened her mouth, but before she could speak, my mobile phone rang. We put the hostilities on hold.

11.11.

Nothing much had changed in the Maternity Annex of the Princess Eugenie Hospital. The workload remained light, the nurses demotivated. Despite the fact that she was sitting directly in front of the telephone, Ellen Drysdale allowed it to ring four times before stretching over eighteen inches of barren desk-top to answer it. Before opening her mouth, she made sure to mark her place in the issue of Take a Break that was spread over her lap.

'Maternity, Staff Nurse speaking.'

'Hi. This is Joe Brown over at Estates Management.'

So what, Ellen though. Although she had never heard of him, she paid the name no heed. She examined her fingernails. They were getting kind of long. 'Uh huh?'

'There's been a security alert issued by the local police. A woman attempted to enter the Maternity Unit of Glasgow Royal and abduct a new-born.'

Ellen sat up in her chair, fingernails forgotten. She listened intently as the man claiming to be Joe Brown from Estate Management continued.

'The woman managed to obtain the access code for the unit and sneaked in unnoticed. She failed in her attempt to abduct a child, but there are concerns that she may try again. At police suggestion, we're doing an immediate security audit on all the hospital's controlled entry doors. There's going to be a memo coming round to remind people not to give out the codes for any controlled access doors to anybody who isn't a current member of staff.'

'Oh. . . right.'

'Anyhoo, that's going to take a couple of hours to organise. In the meantime, the powers that be have asked me to do a quick check on all the secure-access doors in the hospital, starting with Maternity.'

Her mouth was dry. 'Uh huh.'

'You're aware that Trust policy states that access codes need to be changed every two months?'

She wasn't, but the second that the muppets in charge of the trust realised that staff were beginning to understand the way the game was played, they changed the rules. 'That's right, yeah.'

'According to my records, the code for your unit hasn't been altered for the past ten months. The last registered change was made in January. One-zero-six-six.'

She shook her head. 'It's not that any more. It's been changed since then.'

'Can I ask why the alteration wasn't registered with security?'

'I'm sorry. I thought it had been.'

'When was it changed?'

'I think it was August.'

'Who's the ward manager?'

'Sister Janice Caldwell.'

'Can you ask her to make sure that all code-changes are registered with Estates?'

Ellen said that she would. The man wasted no time in hanging up, stating that he had a lot more calls to make. She placed the phone back in its cradle and gave a sigh of relief. She'd forgotten how lucky she had been, almost managing to wipe the memory of that night from her mind. Some people would do anything for a baby...

Within a few minutes, she'd gone back to her magazine. Some poor farmer's wife in Buckinghamshire had found that her husband had augmented the pigs' diet with the chopped-up remains of her ninety-year old mother.

11.12.

The screen on my phone said *Joe*. I stood up. 'It's the boss.'

Audrey said, 'Tell him to fuck off.'

Ignoring her, I made my way into the kitchen, flipping the handset open as I went.

'Hi.'

'Any news?'

'Nothing. Audrey sends her love.'

'You're not going to believe this.'

'What?'

'Sophie Sloan.'

'What about her?'

'She's the one who's got Mark. I'm sure of it.'

'Bullshit,' I said, but only because I felt like I had to say something. I said it again, stretching it for greater effect. 'Buulllllllshit.'

'It's not bullshit. After you left, I did some digging. Opened up quite a can of worms, I can tell you.'

I ignored the mixed metaphor. 'Like what?'

'I had a long chat with Ian Sloan. Get this: he freely admitted having an affair. Sophie knew all about it and didn't care.'

'Wait a minute. . . she knew her husband was having an affair? You sure about this?'

'I am. I spoke to the sister as well, and they're both singing from the same hymn sheet. Now, the question is, if Sophie Sloan knew that her husband was screwing around, why hire us?'

'Maybe she wanted proof? So that she could divorce him?'

'Come on, Cam. If she wanted proof, she'd have asked for it. She'd have wanted photographs and stuff like that. But she didn't, did she? Think about it; infidelity constitutes eighty percent of our work. Everybody knows that.'

'But why?'

'I don't know yet. But I think this woman's been stalking you from a distance. You know what stalkers are like. They get closer and closer. Her coming to the office was just her first attempt to initiate direct contact. She seized on the first thing she thought of as an excuse to meet you face to face.'

'Joe, that's crazy.'

'I know. But remember we both felt like she wasn't the most tightly wrapped of people? According to Ian, Sophie Sloan's got a season ticket to Fraggle Rock.'

Fraggle Rock was the nickname of a local psychiatric hospital. 'What do you mean, a season ticket?'

'I mean she's had four admissions in the past three years. There's been breakdowns. . . bipolar disorder. . . schizophrenia, paranoia. . . delusional behaviour. After you left, Ian and I had a long chat.'

Which had apparently led to them calling each other by their Christian names.

'He might be lying.'

'No way. I got Becky to make a few enquiries – she's still pretty well connected in the NHS. To put it bluntly, Sophie Sloan's madder than a sack of badgers.'

'She can't be that crazy or they would have kept her in.'

'Yeah, you'd think that, wouldn't you? I'm told that as long as she takes her meds, she's relatively O.K., and because she's never harmed anybody, they just stabilise her and send her home.'

It took me a few seconds to digest the information. 'Why the hell would she kidnap Mark?'

'There might not be a reason. If she's crazy, she doesn't need one. Insanity means never having to justify your actions.'

Fair enough. 'Go on.'

'Ian says that he's been concerned – well, more concerned than normal – about her mental health ever since their little boy died. He says that her behaviour has become increasingly bizarre.'

'Yeah, but that doesn't mean that she went out and kidnapped somebody. For goodness sake, Joe, this is clutching at straws. You once told me that by the power of theoretical thinking, you could make a plausible case for Jack the Ripper and Osama Bin Laden being the same person. This is what you're doing here, you're. . .'

'How old is Mark?'

The randomness of the question halted me in tracks. 'Five, Six in February.'

'About the same age as Luke.'

'So what does that mean? She's thinking that because they're the same age, then Mark's a. . . a. . . a replacement Luke? Joe, fucking Sunset Beach had more plausible plot lines.'

'There's something else. She told Ian that a few months ago that she had actually considered abducting a new-born baby from the hospital.'

'That's just talk.'

'He doesn't think so. She told him exactly how she planned to do it, and it didn't sound like she was going off half-cocked. From the way she described it to him, she put an awful lot of thought into it. She even knew the door-access code for the maternity wing at the hospital. It was easy for him to remember. Ten-sixty-six. The Battle Of Hastings.'

'Yeah, well she's obviously a very clever liar. All these details make the thing sound believable but can't be disproved.'

'Except that I phoned the maternity wing of the hospital. Guess what their door-access code was up until two months ago?'

I clutched the phone to my ear, already knowing what the answer was. Joe said, 'Ten-sixty-six. . . Cam? Cameron?'

'I'm still here.'

'What do you think about that?'

'I think I need to sit down.'

Audrey's kitchen was like something out of *Ideal Homes* magazine, all polished surfaces and artificial fruit. Halogen spots lit the whole place up like a mortuary. There was a breakfast nook in the corner by the back door, high-backed stools and a Formica counter. I lurched over and pulled one of the stools out, nearly falling off as I plonked myself down. Sick white light bounced off the waxy, artificial skins of a bowl of plastic apples. 'Joe. . . are you sure it's Sophie Sloan?'

'I think so.'

'But I've never done anything to her.'

'Like I said, if she's as crazy as her husband describes her, then she doesn't need a reason.'

'Joe, this is all speculation. There's got to be something else.'

'There is. Guess what car she drives?'

'Haven't a clue.'

'BMW. A convertible. Not quite a Mercedes, but similar enough to Jason Campbell's.' He paused for effect. 'And it's blue.'

11.13.

The boy went down like a sack of spuds.

Less than two minutes after finishing the doctored Coke, his head slumped forward onto his chest and his breathing deepened. His face, which had grown steadily more pinched and watchful as the hours had dragged on, had evened out, once again assuming the open innocence of childhood.

Sophie watched him sleep, her heart breaking.

What the hell was I thinking?

She felt like she was being torn in two. One part of her – the sensible part that crossed t's and dotted i's and somehow managed to lurch through the days with its hair brushed and its clothes on right-side in – knew that she had gone too far, that the coastline of reality was almost lost over the horizon.

The other part. . . well, that was a different matter. Tap-dancing beside her rational mind was a gibbering chimpanzee of pure, obsessive hate, bug-eyed and drooling with anger.

I'm going to finish it. Soon.

But the boy. . . he was so beautiful.

So was my child.

He was innocent.

So was my child.

11.14.

It took a few seconds for the penny to drop, metaphorically bouncing and spinning, taking forever to vibrate to a halt. Even then, my mind stuttered.

I remembered standing at the window of my burning flat, feeling the increasing tightness in my chest as I inhaled.

Smoke. Fear. The street. Litter blowing in the wind. Broken light bulb in the lamp-post. Lines and lines of parked cars.

A hooded figure running to a parked car. The angle had been steep and the light had been dim, making it impossible to gauge the arsonist's height or build – a fact that a good defence lawyer would have capitalised on.

Headlights flickering on, tyres squealing. I'd recognised the general shape of the car, and associated it with the wrong person.

Jason Campbell.

I hadn't *really* seen him. I'd seen a hooded figure jump into a convertible car and assumed.

And we all know what they say about making assumptions.

By doing so, I had made ass out of myself – and, just for a bonus, broken the arm of an innocent man.

Well. . . relatively innocent.

I clutched the phone. 'Joe, what the hell should I do?'

For once, he was silent.

'I mean, should I tell Audrey?'

'I think you have to.'

'But it'll just give her more reason to keep Mark away from me.'

'Listen, Cam, if Scotty had beamed Mark onto the bridge of the Starship Enterprise, she'd find a way of making it your fault. You need to focus on the bigger picture here. Is there a FPU officer there?'

'Yeah. Somebody called Janice Galloway.'

'I know her. She's good at what she does.'

'Good at what she does? All she's done is make coffee.'

'Let me talk to her.'

I slipped off my stool, making my way across the kitchen into the living area. Both women looked up as I entered. Galloway's eyes were significantly friendlier than Audrey's. I waved the phone at her. 'You know Joe Banks?'

She nodded.

'He's got a theory about who might have abducted Mark.'

She took the phone with a questioning expression on her face. Audrey looked like she was considering biting me. 'For God's sake, Cameron. What's going on?'

I sat down beside her. I had some explaining to do.

11.15.

Forty minutes later, I was on my merry way, driving the streets of Glasgow with no particular place to go. The night was unseasonably warm, causing the rear windscreen of the Golf to steam up. It didn't matter; I was disinclined to look behind me in case all I could see was burning bridges.

Audrey had taken the news in an entirely predictable fashion, remaining silent as I explained the Sophie Sloan case, her lips thinning to a blood-red slash, the vein in her temple growing more and more prominent. When I finished speaking, she started.

This was my fault.

Although it was obvious that the woman was mentally imbalanced, I had ignored the signs and deliberately placed Mark in harm's way.

I was never going to see him again.

Then she threw me out, which was actually something of a relief. I had my mobile phone. Why sit around being miserable and worried at my ex's house when I could be just as miserable and just as worried behind the wheel of my car? And at least there I would be doing something practical. The chances of running into Sophie and Mark were slim, but not non-existent.

I wondered where he was and how he was coping. Mark was a fairly bright kid, but he was so young, too young to be a pawn in a crazy game of chess. I hoped that wherever they were, she was treating him kindly, and that he wasn't too frightened.

Without a destination, I found myself drifting through the city as it put itself to bed. A light drizzle fell, causing the few pedestrians that loitered the streets to hunch their shoulders and share the occasional umbrella. It was the usual Monday-night suspects – couples making their way home from dates, older singletons returning from the weekly bingo pilgrimage. There was even a healthy amount of neds, munching on kebabs and swigging from bottles of Buckfast and Mad-Dog. Most of them were young, barely more than kids. As I hissed by on the damp road, a boy threw a bottle at the car, missing by a few inches, the bottle exploding on the pavement beside me. I shook my head and carried on, wondering how things could have turned out so badly.

It seemed like the world had taken a wrong turn somewhere. I hoped that the song was wrong and that children weren't the future, because if they were, then the future was looking pretty bleak. I worried about the kids wandering the streets when they should have been in bed. When I was sixteen, I'd had rules – in before ten on a school night, midnight on a Friday or a Saturday. No underage drinking, no hanging about street corners throwing half-bricks at the late night buses to see if we could get the driver to chase us.

Of course, I'd done my best to ignore the rules, screwing around, getting into trouble at every opportunity, but I had still been bound by the moral and ethical code that my parents had instilled in me. I never did drugs, I never hurt anybody. I was just a silly wee boy.

These kids, with their shell-suits and their iPods and their dead, glassy-eyed stares – they were different. They didn't give a fuck. About anything. They weren't out wandering the streets at all hours because they wanted to rebel against authority, because they had no authority to rebel against. They were out because they had nothing else to do. Their biological parents barely knew their names, their social workers told them what they should do but not how to do it. If they wanted to work, they could flip burgers in the service industry for minimum wage. Or they could go to college, get an education, except there was no point. They didn't have a chance. Children are like books: the longer they sit on the shelf, the more obscure and difficult to understand they become. Because nobody had ever taken the time to teach them, they were now unable to learn, with an attention span barely longer than the average MTV video. Because of the ongoing absence of authority in their lives, they lacked the discipline it required to sit still and actually learn anything, especially when you consider the fact that most of them could barely read and write. And even if they could, what the fuck for? So that they could be treated like shit for the rest of their lives before being made redundant at the age of fifty, shuffled to one side to make room for the next generation of wage-slaves?

I shouldn't think so much. I was just bringing myself down.

I checked my watch: twelve fifty. The Golf sat steady at thirty-one miles an hour, past the kebab shops and pubs and garage forecourts that had been turned into drug supercentres. I realised that I was hungry and turned into an all night supermarket, parking the car and checking my phone to make sure that I hadn't missed any messages. I hadn't. As I walked through the car-park I messed around with the ring-tones on my phone, making sure that I hadn't put it onto silent.

The supermarket was just another supermarket: bright lights, wide aisles, high shelves, James Morrison in the background whining about having a bad day. I'd like to meet him. I'd teach him about the concept of a bad day. Next to the front door was a chiller cabinet that had probably been filled with sandwiches. Now it was filled with empty space. In one corner was a lone packet of sushi; I decided I wasn't feeling that brave. I grabbed a packet of crisps and made my way to the checkout.

Then I spotted an old friend.

11.16.

He was perched on a high stool behind a till, running items across the automatic scanner, his expression one of intense concentration. His hands moved slowly, as if unsure of themselves. The name badge on the lapel of his blue polo shirt was Sean.

Sean. AKA Shabsy. AKA Celtic Bhouy, confidante and trusty side-kick to Flick-Knife.

His was the only checkout open, and he was busy serving a little old lady who leaned on the handle of a tartan shopping trolley. She had taken full advantage of the promotional offers on frozen meals, stacking at least two dozen cardboard boxes onto the conveyor belt. Behind her was a man with a trolley that seemed to contain about fifty tins of dog food. He took one look at my packet of cheese and onion. 'You can go in front of me if you want.'

I shook my head. 'I'm in no rush.'

'Suit yourself.'

We waited, shuffling our feet as Shabsy ponderously prodded at the buttons of the till as if they were electrified. Eventually he arrived at a total. 'Eighteen pounds sixty-five.'

'Are you sure?' The old lady said in a querulous voice.

'Yeah.'

'I think you made a mistake. It's buy-one-get-one-free, you know.'

Sean nervously touched the keypad. The till beeped at him in an accusing tone. 'I'm sorry, but the total's correct.'

'I won't be able to afford a taxi home.'

'You could always put some back.'

'Let me see what I have with me.'

It took her nearly a full minute to extract her purse from the very bottom the shopping trolley. When it finally creaked open, it appeared to be filled with coppers. After an eternity of fumbling, she waved a handful of change. 'Eighteen pounds twenty-three pence.'

'I need the whole amount. It's the rules.'

The old bat looked hopefully at Dog Food Man, who waved his credit card at her. Her gaze transferred to me. I studied the ventilation ducts. When it became apparent that no knight in shining armour was available, she huffed and turned her attention back to her purse, fiddling away before withdrawing a secret twenty pound note that she had for some reason folded into tiny squares and handing it over to Sean. He laboriously unfolded it and held it up to the light. I wondered if he knew what he was looking for. Dog Food man sighed, shook his head, and muttered something that ended in the word 'sake'. James Morrison faded out and James Blunt faded in. Another singer whose relentless optimism made my teeth itch. Eventually, Sean decided that the twenty pound note was real enough, putting it into the till and counting change with the speed of a plumber who revelled in the fact that getting paid by the hour was the greatest thing since sliced bread. The old woman watched him place the coins on the palm of her gloved hand, her eyes black specks in her wrinkled face.

As soon as she was on her way, Sean turned his attention to the man in front of me. He eyed the cans of Winalot and Pedigree Chum. 'Have you got a dog?'

The man sighed. 'No, son. I've got a restaurant.'

11.17.

Four minutes and thirty-five pounds later, it was my turn. Shabsy passed my packet of crisps over the magic eye of the scanner and said, 'Forty-eight pence.'

'How have you been, Shabsy?'

He looked up at the sound of my voice, his eyes widening as he recognised me. For a second I though he was going to run; his hands grabbed the edge of the checkout and his backside slid off the edge of the stool. I held my hands up. 'I'm not going to hurt you.'

'You're not?'

'If I had wanted to, I'd have waited until the end of your shift and followed you home, wouldn't I?'

He nodded slowly, his hand hovering in mid-air, my packet of crisps held between thumb and forefinger. 'What do you want?'

'How's your little buddy?'

'I haven't seen him for a few days.'

'I didn't know you worked nights.'

'I just started here.'

That explained the hesitancy while using the till. Then again, maybe it didn't; I had a sneaking suspicion that Shabsy would forever be slightly intimidated by anything that had more buttons than the hand-control to his games console. I reached out and took my crisps. 'You and I need to talk.'

'What about?'

'Many things. Shoes and ships and sealing wax and whether pigs have wings.'

'What?'

I'd forgotten; Shabsy had probably never heard of Lewis Carroll. 'I want to know how you knew my name.'

'I don't know.'

I glanced around. The place was almost deserted. Down one aisle a heavily pregnant woman was trying to build a pyramid of disposable nappies. I reached out and grabbed Shabsy by the neck of his polo shirt. 'Your friend. I want to know how he knew my fucking name.'

He pulled away, bumping his arse off the stool and overturning it, sending it to the ground with a clatter. The pregnant girl looked up briefly before returning to her building blocks. Shabsy smoothed his collar. 'Look, I don't want any trouble. I just got this job. I don't want to lose it in the first week.'

'I wouldn't have thought you were so career minded.'

'Look, I got a fright the other night, alright? Dave really meant to cut you. I don't want the jail.'

'So you're trying to go straight. How admirable.'

'Look, I'm sorry about what we did, pal. I really am. It was a stupid, dumb thing to do, and it went way too far. Come on, it's not like you didn't get your licks in. You broke Dave's thumb.'

'Dave? Is that his name? How can I find him?'

'I don't know.'

I considered grabbing him again, but before I could, a couple stepped around the corner of the opposite aisle and started making their way to the checkout. I held up a finger. 'You really want to keep this job?'

Shabsy nodded.

'When's your next break?'

'Twenty minutes.'

'I'll wait for you at the front door. If you're not there in half an hour then not only will you lose this job, but I'll use a few contacts to find out where you're staying. You ever been kneecapped?'

He shook his head.

'It's not very nice.'

I started to turn away. Shabsy said, 'Wait!'

I turned back. He pointed at the crisps in my left hand. 'That's forty-eight pence, please.'

I waved the packet at him. 'Think of them as compensation.'

11.18.

The car park was nearly empty. I'd shifted the Golf to a deserted little corner, close enough that I could keep an eye on the doors, far enough away to avoid undue attention.

Shabsy showed up twenty-eight minutes later. By then, I had eaten the crisps, tossed the packet and checked my telephone messages half a dozen times. They didn't take long to check, because there weren't any. I was listening to the end of the news on the radio when I saw him step out of the main door of the supermarket, zipping up his fleece and turning the collar up despite the warmth of the night. I honked the horn and flashed the headlights at him. He started to trudge over with the enthusiasm of a member of the French aristocracy asked to test the reliability of the guillotine.

I got out to greet him. 'I was beginning to think you weren't going to show up.'

He stuck a cigarette into his mouth. 'It crossed my mind.'

I walked round and opened the passenger door of the Golf. 'Don't bother lighting it.'

He tucked the cigarette behind his ear. 'Where are we going? I've only got fifteen minutes.'

'We're not going anywhere. We're just going to talk.'

He looked up at the sky, from which a light drizzle had began to fall. 'How do I know that you're not going to hurt me?'

'You don't. But I can guarantee two things. One, I can run faster than you. Two, better this than to spend the rest of your life looking over your shoulder.'

He took a deep breath and got in.

I slipped round to the driver's side and slid behind the wheel. He flinched when I reached across to turn the radio off. The two of us sat there in silence for a slow count of thirty. I wanted him to feel the need to break it.

He did. 'I don't know where Dave is. You hurt him bad, man. I had to take him to casualty. I think you even cracked a couple of ribs.'

I rubbed my thumb and forefinger together. 'You know what this is?'

'What?'

'It's the world's smallest. . . forget it. How did he know my name?'

'I don't know.'

I nodded at the cigarette tucked behind his ear. 'Maybe if I let you smoke that then your memory will improve.'

He reached around and removed it. 'Thanks, man. Got a light?'

'Sure.'

I pressed the button for the cigarette lighter.

11.19.

Ten seconds later, the lighter clicked to let me know it was ready. Ever the polite host, I used it light Shabsy's cigarette before sliding it home. He inhaled with enthusiasm. 'Cheers. Listen, it wasn't my idea to give you a kicking. I was just along for the ride.'

'So what happened? The two of you saw me walking home and just decided to chance your luck?'

He unwound the window and blew smoke outside. ' I don't really remember.'

'Try.'

'I'd dropped a wee bit of acid. Everything was kind of blurry.'

'I didn't think people still did acid.'

Shabsy shrugged, apparently unaware of the rapidly-approaching boundaries of my patience. I watched the car park, trying to figure out my next move. Trying to interview the monkey rather than the organ-grinder was a high-risk strategy at best. It would be simple enough to turn the kid upside down and shake him until something of value fell out, but I was getting tired of violence being a solution. Besides, even if I was able to get a location for 'Dave', it was unlikely he would be any smarter than his friend.

'Shabsy, how do things work between you and Dave? Are you equals? Thelma and Louise? Jay and Silent Bob? Or do you just stand there and look pretty while he does the real work?'

'I just hang around with Dave. Or at least, I did.'

'So you wouldn't necessarily know what his business plan was?'

He didn't answer. To be fair, it was a pretty stupid question. Based on observation, it seemed unlikely Shabsy knew what day it was, let alone be privy to the inner workings of what was obviously a highly complex criminal mind. 'Shabsy. . . what you and Dave did to me. . . what you tried to do to me. . . was it just something random? Did the pair of you just see me and decide I looked like an easy target?'

'It was Dave's idea to give you a doing.'

'He said something about it being 'Easy Money'. What did he mean by that?'

Shabsy shrugged.

'Did he mean my money? Or somebody else's?'

'Whassat?'

'Did somebody pay the two of you to hurt me?'

'It was all his idea.'

'It was Dave's idea to try and mug me?'

'Aye. He told me that you deserved a kicking.'

'Did he say why?'

No reply.

'So the pair of you were just hanging around outside. . . you see me walking down the street. . . Dave suddenly comes up with an idea about giving me a battering. . . and you thought, what the hell, it might be a bit of a giggle?' I fought the impulse to punch the side of his head. 'What are you, a sheep?'

'Hey, man, all I know is that the whole thing was Dave's idea. The two of us saw you, like we did almost every night, and he goes, "I heard that cunt killed a wee lassie, let's give him a doing." So we followed you into the close, and that's when. . .' He shrugged, as if to say, you know the rest.

'Didn't quite work out the way you planned it, did it?'

Shabsy gave me a sideways glance. 'Is it true? Did you kill a wee babby?'

I glared at him until he looked away. 'You just followed along like a good little foot soldier.'

'That's how it happened. It wasn't my idea to jump you.'

'Alright, Shabsy, I'm going to make it as simple as I can for you. I'm Chris Tarrant, you're you, all your lifelines are gone and this is the million pound question. Do you think Dave came up with that idea of jumping me all by himself?'

Shabsy looked at me for a long time in the half light of the car.

'Dunno.'

The prick.

I'd been to easy on him, gentle to the point where he thought he could get away with being insolent.

Insolent. . . little. . . wanker.

I reached over and wrapped my left arm around the back of his neck, jerking his head forward, my free hand clicking the cigarette lighter back in. He struggled, but I had been fast, too fast for him, his right arm trapped against the seat by my body, his left flailing in-effectually somewhere near my mid-section. In seconds, the lighter clicked to let me know that it was ready for use. I grabbed it from its socket and moved it to his left eye. 'Shabsy, stop struggling or I'll blind you. I fucking swear it.'

He did as he was told, his head locked underneath my arm. I could see inside the lighter: a corona of red-hot steel glowing in the dim light. I moved it forward until it was less than an inch from his pupil. 'Shabsy, did somebody pay you and your friend to beat me up?'

'I don't know. . . maybe. . . I was just along for the ride!'

'Who do you think it was?'

'I don't know! I don't know. Please! I didn't mean it!'

'Who do you think it was?'

I felt his body tense, as if preparing to renew the struggles. If that happened, I was going to jam the lighter straight into his right eye, into the soft jelly, hearing the hiss of the fluid even over the screams of pain. 'Shabsy, this is your last chance. Tell me something I want to hear.'

'I don't. . .'

I moved the lighter in. He closed the eye in defence; the filament brushed the surface of his lid, giving off a tiny sizzle. He screamed, tried to whip his head to the left. He got lucky; instead of hitting the eye socket, the cigarette lighter bounced off his cheekbone like a rubber stamp. There was a louder sizzle, followed by a wisp of smoke and the smell of burning. I tightened my grasp. 'Hold still.'

'YA FUCKIN' PSYCHO! YOU'RE A FUCKIN' NUTJOB! HELP! HELP! HE'S TRYIN' TO KILL ME!'

I looked around. There were a few parked cars but no people. An empty can of Coke rattled as the breeze skittered it across the concrete like tumbleweed. I strengthened my grip. 'Shabsy, I have a little boy. He's the most important thing in the world to me, but he's gone missing. The person that paid you and your pal to beat me up might have been the one that took him. If I don't get him back, I have nothing left in my life. Right now, you are standing between me and my son, so if you don't stop whining and start helping, then you have nothing to offer me. Given that I genuinely don't give a fuck what happens to me or you, I will probably start with your eyes and make my way down the rest of your body. I know that I'll get caught, but that will provide you with absolutely no comfort whatsoever because you, my friend, will be busy being eaten by flies in a ditch.'

'THERE'S A GUY IN THE SAME BUILDING! ONE OF YOUR NEIGHBOURS!'

I moved the lighter away. 'One of my neighbours?'

'He bought some hash from Dave about half an hour before we

saw you. He had cash. A lot of cash. I remember thinking that he seemed to be paying a lot of money for a quarter.'

'What did the neighbour look like?'

He shrugged. 'Like a dopehead.'

'Dreadlocks?'

'Yeah.'

'Gotcha.' I let go of Shabsy.

Lee.

11.20.

It had been more than three days since the fire, but the smell of burning lingered still. The door to what remained of my flat was black round the edges and criss-crossed with crime-scene tape. On the concrete wall leading up the stairwell to the next landing, somebody had daubed the words BURN IN HELL, BABYKILLER. The mystery graffiti artist had struck again. I ignored it. I wasn't there to rake over old coals, either literally or metaphorically. Nor would I allow myself to feel falsely sentimental over a place that had always felt more like a bolt-hole than a home.

This was nothing more than a business call on an old acquaintance who happened to live in the same building.

I didn't bother knocking, just raised my foot and kicked the door as hard as I could. The bolt gave and the door flew open, slamming into the wall and sticking. The hallway was in darkness. I moved quickly but carefully, mindful that I didn't know what kind of crap Lee might have lying around on the floor. Nothing spoils a dramatic entrance quite as much as tripping over a basket of dirty laundry.

The layout was the same as Liz's flat; bathroom and kitchen on the left, bedroom on the right, living room at the end of the hall. I went for the bedroom, leaping onto the double bed and dropping to my knees on either side of the sleeping figure, pinning it to the mattress. The curtains were slightly open and a sliver of pale light splashed into the room, illuminating the head of the bed. I grabbed a spare pillow and used it to cover the just-waking face, driving it down with all my strength, fully intent on smothering the little bastard. Lee started to thrash weakly from side to side, his movement restricted by my weight and the quilt that pinioned his arms to his sides.

I counted to ten before removing the pillow. In the moonlight, Lee's face was bone pale, the eyes dark hollows filled with white terror. His mouth opened to scream; I filled it with pillow.

Somewhere above my head, a door slammed. My entrance had not gone unnoticed.

Lee made a horrendous, choked sound at the back of this throat– *Ag gh agh*– and I willed him to be quiet, hoping that whoever I had woken would have the good sense to decide that whatever was going on was nothing to do with them. I didn't particularly want to hurt anybody else, but I was done fucking around. I leaned in, whispered into Lee's ear. 'Make a sound and I'll kill you.' Then I took some of my weight off the pillow, feeling Lee's chest rise as he sucked air through fabric. The struggles– pathetic as they were– eased up slightly.

A woman's voice said, 'Everything alright?'

It was the old bat with all the cats. It sounded like she was standing right outside the flat. I called out, 'I'm fine.'

'It was quite a nasty bang.'

'I'm sorry about that.'

'The door seems to be broken.'

'I forgot my keys. Had to break in,' I shouted. 'I'm sorry, I'm in the bathroom. Had a bit of an emergency, if you know what I mean. I ate a bad Doner kebab.'

'Who is that?'

'It's Lee,' I struggled to remember her name. 'Mrs Rankin, now isn't the best of times.'

'I was asleep. I had quite a fright.'

'I'm sorry. I'll try not to let it happen again.'

'I have a heart condition, you know. My doctor says that I shouldn't be subjected to undue stress.'

For once, I managed to resist the temptation of a snappy come-back. Instead, I settled for saying, 'I'm very sorry, Mrs Rankin. I promise I'll be more careful in future.'

I heard a final harumph, then the shuffling of slippers on concrete as she made her way back up to her flat. I leaned forward, whispered into Lee's ear. 'You going to play nice?'

Beneath the pillow, I felt his head nod. I gingerly released the pressure, ready to re-apply it if the bastard so much as crossed his eyes at me. He coughed and spluttered, unable to cover his mouth. I ignored the saliva as it hit my face. 'Morning, Lee.'

'Stone. . . you crazy. . . what the hell. . . '

I raised the pillow. 'Shut up.'

He did as he was asked.

'I'm going to ask you a series of yes/no questions, to which you will either nod or shake your head. Do you understand?'

'Yes.'

I pressed the pillow down for a count of five before releasing it. 'Do you understand?'

'Yes!'

'Obviously you don't.'

I moved the pillow back, this time for a count of ten. When I removed it, I saw that the whites of his eyes were bloodshot. He choked and gasped for a few seconds, the skin of his cheeks leeching from white to a shade of pale blue. From where I straddled him, I could feel his heart beating in the base of my crotch.

'Lee, I'm going to explain it one more time. Do not speak. Just nod or shake your head. Understand?'

This time, he did, nodding so hard that he started coughing again. With relief, I noticed that the blue in his cheeks was fading; for a few scary seconds I had wondered if the kid would die of a cardiac arrest before I was finished. 'Lee, I believe we have two mutual friends. Dave and Shabsy. They used to hang around outside the shop across the road. Is that right?'

Nod.

'Did you pay them to jump me?'

Nod nod.

'Are you the person who's been leaving little graffiti messages on my front door?'

He shook his head, but not before I saw his eyes give a guilty little flicker. 'Do you know who it is?'

Nothing. I moved the pillow in closer.

He nodded.

I leaned in closer, whispered in his ear. 'This time, you can speak. Who?'

His voice was hoarse. 'My girlfriend.'

The girlfriend. The one that none of us had thought existed.

'What does your girlfriend look like, Lee?'

'Black hair. Thin. She's very pretty.'

'Is she the same age as you?'

Shake shake.

'Older? Late thirties?'

Nod nod.

'You said that your girlfriend's name was Jane? Is that right?'

Nod nod.

'Does the name Sophie mean anything to you?'

His head bobbed up and down frantically. 'It's her middle name.'

'No it's not,' I told him, thinking back to the initials on the cheque I had banked. 'It's her first name. Jane's her middle name.'

My inner thigh was starting to cramp. 'Lee, I'm going to get off you now. Don't think of it as an invitation to try anything. It's been a long night and only my kind and generous nature is preventing me from hurting you very badly. Understand?'

He nodded. The bedsprings gave a familiar squeal as I climbed off. Lee sat up in the bed and took a few deep breaths. I flicked on the light, causing us both to blink. His face was ashen. The bedroom was a disgrace, even for a man of my low standards. Clothes were spread across the floor like fabric snowdrifts. Plates of half-eaten food were stacked on a dirty little bedside table. On a shelf directly opposite the bed was a portable television/DVD player, an open DVD case beside it – something called *The Lord of the Rings*. I picked it up and examined the cover artwork: two naked girls wearing wizard-hats and strap-ons. 'This isn't the Peter Jackson version, is it?'

Lee looked at me blankly.

I put it down. 'Although I did hear that the movie version strayed significantly from Tolkien's original book.'

He said nothing, his eyes flicking down to the floor. I pressed the 'eject' button on the DVD player; three seconds later the drawer slid open with a squidgy little whine. I took the disk out and snapped it, not because I had anything against porn but because I wanted to remind him where the balance of power lay. 'Put some clothes on and make me a cup of coffee.'

Thirty seconds later, the two of us were in Lee's kitchen, which was only marginally more pleasant than his bedroom. I leaned against one of the counters, keeping my eyes on him as he went about the business of filling the kettle and spooning coffee into mugs. He behaved himself, although I did catch him eyeing one of the carving knives in the drawer. I tutted and wagged a finger at him. 'Don't be a silly-billy. Tell me about Sophie. Or Jane, if you prefer.'

'What about her?'

'Where did you meet? How long have you been together. Is it true love? Are you going to buy a bungalow in the suburbs and grow sunflowers together?'

He looked at me like I was crazy. 'She's married.'

'I know.'

'She just wanted an affair. No strings.'

'What did she do? Knock on your front door, tell you that she'd just moved in next door, was having a dinner party and had run out of coffee and could you help her out?' I shook my head. 'Not even you're dumb enough to fall for that.'

'She backed into my car, scratched down the one side. There was no real damage, but she was really sorry about it, couldn't stop apologising. I think she thought I was going to go mental about it. She asked if there was anything she could do to make up for it. I asked if she would let me take her out for dinner, thinking that she would shoot me down in flames, but she didn't. That's how it started.'

'She just happened to hit your car?'

He shrugged. To him it was nothing more than a minor car accident that had led to casual sex with a bored housewife who looked like a fashion model. Truly, it was a love story for the ages.

'So what's she got against me?'

Lee took his time to think about it before shaking his head. 'Dunno. One day – it was about four weeks ago, I reckon – we were lying in bed when she told me that she had seen you getting into your car. She told me about how you knocked over that kid, said that scum like you should be thrown in a hole and forgotten about. I said that you were probably just trying to get on with your life and she started to get really wound up.' He shook his head as he poured the kettle. 'I mean, really angry, crazy angry. She started shouting that I was like all the other men and I was just trying to excuse your actions. We ended up having this massive big row and I said as a joke that if she was pissed off at you then maybe she should do something about it rather than take it out on me. She did. I'd been painting my bedroom and had some paint left over. She just grabbed a brush and went crazy, writing all kinds of stuff on the walls.'

'What about beating me up? Whose idea was that?'

'Her again. She had seen those two losers hanging around outside the 24hr store. She offered them a hundred each to give you a kicking. She even showed them your photograph.'

'Where did she get it?'

'Hell, I don't know. Maybe she cut it out of a newspaper or something. Anyhow, she showed them your picture and they recognised you and agreed to do what she wanted. The two of us were watching for you coming home. When they attacked you? On the bottom landing? Ja. . . Sophie and me were standing with the front door open, listening to what was going on. When you sent the two of them packing, she wasn't happy. She was really pissed off.'

'Sorry to disappoint.' I said. 'But it wasn't really her, was it? It was you that paid them off. She might be pulling the strings, but you're the one doing the dirty work, aren't you?'

He paused, taking his time. 'Might've been.'

'Lee, I got to tell you. This one's a bunny boiler. She's got something against me. The crazy bitch is stalking me.'

He silently spooned coffee into two mugs that looked like they had been used as a receptacle for semen-stained tissues. I picked up one of them, emptied the granules into the sink, and washed it carefully beneath the tap before giving it back to him. 'I would rather not catch anything, if it's all the same to you.'

'What do you mean she's stalking you?'

'I mean she's fucking stalking me. She's sport-fucking you because you happen to live next door to me. Do you really think a woman who looks like she does would have anything to do with a loser like you if she didn't have some kind of hidden agenda?'

'Stranger things have happened.'

'Not in this life, son.'

'Yeah, well. So what if she is? I got my hole, didn't I?'

'Lee, the woman's a fucking psychopath. I think she's kidnapped my son.'

He leaned on the kitchen counter, his eyes searching my face. 'You're not kidding, are you?'

'I'm not generally known for my sense of humour.' I nodded behind him. 'The kettle's boiled.'

'She's kidnapped your son? That wee boy that I sometimes see you with? That's your son?'

'His name's Mark. He lives with his mother. He's a good kid, and this woman – Jane, Sophie, whatever the fuck she's calling herself – snatched him as he walked home from school. Pour the coffee.'

He turned to do as he was told. 'Jesus, that's heavy.'

'It's a fucking weight, Lee. It's a gravitational pull of a thousand suns. I want him back. I want my little boy back safe and sound. I want you to help me do this.'

'I don't know anything.'

'I need to know how to get in touch with Sophie. . . Jane. Do you have a phone number for her?'

'I don't. . . wait.' He reached behind, fumbling on the kitchen counter. I tensed, still wary of the sudden knife, but when his hand reappeared, it held nothing but a mobile phone. 'She called me last night, to tell me that she wasn't coming over. I might still have the number.' He prodded buttons before handing the phone to me. 'I think this must be it.'

I looked at the digital screen. 'That's not a mobile number.'

'She said she was low on credit. It sounded like a pay phone.'

Great. A payphone. Only about a million of them in the city. Even so, it was worth a shot. I dialled the number, hoping that somebody would answer.

Nobody did.

11.21.

Ten minutes later, I was back on the road, cruising aimlessly through the city streets. I was tired, and the caffeine had given me a headache. I found a pack of paracetamol in the glove compartment and dry-swallowed two of them.

It was after four, and the streets were devoid of people. The city seemed to belong to the animals – foxes, cats, the occasional stray dog, even a few rats. They would look up in surprise as my headlights washed over them; dull eyes reflecting dumb curiosity before returning to whatever tasty treat the gutter had yielded. Lonely, I kept the radio on, one-hit wonders linked by a smoky-voiced disc jockey who sounded only a couple of tokes away from Art school.

I was lost.

Not *lost* lost. I had drifted south, the glass and concrete of the commercial centre giving way to sandstone tenements as the city changed from one set of clothes to another. I found myself on Victoria

Road, the trees of the park little more than vague shadows in the dark.

I was lost as in aimless. Lost as in directionless. Lost as in having no plan, no ideas, and absolutely no idea what I should do next.

I couldn't go home because I had no home to go to. I couldn't go to Joe's, because I was a guest in his house and guests don't stumble in at four in the morning and wake the place up. Audrey had made it plain that I had outstayed what there had been of my welcome, and I couldn't go to Liz's, because Liz was in hospital recovering from a broken leg that was entirely my fault, yet another person whose life had been negatively affected by my truly spectacular ability to combine poor judgement and bad luck.

I thought briefly about heading north, finding a wooden shack in the middle of a deserted moor, and living off the land. Nothing to occupy me except hunger, pneumonia, and my increasing obsession with persuading the *Sunday Times* to publish my una-bomber style political manifesto.

Sounded fun.

With that thought in my head, I found an empty space in a quiet back-street, tilted my seat back and went to sleep.

Well, tried to, at least.

Chapter 12

Saturday 22nd November

12.1

I was woken by somebody trying to get into my car. A persistent scratching sound dragged me from a thin, dream-filled sleep into a thin, worry-filled reality.

I opened my eyes and found myself staring into the beady black ones of a magpie standing on the right-side windshield wiper. As I watched, the bastard thing dipped its head and pecked at the rubber with a beak that looked as sharp as a vegetable knife. The thing shifted on its perch, extending its wings for balance.

Bad luck to see a single magpie, and certainly no way to start the day. I looked around for its mate. The darkness was lifting, leaving behind a heavy fog that shrouded the world in a shifting grey. The street was quiet, waiting to wake up, the cars beaded with condensed moisture.

No companion. Mr Magpie was all on his lonesome, just like me. He watched me beadily through the windscreen, his head cocked to one side. I raised my hand in a wave. 'Hello there, Captain. How's the wife and kids?'

With a arrogant tilt of the head, the bird took flight, swallowed by the murk before it had travelled ten yards. I watched it go. 'Well, screw you, then.'

Sleeping in the car had done me no good at all. My knees and ankles were fused, my lower back a symphony of aches and pains. My hip felt like it had been hollowed out, the bone marrow replaced with broken glass. Even my arms were numb. I yawned and stretched as far as the small car would permit. My mobile phone was on the dashboard. I grabbed it, checked the display.

No messages – and, just for a bonus, the battery was nearly flat. I had enough power for maybe two minutes worth of conversation.

First thing I did was send a text to Audrey: N E News?

Three minutes later, she got back to me: No. Fuc off.

Good old Audrey, managing to remain ladylike even in a crisis.

I thought about texting Joe, but what would the point be? If there was anything, he would have called me. No reason to go wasting precious juice. Instead, I looked at the last number I had dialled.

It was an 0141, the standard dialling code for Glasgow. Wherever Sophie had called Lee from, it had been somewhere in the city. I dialled it again, doubting that anybody would answer but giving it a shot just the same.

The tone repeated in my ear. I drifted off, making my plans for the day. I needed to find out a little more about Sophie Sloan, if only to make her appear a more attractive suspect to the officers assigned to investigate Mark's disappearance. Janice Galloway had shared my concern, but the police would be doing what they did best – sifting through details, trying to find out if any of the information I had given them tied up with any of the facts that they had discovered on their own. Right now, Sophie Sloan was nobody, just another name among several, another address to be checked. They would have people concentrating on known paedophiles that lived in the area of the school, or near Arnold's house. That meant lots of interviews, lots of alibis to be confirmed, and most of all, lots of man power. It was frustrating, especially. . .

'Herro?'

I started, forgetting I was still on the phone. It was a man's voice, but the inflection was childish.

'Hello, who is that?' I said, in my friendliest voice.

'Herro?'

'Hello. Who am I speaking to?'

'Herro. Who this?'

'My name's Cameron.'

The English wasn't so much fractured as taken to the toolshed at the bottom of the garden and dismembered. 'I Hiro. Hiro Makanura.'

I put a smile into my voice. 'Nice to meet you. Where are you, Hiro?'

'I from Japan.'

'And where are you now?'

'Glasgow, yes please. In Glasgow. Is Miles Better. Is No Mean City.'

'Whereabouts in Glasgow?'

'Horrorday in.'

More of that 'No Mean City' crap, I thought. I wished I could climb into my phone and pop out at Hiro's end like an evil Genie. I'd give him a fucking horror day in. 'Whereabouts is that?'

'Sorry?'

'Where are you just now?'

'Horrorday in.'

'What do you mean?' Beeps sounded in the background; my mobile was telling me it was tired and needed a little nap. I resisted the temptation to hurl it out of the window.

'Horrorday in.'

'Yes, but where?'

'I tell you. Ho. . .'

Gone.

Angry, I threw the mobile at the passenger door. It bounced off the glass with a thunk and landed into the footwell. I put my elbows on the steering wheel and my head in my hands, swearing viciously under my breath. The phone number had been my only link with Sophie Sloan.

Horrorday in Glasgow.

He was on holiday in Glasgow.

Well, good for him. I hoped it fucking rained and his camera got nicked.

Although my bodyclock, like my mobile phone, was telling me that my batteries were low, my watch insisted that it was quarter past seven. Time to begin a brand new day of fun and games. Less than three hundred yards away was a drive-through McDonalds. As it was unlikely she would offer me breakfast, I would stop for a Muffin before making my way back to Audrey's to see if there had been any new developments. Sighing, I keyed the ignition.

After that, I would try to hook up with Joe. If the police weren't going to take the Sophie Sloan link seriously, maybe the two of us would be able to do some digging.

Mark.

I did some quick mental arithmetic. He'd been missing for about thirteen and a half hours. Anything could have happened to him. It felt weird. I wasn't sure how I was supposed to act. I was an active person by nature. It felt wrong to sit at home on the settee and worry. I needed to be out there, looking for him, filling my time with something positive. If I stopped moving, the worry would get to me, would gnaw away in my brain. If Sophie Sloan had been the one that abducted him – and I believed it – then maybe she would look after him. He might be frightened, but she was female. Surely there was something to be said for the maternal instinct? She would comfort him, feed him, reassure him that all was well, even though it fundamentally wasn't.

Amateur night on the Psychology Couch: if it had been Sophie Sloan that abducted Mark, perhaps she was just seeking a replacement child. Perhaps Mark was the spitting image of the one she had lost, and that somehow, in her twisted, delusional mind, she actually believed that she was entitled. If that was so, then I felt sorry for her.

Of course, not sorry enough to not kick the shit out of her for all the fear and worry she had put us through. If Sophie was the one, the bitch was dog meat.

McDonalds was in front of me now, the two golden arches – I

think Stephen King calls them The Great Tits Of America – looming out of the fog. I positioned myself in the drive-through lane. There were two cars before me; within seconds there were two cars behind me as well. I wondered if anybody in Scotland even bothered to make breakfast anymore. Within three minutes, it was my turn. The assistant looked about fifty and had a heavy East European accent. Back in his homeland he was probably a brain surgeon, or a nuclear physicist, and yet he had come to Britain for a better quality of life and found it serving fast food. What a fucking world. I gave him my order and pulled forward to the delivery window. My breakfast was handed to me in a paper sack.

I found a parking space and started to eat. I switched on the radio, but every station was either playing irritating shit Fifty-Cent, or West-life, or Puff Daddy (or Puffy, or Prick-Boy, or whatever the hell he wanted to be called this week), or had some loud-mouth DJ who seemed to think that prank calls was the high point of humour. Disgusted, I switched it off again and started to read the box that had contained my bagel. It was the typical McDonalds promotional tie-in – I could win a trip to California to meet the stars of some movie. Idly, I read through the competition rules and prizes. Included was a rental car and two thousand dollars of spending money. All I had to do was text in a simple answer to a simple question. The text would cost me fifteen pence, which meant that the prize would be paid for by the number of people that entered it and the McDonald's Corporation wouldn't need to shell out a single penny. My bagel box was covered in cartoon characters from the film – smiling bears, grumpy donkeys, wind-surfing unicorns – all with their voices no doubt provided by Hollywood megastars. Yet another movie that Mark would love and I would yawn through.

All assuming I ever saw him again.

Maybe Audrey would let me take him away on holiday. That would be good. I'd love to take him to somewhere like Disneyworld; he was just the right age, and his excitement would stop me from being a grumpy old bastard who thought the place was nothing more than a glorified fairground with extra-long queues. I read the small print of the competition rules, wondering if McDonalds and Disney had thrown in some accommodation as well.

They had. At Holiday Inn, Orlando.

Something clicked inside my brain.

Hiro Makaunura had understood me better than I had understood him. He hadn't been telling me he was on holiday in Glasgow.

Holiday Inn, Glasgow.

12.2.

I was stuck in traffic.

My hands clenched the wheel and a pulse beat steadily in my temple. Hemmed in on all sides, I wondered whether VW made an optional cowcatcher specifically for my Golf, and why the hell I'd never bothered to have one fitted. Horns blared. Radios blared louder. In the lane to my right was a young man who had decided to grind the rest of the world into submission with techno music played at one hundred and forty decibels. The bass was so heavy I could feel it vibrating through the steering wheel. I wondered if I might have a stroke. Nobody would care if I did. The rest of the world would just drive around my corpse, tooting their horns in irritation.

Rush hour.

I'd covered two hundred yards in twenty minutes, which at least gave me time to reflect on the irony.

There were two Holday Inns in the area; one in the city centre, and one near Glasgow Airport, which is actually seven miles out of the city, just north of Paisley. I'd found a payphone – which was harder than you think in this day and age – and asked Directory Assistance to give me the number for both the Holiday Inns in Glasgow. The one based at the airport had the same dialling code as the number Sophie had given Lee. I was glad, because that one was slightly closer.

Although it doesn't really matter how close anything is if you're trapped in traffic.

I swore (no surprise there, then), and wrenched the wheel. There was a bump as the left-side wheels mounted the pavement. Horns honked and fists waved as I barrelled up the inside of traffic, hooking into a side street. One way. Naturally, I was facing the wrong direction. A man in a Toyota furiously waved his mobile phone at me. There were no parked cars or lampposts on the edge of the road. I kept my left-side wheels on the pavement and crawled for about fifty yards, eventually finding a road running parallel to my original starting point. With a sigh of relief, I turned onto it. Traffic was still heavy, but at least it was moving.

It took me twenty minutes to reach the airport, which was actually bloody good time when you consider just how congested the streets were. I used the time to ponder strategy. It would do no good at all for me to go barrelling in like a maniac. Nearly eighteen months ago, terrorists had tried a similar stunt with a jeep filled with explosives. They missed their destination by about two feet, but the incident served as a wake-up call to everybody in Scotland. We all stopped saying that it couldn't happen here.

In the aftermath of the attack, security had been beefed up in the streets surrounding the airport. Unmarked cars, close circuit television cameras, and concrete blockades. If I spotted Sophie Sloan, I wouldn't bother telling security that I thought she might have abducted my child; I would just start pointing at her while shouting the words 'Suicide bomber!' over and over again.

I wasn't the only person heading to the airport. Taxis, land-rovers and BMW's all seemed to have a plane to catch. We behaved ourselves as much as possible, keeping to the correct lane and using our indicators. Eventually I saw the Holiday Inn. It was a typical hotel: shaped like a high-rise block of flats only with a better paint job. I pulled into the car park and motored around slowly. There were plenty of spaces available, but I was looking for something in particular. I found what I was looking for parked next to a green Land Rover.

It was a blue BMW soft-top, parked at an angle to the white lines, as if whoever had been behind the wheel had been in a hurry. I pulled into the space opposite and got out of my car, bending down to peer into the rear window. There was a small ruck-sack in the well behind the seats. After a few seconds squinting, I was able to discern the WWE motif.

A schoolbag.

Mark's.

12.3.

Walking quickly, I made my way into the hotel. The lobby was small and the ceiling was low, the colour scheme a non-descript shade of oatmeal. Behind the desk was a woman in a white blouse. She sneezed heavily, wiping her nose on a minuscule scrap of tissue paper. Her nostrils looked red and raw. As I watched, she refolded the tissue and used it to wipe the screen of her computer monitor. Lovely. She started when I cleared my throat, before recovering well enough to give me a lop-sided smile. Her voice was thick and phlegmy. 'Cand I hep you?'

I reached into my wallet and took out my photograph of Mark. 'I'm looking for this little boy. He might be with a woman, possibly checked in at some point yesterday afternoon.'

She was shaking her head. 'I've beed off for a couple of days. With the cold. I have bno idea.'

'Is there anybody who was on duty yesterday that I could speak with?'

'I'm bnot really sure. Baybe you could tell be what it was regarding?'

I resisted the urge to climb over the reception desk and grab her by the throat. 'Have you seen the news today?'

'Bno.'

'There was a little boy abducted yesterday on his way home from school. The woman who abducted him is possibly staying in this hotel, which means that the little boy is possibly staying here as well.'

She sneezed again, sealing both nostrils with her index fingers to prevent a tidal flow of snot from deluging her upper lip. 'Ard yuh a poweece offither?'

'I'm a detective. Can you check your register and see if the name Sophie Sloan is on it?'

She scrubbed away with the already saturated handkerchief. Her nose was wet and shiny and clogged, like a Golden Retriever with hay fever. 'I'm subbosed to ask for identification.'

'I know that,' I told her. 'But we're desperately short on time here.'

She picked up the phone. 'Juthd let bme thpeak to the hotel manager.'

'Look, don't give me any of that client confidentiality bullshit. If the child comes to harm because you were too frightened to co-operate with a police investigation, I'll make sure that you get charged with obstruction of justice.'

She stood there, opening and closing her mouth.

'Now, all I want you to do is check your little computer and see if there is a room booked to a woman called Sophie Sloan. You don't even need to say anything. Just nod your head if there is.'

The keyboard clattered underneath her fingers. 'Bot to Sophie Sloabn.'

My heart sank. 'Anybody Sloan? Ian Sloan, perhaps?'

More clattering, then another shake of the head. I felt my hope slipping away. Desperately, I said, 'What about Jane? Jane Sloan?'

After a few more seconds pecking at the keyboard, she nodded. I reached forward, grabbed the monitor, turning it to face me, holding it with both hands. She squawked and flapped at my arms, trying to make me give it back. I looked at a screen full of jumbled numbers, trying to decipher them. After five seconds, I found what I wanted and released the monitor. The receptionist grabbed the monitor and turned it to face the correct way, hissing, 'I could lothe bmy job for that.'

I decided not to show how little I cared. Instead, I reached into my wallet and gave her a business card. 'Call this number. Speak to Detective Joe Banks. Tell him where you're calling from. Do it now.'

She took a deep breath. 'I want your badge number and your name. I'm going to complain about your attitude.'

'Do it!'

'I will if you give me your name.'

I was already moving. 'Detective John Coombes. Now fucking well do as I ask.'

12.4.

Too impatient to wait for the lifts, I galloped up the stairs, taking them three at a time. Thick carpeting muffled my footsteps. On the second floor I met a man in a suit. We both did an absurd little side-step that managed to keep us on a collision course, and I crashed into him, shouldering him into the wall without stopping. A few steps later, his companion tried to grab me in a bear hug. I brought my knee up smartly into his groin. The air rushed out of him and he collapsed, falling to his knees and rolling down the staircase. I might have yelled some apologies, but I doubt it. Nothing was going to stop me from reaching the fifth floor. Nothing.

I crashed through a set of double doors and into a corridor. More oatmeal. I was getting tired of brown. Quickly, I started checking room numbers. The computer monitor had said that Sophie was in room 5/H. I followed the signs, my heart in my mouth, roaring, 'Mark? Mark, where are you? It's Daddy!'

Nobody answered. I blew past a chambermaid pushing a pile of laundry on a trolley, through another set of double doors. 5/H was just on the inside. I was moving so fast I nearly missed it, screeching to a halt outside the room. I pounded on the door.

'Mark? Sophie? Come on, open up.'

There was no response. I raised my foot and kicked the door as hard as I could. There was a crash, but it held firm. A sharp pain stabbed my ankle, reminding me that this wasn't the first door I had attempted to kick down in the past few hours. This was different, however. The door to Lee's flat had been a shitty little piece of wood that had been riddled with dry rot and woodworm, while this was a hotel door in a state of reasonable repair.

Fuckit. Let's see what lies behind door number two. I lashed out with my foot again. This time, the crash was even greater, as was the pain in my ankle. The fire doors swung open and there was the chambermaid, her mouth open in surprise. She started yammering away in pidgin English; I paid no attention to her, this time doing the scissor kick that had broken the glass in my bedroom window. My foot sailed right through the door, catching in the wood. Upon landing, my left ankle turned beneath me and I fell heavily on my side, hung up on my right ankle that was hooked in the splinters of the door. The pain was excruciating. Slivers of wood dug into my skin. With a mighty heave, I wrenched my foot free, dragging it out from the hole I had created. Splinters lined the flesh of my ankle like the quills of a porcupine, blood beading where the skin had been penetrated. The chambermaid was still yapping away. I yelled at her to shut the fuck up and she did, clapping her hands over her mouth, her eyes as big as saucers. No doubt she thought I was mad; high on drugs and alcohol, the kind of person she had fled her native country just to escape from. I lumbered to my feet, ignoring the pain, ignoring the blood squelching into my shoe, waving my arms in what I thought might be a conciliatory fashion; it was alright, I wasn't going to hurt her, I was just looking for my son. She retreated, shaking her head, an expression of fear on her face. The room across the hallway opened and an elderly lady poked her head out. 'What's going on out there?'

'Remodelling,' I said shortly, reaching through the hole my foot had created and fumbling with the chain. I felt for the latch with my thumb and forefinger; twisted it to one side. The door swung open. I charged into the room like a stormtrooper, hands clenched into fists and ready to swing.

There was nobody there.

I found myself standing in a very empty, very standard hotel room. The double bed was in front of me, the covers pulled up to the pillows but wrinkled, as if whoever had done it had been a paying guest rather than a paid employee. A dirty mug sat on the small dressing table next to the bed. Lipstick on the rim. I searched the room as quickly as I could – under the bed, in the closets, even ducking into the bathroom in case they were hiding behind the shower curtain. The bath was empty.

The basin wasn't.

It was filled with water, dark, purple splotches floating on the surface. Hair clung damply to the fixtures. A couple of towels were abandoned on the toilet seat. I picked them up and noticed that they were stained with the same inky spots as the water. Caught in a fold in the towels were a pair of scissors; they tumbled to the ground, narrowly missing my foot. Sitting on the edge of the basin was an empty box of something called Coppertone Sunset.

She had cut and dyed her hair. Which meant that she could have done the same thing to Mark, as well. He could look very different.

This woman was crazy.

I dipped the tips of my fingers into the water. Still warm. I wasn't far behind.

12.5.

Two minutes later, I hit the dining room, where I found a waitress who was a hell of a lot more helpful than the receptionist had been.

'Aye, they were here. Her and her wee boy. They were sitting at that table.'

Her badge gave her name as Dawn. She was about twenty, looked nice in a white blouse and dark skirt, a red tabard over her shoulders. 'They had their breakfast and left.'

'How long ago?'

She shrugged. 'Five minutes, maybe? Not long, anyhow.'

If only I had taken a few seconds to look in the dining room before I had headed off upstairs. I wanted to run for the car park, but decided to take an extra few seconds.

'How was the little boy?'

'He looked tired. Kept asking when he was going to get home.'

'What did she say?'

'Just stroked his hair. Told him it wouldn't be long.'

'What did he eat?'

'Not much. He wanted peanut butter, but we didn't have any. He settled for a couple of rounds of toast. Made his mum take the crusts off, though.'

Mark. I felt a savage cheer burst in my heart, although Dawn's unconscious use of the word 'mum' left a bad taste in my mouth.

I thanked her and sprinted for the exit, stopping on the steps at the main entrance of the hotel to survey the car park. It was still half-empty. The BMW was a hundred yards away, still parked in the same space. I was facing the driver's side, but there was something on the opposite side, something moving, something like a person bending down and fiddling inside the car, almost like. . .

It was her.

Sophie Sloan was helping Mark to buckle his seatbelt.

'Mark!'

She bounced up, her face frightened. Her hair – now a weird, orangy shade – looked like it had been cut by a pair of garden shears. She slammed the door and ran round to the driver's side. I leapt down the stairs (more pain for the ankle) and took off, haring through the car park like a lunatic. I pushed myself as hard as I ever had, ignoring the pain in my hip, my heart pounding, my chest expanding, the blood roaring in my ears as I sucked in oxygen to feed my burning lungs. The BMW started, the transmission grinding as she slammed it into reverse with the clutch only half depressed. Tyres squealed as she rocketed backwards out of her parking space, twisting the wheel too quickly and dragging the front left wing of her car down the side of the Land Rover. I was closing – fifty yards, thirty – but she finally got in gear and pulled away, heading down to the end of her row so that she could double back and make for the exit. I switched direction, trying to head her off, squeezing my way down the tiny gaps between parked cars. A wing-mirror smacked off the front of my jeans, numbing my crotch. The BMW revved as she swung left on a direct course for the exit. It was close. I lunged for the car as she passed, managing to get my fingers in the door handle. My wrist was wrenched an opposite direction to the one nature had intended and the door swung open. I reeled, spinning a full three-sixty before hitting the deck. The BMW lurched to the right, the driver's side door yawing open, and for a second I thought she was going to lose it. Then she corrected, missing another parked car by about a foot, the door slamming shut as it crunched into somebody else's fender. She straightened up just in time to bullet through the extendable wooden arm that comprised the exit. The arm was down, but the BMW was low enough for it to just clip the roof. The arm shivered, then was still. With a squeal of tyres she hooked right and was gone.

I lay there on the cold tarmac, struggling to breathe, counting to ten, watching the world spin around. My balls throbbed, and with a choked sound, I threw up the bagel I had eaten less than forty minutes ago. With a grunt, I lurched to my feet.

I wasn't going to give up that easily.

12.6.

Only when I tried to retrieve my car keys did I realise that the index finger on my right hand seemed to be pointing the opposite way to its companions. The damn thing was turned a full ninety degrees into the palm and unwilling to follow instructions. While the other fingers moved in unison, it just wobbled about, registering protest in the form of sickening waves of pain. Like an idiot, I did what they always seemed to do in an episode of Casualty, seizing it with my left hand and trying to snap it back to its original position. The agony was excruciating. I fell back to my knees, the world drifting in and out of focus like a badly adjusted zoom lens. When I was reasonably sure I wasn't going to pass out, I managed to regain my feet.

Sirens rose in the distance. I wanted to believe it was the cavalry, but it was far more likely they were responding to a complaint from the hotel manager.

In the end, I was forced to use my left hand, digging through the contents of my jeans like an upright game of twister. The keys had managed to retreat to the deepest, darkest crevasse of my pocket, and it was only by removing every single item (handkerchief, packet of chewing gum, lottery ticket) that I was finally able to get a hold of them. I limped back to the Golf just in time to see a police car pull up outside the hotel. A couple of uniformed officers leapt out. The receptionist I had made friends with earlier was standing at the front door, shouting and waving her arms around, clearly trying to send the coppers in my direction. I ducked into the Golf and keyed it, over-revving the engine and squealing out of my space. I flew round the car park, following the same route Sophie had taken. The coppers saw me and dived back into their patrol car, lurching forward in an attempt to block off the exit. Too slow. The Golf – higher than Sophie's Beamer – crashed through the barrier, splintering it into smithereens. I wrenched the wheel to the right, rejoining the one-way system that surrounded the airport, the cop car just a few yards behind. With my left hand, I fumbled with the seat belt, eventually locking it in place. Quickly, I tried to think which way Sophie would head. Her best chance of escape lay in sticking close to the airport, hiding in the myriad of cross streets. However, she would be frightened, irrational, preferring to make decisions quickly rather than prudently. In a crisis, people equate escape with speed and distance, wanting to go as quickly as possible and place as many miles as possible between them and their pursuer. The fastest, closest road to the airport was the motorway, and the nearest motorway slip road was Westbound.

Towards Glasgow. Through rush hour traffic.

It was a bit of a guess, and I was probably wrong. It didn't matter.

The game was nearly over, and had reached the stage where the only sure fire way to avoid losing everything was to gamble hard and fast.

Also, the police car was gaining rapidly. It was increasingly obvious that I wasn't going to be allowed to play for very much longer.

12.7.

'Da-ad!'

Sophie glanced to her left. Mark was twisted in his seat, face pressed to the window. The car hit a pothole and he bumped his nose against the glass. 'Ow!'

'That wasn't your father. It was somebody who looked like him.'

'It was him! It was Daddy! I saw him! I don't like this game. Daddy! Daddy! I'm in here, Daddy!'

The boy fixed himself to the door handle, little fingers grasping at the metal. Sophie reached over and grabbed him by the back of his T-shirt, dragging him away from the door. 'Mark! Don't do that! We're going too fast. You'll fall out.'

'I WANT MY DADDY!'

'I promise, I'll take you to him. And your Mummy as well. I promise.'

The little boy was crying now. 'You keep saying that!'

'And I will. I promise.'

She swung the car onto the slip-road. A bus was crawling up it at thirty, a line of traffic strung behind it. She swung the car as far to the right as she could, the wheels well over the white line, and started to pass on the outside. The embankment was a flash of green on her right, falling away as they climbed level with the motorway. Traffic was nose to tail, wheel to wheel. The speedometer read seventy-three miles an hour, only three miles above the speed limit but still thirty miles faster than the rest of the traffic was moving. She spotted a gap and went for it, right at the same time an articulated lorry on the outside lane made the same decision. The driver saw her coming and slammed his brakes on, airhorn blatting. The BMW slid directly in front of the lorry and was lightly tagged on the rear right fender. It pitched into the side of a red people mover that was cruising happily in the middle lane. The impact caused the blue car to straighten, the tyres suddenly regaining traction. Inside, Sophie screamed. Mark wet himself. She fought to keep her hands on the wheel, the lorry filling her rear-view mirror like some kind of beast. Her foot mashed back down on the accelerator, and the car responded like the fine piece of German engineering it was, the engine smoothing out at as control was restored.

At least, for the time being.

12.8.

I tried to work out how many seconds behind them I was. After Sophie had knocked me to the ground it had taken me ten, maybe fifteen seconds to get back up. Then another fifteen seconds playing pocket pool as I tried to recover my keys. Then *another* fifteen seconds to make it to the car and get moving. Maybe forty-five seconds in total. If she made it to the motorway, she could be three quarters of a mile ahead.

The police siren howled behind me. I wondered if the driver had been trained in high speed pursuits. I doubted it; he was hanging too close to my bumper. If I hit my brakes he would slam into me, causing significantly more damage to his vehicle than to mine. For once I was grateful that the British police force aren't as aggressive as the Americans. Our overseas cousins use something called a Pitt Manoeuvre, whereupon the police car taps the rear wing of the escaping car, causing it to spin out of control. Lucky for me, very few people in Britain had been trained in it.

Still, if he was a big fan of Police, Camera, Action, then he might decide to give it a go. I mashed the accelerator against the threadbare carpet, trying to put a little distance between us. The slip road was a mess; traffic was at a standstill. It took me about three seconds to read the situation. Two hundred yards in front of me, an articulated lorry had jack-knifed across two lanes of traffic. Cars trying to join the motorway from the slip road had been forced to come to a halt as the cars that were already on the motorway forced their way through the remaining gap. With nowhere left to go, I jammed the Golf as far to the left as it would go scraping the side off the metal barrier. There was a horrendous screeching rattle, and the Golf vibrated as it was peeled down one side like a tin of sardines. There wasn't enough room, but somehow I made it happen, forcing the shuddering vehicle a further hundred yards up the slip road, the wider police car trapped at the bottom. The closer I got to the top, the closer together were the cars. Soon I was boxed in, barrier on my left, cars on the right. I muscled on anyway, using the Golf like a chisel, simply forcing my way into spaces that didn't exist. Drivers saw me in their rear-view mirror and hauled their way to the right, desperately trying to avoid having me scrape down the left side of their cars. Some of them even succeeded.

Eventually, I was forced to stop. A pick-up truck the size of a small house blocked the way, and it was impossible to squeeze any further. Screaming my frustration, I stamped on the brakes and brought the Golf to a shuddering halt. I leapt out and started to run. I was almost on the motorway. The lorry-driver was in front of me, a large man with a beefy red face, hands shaking. For the first time I noticed a red people mover mashed against the central reservation, two lanes of the motorway littered with debris. Cars crawled by in the one lane that was still usable. It didn't look like there were any casualties. A couple of people had left their vehicles to try to help. The lorry driver was shaking his head, shouting to make himself heard over the hum of engines and the beep of horns. 'Crazy bitch just pulled out in front of me. I couldn't do anything. Nearly killed her.'

I dodged a Transit Van and elbowed my way through the growing crowd of onlookers until I was directly in front of him. 'Let me guess. Blue BMW. Smacked the people mover but just carried on.'

He nodded, his eyes shocked and far away. 'How do you know?' he asked vaguely.

But I had already turned away, scanning back down the slip road I had charged up. The two coppers were marching toward me. Behind them were a group of people who no doubt found my driving style a tad aggressive. I half expected them to light up a couple of torches.

My options were running out. Sophie was probably a mile in front of me, an angry mob forming behind me. I was public enemy number one. Nobody except me in this dreadful little scene gave a shit about Mark. I knew I was in trouble, didn't care.

And then I saw it. Twenty yards away was a motorcycle, heeled over on its side stand. I looked around for its owner, spotted him next to the people mover, trying to force one of the doors open.

I jogged a little closer to the bike. The keys were in the ignition.

12.9.

Sophie was glad of the steering wheel beneath her hands; without it, they would have trembled uncontrollably. She checked her rear-view mirror again, remembering how she had watched the lorry that had clipped her lose control and skid to a halt. As a result, traffic had definitely thinned out behind her.

A pulse beat in her temple. Stone had frightened her. How had he found her? Maybe he was smarter than she gave him credit for.

Or maybe he had just got lucky.

She glanced to her left. The boy had pulled his knees up to his chin and was sucking his thumb. Christ knew what she had been thinking. Her mind was so foggy, filled with a dreadful buzzing noise, with shapeless, shifting images. One minute she was with her son, holding his hand as he slipped from unconsciousness to death, then she was back in the moment. She was owed a child. As long as she loved him and was kind, he would forget about his early life and grow to love her back.

'Luke?'

He didn't answer. Just kept on sucking his thumb.

'Luke, I'm sorry. I never meant for any of this to happen. I'm just. . .

I'm not feeling very well at the moment.'

At last, the boy looked at her. 'My name isn't Luke. It's Mark.'

'It's Luke! Why would you say such a thing to your mother?'

'You're not my mother!'

She reached out and clipped him round the ear. The boy yelped and retreated further into himself. She pointed a warning finger. 'Teach you to speak to me like that.'

12.10.

The bike was a stunner, a real work of art. Shame I was probably going to wreck it.

It was a red Ducati 748. Low at the front, high at the back, it was sleek and aggressive, like a fighter jet. I'd never ridden one, but I knew it well. Before Mark was born I'd been a keen biker, owning one Yamaha R1 and several hundred pieces of Triumph Bonneville that had taken me nearly ten years to realise were never going to fit together to make one complete motorcycle. Underneath the steel trellis frame of the Duke was a Twin-Cam Desmodronic engine, kicking out about a hundred and ten brake-horse power in a package weighing just over two hundred kilos. Top speed of maybe a hundred and fifty, nought to sixty in about three and a half seconds. It wouldn't keep up with a Honda Fireblade, but was plenty fast enough to beat just about any car on the road.

Including Sophie Sloan's Beamer.

Of course, that was assuming that the damn thing started. It may have been a legend, but it was also fragile, and Italian. Trying to look casual, I sauntered over and swung my leg over the raised tail section, rocking the bike off the side-stand. I thanked God it was my right index finger that was broken; had it been the left there was no way I would have had the strength to work the heavy clutch. I pulled it in and thumbed the starter button, the engine exploding into life beneath me. Like Harleys, Ducatis have their own particular sound, and this one sounded like a badly maintained tractor that had been converted to run on used vegetable oil. I checked over my shoulder; the owner was forty yards back, still poking around the people mover. Recognising the sound of his bike, his head swung round. Our eyes locked and with a cry of rage, he started to run towards me. With my left foot, I frantically worked the gear shift, trying to find first, finding nothing but dry clicks. Eventually it wouldn't move any further. Nearly crying, I rolled the throttle as I let the clutch out.

And stalled it. The engine quit with a sickening rattle.

Moaning, I checked over my shoulder again. The owner was closing, his face red and swollen. My thumb stabbed the starter button without success. The engine was well and truly dead. Then I remembered some Ducatis have a built-in fail-safe. The engine was programmed to cut out if the rider attempted to pull away while the side-stand remained down. I shifted my weight, balancing the bike on my right foot while I heeled the stand into place, grabbing at the clutch and stabbing at the starter button. This time, the engine rang out sweetly. The guy was only five yards away, snorting like a bull. I revved the engine and dumped the clutch. The front wheel leapt in the air. I threw my weight forward to push it down. Within a second I was gone, careering through the crash debris on one wheel, my chest flat against the petrol tank. Only when the engine bounced off the rev limiter did the front wheel drop, slamming back to the ground like a concrete block thrown from a great height, the percussive shock causing my wrists to go numb. I could see nothing in the rear-view mirrors, so I risked a glance behind me. The owner stood in the centre of the motorway shaking his fist, yet another person I had managed to upset.

I breathed deeply, trying to focus my mind to the task in hand, working hard to establish a rhythm. Riding a bike isn't the headlong dash that some people would have you believe. Sure, it's easy to ride quickly – right up to moment you make a tiny mistake and smear yourself over the concrete like strawberry jam on toast. To avoid this requires planning and a measured approach. The brain becomes a computer, constantly weighing odds and potential consequence. It was something I had been good at, good enough that, had I not been accepted in the CID, I could have pursued it as a career path as a bike cop. I'm pretty sure that my life would have turned out differently had I chosen more wisely.

I was starting to overtake traffic. Drivers would spot my approach in their rear-view mirrors. Some, concerned that I was not wearing a helmet and seemed to be in a hell of rush, would move to one side. Others didn't care, holding their lane and speed with the dogged determination of a terrorist who has finally made it into the cockpit of a passenger jet. They didn't bother me. The bike was smaller, faster and more manoeuvrable; I had no difficulty getting past them. Without trying, I managed to keep the speedometer needle (analogue, by Christ; it was like being back in the stone age) between one hundred and one hundred and twenty. That would be fast enough to catch up with Sophie.

Assuming that she hadn't pulled off the motorway at the first available exit.

I weaved in and out of traffic, never missing an overtake, never failing to exploit a gap. At one stage, three articulated lorries hogged all the lanes, rolling side by side at a sedate forty miles, a tailback of cars forming behind them. I undertook them on the hard shoulder, hoisting the middle finger of my left hand when I dived in front of them. The landscape was changing as we got closer to Glasgow City Centre: office blocks on the horizon, the skeleton of the Kingston bridge looping to the left and over the Clyde.

And then I saw her.

She was about four hundred yards in front of me, cruising along in the middle land. I could see the blonde of Mark's hair beside her. Fighting the instinct to speed up, I throttled down instead, allowing the Ducati to creep until it was less than a hundred yards behind her. I had no wish to repeat the accident that had caused me to leave the police force. By now we were on the bridge. The traffic was heavy, nose to tail, and every few seconds I would nearly lose sight of them. She took the exit that led to the city centre; I followed. It was another mile before I figured out where she was headed. Gallowgate.

12.11.

Even though it was less than forty-eight hours since I had last been there, it was still weird. Different and yet somehow similar. The buildings were still grey, the traders still managing to eke out a living despite the obvious lack of consumer wealth in the area. Less than a hundred yards away I could see the blue outline of the cash machine that taxi-driver Harry Josephs had stopped at on his doomed charity mission. I watched as the BMW came to a halt and parked less than twenty yards away from the spot where I had killed two people.

Did she know? Did Sophie Sloan *know* I was behind her?

I cruised a little closer. Traffic buzzed around us, so I pulled into an empty space, turning the engine off, remembering to slip the keys into my pocket. Hopefully, the bike's rightful owner would get it back without a scratch on it, although it was by no means a certainty.

I watched as she got out of the car and moved round to the other side to help Mark with his seatbelt. He looked alright: pale, tired, but otherwise unharmed. Sophie was a ghost. Her movements seemed jerky, her face pinched and drawn. She took Mark by the hand, started to pull him closer still to the spot. I followed.

Why had she come here? Here, of all the places?

12.12.

I had two choices. One, I could run at them and grab Mark, hauling him away to a place of safety, while at the same time scaring the living shit out of him. Or secondly, I could walk up to them, talk quietly, and attempt to reason with her. One victim to another.

Option one was the slightly more attractive of the two. Sophie was holding Mark by the hand, standing in the middle of the pavement, watching the road while pedestrians stepped around her. She seemed dazed, lacking in focus. She probably wouldn't fight with me, and if she tried to, I'd give her a sore face.

Except there had been too much of that kind of behaviour recently. I'd hurt too many people in the past twenty-four hours. I suppose there are some out there that would feel my behaviour justifiable, but I wasn't one of them. I was starting to worry that violence was the only answer I had for all of life's big questions.

I walked over until I was about five yards away. 'Sophie?'

She started, and I saw her hand grasp Mark's even more tightly. Then Mark was pulling. 'Daddy!'

She resisted for only a second before letting him go. He ran to me, hitting my legs and wrapping his arms around me in a hug. I held him as tightly as I could, feeling a single tear in my eye. All the fear, all the worry that I had repressed in the past twenty-four hours, suddenly bubbled to the surface. For a brief but incredibly clear instant, I wanted to kill Sophie Sloan for making feel so vulnerable.

She looked at me, and I saw that she was crying too. 'I'm sorry.'

I moved a little closer so that I didn't have to shout. 'Why'd you do it, Sophie?'

She thought about it for a few seconds. 'I don't know.' Her hand waved. 'It's noisy in here. Sometimes I don't know why I do anything.'

For a second I thought she meant the ambient noise of the city. Then I realised that she meant in her mind. In here.

I didn't know what to say, so I rephrased the question. 'Why me?'

'Because you took mine.'

'What?'

This time, she shrieked. Mark buried his head into my waist. 'I said you took mine!'

'Sophie, I don't know what you're talking about. Your boy. . . they told me that he died of Leukaemia.'

Her eyes met mine, and in them I saw the truth.

'I'm not talking about Luke. I'm talking about Maria. I'm talking about Maria McAuseland.'

Oh Jesus. I felt weak. I felt like the world was dissolving into dust. 'Sophie, I don't understand.'

'Well you should. She was mine, you bastard! Mine!' Her voice cracked. 'I gave up a baby for adoption when I was sixteen. After Luke died, I paid a private detective to find out what happened to her.'

The noise of the city faded into nothing. There was nobody else. No pedestrians, no traffic. Even Mark was nothing more than a vague presence against the lower half of my body. All that was left was me and Sophie Sloan and the terrible tragedy that had bound us together for the rest of our lives.

I thought I knew guilt. I thought I understood it.

I was wrong.

I'd killed this woman's daughter, and her grandchild, and I had driven her insane with grief.

'I'm sorry.'

Even as I spoke, I hated the words. They meant so much more to me than they did to her. It's one of the hardest, most bitter truths there is: being sorry doesn't make things right.

She looked at me with hate in her eyes. 'It's not enough.'

'It's all I have.' I looked down. Mark was still holding on to my legs, our conversation passing unnoticed over his head. 'Apart from him, and he's not yours to take.'

'You took mine. You took both of mine.'

I thought about what she said for a long time. I wanted to argue with her, tell her that it was somebody else's fault. A gangster called Alan Grierson. A crooked, lazy cop called John Coombes. Instead, I said, 'I never meant to.'

'You can't imagine what it felt like.'

'Tell me.'

'Fuck you.' She watched me carefully, waiting for a reaction she didn't get. 'You don't deserve to know.'

'You need help, Sophie. Professional help. People care about you. Ian loves you. He wants to see you get better.'

She sneered. 'Ian? He doesn't understand.'

I nodded at Mark, who still clung to me. 'I won't press charges for this. His mother will want to, but I'll talk her out of it.'

Somehow.

I continued. 'But you must get help.'

She nodded at the spot where I had killed her daughter and grand-child. 'Do you ever think about them?'

'All the time,' I said. 'What happened that night. . . there's not a day goes by when I don't wish for something different. I hate myself for what I did. If I could take it back somehow, I would.'

She looked down at Mark, who still had his face buried in my thigh. 'You don't deserve him.'

'I know. And he doesn't deserve me. But that won't stop me doing my best for him. You'll know that when you see how far I went to find you, and what I went through to get him back. I love him.'

'I wish you were dead. I wish you had died in the crash as well. Then you wouldn't be here. Having you alive is a constant reminder that they're not. It's not fair.'

'So do I, sometimes,' I told her. 'More times than you might think.'

She looked straight ahead. Somewhere in the city, a police siren wailed. 'What am I going to do?'

'You can be better.' The words were hollow in my ears. Was I really going to give this woman the standard clichés? Next I would be telling her that time was a great healer. 'If you want.'

'Great. I can book a room in Fraggle. You ever stayed in a place like that? You ever gone to twice daily counselling with a psychiatrist who has no idea how you feel?'

'No.'

'It doesn't help, believe me. I might be better off dead.'

'I don't think so. You're sick. Mentally sick. I want you to get better.'

'What you want is for me to forgive you. You want me to say to you that it's alright, you ran my daughter and her daughter down in the road like they were a pair of fucking hedgehogs or something and you want me to say that it's alright, that you were only doing your job as a policeman. Well, fuck you, Cameron Stone. You're not forgiven. You never will be. I hope you spend the rest of your days in misery because you're nothing. You're a baby-killing scumbag who refuses to take responsibility for your actions. You say that you're sorry, but you don't know what sorry is.' She looked briefly at Mark. 'I should have killed him. I should have overdosed him with the Nembutal. Then you might know how I feel.'

I wanted to speak, but nothing came to mind. We spend our lives reviewing our mistakes, time and time again, from every angle, from every viewpoint. There were so many people I could blame, but that didn't alter the fact that it had been me that had been driving the car that night. It had been me that had wanted to catch up with Grierson. When the car struck Maria and Sonata, it had been me behind the wheel.

It was all my fault.

I started to cry. Sophie watched me coldly. 'I hate you.'

Then she turned. Stepped into the road. An engine swelled, a bus, trying to make up for time lost at road works. It was only doing thirty miles an hour when it struck her.

Plenty fast enough.

Epilogue

Thursday 20th November

1.

I was going to kill her.

The two of us had been sitting in the car for nearly forty minutes, and she had yet to stop talking and draw breath. Subjects had included her childhood, her pet dog called Mongoose (or it might have been a pet Mongoose called Dog; I hadn't been paying close attention), her primary school teachers, her secondary school teachers, her ballet teacher, her first boyfriend, her last boyfriend, how they had built a swimming pool in Inverness but on the first day it opened somebody cut their foot on a piece of glass in the water and there had been blood all over the water and they had closed the pool and it had taken another six months to open it again and when it did it had the best flumes that she had ever been on but she didn't like to go there very often because there was rumour that a little boy had broken in one night and drowned in the water and the cleaning staff found him the next morning floating face down in the water and his ghost was meant to haunt one of the changing rooms and she knew that it was just a story but still it gave her the shivers and there was also meant to be a ghost in the field behind the farm where. . .

'Susan?'

'What?'

'Stop talking, please.'

'I'm just nervous. I get like this when I'm worried about something. I was like this when they sent me for the CAT scan and the sister said that I shouldn't worry but of course the minute a nurse says you're not to worry then it's all you can do. . .'

'Susan?'

'What?'

'You're still talking.'

'I'm sorry.'

'Please don't think I'm being nasty, but shut the fuck up, alright?'

She gave a tiny squeak and did as she was told. My brain sighed with relief. I counted to ten, half expecting her to forget and start wittering.

I'd collected her from the hospital two days ago. The bruises had faded, and the cuts on her face had almost fully healed. With enough time, she would be a pretty girl again, although I suspected that her eyes would always be twenty years older than her face. In my wallet was a train ticket to Inverness. Her father was going to collect her from the station, and the McPherson family was going to be reunited so that they could live happily ever after, if such a thing is possible. It's nice to think that endings like that aren't just things found in books.

We managed a whole three minutes of silence before Susan broke it. 'This is a nice car.'

We were in Elizabeth Banks' Mini. After its adventure on the sliproad, the Golf had been a write off. I wasn't especially sorry; more than anything, it felt like it was time to move on.

'It's not mine,' I told her.

'Whose is it?'

'A friend's.'

'Whose?'

'A woman called Becky Banks. She's the wife of my best friend. She's the one that's picking up your bills in that Bed and Breakfast place.'

'I'm very grateful. To both of you. I know you were just paid to find me. You don't have to help me.'

'Don't worry about it.'

I felt her watching me and turned my head. She blushed. 'You're so quiet. I feel like I'm talking to myself.'

'It's been a long week.'

'Do you do things like this often? Come to the rescue of damsels in distress?'

'Not often, no.'

The truth was, I felt like I owed the world a favour. Now that the dust was beginning to settle, and I was able to be slightly more objective about the whole affair, I felt nothing but pity for Sophie Sloan. She may have been a fruit-loop, but it had been my mistake that had sent her spiralling out of control. It would be easy for me to hate her, a pathetic attempt on my part to dodge any responsibility I may have had by laying all the blame at her feet.

Too easy.

Naturally, that hadn't prevented Audrey from doing her share of shifting blame. As soon as Mark had been safely recovered, she had engaged the services of a lawyer and started to sue his primary school, claiming they had neglected their responsibilities by failing to supervise Mark properly and allowing him to be abducted by a woman with serious mental health issues. The school had responded by pointing out the number of times Mark had arrived late, or been left waiting at the school gates for her to collect him. Although they didn't come right out and say it, they implied that Audrey was a pretty disinterested mother who was attempting to cash in on what was an extremely unfortunate incident. The whole thing was a hair away from degenerating into an ugly slanging match.

Audrey's motives for suing were slightly unclear, but then, her life was changing as well. Arnold had kicked her out. In the course of their investigation into Mark's disappearance, the police had looked into everybody that may have had contact with him. One of the names that came up was a guy called Keith Mulligan, who happened to be boyfriend of the week for Audrey's sister, Lynne. The second his name was fed into the computer, it exploded in a cacophony of alarm bells and whistles; in ninety-one, Keith Mulligan had been arrested after he had sex with an underage girl.

Of course, this little titbit of information had caused the cops to have kittens, and a quick chat with Audrey's neighbours came up with the worrying fact that both Keith and his car had been spotted hanging about the street at odd times, almost as if he was watching the place.

Without further ado, poor Keith was huckled in for questioning. He admitted that he was the same Keith Mulligan on the computer, but absolutely denied abducting Mark. When asked whether he had been staking out the house, he grew strangely reluctant to chat, leaving the police to dig through the dirt the hard way.

After a few hours, it turned out that things were not quite as sinister as they first appeared. In nineteen ninety-one, Keith Mulligan had been a young eighteen-year old, the girl had been a willing (and extremely mature) fifteen year-old who, unfortunately for Keith, also happened to be the daughter of a now-retired chief inspector. Since the incident, Keith had been a good citizen, building a reputable business as a painter and decorator. Reading between the lines, the whole business smelled of overkill, nothing more than a case of a well-connected father who, unhappy at his daughter's choice of boyfriend, had used his contacts to force a result on a case that had very little going for it in the first place.

It was eventually proved that Keith had a cast iron alibi for his whereabouts on the afternoon Mark had been abducted. However, in a final twist, it also turned out that not only had he been shagging Lynne (though, to be fair, so had half of Glasgow,) but he had also spent his afternoons entertaining Audrey as well, which explained why the neighbours had been so keen to point the finger. Like a particularly juicy episode of the Jerry Springer show, it all came out in the wash. Keith was released from custody and decided to come clean, immediately heading over to Lynne's and admitting the truth. Lynne lost no time in sharing the news with Arnold the Surgeon, who immediately suggested that it would be better if Audrey found somewhere else to live.

Ha ha.

I knew that it was wrong to gloat, but it was too much to resist, especially when you consider that Arnold was the one that paid for all of Audrey's legal fees. I laughed so much, I sent the poor guy a bottle of Laphroaig in the mail.

Mark was fine. He seemed to have recovered from the whole incident remarkably well. Audrey still mumped and moaned about providing access, but she had moved back in with her mother, who somehow managed to defy the stereotype and be a much nicer person than her daughter. Now, when I went to collect Mark, I was being offered tea and biscuits and friendly conversation. The whole thing was weird, but I wasn't about to look a gift horse in the mouth.

Sophie Sloan was currently being tube fed in a high-dependency hospital ward. The bus plastered her over the front windshield like a bug, snapping her spine and causing extensive head injuries. Doctors thought she would live, although she would require continuous care. Liz had made a few calls, and the general opinion was that Sophie was going to be a vegetable for the rest of her life. I wanted to go and see her, but I wasn't sure why, or even if it would be appropriate, so I had kept my distance.

I was told that I would face no charges. Nobody wanted to prosecute a father who had been acting out of concern for his son. The guy whose bike I had stolen had turned out to be riding without insurance, and the owners whose cars I had damaged in my charge up the motorway slip road were being told to suck it up. It was a shame for them, but I really couldn't bring myself to care. Nor did I give a damn about the rest of the people I had stepped on in my hunt for Mark. Lee was a dope-smoking waste of space and Jason Campbell was a known paedophile; I wasn't proud of my behavior, but it certainly wasn't causing me any loss of sleep.

Liz was going to be discharged from hospital in the next three days. She expected to be off work for another four weeks while her ankles healed, and had made it plain that she expected me to be at her beck and call. 'I expect you to be available to attend to my every need,' she had told me. 'Emotional, physical, nutritional, and sexual,' she had said. 'But mainly sexual.'

I couldn't wait.

2.

That left only one loose end. Susan McPherson, and her pal, Rosie. Which explained why, at just after midnight on a Thursday night, Susan and I were sitting in a car outside a brothel in the city's West End.

'So what are we going to do?' she asked.

'I haven't a clue.'

'We can't sit here all night.'

I took a deep breath. 'You're right. Come on.'

We got out of the car. The streets were cobbled, lined with the parked cars of local residents. Of the local residents themselves, nothing could be seen. They were probably all tucked up in bed, safe and sound, sleeping the sleep of the just. I wondered how they felt about having a knocking shop on the same street. No doubt the women pretended to be shocked and the men pretended not to care.

The door to the Champagne Angel Club was made of some kind of metal that had been treated to make it look like some kind of heavy wood. It looked strong enough to withstand a battering ram, and probably had done in the past. In the plastic box that people used to identify separate flats within the building, there was only one nameplate, reading PRIVATE CLUB. Very discreet. A closed circuit TV camera was fastened to the wall directly above the door. Susan reached out to press the buzzer, and I put up a hand to stop her. 'Not yet.'

'What?'

'This is what will happen. You're only here because of Rosie.' We'd discussed it in detail, and had both agreed that it would be less traumatic for the girl if there was somebody she knew and liked present. 'So you concentrate on her and nothing else. The second we find her, take her back to the car. Don't stop to get anything you don't need, don't stop to talk to anybody. Alright?'

'Alright.'

I went and stood in the blind spot directly underneath the camera. Unless they had somebody continually watching the attached monitor, then whoever answered the buzzer would have no idea that I was there, which suited me just fine.

As a point of fact, there were two tickets to Inverness in my wallet. The plan was that Rosie would go with Susan. Susan claimed her parents wouldn't mind a houseguest. I was unconvinced – Rosie sounded like she needed more help than just a place to stay – but felt that anywhere was safer than where she was just now. They could sort out the fine print between them.

Susan waved a hand at the button. 'Should I?'

Hell no, I thought. *Let's get out of here. I'll buy you a Big Mac and put you on the train alone, and stop sticking my nose in other people's business before it gets broken.*

If only. 'Let's do it.'

She pressed the button. A few seconds later, a female voice said, 'Yes?'

She leaned in to speak to the microphone. 'It's me. Susan. Can I come in?'

'Hold on.'

We waited for thirty seconds before the door lock clicked. I pushed it open slowly. If Kenny the bouncer was there, I was going to take him down hard and fast. There was nobody; just a dimly lit staircase that led up to the first floor. I motioned to Susan. 'They're expecting you, so you better lead the way.'

The two of us made our way up the stairs, our footsteps swallowed up by the heavy carpet. We found our way into the reception area. It hadn't changed any since the last time I had been there. Red carpet, red-panelled walls. Only the receptionist was different. She was a woman in her late forties. Her hair was a glorious shade of orange, her face a carefully applied mask. She spotted me, and fingernails like talons drummed the wooden surface of the desk.

'Who's your friend?'

'Beverley, this is Cameron.'

The woman looked at me closely. I gave her the fish-eye back, and eventually she turned her attention back to Susan. 'You can't work looking like that.'

'I'm not planning to. I'm leaving.'

'You can't leave.'

'I'm leaving.'

'You can't leave unless I say you can leave.'

Susan's voice shook with fear. 'I'm taking Rosie with me.'

The woman called Beverley stood up and walked around the desk. Underneath the make up, her face was hard and calculating. My guess was that she either owned the business, or was a close friend of the person who did. Probably an ex-hooker, she had hard eyes and a sullen face that made me think she been in the business for a long time. If I was a betting man, then I would have placed money that Kenny had been acting under her instructions when he beat the crap out of Susan.

Beverley examined me more closely, trying to figure out what role I had in our little play. She smiled. 'Let me guess. This little bitch comes here and gives me an ultimatum and you're the muscle that's meant to make me go all scared?'

I smiled back. 'That was the general idea, yeah.'

'So what's the deal?' She nodded in Susan's direction. 'Is she fucking you for free? Are you Richard Gere come to save Julia Roberts here from a life of sin and debauchery?'

'Something like that. I'm afraid I don't have a limo.'

'By the time I'm done with you, you'll need a hearse.'

'Now, there's no need to be unpleasant.'

She stepped even closer so that our faces were less than six inches apart, me looking down on her. 'You think you're big,' she said. 'But you're skinny. I've got a man that will eat you for breakfast.'

'I've met him,' I said. 'Charming fellow. Good with his hands, if I remember correctly. He is big, but he's not exactly. . . sophisticated. He's like a badly trained pit-bull.'

'No need for sophistication in his job.'

'Or in yours.'

Beverley nodded at the desk. There was a panic button on the side. Red, naturally. 'All I need to do is press it and he'll come running.'

'Let's hope he doesn't catch his knuckles on the door-frame.'

Beverley spoke to Susan. 'I'll tell you what. You're not much to look at, and you always were a bit of a snotty cow. I'll let you walk away. You and your friend here can skedaddle off into the sunset and never be seen again. How's that for a happy ending?'

Susan was shaking now, but when she spoke, the resolve in her voice made me proud. 'I'm taking Rosie with me.'

'No chance.'

'I'm taking her with me.'

Beverley threw her head back and laughed, one hand clutching at my arm. 'Oh, that's rich. You really are a Samaritan, aren't you?'

'She shouldn't be here. She doesn't know what's going on. For Christ's sake, she's got learning problems.'

'Tell me about it. She's in one of the few jobs where being a retard is actually an advantage. She never complains, she never whines. She just wipes herself down and moves on to the next cock.' Beverley said. 'I wish you were all like her.'

I was disgusted. 'Look, we don't want to cause trouble. Just let us take her and we'll be on our merry.'

'You don't get it, do you? She's not yours to take.'

'She's not yours either,' Susan said. 'She doesn't belong to you.'

Beverley ignored her. 'Of course she does. We paid good money to bring her over here. You think I'm going to let her go?'

I spoke. 'Beverley, this is getting boring. Look, we're not leaving without Rosie, so you might as well just make it easy and tell us where she is.'

She looked at me like I had just crawled out from underneath a rock. 'No chance.' Then she turned and pressed the button on the side of her desk.

I moved fast, grabbing her by the hair and jerking her head back, putting my knee against the base of the spine so that she fell loose-limbed to the floor. I'd met her type before, back when I had been a member of the police force, the constraints of the uniform meaning I was unable to treat them the way that they deserved. She was nothing – a soulless, dead-eyed, amoral hustler, living off the sale of flesh, the more demeaning the act, the higher the price and the greater her cut. Left unchallenged, she would continue, forever lowering people until they were nothing more than animals. I blamed her for the shit state of the world, and for the fact that everywhere I looked, people were becoming more and more disposable. Every day, in every walk of life, we're surrounded by people like Beverley, dealers of flesh, peddlers of skin, perpetuating the awful fact that everything – and I mean every-thing – can be bought. The world's a sad place, and the saddest thing of all is the fact that the only thing that's not going up in price is the value of human life.

I punched her in the face as hard as I could.

Not the proudest moment of my life, I'll admit, but it had been a long night,

Besides, she fucking well deserved it.

3.

Then a door crashed open and Kenny the bouncer was upon us, larger, hairier and more aggressive than I had remembered. He took a second to survey the situation before leaping at me, his mouth open-ing in a silent scream like an attack dog.

I had one final trick up my sleeve – or, in this case, in my pocket.

When you become a cop, they give you lots of cool new toys to play with. A warrant card that opens doors. A uniform so that people will respect you (in theory). A truncheon to protect you. Handcuffs that will help you to arrest criminals. Of course, in the eyes of some the people you swore to serve, the uniform makes you a target, and the truncheon makes you a thug, but that's not your fault.

When you leave the force, they expect a lot of this stuff back, but in reality, a lot of it goes 'missing' – actually finding its way into the private collection of many an ex-copper.

Before going out, I had borrowed such an item from Joe. Holding it with my thumb on the top, I raised, pointed, and fired.

Pepper spray.

The liquid arched across the rapidly decreasing gap and hit him directly in the face. He ploughed into me, his momentum causing both of us to crash to the ground. It was like having a cement mixer dropped on me. I rolled out from underneath him and looked for something to hit him with. There were plenty of things I could use – a fire extinguisher, the computer monitor – but they were all too heavy. I didn't want to kill him. Much. Eventually I selected the hand-set to the cordless telephone. It was ideal: hard, smooth plastic, with just enough weight to turn the lights out for a few minutes. Kenny was rolling around on the floor, rubbing furiously at his eyes, whimpering like a kicked dog, which was a fairly apt analogy. I got down on my knees and picked a spot on his smooth, shiny cue-ball of a skull.

'It's for *you*.'

(WHACK!)

'It's your *mother*.'

(WHACK.)

'She says you've been a *very*

(WHACK)

naughty

(WHACK.)

BOY!'

(WHACK!)

And with that, he passed out.

C. DAVID INGRAM

4.

I looked up, breathing heavily. Susan was watching me, her face shocked. So was Beverley, her mouth a red-rimmed ruin of smeared lipstick and broken teeth. I watched her bleed for a few seconds before brandishing the phone at her. 'Rosie. What room?'

She tried to speak, but all that came out was a mushy sound. Her eyes found mine and pleaded. I was unmoved. 'Try again.'

'Ayeeee. . . Aye. . . ' Her face twisted with the pain of effort.

'Eight?'

Nodding frantically, she rolled to her hands and knees, blood falling from her face to the floor. I pointed a finger. 'Don't fucking move. Susan, where's room eight?'

She indicated a door opposite the entrance. 'Through there.'

'Lead the way.'

I followed her down another corridor, past closed doors. We saw nobody, but all around us were traces of human presence. Scents filled the air – perfume, aftershave, sweat, incense. With them came emotion – hope, despair, guilt. From one room came the sound of leather on flesh, followed by a gentle cry of pain – male, or I wouldn't have been able to stop myself. From another came the unmistakable sound of ugly sex – pig grunting and a noisy, faked yell of delight. I wondered how many people had passed through this corridor, how many punters, how many girls. Did they all find what they were looking for? Was the pleasure worth the price? The humiliation worth the cash? I hoped so, but knew it probably wasn't.

Susan came to a sudden stop. 'This is it.'

I didn't, kicking the door open. I found myself in a room almost identical to the one I had first met Susan in. There was the futon, there was the massage table, there was the bedside cabinet with the cheap stereo on it – playing, of all things, a pan-pipe version of Bon Jovi's *Living on a Prayer*.

There was the girl, kneeling on the floor in front of the futon, her head in somebody elses' lap.

Her eyes rolled to meet mine, and for a brief instant, there was a sense of deja vu, of a key turning in a lock somewhere. I'd seen her before, but I had no idea when. She was pretty, but there was something in her face that broke my heart a little. Blank misery. A desolate void of pain. An acceptance that this was it, this was all she would ever have. This was life, and all it held for her was degradation and humiliation.

In my life, I'd never seen a person so without hope.

Susan moved forward. The man who was on the receiving end of Rosie's attention turned from where he lay on the futon. His voice was offended, as if we were somehow inconveniencing him. 'What's going on? You can't just barge in here like this.'

And in that instant, I realised where I had seen her before. It had been a long time ago. Just before the accident. She'd been a passenger in a black Mercedes that had belonged to the man whose penis she was currently polishing with her tongue.

I wondered about the circular nature of all things. It's not true what they say; sometimes two wrongs do make a right.

Sometimes.

And even when they don't, they at least complete a chain. I had been wrong when I said that Susan and Rosie were the final loose ends to be tied up. The final loose end was *him*, Rosie's customer, the man who had set this tale of woe in motion.

I put my hand in my pocket, moving my fingers over the heavy links of the dog lead, feeling for the nylon loop. I remembered the night I had been mugged in the stairwell, and the damage it had caused. This time, I would not be so gentle. I took the chain out of my pocket and let it dangle by my side, the weight pleasant and reassuring. The man's eyes widened in fear. 'Do I know you?'

'No. But I know you.'

Realisation dawned on his face. He'd recognised me.

With my foot, I gently pushed the door closed. 'Grierson, you and I have some unfinished business.'

Acknowledgements

Writing may be a solitary act, but writers tend to forget that there's a lot more to publishing a book than simply coming up with the words. *The Stone Gallows* is no exception, and could not have happened without the help of a great number of people.

I am extremely greatful to Ed and Julie Handyside for spotting me and giving me a chance, and to all the staff at Myrmidon Books who have worked so hard. A particular mention is due to my editor, Anne Westgarth.

While writing Gallows, I worked in three different nursing homes: Breamount Nursing Home, Craigielea Care Centre, and Elderslie Care Home. All three establishments are uniformly excellent; staffed with kind, hard-working people who care very deeply about the welfare of the people in their care. It's important to point out that none of them provided a model for Inchmeadows, which is – of course – entirely fictional. I should also mention a couple more names here: Eileen Docherty and Madge Cluckie.

Thanks are due to my old pal Philip Gray for all the advice and beer, usually at the same time, which meant that by the time I had finished the latter I had usually forgotten the former.

I'd like to thank my family – my mother, my sister, my aunt, my brother, and my father, who gave me the idea in the first place.

I'd like to thank my lovely wife, Karn, who puts up with me long after she should have told me to pack my bags and leave. Every writer should have a partner like her; not all of us deserve one. I'm damn sure that I don't.

Finally, I'd like to thank the readers. For any of you who were wondering, Cameron Stone *will* be back – he does, after all, have some unfinished business.

MORE GREAT CRIME WRITING FROM MYRMIDON

A gripping, *twisting* crime thriller set on the streets of Newcastle

The Editor
by Mari Hannah

Grace Daniels is a dedicated, single-minded Detective Inspector in the murder squad. Commanding the respect and loyalty of her team, she seems destined for great things in the Northumbria force.

Then, on November 5th, as crowds of revellers throng the banks of the Tyne, the noise of fireworks smothers a gunshot as a prominent businessman has his brains spattered over the furnishings of his luxury Quayside flat.

Being assigned to lead the high-profile murder inquiry is the biggest break of Daniels' career. But there's a catch: Daniels discovers she *knows* the victim personally; she should tell her boss and be taken off the case. Instead she stays silent.

There are fresh complications: someone very senior in the force is being deliberately obstructive and there's a mole in Daniels' team- someone out to undermine and discredit her at every opportunity.

Then there's Daniels' own secret: what is her relationship to the victim and why is she desperate to hide it? The truth is that the tough-minded inspector is far more vulnerable than she appears and mired in the kind of trouble that threatens far more than her job.

£7.99   ISBN 978-1-905802-32-6

Stylish menace from the author of *The Painted Messiah* and *The Blood Lance*

Cold Rain
by Craig Smith

"I turned thirty-seven that summer, older than Dante when he toured Hell, but only by a couple of years. . ."

Life couldn't be better for David Albo, an associate professor of English at a small mid-western university. He lives in an idyllic, out-of-town, plantation-style mansion with a beautiful and intelligent wife and an adoring teenage stepdaughter. As he returns to the university after a long and relaxing sabbatical, there's a full professorship in the offing- and, what's more, he's managed to stay off the booze for two whole years.

But, once term begins, things deteriorate rapidly. The damning evidence that he has sexually harassed his students is just the beginning as Dave finds himself sucked into a vortex of conspiracy, betrayal, jealousy and murder.

Unless he can discover quickly who is out to destroy him, all that he is and loves is about to be stripped away.

£7.99   ISBN 978-1-905802-34-0